TELL
ME
LIES

TELL ME LIES

A NOVEL

Carola Lovering

ATRIA BOOKS

New York ··· London ··· Toronto ··· Sydney ··· New Delhi

ATRIA
BOOKS

An Imprint of Simon & Schuster, Inc.
1230 Avenue of the Americas
New York, NY 10020

First Atria Books hardcover edition June 2018

ATRIA BOOKS and colophon are trademarks of Simon & Schuster, Inc.

For information about special discounts for bulk purchases, please contact Simon & Schuster Special Sales at 1-866-506-1949 or business@simonandschuster.com.

The Simon & Schuster Speakers Bureau can bring authors to your live event. For more information or to book an event, contact the Simon & Schuster Speakers Bureau at 1-866-248-3049 or visit our website at www.simonspeakers.com.

Interior design by Laura Levatino

Manufactured in the United States of America

10   9   8   7   6   5

Library of Congress Cataloging-in-Publication Data

Names: Lovering, Carola, author.
Title: Tell me lies : a novel / Carola Lovering.
Description: First Atria Books hardcover edition. | New York : Atria Books, 2018.
Identifiers: LCCN 2017040924 (print) | LCCN 2017050875 (ebook) | ISBN 9781501169663 (eBook) | ISBN 9781501169649 (hardcover)
Subjects: | BISAC: FICTION / Contemporary Women. | FICTION / Coming of Age. | FICTION / Psychological. | GSAFD: Love stories.
Classification: LCC PS3612.O855 (ebook) | LCC PS3612.O855 T45 2018 (print) | DDC 813/.6--dc23
LC record available at https://lccn.loc.gov/2017040924

ISBN 978-1-5011-6964-9
ISBN 978-1-5011-6966-3 (ebook)

For my mother, the original Lucy—
you are the light of my life.

And to everyone who's ever had a Stephen DeMarco—
this book is for you.

Sometimes you make up your mind about something without knowing why, and your decision persists by the power of inertia. Every year it gets harder to change.

—Milan Kundera, *The Unbearable Lightness of Being*

I shiver, thinking about how easy it is to be totally wrong about people—to see one tiny part of them and confuse it for the whole . . .

—Lauren Oliver, *Before I Fall*

PART
ONE

1

LUCY

AUGUST 2017

I wake two minutes before my 5:45 a.m. alarm goes off, on instinct, like the neurotic, sleep-deprived New Yorker I've become. My head kills from the wine—Dane and I split two bottles with the dinner that *I* paid for—but I force myself out of bed anyway. Three Advil, two cups of coffee, and an Adderall and I'll survive the day. And isn't that what New York is all about anyway—surviving?

Dane stirs in the bed while I'm putting on my Lululemons. The new ones—size 4, not the 2s from senior year. Ugh.

"You crazy?" he slurs, half asleep. "Get back in bed." With his face buried in the pillow he reaches out and grabs for my leg.

"I'm going to six thirty SoulCycle." I fling his hand away. "I already signed up." I squeeze myself into a workout top. I feel disgusting, last night's food baby protruding underneath the spandex.

I splash some water on my face in the bathroom and brush my teeth for thirty seconds. My watch reads 5:56. I'm running late. In New York, no matter how fast I go, I'm always running late. I grab my work stuff, shower stuff, change of clothes, and my weekend bag for Bree's wedding—thank God I had the foresight to pack before getting drunk with Dane.

"Bye," I tell Dane, half hoping he's fallen back asleep.

"Babe . . . c'mere." He rolls over and opens his arms. Dane has been calling me "babe" since the day we met three months ago, that drunken afternoon I stumbled into him at the Frying Pan and couldn't help but nuzzle up to his tanned, good-smelling neck as the sun dropped into the Hudson River. *Corona, babe?* He'd smiled dumbly, one front tooth longer than the other. Babe is cliché, of course, coming from a guy like Dane. Still, he looks all sleepy and handsome, and I let him pull me in for a kiss goodbye.

"So I won't see you until Monday?" he mumbles.

"I'll be back Sunday night."

"Okay. Let's do something then. Have a blast, babe. You're gonna be the sexiest bridesmaid. Wish I could go with you."

"Me too, babe," I say, trying out the nickname. I'm sort of making fun of him, but Dane is too oblivious to notice. I do wish he could be my date for the wedding, but Bree and Evan aren't giving plus-ones unless the couple is engaged. And Dane and I are about as far from being engaged as you can get.

I leave my apartment in the dark. The kitchen is a mess, mostly from Dane and me, but I know Dane won't bother doing the dishes. He's not at all helpful when it comes to that kind of stuff. My new roommate, Julie, probably thinks I'm a slob. If Bree still lived here it wouldn't matter, but she doesn't. She moved in with Evan three months ago.

By the time I get down to the street it's 6:08, and I don't trust the subway to get me uptown on time. I hail a cab. It's irresponsible, spending ten dollars on transportation that could be free—work pays for my unlimited MetroCard—but I can't miss Soul.

The class is full, of course, because Courtney is teaching and her classes book up at exactly 12:01 p.m. on Mondays, one minute after weekly sign-up opens online. I set an alarm for 11:55 a.m. on my phone every Monday, so I can be ready.

Courtney is really working us this morning, and my head feels like it's going to explode. I didn't drink enough water.

"Tap it back! Tap it back! TAP IT BACK!" Courtney is screaming through the microphone, a Wiz Khalifa remix blaring through the speakers. The pain in my thighs is excruciating, but the calorie burn is always worth it. I turn up the resistance even higher.

"Cardio is your *friend*!" Courtney is pedaling faster than anyone else in the class, a ginormous smile plastered to her face. I wonder where she gets the energy at 6:30 a.m. She probably didn't stay up until one in the morning drinking copious amounts of sauvignon blanc and eating sweet potato fries with her new, hot, but slightly ridiculous maybe-boyfriend. Dane barely goes to work. He'll probably lie in my bed for half the day watching surf videos on YouTube before turning his attention to his "remote marketing" job.

After SoulCycle I can barely walk, but I'm thrilled it's over and done with. I shower in the locker room and pull myself together for work—some makeup, not too much. I walk seven quick blocks northeast to my office on Forty-Seventh and Madison.

"You're early," Alanna sneers when I walk in. She's really saying: *You're early but not earlier than me.* Alanna is on a complete power trip because she's an *account manager* and I'm an *account executive*, and she pretends to be my boss even though we both have the same boss, Melissa, *director of sales.* God, I hate titles in the corporate world.

"I went to SoulCycle," I say, watching her eat a strawberry Chobani. Alanna probably thinks she's being healthy, but everyone knows those yogurts are loaded with sugar—you have to buy plain.

She ignores me, unattractively licking the top of her yogurt and sticking the whole thing in the trash. I want to tell her that she should recycle, but she goes back to click-clacking on her keyboard with her burgundy shellacked nails. Alanna's long black hair is pinned up in a bun on top of her head, the way she wears it when she's too lazy to straighten it or create perfect, Victoria's Secret waves. As usual her eyes are coated in black makeup that makes them pop harshly from her face. She isn't naturally pretty, but like lots of girls in New York City, she does everything right. Tweezes and plucks and highlights and diets and morphs herself into something she isn't. I'm not saying I do everything naturally—I still can't help monitoring everything I eat, and I've gone through more Hoola bronzers than I can count—but I would never get biweekly blowouts like some girls I know, or waste $140 on eyelash extensions. There is a level that certain girls take it to in Manhattan, and I don't have the time or the salary to go there. Plus I think the caked-on-makeup look is frightening. I'm not a supermodel or anything, but I can get away with being a girl who is pretty-without-trying-too-hard. Mascara and a touch of eyeliner and call it a day.

I check my email, my eyes burning with exhaustion. The Adderall is barely helping. I'm going to be a wreck for the rehearsal dinner.

Melissa sneaks up on us without a greeting, her social awkwardness waning as she switches into boss mode.

"Lucy, did you print the meeting agenda?" she asks tersely, averting her eyes. Melissa is on even more of a power trip than Alanna, which, coalesced with her social dysfunction, is a frightening combination.

I hold up a manila folder with ten stapled copies.

"The Expedia client will be here in twenty. Alanna, run down and pick up some pastries from Financier. And a fruit platter if they have it."

"Sure." Alanna hates being the one to get sent on errands, and I can feel her seething. That's the one thing Alanna and I have in common—we both dislike Melissa, and Melissa seems to dislike both of us.

"Lucy." Melissa turns back to me. "Run me through the agenda."

"Shouldn't we wait for Harry?" Harry is VP of marketing, Melissa's boss, who used to be my boss before he and Melissa both got promoted. Harry is my favorite person at *The Suitest*, the middlebrow online publication by which I am employed and "the Internet's comprehensive guide to the best hotels around the globe." Harry wears Pucci ties and takes me to sample sales during lunch. His husband, Dominick, is an editor at *Departures*, and they live on the eighty-first floor of the new skinny building on Park Avenue. Harry lets me hide in his office when Melissa is at her bitchiest. He can't fire her because she's so good at her job—the woman gets shit done, and fast—but he agrees that she's got a giant rod up her ass. Harry says a lot of people in our industry have rods up their asses but that you can't take things personally.

"Harry isn't getting involved with Expedia," Melissa tells me importantly, even though he attended last week's meeting.

"But he always attends client meetings."

"Not anymore," Melissa barks. "He has me leading this account now. I'm the one who landed it."

I resist the overwhelming urge to roll my eyes. Melissa never misses an opportunity to remind everyone that *she's* the one who landed us Expedia. I honestly have no idea how she pulled that off.

We run through the agenda; Alanna comes back with a platter of shiny pastries; the clients are on time, and the meeting begins. The Expedia people like to keep our meetings speedy, which I appreciate, because my head is still throbbing. I'm on my third coffee. I don't touch the food, though I want a chocolate croissant beyond badly. I observe Alanna observing the pastries, and I bet she wants one as much as I do. Maybe she even snuck a bite at Financier. Melissa digs into an apple fritter without shame—she is oblivious to the harm of carbohydrates in a way that almost makes me envy her, except that I really, really don't. Melissa is thirty-one and single and odd and spends all her free time alone with her cat or Instagramming selfies with her cat—I'd feel bad for her if she wasn't a raging bitch.

After the client leaves I type up the meeting notes for Melissa and then remind her that I'm leaving early. She gives me a look like this is brand-new information, even though I told her a month ago and have reminded her every day this week.

"For my friend's wedding in New Jersey? I'm a bridesmaid and the bridal lunch is today. I reminded you yesterday? I have to make the 11:02 out of Penn Station?" Everything I say ends up sounding like a question. I wish Melissa didn't make me so nervous.

"Right." Melissa scowls and darts her eyes away weirdly. Alanna spills coffee on the sleeve of her shirt and scowls. In sales, scowling is protocol.

"Before you take off, I need to see you in my office." Melissa uses every opportunity imaginable to let the world know she has an *office* now that she's director of sales, even though her promotion was more than a year ago and even though her "office" is essentially a cubicle without a door, three feet from my own desk.

"Now?" My stomach plummets instinctually.

"That would be ideal." Melissa sneers, and I can feel Alanna smirking behind me.

I follow her into her "office."

"Want to tell me what the hell this is?" Melissa swivels her laptop screen toward me, displaying an article on Departures.com: "Is It Worth It? The Risks We Take for Travel's Sake" by Lucy Albright.

"It's an article I wrote."

"I can see that." Melissa's face morphs into something ugly and livid. I can see the bad foundation job, the way the yellow skin around her mouth looks like it's cracking. I always feel strange when she confronts me in person. She loves using her authority to get pissed at Alanna and me, but it's usually from behind the security of her computer screen, where she sends passive-aggressive emails or IMs from fewer than three feet away without a spoken word. Melissa has done well enough at *The*

Suitest—Expedia is our biggest client—but she's too uncomfortable to have an actual, verbal conversation about anything other than meeting agendas.

"I didn't realize you were trying to be some kind of global health journalist." Her face is practically twitching with rage or discomfort; I can't tell which.

"I just freelance on the side. The article ran two weeks ago. How did you find it?"

"It's on the Internet, so it's not exactly hidden material. Alanna brought it to my attention."

Alanna. Of fucking course.

"It's a piece I wrote and submitted months ago. Dominick gave me the tip."

"*Harry*'s Dominick?"

"Yes."

"Does *Harry* know about this?"

"He knows I like to write and that I'm trying to do more freelancing, so he connected me with Dominick. I don't see what the problem is."

"The *problem* is, Lucy, that you wrote an article about Cabo San Lucas and did not mention our Cabo San Lucas *client*, Las Ventanas al Paraiso. You are first and foremost an employee of *The Suitest*. Do you have any idea how this makes us look? What if Sonja sees this? I know Harry would agree, had he read the article, which clearly he has not." Melissa's lips are curled into a snarl, and I can see just how much she cherishes the opportunity to make me feel like an idiot. It's disconcerting to hear so many spiteful words coming out of her mouth rather than seeing them typed out in long, pointed paragraphs on instant message. I can tell she's pleased with herself for handling this offline.

"I couldn't have included Las Ventanas in the piece, Melissa. I work on the account. It would've been biased and unprofessional."

"*This* is unprofessional." She stabs her finger at my name on the computer screen. "You include Casa Dorada, one of Las Ventanas's main competitors. Have you lost your mind? Please tell me this didn't run in print?"

"It didn't."

"Oh, thank God," she breathes, as though we've just avoided a nuclear war with Iran. "This needs to come down immediately."

"Are you serious?"

"I am so serious, Lucy." Melissa folds her pale, flabby arms and focuses her socially anxious gaze somewhere past my left shoulder.

"Melissa, the article is a think piece on the Zika virus and the state of tropical vacationing right now. It has nothing to do with my stance on Cabo hotels. It's not even *about* Cabo. I only mentioned the other hotel because there was an outbreak there. It's not even good press for the resort."

"I don't care. If Sonja sees this we could lose the account. And if you're trying to write I don't know why you're working in *sales*—"

"Melissa, it's *one* article. You know I like to write—I've done some freelancing and I wrote that post for *The Suitest* last year. But I love working on the sales side." I taste the lie as it slides from my mouth, bitter as metal.

It's the lie I've lived for more than three years now, sustained by Harry's advice: *You want to be a travel writer? This is a good place to start and your foot's in the door, baby. You do sales for a year, make some contacts, then hop right over to editorial. Easy with a side of simple.*

But it hasn't been easy with a side of simple; a year went by and the sole entry-level editorial opening was given to the publisher's goddaughter. Vance, *The Suitest*'s editorial director and a friend of Harry's, agreed to let me write a monthly post reviewing a local hotel bar or restaurant, but the stint didn't last long. Once Melissa got wind that my review of the William Vale's new rooftop bar had gone live on *The Suitest*, she informed Vance that I worked for her in the *sales* department and that I didn't have time to be helping out with editorial projects. Harry says I shouldn't worry so much, that I should be patient. Get Melissa to love me. *Ha.* Melissa hates me. No matter how hard I work or how much ad space I sell, Melissa will continue to hate me.

"Lucy," Melissa spits. "You've overstepped serious boundaries and the article needs to go, now. Call Dominick or whoever you worked with at *Departures* and make sure it's down by the end of the day."

"I think I should at least run it by Harry."

"Unfortunately Harry is no longer your supervisor," she spits. "Nor does he lead the Las Ventanas account."

"But—"

"We're done." Melissa turns her computer back in front of her face and pretends to already be engrossed in something on the screen. This is my problem with sales—it's full of hotheaded, self-important people like Melissa and Alanna who think clients are demigods, who get off on creating problems out of nothing and act like they save the client's fate, and in turn the world, by solving them. And despite Harry's encouragement and a promotion that essentially just replaced the word *coordinator* with *executive*, I'm no closer to the editorial door than I was three years ago, especially not with Melissa as my boss. But this job pays the bills, and the $150 I got for the *Departures* piece didn't make a dent.

I leave Melissa's office and grab my bags, resisting the urge to knock Alanna in the back of the head on my way out of the building. Getting my name in *Departures* was a huge step up from the other freelance writing I had been doing. After Dominick had given me the tip, I'd spent two whole weekends researching and writing the piece. It was *Departures*! That's basically *Travel + Leisure* or *Condé Nast Traveler*—same tier, at least. No way was I having Dominick take it down.

Outside it's muggy and Madison Avenue is clogged, but I manage to flag down a cab. My meeting with Melissa has set me behind schedule and I'm worried I'll never make my train if I attempt the subway.

Penn Station is like the crack den of New York transportation hubs. It's a windowless, drab rat maze with low ceilings, and it's always so crowded you can barely lift an arm. With my rolling suitcase, tote bag, purse, and the Bergdorf Goodman bag holding Bree and Evan's wedding present—I still can't believe *Bree* registered at Bergdorf's—it's that much worse, and by the time I find an empty seat on the 11:02 train headed toward Tewksbury, New Jersey, I'm in a full sweat.

My phone vibrates on my lap.

DANE: Come back, babe.

Jesus. One of my best friends is getting *married* tomorrow, and I'm dating Dane: a surf-obsessed skater bro who thinks my name is Babe, consistently "forgets" his wallet, and has a tattoo that reads *DON'T TALK ABOUT IT, BE ABOUT IT* in block lettering on one of his beautiful, muscular shoulders. Such is the strange reality of life at twenty-five: the newfound threat that everything—jobs, people, decisions—*matters* in a way it never seemed to before. Wasted time is a luxury I'm worried I can no longer afford.

I watch the city slink away from the window of the train. I close my eyes, still exhausted, but I know I won't be able to sleep. I can never sleep on any form of transportation. I'm too frantic to read, so I listen to Fleetwood Mac in a nervous frenzy and pray that the bruise-colored bags under my eyes will magically disappear before we reach Tewksbury.

Now that I'm on the train, actually going there, I'm too preoccupied to think about Melissa and the *Departures* article and what I'm going to do. Because Bree is marrying Evan. Bree is marrying Evan, and *he* is going to be there; *we* are going to be there, sans plus-ones, and I don't know if I can stand that. The sickness in my stomach is growing worse by the minute, the familiarity of the pain creating a nauseating déjà vu. The same gut-wrenching dread I lived with for years.

The rehearsal dinner is in a matter of hours, and even though Bree promised only the bridal party and family would be there, she could be wrong. She wasn't looking at the actual list when she said that.

I still can't think about him without thinking about sex. Even after a lot of the emotional residue has cleared, the physical stuff continues to sneak up on me. I close my eyes and there I am, on my hands and knees with him behind me, and I picture the hungry expression on his face, and it has nothing to do with love or missing him, it's just raw and animalistic and I like to think about it. There is something about that kind of sex that bites into me, that causes the memory to shoot up every once in a while, like something chronic. He's not the only person who's fucked me like that; he was just the first.

My phone vibrates again. It's my group text with Jackie and Pippa. Their flight got in from LAX this morning.

> PIP: I think we're close, but our Uber driver is confused. How do you spell Tooksberry, Luce? Tooksbury? We can't wait to squeeze you!!!

Tewksbury, I text them. Underneath my anxiety I am ecstatic about seeing Jackie and Pip. I chug water from the liter I bought at Duane

Reade and remember to cut myself some slack. If it was anyone other than Evan who Bree was marrying, none of this would be happening and I would be a good, normal friend and bridesmaid instead of a panicked, perspiring wreck busting out of a size 2 Self-Portrait dress. I'm not a size 2 anymore, and, after three years of therapy and numerous conversations with my nutritionist involving the potential harm to my fertility, I can live with that, but for this wedding, I had to make a size 2 work.

Part of my panic is missing Bree, I know. Watching Bree pack up her half of our apartment after two years together, having *Julie* move in with her frilly couch pillows and loud food processor.

The train rolls into the stop for Tewksbury, my head pounding harder with the brakes. Outside, the August air is hot but less humid than Manhattan, thank God. I haul my bags into the first cab I see and give the driver Evan's parents' address. They decided to have the wedding in Evan's hometown in New Jersey instead of Darbydale, Ohio, where Bree was born and raised. *A more convenient location—just outside the city— it's easier for everyone*, Bree had explained. And the unspoken: Evan is the one with the stunning, ivy-adorned mansion in one of the most expensive counties in suburban New Jersey. Or maybe it is spoken—it probably is. Bree doesn't come from much money, and she's open about it. Her grades won her a scholarship to Choate for high school and then a full ride to Baird College. But she's the opposite of a gold digger—Bree wouldn't marry Evan for his money. Since day one she's been determined to become self-sufficient, and now she's an associate at J.P. Morgan. She would be just fine without Evan, financially.

Evan's house is at the end of a long, curved driveway, nestled into a green hillside. It's gorgeous, and at least twice the size of my family's house in Cold Spring Harbor. I let the driver swipe my Visa and then haul all my crap out of the cab like a crazy bag lady. A butler, or someone who seems like a butler, rushes to help me. The foyer is giant and airy and extends to the back of the house, where I can make out Bree's profile on the terrace. She is chatting with Evan's parents, who I met at the engagement party at the Pierre. Her white-blond hair is swept back in a low bun and she's wearing dark, stylish sunglasses that must be a recent purchase.

As I watch this new, sophisticated version of Bree talking closely with her soon-to-be in-laws, I can't help but feel nostalgic for the girl I met the first night of freshman year seven years ago—the scrappy, never-done-drugs, never-had-sex Bree.

I don't miss college—I basically took my diploma and beelined for my packed U-Haul. Still, nostalgia has my stomach in knots, because I remember that first night by heart.

My mother stood in the doorway of my dorm room, shifting her weight from one foot to the other, glancing around as though something had been forgotten. My dad was calmer, smiling his usual *I'm comfortable anywhere* grin. I sat on my freshly made twin bed, because the room was tiny and there was no place else to sit. My roommate, a tennis player named Jackie Harper from Wilton, Connecticut, sat across from me on her own bed. Her parents had left hours earlier, and I wished mine would take a hint and do the same.

"Oh, I almost forgot," CJ said. She pulled a liter of Diet Coke and a handle of Absolut vodka out of her oversize purse and placed them on one of the desks. She looked at me with annoyingly pleased eyes—it was her parting gift, her attempt to keep the peace between us and say to the world: *I'm a cool mom.*

Jackie looked impressed. A flash across my dad's face told me he didn't agree with his wife on this one. But my dad never crossed CJ.

"If you're going to drink, you should drink your own stuff," CJ said. "Don't *ever* drink from a cup that's been sitting out at a party. That's how people get roofied. And if you're going to try drugs, call me with questions. I'm not a dinosaur. I know that college is about experimenting."

My father's mouth formed a straight line, and he looked at his watch. I hadn't heard this side of CJ in ages—she was usually a warden when it came to my drinking—but deciphering her unpredictable personality was like trying to order dinner from a menu written in foreign characters. She was probably just trying to impress Jackie because she thought Jackie was pretty, and because Jackie's mother had been wearing Gucci loafers.

"Lucy." CJ crossed her thin, tanned arms, her aqua eyes wide. "Last chance. Are you *sure* about Baird? You don't have to go to college *all* the way out in California, you know. If you went to college on the East Coast, you'd still be away at school, but you could see your friends and sister whenever you wanted. Isn't that worth considering?"

CJ always asked questions like this, illogical ones with no answers. I'd already unpacked; she'd already made up my bed with her lid-tight hospital corners. Freshman orientation had already started. CJ wasn't done being pissed that I'd turned down Dartmouth for Baird (a lot of people seemed shocked by that), but what she didn't understand was that if I didn't get as far away from her and the tri-state area as soon as possible, I was going to implode.

"CJ . . . ," my father started. I could tell he was getting antsy. It had been a long day.

"Okay, okay. *Ugh*." She looked at me. "I'm just going to miss her too much. Fuck, Ben. We're empty nesters now."

CJ swore a lot, which was kind of nice because, growing up, my older sister, Georgia, and I could swear as much as we wanted. Whenever we went out, Georgia and I knew to tame our speech, but CJ didn't, and her swearing could be embarrassing.

Jackie was sitting on her bed chewing gum and pretending to read from the orientation packet, but I could tell she was listening.

"One more thing." CJ pulled out a small white box and handed it to me. Inside were two tiny gold studs—one letter *L* and one letter *A*, my initials.

"For your second holes," CJ explained. CJ had flipped her shit when I got my second holes pierced over the summer. She'd said they were "extremely tacky," but now, apparently, she had decided to support them.

"Thanks, CJ. I love them."

CJ flinched. She's used to the fact that I don't call her Mom anymore—I haven't in years—but she still hates it, especially when we're around new people. "They're going to think I'm your stepmom," she once said, and I'd shrugged, because after she did the Unforgivable Thing, I stopped caring what she thought.

"I'm so glad. Here, try them on."

CJ placed one stud in each second earhole. Then she hugged me so hard I could barely breathe. For such a small woman she's freakishly strong—it's all the Pilates. I inhaled the scent of her Fekkai shampoo and swallowed over the lump lodged in my throat. I couldn't see her face, but I could tell from her short, uneven breathing that she was crying. I bit the inside of my cheeks so I wouldn't cry, too.

My dad is less complicated. He hugged me like he always did—lifting me off the ground and giving me a butterfly kiss with his eyelashes. As usual, his face smelled like Noxzema. He placed me back down and I took in the sight of him—kind blue-gray eyes, dark hair sprinkled with gray. I felt grateful for him in a way I no longer could for CJ.

"Be good, Sass." He winked. My parents have called me Sass since I was two and used to parade around the house wearing sunglasses and a feather boa.

When my parents finally left, Jackie and I looked at each other. Our dorm room was small, but it was all ours. I felt a stir in the base of my stomach at the knowledge that I could finally do whatever I wanted. No curfew, no sneaking around, no asking permission. The expression on Jackie's face revealed a mutual feeling. We were exhilarated and terrified, all at once.

We decided to put CJ's vodka to use immediately. Jackie mixed the drinks in a couple of mugs she'd brought and accidentally tipped one over, spilling the spiked Diet Coke all over my bed. The soda hissed and I watched as the tar-colored liquid soaked my new white sheets and duvet. CJ bought all my bedding at Saks—it was some European designer she loved. CJ always spent *way* too much on stuff like bedding. My father never seemed to mind.

Jackie covered her mouth. "Shit! I'm an idiot. Sorry, Lucy."

I shrugged, barely caring. I kind of liked seeing CJ's efforts unexpectedly negate each other. "It'll come out in the laundry."

"We should wash them now, to be sure. I'm an idiot," Jackie repeated.

"You're really not."

Jackie stripped the sheets. The hospital corners would never be as perfect again—I don't even tuck in my top sheet when I make the bed, which CJ hates.

I could tell Jackie felt really bad, and I wished that she didn't. I watched her rub a Tide stain stick over the ruined part of my sheets.

She was beautiful in that idyllic way—the effortless blond, blue-eyed, stops-you-in-your-tracks beautiful like CJ and Georgia. My sister looks much more like CJ than I do. I have brown hair and my dad's eyes, a darker, grayer blue than CJ's and Georgia's translucent, shocking aqua ones. People tell me I'm pretty, but I'm not Georgia pretty. People tell me I look like the brunette version of Georgia, but nobody ever says that Georgia looks like the blond version of me.

Jackie insisted on washing my bedding (blue-blood manners—I could tell), and I mixed us new drinks while she ran down to the laundry room. When she got back we sat on our beds, talking, playing the do-you-know-this-person? game for a good half hour, because Wilton, Connecticut, isn't that far from my hometown in Cold Spring Harbor, on Long Island. The vodka made us chat faster and deeper, until we were both stretched out on our beds, the last of the light spilling through our single window. We had a view of palm trees and in the distance the San Gabriel Mountains, a purple ridge in the dusk. Mountains were still so new to me then, and I shivered at their potential, at whatever it was they would promise.

Talking to Jackie was almost as easy as talking to Lydia, my best friend from home. I knew I'd lucked out on the roommate front. Georgia's freshman-year roommate at Yale had been from a farm in Kansas, and she said they'd never had anything to talk about besides chickens and organic fruit.

"Your mom is awesome," Jackie said, gesturing toward the half-empty bottle of vodka.

As usual, I hated hearing this. But I didn't hold it against Jackie, because if I didn't know CJ, I'd probably say she was awesome, too.

Jackie opened her laptop and turned on "Rhiannon." I felt even surer about her.

"You like Fleetwood Mac?" she said when I smiled.

"If I could have lunch with one person in the world, it would be Stevie Nicks." I tucked a strand of hair behind my ear, hoping my answer didn't sound too rehearsed. It had been the personal-essay question on my application to Dartmouth (I was surprised they'd accepted me based on that answer—Stevie isn't close to being intellectual enough for Dartmouth). I grew up listening to Fleetwood Mac like it was a religion, especially that really bad year, the year that followed the Unforgivable Thing. Lydia and I used to play *Rumours* from start to finish and smoke cigarettes out her bedroom window. Well, I smoked. Lydia never smokes.

Jackie grinned. "Stevie's the queen."

The Absolut was making my limbs pleasantly heavy, and I felt as though I could stay there talking to Jackie forever. She asked me about boys, if I had a boyfriend, so I told her about the Parker part of my past, making sure it sounded like I cared more than I did. It actually bored me to talk about Parker—I'm much more interested in other people's love lives—so I quickly moved on to ask Jackie about her own love life. She'd broken up with a high school boyfriend over the summer, she said. He was going to college in Virginia and they didn't want to do long-distance, so it was mutual.

I wanted to ask more questions, but our door swung open and a tall girl with long, glistening black hair walked in, followed by a skinny girl with white-blond hair, the color of saltine crackers.

The dark-haired girl's eyes were so crystal blue they looked fake.

"*Finally*, Bree," she said. "I think we found normal people." She ran her fingers through her dark hair and looked at Jackie and me. "I thought I heard 'Rhiannon.' Have you guys noticed that everyone in our hall is either international or a dreadlocked lesbian?"

"*Pippa*, you can't talk like that," the blond girl said. She shifted her weight to one foot and placed her pale, pin-thin arms on her nonexistent hips.

"Why not? I have nothing against lesbians. My cousin is a lesbian. For a while I thought *I* was a lesbian. I'm just *saying* that I don't have anything in common with someone who chooses to do that to their hair."

"Not all lesbians have dreadlocks," the blonde said.

"I know *that*, Bree."

The dark-haired girl looked at us and rolled her enormous eyes. "I'm Pippa McAllister. And this is Bree Benson."

Jackie and I introduced ourselves.

"Are you roommates?" Jackie asked.

"No," Bree said. "I have a single in Pitney. I wish I were in Kaplan, though. This dorm is so much nicer. But I met Pippa last week. We were on the same Orientation Adventure."

I nodded. Orientation Adventure was part of Baird's freshman orientation program—camping trips that took place the week before the semester began. They were optional, though, so I opted out. I hate camping. Turns out Jackie did, too.

"My dad made me go," Pippa sighed. "It was kind of brutal. Two of the girls on our trip didn't shave their armpits. Thank *God* I found Bree."

The way she carried herself, I could tell Pippa had been popular in high school. She seemed like someone who did whatever she wanted without worrying too much about the consequences. I liked her instantly—probably because I've always lacked that *I don't give a fuck* quality in myself. Even if I don't want to give a fuck, even if I convince myself I don't, I always do.

"And I live on this hall," Pippa continued. "My roommate is from Seattle, and she and her boyfriend came here *together*, so she's like, off with him somewhere. He came to the room earlier, and they were basically making out in front of me; it was dis*gust*ing. He's one of those dudes with the big holes in his ears."

"Gauges," Bree corrected. She sat down in my desk chair and crossed one of her chopstick legs over the other. She was so thin she looked like a thirteen-year-old boy. "Have you guys eaten? Maybe we should order a pizza? I'm starving."

"I *cannot* eat pizza," Pippa whined. "I've already eaten a muffin today *and* a sandwich. I refuse to gain the freshman fifteen."

"Pippa, you had a gluten-free muffin this morning and like, one bite of my sandwich. You're fine."

"Easy for you to say, you can eat whatever you want and not gain weight."

I eyed Pippa, who wore a black cotton dress. She wasn't fat by any means, but she wasn't super skinny like Bree. It's how I would've described my own body, until Pippa turned to Jackie and me and said, "But you're both rails, too. Ugh! Not fair. My metabolism is failing me with age."

I looked down at the tops of my thighs, tanned from the summer but suddenly fleshy-looking. Fleshier than Jackie's, and definitely fleshier than Bree's. It hadn't even occurred to me to think about the freshman fifteen. I'd heard Georgia mention it, but only in passing—*the inevitable fifteen pounds everyone gains their freshman year because of all the beer and pizza.*

I'd eaten a cheeseburger and a bowl of ice cream at the orientation barbecue earlier that day. CJ had nibbled on some potato salad. I'd never had to think about what I ate, but maybe I needed to start.

"Anyway," Pippa said. "We're supposed to find people to bring to this party. Some guy invited us and said to bring more freshman girls. 'Fresh meat' is actually what he said, which is kinda gross, but hey, it's a party. Wanna go? It's at a house on Hutchins Street."

"Sure," Jackie said.

"Now? Should we change?" I was still wearing jean shorts and a white tank top, grubby from moving in all day. Pippa and Bree were in sundresses, and Pippa was wearing eyeliner and something glossy on her lips.

"If you want." Bree shrugged.

"Nah, let's just go," Jackie said. She untwisted and retwisted her blond hair into a messy bun and stood. In a navy T-shirt and track shorts, she looked like a gorgeous tomboy—the kind guys are obsessed with. I wanted to at least put on some mascara and change my shirt, but I didn't say anything. I didn't want to come off like some superficial girly girl who can't go to a party without makeup on.

"Let's take a shot before, though?" Pippa said, gesturing to the Absolut. "If it's okay with whoever's vodka that is."

"Mine," I said. "Go for it."

The four of us passed the bottle around. When it was Bree's turn, she hesitated before taking a swig, then her expression morphed into one of disgust.

"Yuck." She passed the bottle to Jackie.

"It gets easier," Pippa said.

"Easier?" Jackie asked.

"I didn't drink that much in high school." Bree blinked her hazel eyes.

"Well, there's plenty of time to catch up now." Jackie smiled.

"What *did* you do in high school, if you didn't drink and you didn't have sex? You went to boarding school. Isn't that what people do there?"

"Pippa, you're annoying." Bree glanced away before looking at Jackie and me. "I went to Choate and spent most of the time studying my ass off so I could get a good financial aid package for college. I'm not trying to make you feel bad for me; I'm just telling you," she said quickly, as if she had rehearsed it. Then she looked down and smiled ruefully. "But yeah, I've got to lose the v-card."

"Well, don't give it up to just anyone," Jackie said.

I nodded in agreement, though I felt bad for Bree for getting put on the spot. I would've hated going to college a virgin.

"We'll get her laid, ladies." Pippa grinned. "And with someone worthwhile. You're gorgeous, Bree. You can afford high standards."

I wouldn't have called Bree *gorgeous*—she was more *cute*, with her freckles and button nose—but I understood that Pippa was trying to redeem herself for making Bree feel self-conscious. Bree's prettiness was mostly accentuated by her thin figure. Skinny people just look better, I realized then.

Jackie took her swig of Absolut, and my stomach churned in anticipation. We were going to a party, and there wouldn't be a curfew. I would probably never have a curfew again. I felt the corners of my mouth poke into a smile. I fingered the backs of my new earrings, twisting them around and around as I waited for my turn to take a pull of the lukewarm Absolut. Jackie handed me the vodka and I winced as I swallowed it down—not a new feeling. I'd done my fair share of vodka pulls in high school, first for fun and then just to dull everything away. But things were going to be different now, I knew.

I felt a pleasant rush to my head as I stood. I was still touching my new earrings as I caught a glimpse of them in the mirror hanging on the back of the door. *L. A.* They looked expensive—definitely real gold. I actually liked them a lot (I'm a sucker for a tasteful monogram), but they screamed *gift from CJ*. They would never be anything else. I pulled them off discreetly, quietly dropping them into the trash bin as we left the room.

2
STEPHEN

The first time I saw Lucy Albright was at a party at Wrigley's house on Hutchins Street. Wrigley and his roommates threw down a lot our junior fall, and the best-looking freshman girls always showed up wasted, wearing tight jeans and revealing tops. But Lucy was different from the rest of them. She's beautiful, but it's more complex than that. Lucy is beautiful in the way that makes it hard to stop staring, in the way that the attractiveness becomes something you have to *figure out*. The best part is, she has no idea.

She stood in the living room by the fireplace, holding a plastic red cup and wearing shorts, I forget what color, but I remember that they were shorts because I took note of how long and slim her legs were. Not too skinny, but perfect. Tan, creamy skin, like a coffee milk shake. Her arms were the same, lengthy and thin like string beans. Every move she made seemed graceful and honed; she was feminine and delicate in a way that made me want to hold her hand. I couldn't stop watching her.

Her face was incredible, too. Perhaps not perfect—no, not perfect—but holy hell pretty. Dark blue eyes, a straight nose between defined cheekbones. Her long, chestnut-colored hair spilled down over her neck and down through the middle of her exposed shoulder blades.

I watched her for a long time. Sometimes I catch myself staring at people for too long without realizing it. I'm only curious. Why do they laugh? How do they speak? What do they do? What do they feel? I want to know.

Lucy's smile spread across her whole face. It was pretty, like the rest of her. You have to be careful of girls that are too pretty, though. They hold a power that they never had to earn.

I finished my seventh beer. I'd already had two whiskey shots, but I still felt a creeping sense of anxiety right at the base of my brain, so I did another with Wrigley in his room. Charlie took out the little white bag and shook a small pile of blow onto the mirror lying on Wrigley's table. He used his driver's license to cut us each a generous line. Long and thin. Like Lucy's arms, I thought, as I inhaled and felt the *whoosh* hit my brain. Like a blast of cold, sweet air that made life come into focus.

I didn't talk to her that night. Not because I was nervous—I don't get nervous talking to girls—but because I got shitfaced and ended up in Diana's room again, fucking her, and then sitting up in bed until three in the morning listening to her whine about what a horrible person I'd become.

I did catch Lucy's eye, though, across the room, and I held her gaze for a couple of seconds. She looked at me with an expression mixed with interest and fear, like I was going to do something terrible to her. But when I smiled, her expression softened. That was when I knew. It's usually fairly easy to tell, but with Lucy I knew for sure. There was something about her, a fragile sense of blind conviction. I knew that she would trust me.

3
LUCY
OCTOBER 2010

Pippa started seeing Mike Wrigley the second week of freshman year. Everyone called him Wrigley, not Mike. Wrigley and his friends were in charge of planning the annual trip to Lake Mead the first weekend in October. They were part of the underground fraternity Chops, short for Lambda Chi Alpha, Pippa explained. Baird had shut Chops down a few years ago after a drug bust, but Wrigley had since spearheaded its underground revival. Freshmen weren't supposed to go on the Mead trip, but with her new semi-girlfriend status, Pippa got the four of us invited.

We hit the road at dawn on Friday in Pippa's Touareg, tailing Wrigley in the weak gray light, the sun a thin orange line on the horizon. Pippa offered to drive while the three of us slept, but I can never really sleep in cars, so I talked to her while she chased Adderall with her latte and balanced the wheel in cruise control—it was a straight shot on I-15 across the border into Nevada.

I'd been perplexed by the collective enthusiasm surrounding the five-hour drive to a random desert lake, the Pacific Ocean being a mere fifty miles from Baird. But pulling into the marina midmorning, the sun a giant tangerine orb casting rays onto the velvety blue water, I understood. Mead was more than just a lake. Massive red cliffs rose around the shorelines like something from another planet, the surface of the water iridescent under the cloudless dome of pure blue sky. It was a landscape starkly different from anything I'd ever laid eyes on. New frontiers. The possibilities filled me. I watched as the rest of the cars pulled in and bleary-eyed kids climbed out, yawning and stretching in the sun. There must've been sixty of us, maybe seventy. Some were cracking open beers already. Wrigley appeared from the marina office with two keys and tossed one to a guy with longish dark hair. Someone else in Chops, most likely. They were wearing matching captain's hats.

"Anchors aweigh," Wrigley said, and everyone followed him and the dark-haired guy onto two houseboats at the end of the marina.

Lake Mead was the most spectacular place I'd ever been, I decided after day one of cruising through the endless lake, through canyons that seemed to stretch on forever. It was October but still summer weather on the lake, even hotter than my first month in Southern California, and I could feel the sun baking me a shade darker. There were fresh thirty-racks in every corner and plastic pouches of pink Franzia dangling above our heads. Wrigley turned up the music as loud as it would go and it didn't matter—there was no one else around for miles.

At night the two boats docked on a wide-enough beach. When Jackie, Bree, and I couldn't keep our eyes open for another drink, the three of us crawled into whatever vacant space we could find and crashed into sleep. Pippa slept with Wrigley in his tent on the beach. The queen of Mead, I heard one girl deem her, because Wrigley was the king.

I felt farther away from home than I ever had, and happier than I had since before the really bad year, before the Unforgivable Thing. Baird kids seemed to have a kind of fun that was new to me, the fun that came with open-mindedness and experimenting and genuine self-confidence, an entirely different kind of fun than the Cold Spring Harbor, Southside-induced fun we had in cocktail dresses on the golf course, where fun had become another word for *competition*—a night out was a contest to see who wore the cutest outfit and who flirted successfully with the most attractive guy. I'd gotten so sick of all that at the same time that Lydia and Helen and my other Long Island friends had absorbed it into their identities. They would build their lives around it—preppy Long Island kids turned preppy Long Island moms. I wanted to run away from it; I was afraid of what might happen if I didn't. I craved something more when I put my head down on the pillow at night, and the longing stretched all the way to my toes.

I had tried to explain all this to Lydia without sounding condescending, but I never succeeded. I knew I sounded spoiled, patronizing, criticizing a life I should've felt lucky to have. It wasn't that I wasn't grateful—I was, I tried to be—but by the beginning of senior year I knew that if I didn't get out of there, I would shrink. It was a point of contention between Lydia and me right up until the day I left for Baird and she for Amherst. She wanted me to want the things she wanted, but I just didn't.

Except for a few of the older girls who stared at us like they wanted to throw us overboard, the kids at Baird were sincerely nice. Funny and interested and offbeat and smart—a collection of personalities that inspired me, that made me feel a new part of myself. I watched them take drugs like it was nothing, and not because they were trying to impress anyone. If you didn't do drugs, no one cared, either. There were loose social circles but no cliques; it felt like you could really do whatever you wanted and no one was going to judge you. Baird kids wore neon one-pieces and gold shorts and said things like *hella* and *let's kick it*. Lydia and Helen would've thought they were weird.

The third and final day on Lake Mead, I leaned against the railing on the upper deck of one of the houseboats. I was physically exhausted but still mentally jacked up, fueled by beer and adrenaline. Pippa leaned over Wrigley, her hands pressed to his sun-kissed shoulders, as he used a credit card to separate a mound of white powder on a hand mirror. Pippa had been doing coke with Wrigley all weekend. I watched her suck the skinny white line up her nostril with a rolled twenty-dollar bill.

Pippa passed the mirror to Jackie, and I felt a stab of betrayal when Jackie sucked up one of the lines. Until this weekend, I hadn't known Jackie did coke. She said she doesn't "do" it (i.e., doesn't buy it), but that if it's there, she might dabble. I was relieved when Bree declined and passed the mirror to me, because it meant I could do the same. Part of me wanted to try it, but there are those stories about people passing out and never waking up the first time they do coke, and I just knew I'd be one of them.

I passed the mirror to the guy next to me and stood. My fingers gripped the thin railing of the boat, and it was then that I turned around and saw his eyes. I'll never forget his eyes. I think I'll lie in bed years from now, when I have children and my children have children, and I'll see those two bottle-green orbs, watching me, on the precipice of changing everything. The eyes were small but luminous—they could've been woven with strands of silk they were so bright. They pierced me from the deck of the other houseboat, a good twenty feet away. It was crowded—people stood all around, wet elbows bumping into sides and heads turning, shielding the eyes from my view every couple of seconds, like clouds passing over the sun. But the eyes never looked away.

"Luce, we're funneling!" Jackie yelled. The coke was finished; there was a new activity. "You first."

Everyone was shouting my name, and Jackie grabbed my hand, pulling me down. I anticipated pain as my knees scraped the rough fiberglass surface of the deck, but in my drunken blunder I was having too much fun to notice if it hurt.

Jackie handed me the plastic tube and lukewarm beer rushed down my throat so quickly I nearly gagged, but I managed to swallow it in full, fast gulps until the can above my head rattled empty. Jackie helped me up, my head so dizzy that I lost footing in the sunny haze, falling backward, when a thick arm caught me from behind. Thick but soft, like the punching bag my dad keeps in our basement.

"Watch it." The voice was hard and quick.

I looked up, my heart hammering in my chest. The bright green eyes stared down at me sharply. I felt as if they could see into me, as if they had jumped inside my body and were wandering around the inside of my soul, taking notes.

"Have we met?" He released me.

I recognized him. I'd seen him at a party once, and he was the guy Wrigley had tossed the other set of keys to on the first morning of Mead. Chops captain number two. He was taller up close, with curly dark hair all over his chest. Parker didn't have any hair on his chest.

"I don't think so," I answered. "I just saw you—on the other boat? How did you get over here so quickly like that?"

"Magic." He winked. His dark hair was shiny and coarse. It fell in tousled waves around his face. Olive-toned skin.

I couldn't decide if he was handsome. He looked like a younger Christian Bale, maybe, but thicker. A weaker chin. Not as overtly good-looking. But there was Something About Him. A pinch in my stomach.

"You must be one of the aesthetically pleasing freshman ladies Wrigley brought along, bless his heart. I'm Stephen DeMarco." He held out a hand, his eyes locked to mine.

"I'm Lucy Albright."

His hand felt thick and cold from the beer he'd been holding.

"Lucy. Like the song?"

"The song?"

"'Lucy in the Sky with Diamonds.'" He smiled, using his hands to make a panorama in the sky.

"My dad used to sing me that song."

"'Picture yourself in a boat on a river, with tangerine trees and marmalade skies . . .' And we're on a boat on a river. It's too perfect." He laughed. I noticed a little pudge spilling over the waistline of his red bathing suit.

"Except we're not on a river. It's a lake."

Stephen tilted his beer bottle in my direction. "That it is. You're smart. I see why Baird had the good sense to accept you."

I couldn't think of anything to say. I grabbed another beer from an open case at our feet. I felt like I was surviving on beer at that point. I'd barely had anything to eat in three days. I'd been eating less in general, actually, ever since the freshman-fifteen conversation. My stomach grumbled.

"So what do you think of Lake Mead, Lucy in the Sky with Diamonds?" Stephen asked. The sunlight was splintering, but he kept his sunglasses on top of his head, his eye contact unyielding. I knew if I looked away it would seem rude.

"It's amazing," I said.

"You never forget your first trip to Mead."

"I don't doubt it. Nice hat, by the way."

"Thanks. Wrigley is the true captain, but I convinced him that the cocaptain deserves a hat, too."

"Of course. Your efforts are appreciated. Thank you for keeping us afloat."

"Not a problem. Only following my orders, Lucy." When he said my name, there was a jolt in the nerves wrapping my spine. "It was nice to meet you."

"You, too." I was locked in my head, momentarily stunned by a foreign feeling. I was relieved when he wiggled three thick fingers before turning away.

Then he looked over his shoulder, piercing my gaze again. "By the way. You look so good in that bikini, it hurts."

4

STEPHEN

I knew it when Lucy became interested in me. I could sense it at Lake Mead; when we talked, I could taste it in the space around her, like salt in the air.

The only problem was that Lucy's interest was, for her, a subconscious yearning. A feeling she would not yet face, one that clashed with her naïveté and limited sexual scope. She wasn't a virgin—there was no way—but her demeanor seemed raw, youthful. I need to know more. I needed to know what it was like to fuck her.

I knew how to catch the interest of girls like Lucy. It would take time and effort, like most good things in life, but I wasn't in a rush. I had plenty to keep me occupied, including the dilemma of Diana Bunn.

Diana has been my on-off girlfriend throughout Baird. I never envisioned myself staying with the same girl for all of college, but whenever Diana and I broke up, life turned into an exhausting series of long, drawn-out conversations that stalled my productivity in other areas. Our worlds had become so intricately intertwined on the tiny campus of Baird—same friends, same schedule—that I literally couldn't imagine my life without her.

Diana was a sociology major, so most of her classes were in the Edmonds Center, and as a political science major mine were mainly in Fielding Hall. Our routine was on lockdown. I left class in Fielding and walked across the quad to Edmonds, where Diana waited for me to walk to lunch. Charlie or Evan or one of the science majors saved the corner table in the dining hall. All the buildings were made of the same pale gray slate. All the quads were well-kept squares of kelly-green grass year-round, the Southern California climate void of seasons. I ate at the same lunch table with the same kids. Had the same shitty beefsteak sandwich on rubbery bread. And the same unwavering girlfriend.

No wonder I'd become restless. But last time Diana and I did take a time-out, she went into a histrionic state, everyone else got involved, and it was all completely draining. I escaped by going into town and eating lunch alone at the deli, which was fine except that paying for my own meals started to get expensive. But if I ate at another table in the dining hall, I'd spend the entire meal being stared down by Keaton and Josie and all of Diana's friends (who are *my* friends, too, I should add). I could have made Wrigley come sit with me, but then everybody would've hated him, too. It was just a big mess.

So dating Diana made everything easier. And we got along well when she didn't hate my guts. At times I have even loved her. Not in the way most people portray love, which is fine by me, because that kind of love is just a form of weakness. It holds people back.

I've always been attracted to Diana, even though she isn't Miss America. She has curly, caramel brown hair that falls just above her shoulders and almost precisely matches the color of her eyes. Her chin is a little too prominent, but it gives her character. The thing is, I know I'm no movie star. I'd be better looking if I lost fifteen or twenty pounds, but I carry most of the extra weight around my middle, so it's not as noticeable, and most girls don't seem to mind. That was another good thing about Diana—she didn't nag me about going to the gym like my ex from high school had. And though Diana knew about Nicole, she was willing to talk about it—which probably meant that she didn't know about the others. Hence the overly dramatic breakup that was four hours of a precious September Saturday.

Diana: I know you slept with Nicole Hart after Hawaiian Luau last year. Don't even try to deny it, because I know.
Me: It was a mistake, but I did. *I did.*
Diana: You're a fucking piece of shit.
Me: I am. *I am.*
Diana: Seriously, you are beyond selfish.
Me: I know. *I knew.*

Diana: You're a disgusting, worthless excuse for a human
being and I hope you rot in hell.
Me: I understand why you say that. *I understood.*
Diana: This is over.

I hate when Diana tries to call the shots in our relationship. It was a month ago that she called me out, right when we got back to school, after Wrigley's party. She didn't even come to Lake Mead she was so mad at me, despite the bouquet of white lilies (her favorite) I'd placed on her doorstep alongside a heartfelt, handwritten letter. But now that some time had passed, I could tell she was ready to forgive me and get back together. Diana is emotional, and emotional people count on time for fucking everything. It takes *time* for them to regain their so-called sanity. Diana was always testing me with her so-called needed *time*, as though *time* may or may not be enough to save our relationship. It was hypocritical. She always came back. Despite her threatening declarations, she would never have the final call—I made sure of that.

Diana finally stopped by yesterday afternoon, while I was sitting on my couch reading articles online. I love being by myself in the afternoon, after class is over and I've eaten a good lunch. My roommate, Evan, was normally at lacrosse practice until dinnertime, so I usually had the room to myself.

I was reading about the guys on the "30 Under 30" list in *Forbes*, about how they climbed the corporate ladder quickly and effectively. I've always known that I wanted to be a lawyer, and I know I'll make a good one. Everybody says do what you love, and I love the law. It's fun—it's like a game, the way you work your way around the different constitutional limits and push the boundaries to work in your favor. People like to speak about justice as some fantastical idea, some invisible measure of what is "right," but justice is following a fair procedure—that's all. In that sense, the most successful lawyers craft justice. They configure it. What many people fail to understand is that the world is carved by nature's laws, not moral values.

Plus if there's one thing I'm sure of it's that I'll make a shit ton of money. My father has never been successful—he's a very mediocre accountant who's poured most of his energy into dealing with the nutcase that is my mother. My mother was diagnosed with bipolar disorder the year after I was born, and they thought it was going to be manageable, but she refused to take her damn medication. So you'd have thought my father would've divorced her *then*, but no, my parents decided to stay together and to have a third child together—my little sister Sadie—before finally splitting up when Sadie was four. When my parents did divorce, the judge took one look at my mom's medical history outlining her numerous manic episodes, and full custody went to my father. My mother proceeded to buy a house on the water in Port Jefferson with her half of the divorce settlement, which had been most of our college savings. The house is nothing insane, but a place ideal for one person, and my father didn't even put up a fight. He borrowed money from my uncle to cover our mortgage, and my older brother Luke and I had to take out student loans. We're not in *poverty* or anything, but we're not exactly rolling in it, and I sure as hell am not going to have a life like that when I'm out on my own.

Anyway, I was dreaming of seeing my own picture on the "30 Under 30" list: a twenty-nine-year-old associate at a top firm, well on my way to partnership, a brownstone in the West Village and a wife with a banging body who cooks me steak. Who lets me fuck her in the ass once a week. Maybe we have a kid on the way or something. That's the dream.

The fantasizing was getting me pretty turned on. So I was just about to put on some porn when my door flung open and Diana stood there, her curls damp from the rain.

"You could knock." I hate when people barge in without knocking.

"Sorry," she said.

"What's up?" I eyed her, trying to gain a read. She stood in the doorway, her bottom lip trembling a little. "Di? Come here." I knew she was going to start crying.

She closed the door and sat down next to me on the couch, and it was already waterworks central. Porn would have to wait, but that was okay. Crying girl next to you on the couch leads to sex, regardless of the circumstances. I swear. Ask any guy.

"I miss you," she choked through tears.

"I know. I miss you, too. But you broke up with me, remember?" I smoothed the side of her wet hair. I knew it; she was considering a reconciliation. Probably because Nicole was the only cheating episode she knew of.

"I know, but I think I made the wrong decision," Diana blubbered, her toffee eyes watery and red around the rims. "I just want everything to be okay again. Like it was in the beginning."

In the beginning. I only remember things when someone reminds me—I'm not a naturally reflective person. But when Diana said that I suddenly saw her, two years earlier, standing in Charlie Rosen's dorm room wearing jean cutoffs and a white tank top, drinking a red plastic cup of something. Her soft curls were tangled where they hit her shoulders, and she wore a clump of silver bracelets on one of her arms. I remember admiring her small, athletic build, thinking she was cute in a messy sort of tomboyish way. There was something about the manner in which she carried herself that drew me in—I think it was the way she smiled at the things she thought were worth smiling about, and not about the things she didn't. I could tell she did that, just by observing her in conversation. At the end of the evening I walked her home and kissed her in front of Kaplan. I was pretty confident she'd let me. She did, and afterward I asked for her phone number.

When I decide I like someone, my first step is to gather as much information as possible about every aspect of her life in order to more closely resemble her ideal partner.

I found out as much as I could about Diana: she was born and raised in the suburbs of Milwaukee, wanted to be a sociology major, had two younger brothers, went to Lake Winnebago in Wisconsin every summer with her family, had a cocker spaniel named Lola and a cat named Madge, went to sleep-away camp every summer until she was fifteen, loved hiking, canoeing, the Green Bay Packers, and baked brie. Her father was a high school history teacher, her mother a real estate agent; they had some money but not tons; one of her brothers had Celiac disease, and she tried to support him by avoiding gluten; she'd read *Hooking Up* over the summer and adored anything by Tom Wolfe; her favorite storybook character as a child was Stuart Little; she loved silver jewelry, not gold; she'd had a boyfriend junior year of high school but it had lasted only three months.

I memorized the clothes she wore; the titles, times, locations, and

professors of her classes; where she lived on campus; who her roommate was; who her friends were; and where and what she ate for breakfast, lunch, and dinner most days. I knew she put milk and two Sugar in
the Raw packets in her coffee, liked whiskey, hated cigarettes, and that
she'd made out with two guys so far that year, one of whom, a skinny
sophomore on the track team named Joel, was interested in her.

It wasn't difficult information to find. Some of it I garnered through
that first conversation with her, from people I knew who knew her, and
bits and pieces were obtained through a variety of accessible sources:
our class directory, Facebook, and a thorough Google search.

The second time I saw Diana was when I invited her to pregame in
my dorm room the following week. She seemed hesitant about coming,
so I mentioned that I'd recently finished reading *A Man in Full* by Tom
Wolfe. Did I like it? she wanted to know.

"I thought it was an engaging commentary on American culture."

Diana looked impressed, so I continued.

"I mean, Tom Wolfe is first and foremost a social commentator, and
this book is no exception. I generally avoid modern authors, as the con-
temporary ones are weak writers, but this book is awesome." (Full dis-
closure: My rave review came from a random reader, extracted from a
random Internet website.)

"Hey, Princess Diana, why don't we take a shot of tequila in celebra-
tion of the greatest American novelist, I mean, social commentator, of
our time?" I suggested.

"Princess Diana?"

"Princess Diana of Wales, duh." I touched the tip of her nose and she
smiled at the nickname. They always do.

There was no tequila, so we did Bailey's instead. And that shot of
Bailey's went down as easy as the start of our relationship—creamy and
sweet, so much so that you couldn't taste the toxicity underneath.

I reminisced while Di cried on my shoulder, her tears soaking my
shirt. I studied the back of her head as her face convulsed into my arm-
pit. I did miss having her around. I would've tried some tears out myself
but knew it was hopeless. I recall crying only once in my life, when I was
five years old and ran into a hornets' nest in our attic. I got about forty
bee stings and was rushed to the ER. My dad was away for the weekend,

so my mom had to take me, and I remember her yelling at me that I was ruining her day because she was supposed to go into the city with some friend. I don't remember if I was crying because of that or because the bee stings hurt so fucking much, but I haven't cried since. Not even any of the times my mother came home out of her mind during an episode, screaming at all of us to be silent because she was "being chased," and shattering dishes against the wall next to my father's head when he'd try to calm her down.

Since I couldn't cry I kissed Diana; kissing counts as an emotional gesture. Minutes later we were having sex on my bed. I didn't end up needing the porn.

5

LUCY

OCTOBER 2010

The week after the trip to Lake Mead, I lay in my bed feeling restless. Jackie's bed was empty. She'd met a guy, a freshman named Stuart, and they'd been spending more and more nights together. The other day, she'd called him her boyfriend.

Pippa and Wrigley were still an item. She said he lit candles and dripped the hot wax on her when they had sex. Bree had made out with two different sophomores (still no sex). I had yet to even *kiss* anyone at Baird.

It's always been like this for me with boys. I'm not picky, per se—I don't need a bunch of specific boxes to be checked. I just need a feeling to be there, and if it isn't, then I can't do it. Some girls play it safe and look for uncomplicated, but uncomplicated can be a death sentence—I learned that after the Unforgivable Thing, and after Parker. I gazed out the window at the fading sunlight, wishing that things could be different, that *I* could be different. But I made that big promise to myself after I broke up with Parker, huddled under my quilt, still in my dress the night of spring formal, eyeliner smudging my face in a mask of black tears; I swore that I'd never date anyone again unless I had that *feeling*—the feeling that everything had been flipped inside me, for the better.

I went out with Parker Lines for a year and a half because I had to. It was getting late in the game and I still hadn't had a boyfriend and Parker was *so cute* and *so nice* and I was *crazy* not to. I maintain that we never really had chemistry, but maybe Lydia was (partially) right in saying that the real reason I wasn't ever into Parker is because I was hung up on Gabe Petersen.

I met Gabe the summer after eighth grade (the summer before the Unforgivable Thing). It's ridiculous, but I loved him before I even talked to him, and that's the only time that has or will ever happen to me—I'm sure of it. It's the kind of thing that's only possible when you're fourteen and delirious from the dramatic effects of pubescent hormones.

I knew who Gabe was—the Petersens lived in Oyster Bay, and their daughter Macy was my year. Our families were both members of the Cove Club, the country club where I'd become friendly with Macy during childhood summers of camp and swim team. But Gabe was significantly older than us and never around when we were kids; I only knew of him in passing as Macy's older brother, and had a vague idea of him from the Petersens' Christmas cards. Macy told me once that she was sure she'd been an accident, since Gabe and her sister, Eleanor, were so much older.

The first time I saw Gabe in the flesh he was playing golf with Lydia's cousin, Andrew Montgomery. Lydia and I used to spend every summer day sunbathing by the club pool, charging Arnold Palmers and Caesar salad wraps to our parents' accounts and watching boys come in for lunch after eighteen holes. Gabe was wearing a white polo shirt and seersucker shorts. Macy had her father's deep red hair, but Gabe looked more like his mother, with light brown hair and honey skin. His face was so perfect I could hardly look at it. Blue eyes, a ski-jump nose like Macy's, and full, ultra-kissable lips. I loved him instantly.

"That's Gabe Petersen, isn't it?" I asked Lydia while I watched him and Andrew order lunch at the snack bar.

She glanced up briefly. "Yeah."

"Is he Andrew's year?"

"I think so."

"And how old is Andrew?"

"Like, old," Lydia said, eyeing me. "Already-out-of-college old."

Andrew came over to say hi when he noticed Lydia and me on our chaises, and Gabe followed. We were introduced. He looked at me in a way that made my stomach wobble so badly I had to sip my Arnold Palmer and stare at my fingernails. I listened to Gabe explain that he was in between jobs and would be teaching tennis at Cove Club all summer. He'd played at UNC.

"Lucy and I won the girls' doubles championship three years in a row," Lydia bragged.

"Oh yeah? Well it doesn't sound like you need 'em, but if you ever want lessons I teach a mean backhand." Gabe smiled, and he was looking at only me.

That was how things worked in eighth grade. Subtle insinuations that felt more romantic than anything. Gabe was the most perfect guy I'd ever seen. I went home and told CJ I needed tennis lessons.

"I should take them with Gabe Petersen, though," I said. "Macy's brother. He played at UNC, so he's really good. Apparently."

CJ shrugged and said I was already a fine tennis player but that she'd love to see me do something other than lie by the pool all day.

I signed up for weekly lessons with Gabe. Every Thursday afternoon we went out on one of the green clay courts, just the two of us. Gabe was cinnamon brown from spending his days in the sun. When he lunged for the ball, his shorts rode up and I saw the white skin of his thighs. I could've melted right into the court. When I practiced my serve I could feel him watching me, standing closer than he had to. Sometimes he'd come up behind me and place his giant hand over mine, repositioning my grip on the racket handle.

"Like that," he'd say gently, his breath prickling my neck and shoulders.

I played sloppy, nervous tennis that summer because I was too preoccupied with being near Gabe. Our lessons always flew by, and I almost couldn't stand it when the hour was up and I'd have to wait a whole week to be near him again, to be close enough to smell his perfect Gabe smell—a mix of sweat and new tennis balls, fresh from the can.

My feelings for him swallowed me whole. I thought about him constantly—his perfect hair and beautiful face and the way he smiled at me and the magnetic way my body responded to him.

I told Lydia everything, and she said he was *way* too old for me and that I'd better be careful because if anything happened between us, Gabe could go to jail for statutory rape. I told her that was nuts—I wasn't ready to have sex anyway—but I did want to kiss him. I wanted his hands all over me.

One Thursday near the end of the summer, slate-colored clouds gathered in the sky halfway through my tennis lesson, and soon rain was pounding down in sheets. Gabe and I ran into the tennis hut for shelter.

He turned to me. "Doesn't look like the rain's gonna stop, and it's almost five. Maybe we should call it."

I nodded. Rain crashed on the roof above our heads in loud blasts.

"Do you want to call your mom to come get you?"

"She's teaching Pilates till five. I'll just wait here."

"I can drop you off, if you need a ride." Gabe's eyes flickered, cornflower blue.

We climbed into his car, a navy Jeep. It was messy and littered with beef jerky wrappers, but it smelled like Gabe and I loved it. I buckled my seat belt and was so aware of myself, of just the two of us in the tiny, confined space of Gabe's car.

He asked where I lived and I told him, even though my house was only ten minutes from Cove Club and I wanted to make something up, some faraway address that would maximize our time together. Out of the corner of my eye I stared at Gabe's cheek, which looked like it had just been shaved. The hairs on his arms stood on end as he used his strong, tan hand to shift the gears.

"I want to learn to drive stick," I said, breaking the silence.

"Stick is the way to go. You can't drive yet, can you?"

"No. But I get my learner's permit next summer." I cringed at how young I sounded.

"Ah." The car accelerated, rain still pitter-pattering on the windshield. I was running out of time.

"How old are you?" I asked, feeling suddenly gutsy.

"Oh, man." Gabe laughed. "Not answering that."

"Just tell me."

"I'm twenty-three, Lucy."

"I'm seventeen," I lied, grinning.

"No way. You're Macy's age. Which makes you . . . fourteen."

"A *mature* fourteen, though, don't you think?"

"This is your road." Gabe pressed the brake, ignoring my question. "Where's your place?"

I pointed ahead to the green mailbox, number 34, and Gabe drove up the winding driveway and stopped in front of the house I'd lived in all my life, limestone nestled with blooming hydrangeas—CJ's favorite.

"Pretty spot," he said.

"Gabe." I stared at him, overcome by something unbearable. I just liked saying his name. *Gabe.*

"It's not raining anymore."

"Thanks for driving me."

"Lucy," he said, and chills prickled every inch of my skin as he took his index finger and lightly brushed it against my cheek. "You're beautiful." He said it slowly. I savored each syllable. I was floating. When a guy calls you beautiful, there's nothing quite like it.

I wanted him to kiss me so badly that I must've willed it to happen, because then he was leaning down and his pillow lips were touching mine, soft as a cloud, and in that same motion his hand moved up inside my shirt, under the elastic band of my double-A bra and over the buttons I had for breasts. But it didn't last nearly as long as I craved, and all too quickly he pulled away, his breath shallow, something sorry flashing in his eyes.

"I'm not really close with Macy," I offered, panicky, half shaking. "We've never gone to the same school."

"Lucy, I'm sorry. I shouldn't have, you—you're gorgeous, but—you're so young."

Just then CJ's Lexus pulled up, a crunch of gravel that jolted me alert as Gabe rolled down his window and our perfect moment evaporated. CJ climbed out of the car in her black spandex holding a bunch of shopping bags.

"Hi, Mrs. Albright," Gabe said, his voice rushed. "It poured rain so we had to cut the lesson short. Lucy needed a ride."

"*Please*, Gabe, call me CJ. It was raining buckets, no? I got soaked just walking to the car. Well, thank you, Gabe; that was super sweet of you to drop off Luce. Tell your parents I said hi, will you? I owe your mother a phone call."

"Of course."

CJ seemed to be waiting for me to get out of the car, and unwillingly I detangled myself from the air around Gabe. I told him I'd see him the following week.

"Next Thursday is her last lesson," CJ said. "Because we're going to the Cape for ten days and then school starts. School! Can you believe it? The summer flies, every time."

But the next week Gabe didn't show for our lesson; he'd called in sick that day, apparently, and I was stuck with another tennis instructor, named Hugh, who was short and bald and nothing like Gabe. I waited until after the lesson to run into the women's locker room and burst into tears.

High school started in the fall, and girls started getting boyfriends. There were lots of interlocking hands and tables of two in the cafeteria, but by then, the Unforgivable Thing had happened, and the relationships unfolding before me seemed dishonest and laced with betrayal, or the promise of betrayal. They were too easy, too carefree. I was sure of the inevitability of the pain they'd all cause; I felt it hot and deep in my bones.

By the end of sophomore year enough of my friends had started having sex that I knew I wanted to do it, too. I didn't want sex to get off—I'd figured out how to do that on my own, pressing that sweet spot, images of Gabe blurring my vision until the world fell away. It was easier with a vibrator, which I'd bought with my "edgy" friend Antonia at a sex shop in the city (I didn't think Antonia was edgy, but Lydia and Helen said she was. Lydia and Helen would never buy vibrators).

Still, I wanted real sex. Some boys liked me, but I didn't like any of them back. Sometimes I hooked up with them, but usually I just thought about Gabe and wished that I could feel that again. I'd just about had it with myself when blond-haired, squash-playing Parker Lines asked me to the hayride junior fall. There was nothing wrong with Parker, no flaw that I could point out to Lydia and Helen other than the fact that I wished he were three inches taller. They told me I wouldn't find anyone better to date in Cold Spring Harbor, and I couldn't argue. I needed something. Antonia's father had gotten a new job and they'd moved to Michigan at the beginning of the school year, so I was no longer spending weekends getting drunk with her. Parker was popular, attractive, athletic, and decently smart—all the good-on-paper stuff. I have no idea why he liked me so much, but by spring he was telling me he loved me, and I was saying it back, the words meaningless syllables gathering in my mouth.

We slept together in April. I was ready, and it was underwhelming. It hurt less than I expected, but even after months it never felt like anything special; I knew I was doing it for the sake of doing it. I was going through the motions of having a serious boyfriend without really *having* one. CJ was over the moon. She loved Mrs. Lines—they played tennis together. She thought Parker was *absolutely perfect* and invited him over to our house for dinner more than I ever did.

By senior winter I was so miserable with Parker that I could barely be around him. His touch had started to feel like a child molester's. I wanted to break up with him before spring formal in May, but Helen persuaded me to wait until after because *the pictures, Lucy! Think of the pictures.*

I had taken all the APs our high school offered and gotten good grades because it was easy enough, and if nothing else, I wanted to have choices. When my college decision came down to Baird outside Los Angeles and Dartmouth in Hanover, New Hampshire, CJ offered to buy me a Range Rover if I chose the latter. I knew it was just because she wanted to increase the chances that I'd stay with Parker. He'd been accepted early-decision to play squash at Bowdoin. She said she thought he would have trouble with the distance—Maine and California "will be tough." I wanted to laugh in her face at the same time that I felt horrified. I didn't even want a car. Dartmouth was ranked higher, but I just had to get out of the northeast, and I sent my acceptance to Baird the next day. When CJ threw a fit, I emphasized my interest in the smaller liberal arts environment and Baird's esteemed English program, especially one course, called Writers on the Riviera: From Hemingway to Fitzgerald, taught abroad on a sailboat on the Mediterranean coast of France. The course *was* the main reason I'd applied to Baird; it was a six-week immersive study of Riviera-inspired literature, particularly that of Hemingway and Fitzgerald, who both lived and wrote in the South of France. Spaces were competitive, but I'd get into the program if it killed me.

On the evening of spring formal, my hands shook as I applied mascara. CJ had bought me this beautiful, expensive dress—the cream-colored Shoshanna one that I wanted—and I could barely step into it, my whole body was teetering with dread. Parker would arrive in thirty minutes to pick me up. We would go to the Montgomerys' for pictures and sips of champagne, and then we would spend all night together, dancing and eating cake, followed by an after party at Kelsey Nelson's, followed by ten minutes of mechanical, clinical sex in whatever room we could find. The whole thing was a lie, a stage, a trap I'd been too insecure to avoid. And worst of all it was cruel to Parker—my friend turned boyfriend who now filled me with disgust. All of it was unfair, and all of it was my fault.

When the doorbell rang and I opened it to Parker, handsome in his tux, holding a corsage that perfectly matched my dress, I knew what I had to do. Except that in these situations my emotions have always been one step ahead of my logic, and so I just collapsed right there on the front stoop, my face breaking into a mess of tears and makeup. I told him everything I had rehearsed—that he didn't deserve me, that it was my fault, that I was so sorry I felt sick. He still hated me, though. He didn't understand why I was doing it then and there, leaving him high and dry the night of our senior spring formal.

"The world doesn't revolve around Lucy Albright, did you know that?" he spat. "You're not that fucking special. I don't understand one fucking thing that goes through your head." It was a particularly harsh blow, because Parker never swore.

I didn't blame him. I didn't understand me, either. I considered telling him about CJ and the Unforgivable Thing; I thought that it might help him get me. But I could never use the Unforgivable Thing to my advantage; I could never give it that kind of power. And regardless, I could never tell Parker. I had always known I could never tell him. I couldn't tell anyone.

And so I spent spring formal in a ball underneath my covers sobbing, Parker's corsage wilting on top of the trash. I lay there feeling sorrier and sorrier for myself, wishing I could love Parker the way I'd loved Gabe, wondering what was wrong with my stupid, stupid heart. CJ was hysterical, of course, but I couldn't make myself talk to her—I said only that Parker and I'd had a fight and I wasn't going to formal.

Ironically, my sister, Georgia, was the one who made me feel better that night. In the three and a half years since the Unforgivable Thing, Georgia and I had become strangers. But she was already home for the summer after her freshman year at Yale. She came into my room, sat down on my bed, and smoothed the back of my head. I peeked up to see a curtain of her blond hair, her flawless face. My perfect, premed, saving-the-world-one-African-baby-at-a-time sister.

"Tell me what's going on," she said calmly.

I told her. Georgia wasn't frenetic like CJ, so it was easier to talk to her. I explained about Parker and how I'd felt about our relationship since day one, the pressures I'd let crush me.

Georgia was quiet for a while. She's one of those people who thinks carefully about what she's going to say before she says it, so she always says the right thing.

"Lucy, promise me something. Promise *yourself* something."

"Yeah?"

"Don't ever settle again. What's the point? Everybody gets hurt. Besides, life is too short. Wait to find someone you're really crazy about, even if it takes time. It's just better that way."

I knew Georgia was right, though I wondered if she really took her own advice, or if love just came more easily for her, the way I wished it would for me. Georgia was a serial dater—her boyfriends were all serious, slightly boring intellectuals, and one always came right after the next.

"I promise," I told Georgia anyway, meaning it.

That promise carried me through graduation. I clenched my teeth as I walked across the stage to accept my diploma and felt Mrs. Lines's seething glare on me from somewhere in the crowd. *I will not settle.*

Lying in my bed at Baird, I glanced out the window at the dark outline of the mountains. Even at night you could see that they were there, sustaining, enduring. I fingered the knotted fabric on Puff, my ratty, old half of a blanket and lifelong sleeping companion. Georgia has the other half. Puff was originally Georgia's, but we both loved it so much that one day CJ just ripped it right in half so we could each have a piece. I cried at Puff's mutilation, but Georgia didn't—even as a four-year-old she calmly accepted CJ's rationale.

An unexpected wave of homesickness clobbered my chest, sinking down like a paperweight. I had the urge to call Georgia, to hear the composed, melodious rhythms of her voice—but then I had to remind myself that, in spite of that night we bonded over my breakup with Parker, we weren't close anymore, that we hadn't been for years, and that my calling at eleven on a Tuesday would be so unexpected she'd think something was seriously wrong.

Suddenly my phone buzzed on my nightstand atop *Anna Karenina*, which we were reading for Professor Tittleman's nineteenth-century Russian literature class.

A 516 number flashed on the screen—the same as my home area code in New York.

"Hello?"

"Lucy."

"Who is this?"

"Have you heard of the new sushi restaurant downtown, Sakamoto?"

"No. Who is this?"

"It's supposed to be fantastic. Want to go tomorrow night?"

"*Who* is this?"

I sat up straighter in bed. Pale yellow moonlight filtered through the blinds, striping my sheets.

"Oh, excuse me. This is Stephen DeMarco. We met at Lake Mead."

The Christian Bale guy. With the green eyes. Stephen was from Long Island, like me? My skin suddenly felt coated with electricity. I had been wondering about him ever since that last day at Mead, but not because I liked him. It was just curiosity.

"Yes, Steve. I remember."

"Ste*phen*. I don't do Steve."

"Stephen. Sorry."

"You're probably wondering how I got your number."

"I wasn't, but now I am."

"Ha!" He laughed throatily on the other end of the line. There was a satisfaction in making him laugh.

"How, then?"

"I'll tell you tomorrow over sushi. How about it? The weather's supposed to be gorgeous."

"The weather always seems to be gorgeous here."

"Valid point. Sunshine and palm trees and mountains, can't hate it. Temps drop a *little* in the winter months. You'll see."

"Ah."

"So tomorrow, seven thirty?"

"Well . . ." I bit the insides of my cheeks.

"Lucy. Do you want to get dinner with me or not?"

I didn't think I should go. He wasn't really my type. Plus something about him worried me, made my stomach flip in a funny way.

"I don't think I can. Sorry."

"Bummer. All right." He didn't sound fazed.

"Is that it?"

"That's it."

"How did you get my number, though?"

"Well, my friend Wrigley is fucking your friend Pippa. I wanted your number, and . . . voilà."

"Wrigley and Pippa are more than that." I knew that Pippa liked Wrigley a lot, and I felt an obligation to defend her.

"More than what?" Stephen asked.

"More than . . ."

"You can say it." I could nearly hear him grinning, and the pit inside me deepened.

"*Fucking*." It came out in an embarrassingly low whisper.

"Okay, I'm sorry," Stephen said. "Wrigley and Pippa are *making love*."

"That is *not* what I meant."

"What did you mean?"

"I meant—I just meant that they also go on dates and stuff."

"I'm trying to take *you* on a date."

An image of Stephen DeMarco in his red bathing suit flashed across my mind. Hairy, overweight, crass. Sure, handsome in some obscure way, but I hadn't felt attracted to him. Had I? I couldn't remember.

"I don't think now is a good time," I said.

"Don't sweat it, Lucy in the Sky with Diamonds," Stephen replied evenly. "But don't show up to any house parties wearing a bikini, or I might not be able to restrain myself."

The base of my stomach pinched again. He made the most ordinary sentences so directly sexual. Talking to him made me feel like a child.

"Why would I wear a bikini to a house party?"

"Touché, pretty girl," he said.

I hung up the phone and rolled over in bed. I felt clueless, even turning down a date from a guy I wasn't interested in. I knew nothing about dates. Parker never took me on actual dates. We grilled dinner in his backyard and got brunch on the weekends, but those weren't real dates. Or were they? Was I supposed to go on a date with a guy who asked, just for the hell of it, even if he made my insides lurch in a peculiar way? Was that what you did in college?

For a brief moment, I wished I could ask CJ, because she would probably know. But just thinking about that made me grit my teeth together, made me forget to blink for a whole minute, which is what happens when I think about CJ for too long. Because when you have a mother who did the Unforgivable Thing, you can't ask her those kinds of questions.

6

STEPHEN

OCTOBER 2010

It was a Saturday evening and I was staring at the familiar paisley print on Diana's quilt—orange and yellow and pink swirls—and focusing on my arousal. I love sex, but I'd fucked Diana so many times that it had become as familiar as jerking off. It was *good*, but no longer *unreal*—the word we'd once mutually used to describe it. I pulled her on top of me, but she wasn't having it. Yet again she was too pissed at me to focus on having an orgasm. So I sped up to reach my own end, came inside her, and rolled away.

I felt the stirrings of another argument. That is what my relationship with Diana had become: argue, sex, argue, sex, argue, argue, sex, argue. Nothing else in between.

"We have to stop doing this," she mumbled, propping up on one arm. Her messy hair fell in front of her eyes, and I pushed it behind her ear.

"Maybe if you concentrate on something other than being mad at me, you could actually enjoy yourself one of these times." I climbed off the bed to look for my boxers.

"Fuck you, Stephen." She picked up the box of Kleenex sitting on her bedside table and chucked it at my head. "Maybe if you stop sticking your dick in everything with a pulse, I wouldn't be so worried about getting some gross STD and I *could* enjoy myself."

Diana was crying now. I put on my clothes, grabbed the open can of beer on her desk, and chugged it in a single take. Then I sat down on the edge of the bed and dried her tears with my thumbs.

"Princess Diana, stop it. Nicole was a mistake, I've told you. I love *you*. How many times do you want me to tell you? I want to be with you."

"I'm not ready for that."

"So why are you sleeping with me?"

"I don't know. I ask myself that question every day. Maybe we should cool it for a while."

"Is that really what you want?"

"Yeah." The sheets had fallen below Diana's breasts and I stared at them, small and pale with rose-pink nipples, as familiar to me as my own hands.

"Diana, c'mon. I'm going to Wrig's birthday party. Will you come with me? Hold my hand? Be my girl again?"

"Go with you and watch you flirt with freshman sluts?"

"Oh Jesus, Diana." I pinched my sinuses. I didn't have the energy to stick around for another two-hour fight, so I grabbed my jacket and left. Let her call me selfish and mope around her house all night. She and Keaton and Josie would drink a case of red wine and talk about how much they hated me. Give it a week or two and she'd be calling me again, begging me to come over.

I let the screen door slam shut behind me, louder than usual, and walked south down Perry Street, toward Wrigley's house on Hutchins. It was a hot night, and I walked quickly toward the shelter of the air-conditioning unit at Wrigley's. His twenty-first birthday was bound to be a big bash. I stuck my hand in my pocket and cupped the little baggie of coke I'd bought him as a present. Maybe it was a good thing I was going by myself. I could do as much blow as I wanted. And according to Wrigley, Lucy would be there.

7

LUCY

Pippa dragged me to Wrigley's birthday party.

"You have to come. Wrigley has cute friends. You should really go for Stephen DeMarco, Luce. He's single now, and Wrigley says he likes you. *And* I hear he's good in bed." We were walking toward Wrigley's house near the south side of campus, Pippa clomping along in her wedges, towering above me. Pippa is only a couple of inches taller than me, but in heels she's a giant.

Even though the sun had set hours earlier, the Southern California heat was unrelenting, and I wiped a layer of sweat from my brow line. Pippa handed me a Nalgene filled with vodka.

"How do you know that?" I took a swig and winced at the taste. We always bought the cheap stuff.

"Wrigley says. It's just a known thing. Plus he looks like he'd be good at sex."

"And you believe Wrigley?"

"Come on, Lucy. Besides, how long has it been?"

I wasn't going to answer that question, so instead I asked if she thought Stephen was attractive.

"Maybe not conventionally, but yes. He has nice green eyes. And his personality makes him more attractive."

"He's kind of fat."

"All boys are fat. And they're just going to get fatter." Pippa seemed to know everything.

"Wrigley isn't fat. He plays water polo."

"Have you seen his stomach?"

We were late for the party, but Pippa wanted to be late because she and Wrigley had had some tiff and she was "playing it cool." Like most of the off-campus houses at Baird, Wrigley's place on Hutchins was falling apart. Beer bottles littered the floor, and there was no furniture except for a worn brown couch and a huge flat-screen TV. The Chops logo was painted on one of the walls. A keg stood in the corner next to the bar, which was a flimsy fold-up card table supporting cheap handles of liquor and liters of flat soda.

By 1:00 a.m. the keg was done and the plastic bottles of liquor were empty except for the raspberry Burnett's, which no one dared touch. Someone would have to make a liquor run soon, or everyone would begin to filter out to other parties.

Pippa was in the corner talking to Wrigley, their bodies pressed close together like Twizzlers in a pack. They'd gotten over their tiff apparently. Pippa ran her hands through Wrigley's blond crew cut. Sometimes I couldn't tell with Pippa—did she really like Wrigley, or did she just enjoy the attention of an older guy on the water polo team with an abundant supply of cocaine? I still hadn't tried coke, but I could tell when Pippa had done it, the way she clenched her teeth afterward.

I wished Jackie was there, but she had a team dinner for tennis, and Bree was in the library studying for her statistics exam. I'd meant to work on my application for a staff writer role at *The Lantern*, Baird's student newspaper, but Pippa was dreading going to Wrigley's party alone—she claimed the junior girls hated her—so instead I found myself at 404 Hutchins Street in a room full of people I barely knew.

I scanned the bottoms of the bottles for remaining traces of alcohol—I needed one more drink—when I heard the voice, familiar in its level of unmerited confidence. "What, you don't like raspberry vodka?"

I turned around to meet Stephen's face. His dark hair was thick with wispier pieces falling past his ears, and his chin was covered in dark stubble. He stuffed a hand into the pocket of his jeans and produced a silver flask.

"You want?" His eyes scorched mine.

I held out my empty cup, and he poured. I sniffed the rim.

"Tequila." I took a small sip and felt it burn the back of my throat.

"Do you like tequila?"

"Sometimes."

I stood on my tiptoes to try to spot Pippa. She was hanging on to Wrigley's arm like a tree monkey. We made eye contact, and she flashed me the thumbs-up.

"Looking for someone?" Stephen asked.

I shook my head. He poured more tequila into my cup.

"So, Lucy in the Sky with Diamonds, what do you think you'll major in?"

"English. Journalism minor." I looked up at him, his plain yet oddly captivating face. Those thick dark eyebrows, the small bow-shaped mouth. I had those wishy-washy butterflies in my stomach again, but felt drunk enough to ignore them.

"English and journalism. Are you sure?"

"Yes. I want to be a travel journalist. Why?"

"You sound very sure."

"Well, I am. Is that so bad?"

"Not bad at all. It's good to know what you want."

"I mean, I don't know everything I want."

"Of course you don't. You're not supposed to. You're only, what, eighteen?"

"Yeah."

"You're an infant."

"You're probably only two years older than me."

"I look older than I am, though."

"You do look older. No offense."

"None taken. I bet you've never even voted."

"Why are you giving me shit about my age?"

"She swears!" He fake gasped. "I didn't think you had it in you."

"I swear more than you would think."

"You surprise me then." He grinned. "I just thought from the Barbour jacket and the gorgeous, preppy face that you were, you know, a little straight edge. Joey Potter meets . . . Blair Waldorf?" He cocked his head.

"How did you know I have a Barbour jacket?"

"I've seen you wearing it around," he said. "On cooler occasions, I suppose. It's a sauna out there. I've been sweating all night."

"My mom gave me that jacket, all right? And I *don't* have a preppy face." I hate when people automatically assume that I'm preppy. My dad *is* from a Waspy family and I *used* to wear cable-knit sweaters and pearls in middle school, but now I hate pearls. I wouldn't be caught dead wearing them.

"I said you have a *gorgeous* face. You don't listen." He tapped his ear with his pointer finger.

"You said preppy, too."

"You're very hard to please, do you know that?"

"Your compliments are backhanded. I'm not an idiot."

"I know you're not." He poured me another shot of tequila.

I'd had a lot to drink. There was a tingling sensation at the base of my spine. Half of me wanted to ditch my cup and make a run for it across campus, back to Kaplan. But my feet felt heavy, glued to the ground. A magnetic force suctioned them down from inside the floor.

"We're both from Long Island, you know," he was saying. "I noticed when Pippa gave me your number."

"I noticed when you called me. What town?"

"Bayville."

"*Bayville?* That's twenty minutes from my house."

"Let me guess. Oyster Bay?"

"Cold Spring Harbor."

"I was close. Giants or Jets?"

"Giants, duh. I have an Eli Manning poster in my room. Is that embarrassing?"

"As long as it's not on the ceiling above your bed and you get off to him every night. Actually, that would be kind of awesome." He parted his lips and looked me hard in the eye. Stephen made more overtly sexual comments than anyone I'd ever met.

Picturing Stephen picturing me getting off to Eli Manning made my insides stir deep down.

"I bet you have an Eli Manning poster, too." I smiled dumbly.

"Actually I do. But I don't jerk off to him. I have the Penelope Cruz poster for that."

"Can we change the subject?"

Stephen laughed, and I felt a warm glow coat my chest. He ran his fingers through his thick, glossy locks.

"You need a haircut," I said, feeling bold.

"I was at the barber two weeks ago. My hair grows like I wash it with fucking fertilizer." He pulled at the ends.

"That's a pain." I laughed softly.

"Well, Lucy, it's a shame you won't go out with me, given that we have so much in common." He sounded amused rather that disappointed. "New Yorkers in LA need to stick together, you know. These new age, hippie sun chasers are not our people."

I shrugged and smiled, thinking of Pippa, who was from Pasadena. I had only known Pippa for six weeks, but she already felt like my people.

"You really won't go out with me?" Stephen leaned in a little too close to my face. He smelled like tequila and Old Spice. His eyes—the eyes—settled on mine.

I suddenly realized that everyone else had disappeared from the party. Even the music had stopped. It was just the two of us, standing against the white Formica countertop in Wrigley's dimly lit kitchen, the AC unit humming.

"What time is it?" I asked.

"I dunno."

"Where did everybody go?"

"Probably to another party."

"Oh."

"Do you want to go find another party?"

I was suddenly nervous. I hadn't meant to get myself into this situation.

"Or we could hang out in my room," he said before I could answer. "It's in Copeland, right around the corner, on Carroll."

It was one of those moments I would look back on for years to come: a blurred image in a magnifying glass; a memory distorted in a fishbowl. Maybe everything would have been different if I had listened to the half of me that wanted to run away.

"Or we'll do it some other time," he started to say, but I was already nodding, because the other half of me was proving stronger, the half of me that wanted to see what would happen with this stranger who was not my type but who was making my spine melt like a candlestick. I hadn't felt that in years—not since Gabe.

I followed Stephen outside and down the street and into Copeland, one of Baird's older, smaller dormitories. The wooden staircase creaked loudly as we climbed up to the third floor and walked down the hallway.

"This is me," he said, cranking the door open. "You're in luck. I have the AC blasting."

"Why does Wrigley live off campus and you don't?" I stopped in the doorway to his room.

"Because he's luckier than me." Stephen leaned down and kissed me, so suddenly it caught me off guard. His mouth was warm and wet and the kiss felt surprisingly good. He whisked me up off the floor in one fluid motion, kicking the door shut behind him, and carried me over to his bed.

"You have a roommate?" I asked, glancing toward the other bed.

"Yeah. Evan Donovan. Do you know him?"

I shook my head.

"He's all right. He plays lacrosse, and he has a girlfriend, so he's never really here."

"You don't like him?"

"I do. We're just different. He can be difficult. He's my friend, but he wouldn't have been my first choice as a roommate."

"Then why do you live together?"

"We got similar numbers in the housing lottery and it just worked out."

"Why is he difficult?"

"Lucy . . . ," Stephen whispered. "I don't really want to talk about Evan right now." He leaned in, the edges of his lips brushing mine. "I've thought about kissing you since the moment I saw you on that houseboat." He tasted like tequila and something minty. His hands slid underneath my bra, fumbling with the clasp. His mouth was hot on my neck, then my abdomen, then lower.

"I don't want to have sex," I said.

"I know."

"How do you know?"

"I can just tell." He laughed. "It's not a bad thing. No reason to rush it. I just want to go down on you."

I'd never loved the feeling of a guy going down on me, but maybe it was Parker's ineptitude. Pippa loved it. So did Jackie. Even Lydia liked it. Still, the idea of Stephen doing it didn't sit right, not then. I barely knew anything about him.

I shook my head, suddenly feeling too drunk. The room seemed to be rotating. The sour taste of old tequila filled the back of my throat.

"I just need to sleep."

Stephen laughed. "Okay. You're the boss."

He kissed me again, sliding his tongue expertly into my mouth. He was such a good kisser, but the bile was already rising, and I pushed him away.

I knew I wouldn't make it to the bathroom in time. I covered my mouth and pointed to the trash bin. Stephen grabbed it and moved it under my face just in time.

"Shit," I managed, mortified by the intensifying smell. "I'm so sorry. I need to go . . . home. I'll go wash that for you first."

"Are you crazy? Lucy, I am not letting a young inebriated girl walk across campus alone in the middle of the night. There could be rapists lurking in the shadows."

I mumbled something incoherent. He left the room and came back minutes later, with a clean trash bin and a bottle of Listerine that he made me swish around in my mouth. He handed me a glass of water.

"Sleep here tonight. No funny business, I promise."

My eyelids drooped, singeing with exhaustion. I could fall asleep there. Just one night.

"Good night, pretty girl," I heard him say as sleep tugged me under.

When I opened my eyes the next morning, pain split through my head like a bolt of lightning. The inside of my mouth tasted like a dead frog. I propped up on one elbow and glanced around, disoriented until horrifying snippets of the night before began to surface. Stephen's dorm room was a mess and smelled like old Thai food and dirty laundry. He lay asleep next to me, snoring as loud as a lawn mower. His mouth parted over a double chin, and drops of sweat clung to his forehead despite the air-conditioning. With another thunderous snore he rolled over. My palms felt damp; a fresh wave of sickness swelled inside my stomach, and I racked my brain for a silent exit strategy. What had I been thinking? I wasn't attracted to Stephen. I was just a drunk idiot mistaking nausea for butterflies. Pippa was going to be thrilled, though. I pulled out my phone, which was miraculously still intact, and texted Lydia.

LUCY: I just hooked up with the randomest guy. And I puked in his trash bin.

8

STEPHEN

I spotted Lucy in the library, down on the second floor, bent over a notebook in her olive-green Barbour jacket, her chestnut hair a shiny coat across her back. I watched her write carefully in a notebook for several minutes until she rose up out of her chair and headed toward the staircase. She trotted up to the third floor, her hand sliding up the varnished banister, and around the corner, toward the spot where I stood. She bumped right into me.

"Oh, hi," she said, her gaze unsteady. She chewed the edge of her thumb.

"Hello." I leaned in close to her. She smelled like freshly sharpened pencils. "A jacket in eighty-degree weather?"

"They crank up the AC in here."

"I never noticed."

"I'm looking for a book."

"For what?"

"A book."

"I know. I meant, a book for what?"

"For a paper for my Russian literature class."

"Oh. Russian lit with Professor Tittyman or whatever?"

"Tittleman. Yes."

"Tomato to*ma*to. I've had the dude before. He's a stickler for properly formatted footnotes."

"I know," she sighed. "It's the bane of my existence."

"It's stupid is what it is. I have a pretty helpful footnote guide that got me through his class, if you want it." The footnote guide was Diana's, but I could probably find an excuse to snag it from her room.

"That would be great, actually." Lucy smiled. Straight white teeth. "You're not an English major, are you?"

"Hell no."

"Didn't think so."

"Political science. Economics minor."

"You want to be a lawyer?"

"How did you know?"

"Just a guess. My dad majored in poli sci, and he's a lawyer."

"Is he? Interesting. What kind?"

"Criminal defense."

"Public?"

"Now, yeah. He used to work at a firm, but he wanted to do more than just white-collar stuff."

"Interesting." I sneered internally. Public defenders get paid shit money in exchange for having a conscience. I don't know why anyone in their right mind would invest so much time and money in law school and then choose a career as a public defender. You might as well save the money and volunteer for UNICEF or something. But as far as I can tell, from her Barbour jacket and expensive-looking jewelry and the tiniest bit of googling, Lucy's family has money, so clearly Lucy's father can afford to be an upstanding citizen.

"You didn't want to follow in his footsteps?" I asked her.

"I wouldn't make a good lawyer. And I couldn't major in poli sci. My mind just isn't wired for it."

"I don't blame you. English is definitely far less dry than poli sci."

"Well, English can be dry. This class is brutal. Tolstoy feels like reading the Bible backward."

Her reference was not all that comical, but I laughed anyway. When you're trying to fuck a girl, you laugh at her half jokes. You laugh at fucking everything she says.

"What I really want to get into is journalism," she continued.

"That's right." I nodded. "Journalism minor. I remember. You should try to write for *The Lantern*."

"Funny you should say that." She tilted her head adorably. "You're looking at *The Lantern*'s newest staff writer."

"No *way*." I feigned surprise, though I'd known to mention it after seeing her byline in the latest edition. "Small School, Big City: How Baird Students Really Feel About Los Angeles," by Lucy Albright. "That's fantastic, Lucy."

"Thanks." She coursed her fingers through her long hair. "I'm trying to build up my résumé. I'm really hoping to get into this course the English department offers majors and minors the summer after sophomore year, but apparently it's supercompetitive—"

"Let me guess. The one where you live on a boat and sail along the French Riviera?"

"And read Hemingway! And Fitzgerald! Yes! I'm *dying* to go. That's what first inspired me to apply to Baird, actually. I read about the course junior year of high school after we read *A Farewell to Arms*. That book totally broke my heart, but I loved it." Lucy's face brightened, her eyes popping wide with an absurd amount of enthusiasm.

God, how the hell do people get so worked up about fictional books? I can only read nonfiction.

"That's the most coveted course at Baird, probably," I said. "Sounds unreal."

"Yeah, apparently you have to have at least a three-point-seven GPA," Lucy continued. "And even then they accept only twelve students."

"I have heard that." I nodded. It was true—spots in the course were extremely competitive. Diana was an English minor, and her GPA fell one point short of the requirement. She'd whined about it for weeks.

"But God, to get to spend six weeks sailing through Antibes and Cannes and Saint-Tropez, and for *school*." Lucy tucked a strand of glossy hair behind her ear. "It's a long shot, but you never know."

"Well, Lucy in the Sky with Diamonds, if you keep up the hard work, it sounds like you have a good shot."

"Why do you keep calling me that?" She raised a dark eyebrow.

"Because of the song, I told you. I think it fits you."

"You know it's a song about tripping on LSD?"

"Maybe that's one interpretation, because of the acronym." I frowned. "But it's supposed to be about a drawing of a girl named Lucy that Lennon's son made in nursery school."

"That's random. How do you even know that?"

How did I know? I'd looked it up after Lucy and I first met, should I

ever need to bring it up in a conversation such as this one. I could tell
Lucy was flattered by her nickname—*Lucy in the Sky with Diamonds*. It's
a cool song. And it's the Beatles. Everyone fucking loves the Beatles.

"I haven't been able to stop thinking about that song since that day
on the houseboat. When I couldn't find out more about *you*," I mockingly
accused, "because you refused to let me take you to dinner, I researched
the song instead."

Lucy glanced over the railing edge, then peered up at me.

"You're a very interesting person," she said. "By the way, I'm sorry I
never returned your messages."

"God, don't make me sound so desperate. You could just say *message*.
Singular."

"But there were several." One corner of her mouth curled.

"Well, I wouldn't be much of a gentleman if I hadn't called to check
up on you after the whole puking incident."

"I know. I'm sorry about that. That was a low moment."

"Don't be sorry, it happens. I was the bastard feeding you tequila.
Anyway, I'm still hoping to take you on a proper date. No tequila, I
promise. Sushi? *Français*? *Italiano*? Zimbabwean? Your pick."

"Zimbabwean?"

"They have food in Zimbabwe."

"Stephen, I'm not sure. I'll let you know? I should really get back to
wor—"

I leaned in and kissed her, midsentence. Not enough guys take advantage of the midsentence kiss. Girls go crazy for it—romantic in any
and all scenarios.

I pushed her back a little, toward the corner behind one of the book-
shelves. I ran my hands over the back of her jeans and had to think
of Wrigley's droopy ball sack to keep from getting too excited. God, I
couldn't wait to fuck her. It would happen. I could feel her surrender as
I kissed her. She opened her mouth a little wider than the time before.
I could feel her heart racing against my chest. She let me kiss her for a
whole minute before she pushed me back, an expression of shock pooling in her blue-gray eyes. She didn't hate it.

9

LUCY

NOVEMBER 2010

I was helping Jackie craft a text to her ex-boyfriend—he'd asked to see her over Thanksgiving break, but she had yet to tell him she was dating Stuart—when my phone rang. It was lying next to Jackie on her bed.

"CJ Cell is calling." Jackie handed me the phone. "I still don't get why you call your mom by her first name."

"It's just a thing." I avoided Jackie's gaze because I could feel her staring at me, and I could tell she knew I was lying. I turned the phone on silent. "I'll call her later."

"You can call her now, if you want. I think this is fine to send Matt, right?" Jackie looked down at the carefully constructed message on her phone.

"It's perfect." I nodded. "And I'll just call her back later; I have so much reading. Russian lit is *killing* me."

"Okay." Jackie took out her own homework and said nothing else on the subject, though I sensed her wondering.

My mother's name is Cornelia Jane Clifford Albright, but she despises the name Cornelia and has gone by CJ since high school, when she ran away to San Francisco to live with her aunt Marilyn. CJ grew up in a solidly middle-class neighborhood in Rhode Island (a dump, as she refers to it), and hated it there. She was close with Marilyn, her father's sister, who had no children of her own and had always adored CJ like the daughter she never had. Marilyn also had a lot more money than CJ's parents (an unimaginable sum she received in a settlement after a nasty divorce from her gazillionaire ex-husband). Marilyn died of cancer when I was four, so I barely remember meeting her, but I've seen lots of pictures. She had chocolate-brown hair and a big, wide smile. She wasn't as pretty as CJ, but almost. I have one of her sweaters. She had really nice clothes and when she died, CJ got to keep some of them, including Marilyn's famous jewelry collection. Marilyn traveled all over the world after her divorce, and she never married again—she told CJ that life was too short to waste on men. She usually built her trips around advocacy work in developing countries in the fight against AIDS—that was her real passion. CJ said Marilyn used to sleep in huts with AIDS-infected families and counsel gay patients in clinics in Eastern Europe. For every country Marilyn visited she bought a piece of jewelry as a souvenir. She brought CJ with her when she had time off from school (because CJ's parents couldn't afford family vacations), and the two of them continued the jewelry collection together, most pieces reflective of their origin. A lot of it is costume jewelry—funky pieces from markets in Africa and Central America or pawnshops in Romania that Georgia and I used to wear playing dress-up. Then there's the valuable stuff—the ivory-and-gold-twisted bangle from South Africa, the aquamarine choker from Brazil, yellow diamond studs from Kenya, Celtic torques from Ireland, the jade ring from Guatemala, the gold-and-leather cuff from Florence, authentic gold kamarbands from India, freshwater pearls from Japan, diamond-encrusted emerald earrings from Madagascar.

When Marilyn died, CJ poured the jewelry all over her bed and slept in the sea of it, convinced she could still smell Marilyn's Chanel No. 5 lingering on the gems. She slept like that for a week before putting it all back in its big teak jewelry box. My dad didn't complain, not that he ever does.

When I was twelve, I was examining some of Marilyn's gorgeous clothes in CJ's closet, and I tried on an ivory cashmere sweater, softer than a cloud. CJ found me wearing it and she didn't even get mad at me for going through her stuff. She said I could have it, just because. It smells like mothballs, but it's the best piece of clothing I have. I keep it in the top of my closet and wear it when I need a little extra strength. I don't remember Marilyn, but I've heard enough Marilyn stories, and I know I would've liked her. Examining her exuberant collection of global jewels and hearing about her adventurous life ignited something in me. From a young age I began hoarding CJ's travel magazines—stacks of *Travel + Leisure* and *National Geographic* piled around my bedroom in chronological order. I was in awe of the glossy photographic spreads of the world's most exotic destinations—the pink-sand beaches and lush, prehistoric-looking mountain ranges and intricate architecture and tribal regions—and especially the stories behind them. I told CJ I wanted to be a travel writer when I grew up, that I wanted to explore the hidden corners of the world and write about them, and she said it sounded a lot like something Marilyn would've wanted to do, which I knew meant she approved.

When CJ moved to San Francisco she didn't ask her parents' permission; she just packed a suitcase and bought a one-way ticket to California. She said her father was always working and her mother was too busy smoking and playing bridge to notice. (Whenever I push her on this, she sighs: "Oh, Lucy. My mother wasn't a mother to me the way I am to you and Georgia. It was different for her. I just had to get out of there.")

CJ stayed in San Francisco. She got good grades in high school and received a partial scholarship to Berkeley—Marilyn paid the rest of her tuition. The year after she graduated, CJ met my father at a Fleetwood Mac concert at the Cow Palace. Or my father found her, so he says. He was in San Francisco for the weekend visiting friends. CJ was in her hippie phase, and she was twirling around in a long skirt and flower crown trying to be Stevie Nicks's gypsy, so stoned she knocked right into my dad, spilling beer all over his nice white oxford. I hate that I ended up loving Fleetwood Mac as much as CJ does, but the love has always been unconscious—CJ says she used to play "Dreams" to get me to stop crying in my crib.

CJ had a lot of boyfriends in her time, but Ben Albright was the jackpot. She says that when she met him, she thought he looked like John F. Kennedy Jr. More important, he came from money, grew up on the water in Locust Valley, New York, had a summer house in Chatham, Massachusetts, was on the brink of a successful law career having graduated magna cum laude from Columbia, and he wanted to take care of her. He was wealthy but not spoiled; he mowed his own lawn and had a masculine knack for odd jobs, like assembling a bookshelf or fixing a leak. It was a perfect match. CJ was tired of California, but if she was going to go back east, she wanted to go back on her terms and live a certain way, the *well-off* way—the opposite of her childhood in the northwest corner of Rhode Island. So she traded her flower crown for a Ralph Lauren sweater set, and Ben bought her a one-way ticket to New York. He met her at LaGuardia Airport holding a sign that read: *The most beautiful girl in the world.* She loves to tell that part of the story. They got engaged six months later.

CJ was twenty-four when Georgia was born; twenty-five when she had me.

CJ was *Mommy* when I was really little, pouring warm water over my fine hair in the bathtub, drying me off with a towel in her arms. Then she was *Mom*, who packed my lunch box and French-braided my hair before dance recitals; *Mom*, who made me finish my milk every night; *Mom*, who took Georgia and me shopping for bell-bottoms at Limited Too; *Mom*, who showed me how to shave my legs in the bathtub the day I came home from sixth grade, crying because everyone else had started doing it, and I felt like a hairy beast.

But one afternoon in September, the second Thursday of my freshman year of high school, *Mom* died forever. She became CJ.

10

STEPHEN

DECEMBER 2010

I noticed Lucy crying outside the football house the night of the Ugly Christmas Sweater party. She was sitting on the back stoop wearing a big red sweater, smoking a cigarette, which surprised me, because I hadn't taken her for a smoker. The cigarette trembled in her fingers. She wiped her eyes with one of her big red sleeves. It had been two months since Lucy's drunken sleepover after Wrigley's birthday, and one month since our library kiss, but this was my golden opportunity.

"Lucy?" I stood in front of her in my own ugly sweater, which was green with a felt reindeer on the front. "Here." I pulled a handkerchief out of my back pocket. I always carry a handkerchief with me.

"It's okay." She shook her head. "But thanks."

"Come on, do you really want to ruin that beautiful sweater?"

"Thanks." The faintest hint of a smile showed on her face.

I sat beside her. I was feeling drunk from about fifty games of flip cup, and a little dazed from the weed brownies I'd just eaten upstairs with Wrigley.

"I can't believe you smoke cigs," I said.

"Hardly ever." She exhaled a stream of air. I watched it dissolve into the black night.

"Those things'll kill you, you know."

"I barely smoke; I told you." There was an edge to her voice that intrigued me.

"Let me guess. Only when you're having a rough day?"

"I don't really want to sit here," she said, ignoring my question.

"Do you want to walk?"

"I'm just going to walk home." She stood.

"I'll walk you."

"Don't you want to stay at the party?"

"Nah. I'm not a football-house fan, to be honest." It was true—football-house parties were dominated by slutty girls lusting after loud, meathead football players. I'd never enjoyed them much.

"Oh."

"So I'll walk you?"

"If you want."

"Do you want to talk about it?" I asked again.

"Not really."

"Try me, Lucy."

"Believe me, you don't want to know."

"Let me guess. Boy problem?"

"No." She shot me a playful glare.

"Friend fight? Girls can be dramatic."

"It's not that."

"Family?"

Lucy was silent. We were taking our time walking toward Kaplan, even though it was cold.

"Aha! I got it. Family. Well, you are *in* luck. My family just happens to be about the most dysfunctional one around. So I'm the perfect person to vent to. Spill the beans."

"I can't, Stephen."

"You can, actually."

"Well I don't want to."

"Fine. I won't press. Just trying to help."

"I know you are," she sighed. "But it's beyond complicated."

"Yes, I know. Familial matters tend to be complex."

Lucy was quiet. Tear remnants stuck to her flushed cheeks.

"For example," I continued, sensing a bit of receptiveness on her end. "My mother is bipolar. My father finally kicked her out when I was eleven, after she drove off with my then four-year-old sister for a week without telling anyone. My dad thought my sister was dead until the cops found them in a random hotel in Charleston. It was one of my mom's manic episodes—one of hundreds, but the last straw for my dad, I guess."

"Jesus," Lucy replied, looking me in the eye for the first time all night. "I'm really sorry."

"Don't be. It's old news at this point. I'm just glad she's out of the picture. It's better for all of us."

"Is your dad remarried?"

"God no. That's the worst part—he's still fixated on my mom. After a *decade*. After she blew *all* the money in their savings account. After all the shit she's pulled. Like he's always trying to reach out to her and stuff, like there's still some chance it can all be fixed and she'll come back and have magically morphed into this dependable wife and mother. It's very delusional thinking on his part."

"I'm so sorry, Stephen."

"I told you, don't be. Seriously."

"I can't imagine that, though."

"Dare I ask if your parents are divorced?"

She shook her head. "They're not, but they probably should be."

"Gotcha."

"But unfortunately, I doubt that will ever happen."

"So you want them to get divorced?"

"It's complicated."

"Sorry, I didn't mean to pry. It's your business."

She stopped and turned to face me on the sidewalk, her expression sharp. "If I tell you this, you have to promise not to tell a soul."

"Swear to God." I mime sealed my lips.

"And I don't even know why I'm telling you, because I barely know you and I literally haven't told anyone. *Anyone.*"

"I can keep a secret."

"What's up with this weather?" She rubbed her arms through her sweater. A gust of wind swept a piece of shiny brown hair across her forehead.

"It is chilly tonight, isn't it? I would offer you my jacket, but I don't have one."

"I thought Southern California was supposed to be warm, like, all the time."

"It can get a little cool at night in the winter months," I said. "Especially since we're close to the mountains. Do you want to go inside somewhere? Just to talk?"

"I don't know. It's late." She glanced away. "All right. Just for a few minutes."

We walked toward my dorm. Evan spent most nights at his girlfriend's, so I doubted he'd be home. When we got to my room Lucy sat down on the couch and I took a half-empty bottle of white wine out of the mini fridge. I was already feeling fucked up, but being around Lucy made me crave another drink. I checked my phone while I poured the wine into two mugs. No texts from Diana, even though I'd left *another*, even nicer bouquet of white lilies and *another*, even longer handwritten letter on her doorstep that morning.

"Liquid courage," I said, handing her the wine. "Now, spill."

I plopped down on the couch and felt thoroughly stoned, like I was sinking right into the cushions. The air in the room suddenly felt hazy and languid. Pot kind of debilitates me.

Lucy took a sip and looked at me, the lower half of her face spreading into a smile. "It's funny, but I feel better. I haven't even told you yet and I feel better."

"So tell me and you'll feel much better."

"It's hot in here."

"I thought you were cold. I turned the heat on. Sorry."

"That's okay." I watched her peel off her goofy red sweater and toss it on the floor. I could see her nipples through her thin cotton shirt. A black bra strap was visible over the exposed part of her shoulder blade. I felt a warm judder between my legs.

"Tell me, Lucy."

"All right," she started, launching into a long, winding story about her mother that I did a poor job following, because her cheeks were too flushed and her nipples were too hard and I wanted to tear her flimsy cotton shirt off using just my eyes, because I was too stoned to move.

It was Lucy's mother who was the criminal, I understood as I watched her speak, her mouth moving quickly, the anger intensifying in her voice as the story unfolded. I didn't catch all the details but I do understand how it is to despise your own mother, so I responded with another anecdote about my psychotic wreck of a maternal figure, providing a sense of kinship that seemed to console her. I did my best to keep my eyes fixed on Lucy's—solid eye contact gives the impression of a committed attention span. It was easy to watch Lucy, easy and torturous at once to imagine her naked body under that wispy little shirt.

"Stephen," she was saying. "You really have to promise not to tell anyone what I just told you. No one knows this about my mother. I didn't even tell my sister or my best friend or my boyfriend. *Ex*-boyfriend."

"I'm the first to be let in on this secret? I'm honored. And I won't tell. I promise."

"I have no idea why I told you. Maybe because you're so far removed from the situation; it's safe."

"Or because I lured you to my dorm room with chardonnay?"

"Ugh, I know." Lucy gazed into her mug and frowned. "This is what CJ drinks. Chardonnay."

"CJ?"

"That's my mom's name. That's what I call her now."

"So after this whole . . . incident, you demoted her to her first name?"

"It just sort of happened. She hates it, but I hate her."

"Bold move. I like it. Maybe I should start referring to my mom as Nora."

"Oh, you should." She tipped her wineglass in my direction. "It's very therapeutic."

"I bet I can get my siblings on board."

"How many siblings do you have?"

"Two. An older brother and a younger sister."

"God. I'm so sorry about your mother, Stephen. That must be so hard for all of you. I feel like you've gone through worse than I have."

I became aware of Lucy's stance toward me softening; I could hear the concern in her voice and could see the compassionate expression forming in the contours of her face. The truth was I didn't care much about my mother's dysfunction—I rarely had to deal with her anymore, and when she did have an episode that involved the family, I found her behavior to be more embarrassing than emotionally draining. But it was working like a charm; Lucy was beginning to feel a bond between us, a mutual empathy that translated into a newfound affection. And she was starting to trust me. Like I knew she would.

"Which experience is worse is irrelevant," I said slowly, taking extra care to make sense in my weed-clouded musings, especially since I was fuzzy on the specifics of Lucy's story. "Point is, I don't want Nora's actions to define me. And you shouldn't let CJ's define you."

"I know. You're right."

"And don't keep everything bottled up inside."

"You sound like my therapist."

"Your therapist?"

"My parents made me see a therapist after I started calling my mom CJ."

"Oy. My dad has tried to get me to go to a shrink so many times about my mom. I refuse."

"It's dumb."

"It's a waste of money. I'd much rather vent about my problems to friends than a random old geezer with a bullshit certification. But in your case . . . you'd rather tell no one."

"I just couldn't. I can't explain why. It was like . . . if I said it out loud . . ."

"Then it would become real?"

"Yeah." Her eyes landed on mine. "Exactly."

"But your boyfriend, you couldn't have even told him?"

"*Ex*-boyfriend. I don't know, he wouldn't have understood something like that. His family is so cookie-cutter. He wouldn't have known what to do and would've just acted bizarre and tense."

"I know people like that. Is that why you broke up?"

"No." Lucy yawned and placed her empty mug on the coffee table. "We broke up because I didn't love him."

"Ah." Silence hung in the air between us. God, it makes me uncomfortable when people talk about love like it's some concrete emotion, something you can or can't feel. The be-all and end-all of human existence. As though life without it is nothing.

"Hey, Stephen?"

"Yeah?"

"I'm so tired."

"I can walk you home." I felt like I'd been suctioned to the couch for hours talking to Lucy, the pot brownies distorting space and time. Their effects were finally wearing off, and I forced myself to stand.

"Maybe I could stay here," Lucy said delicately. "Just to sleep."

"Sure." I nodded, surprised, my mind already jumping ahead of me, my dick two steps ahead of my mind. "You want a T-shirt?"

"Thanks."

I walked over to my closet and grabbed a clean New York Giants tee. "Here you go."

"Eli Manning. Number ten." She grinned.

"I knew you'd like that one."

I watched her turn away and remove her shirt and bra, exposing her long, slim back. Her skin looked as smooth as caramel, and I desperately wanted to reach out and touch her. But I restrained myself, holding my breath and forcing thoughts of Wrigley's balls again. As she slipped the T-shirt over her bare chest, took off her jeans and climbed underneath the covers, I knew I wouldn't have to wait much longer. After a girl willingly gets into your bed, the rest is history.

PART
TWO

11

LUCY

AUGUST 2017

"What do you think?" Bree spins around, revealing her ivory Monique Lhuillier wedding dress, the sheath style hugging her close. Tasteful lace with a V-cut back that dips low, accentuating her thin figure. Bree is a stick, always has been, but she eats whatever she wants. She's one of those girls who's actually not lying when she says she's thin because of a fast metabolism. To say I'm jealous is an understatement. Surrounded by her bridal party in one of the Donovans' guest bedrooms, Bree is trying on her dress for the final time.

"Meh." Pippa shrugs. "You can find a better one."

"*Pippa.*" Bree frowns. "The wedding is *tomorrow.*"

"I'm kidding, lighten up. You look insane." Pippa flips her shiny dark hair, enviably long as always.

The other bridesmaids, Bree's cousin and two childhood friends from Ohio, flash Pippa disapproving stares. They don't know Pippa and they don't know her sense of humor. Pippa is not everyone's cup of tea.

"It's perfect, B." I nod. Bree does look insane. Her dress is feminine and delicate and elusive. It's so Bree.

"It's so *you*," Jackie says, reading my mind as usual.

Lauren, the hyper wedding planner, looks like she's on ecstasy.

"You look . . . I mean . . . just unbelievable." Lauren's face does something weird, and she looks like she might cry. We don't even know Lauren. Her enthusiasm is superfluous. I don't like her.

My phone dings in my purse, and Lauren looks at me like I'm the most disruptive person she's ever laid eyes on.

I sneak a peek at the text.

DANE: Miss u babe. What color undies u wearin? :-)

Lauren is still peering at me. I shove my phone back into my bag and stifle a yawn.

"Luce, are you tired?" Bree asks as Pippa helps her out of her wedding dress. She puts on her outfit for the luncheon—white silk shorts and a navy silk top. Even though we were roommates for three years, I still can't help but observe Bree's body when it's uncovered. Her thighs are so thin I think I could fit my whole hand around one of them.

"Kinda tired," I say. "I should've slept on the train."

"You can never sleep on trains, though." Bree gives me a sympathetic look. "I would say nap before the lunch, but I don't think there's time."

"There isn't." Pippa looks at her watch. "It's almost one."

"I'll be fine." I squeeze Bree's hand. "Don't worry."

The bridal luncheon takes place on the Donovans' terrace, overlooking the swimming pool and acres of lush green grass. Lauren and her crew have set up round tables underneath the pergola, each draped in a white linen tablecloth and decorated with lilac hydrangeas and matching lilac place settings. On the bottom of each napkin *Bree & Evan: August 26, 2017* is printed in an identical hue of lilac.

"I've never seen her so fucking happy," Pippa says, sinking down into one of the cushioned wicker chairs. "And I've never seen so much fucking lilac."

"She deserves it, though." Jackie sits next to her, twirling a piece of butter-yellow hair around her pointer finger.

"Deserves what?"

"Happiness?"

"Of course she does," Pippa agrees. She grabs a bottle of Veuve out of the ice bucket next to the table and pops the cork, filling our flutes. Bree's cousin shoots Pippa a disapproving look again—none of the other tables have opened their champagne yet. But I'm grateful for Pippa, because I really need a drink, and I down half the glass before she tops me off.

"I'm just surprised that out of all my best friends, *Bree* is the first one to lock it down." Jackie picks at a clump of mascara stuck to one of her eyelashes. She hates wearing makeup.

"I'm not," Pippa says. "This is what Bree wants. She came to college a *virgin*. She's a good girl. Of course she's going to settle down as soon as possible."

"But she does love Evan," Jackie says.

"Of course she does," Pippa agrees. "I love Evan, too. He's a total catch. I'm not saying she settled *for* him. I just think she wants to be settled. Think about it—they've only been dating for three years."

"Less than three years," I say, because I know exactly when they started dating, almost down to the minute.

"Right." Pippa nods. "And they got engaged after only a *year and a half.*"

"I thought it would be you, honestly," I tell Pippa.

"Me?"

"I thought you'd be the first of us to get married."

"Are you kidding? I just turned twenty-six. I don't want to get *married* right now." She says it an octave too loud. Lauren looks over and frowns.

"The last guy I dated was addicted to painkillers," Pippa continues, ignoring Lauren's disapproving glare. "*And* he stole my trazodone. *And* he told me I was fat."

"Derek told you that?" I ask. Pippa had recently dated a self-destructive ex-Hobart lacrosse player with a drug-slash-kleptomania problem.

"Yes, he did. Isn't that nice? So based on the men I've been selecting, I'd say marriage is not on the horizon."

Mini quiches are placed in front of us. Course one. My stomach is growling, despite the Adderall. I carve out one crusty, carb-filled bite, and it takes everything in my power to lay my fork down after that. I pour more champagne into my flute.

"Lucy, are you okay?" Jackie whispers. I can't help but notice she's already halfway through her quiche. I'll never stop noticing what other people eat.

"I'm fine. Why?"

"You're barely eating."

"I have a stomachache."

Jackie rolls her wide blue eyes and turns to talk to one of Bree's Ohio friends. I've lied to Jackie about food too many times to count, so naturally she doesn't believe me. I've gotten better about eating, really—but wearing a strapless lilac bridesmaid dress in front of 250 people is a diet emergency.

Still, my lie to Jackie is only a half-lie, because I do feel sick. I've felt nervous-sick about this wedding for months. I chew the edge of my thumb, a habit CJ frequently reminds me is disgusting.

Bree flashes across the terrace in her white shorts. She makes eye contact with us and smiles, then sits down at the adjacent table, next to Evan's mother. Her almost *mother-in-law*. I can't help but agree with Pippa about marriage. I don't think I could be somebody's wife right now.

Having lived with Bree when she started dating Evan and when he proposed, I've seen this relationship all the way through. I watched Evan come into her life and brighten it at the same time that my own life was collapsing in my hands.

"Are you okay?" Jackie whispers again. "It's Stephen, isn't it?" Her ability to read my mind can get annoying.

Stephen. The sound of the name doesn't make my skin prickle as intensely as it used to, but it holds a power over something inside of me. It still evokes the remarkably lucid image of his arm hooked in *Jillian's* two months after our breakup. Bree had dragged me to Baird's New York alumni Christmas party at the Princeton Club and there he'd been, alive and well.

I'll tell you later, I mouth to Jackie. This is Bree's weekend, and I promised myself I wasn't going to ruin it by being overly dramatic about the past.

I glance down at the lilac napkins again. *Bree & Evan.* It was never supposed to be Bree and Evan. I exhale too loudly, wishing for the billionth time that I could accept that Bree getting what she got shouldn't mirror what I didn't get, and everything happens for a reason and *blah, blah, blah.*

One of the caterers clears the quiches and sets down plates of kale salad, which I'll allow myself to eat freely. She gestures to the empty Veuve bottle.

"Would you ladies like another bottle of champagne?"

"Yes," Pippa and I say at the same time.

The first time I slept with Stephen, I hadn't planned on it happening. I would've been less shocked if CJ had stopped highlighting her hair.

It was the morning after the Ugly Christmas Sweater party at the football house, and I had spent the night in his dorm room. I had meant for it to be platonic—really. CJ had been calling me, even though I wasn't answering, and finally she texted me that it was urgent, which sent a stab of panic into my chest, because I thought it might be something to do with my dad or Georgia or our yellow lab, Hickory. But when I slipped into the kitchen, it was only to hear CJ blabber on about a surprise trip she was planning for my dad for his fiftieth birthday. Did I think they should go to Antigua or Lyford Cay, because even though Lyford was more accessible, the Pratts *and* the Delanos were going to be in Antigua, so . . .

I wanted to tell her the truth, that it didn't matter because they were either going to be drinking rum punches at the Lyford Cay Club or the Mill Reef Club, and if it wasn't the Pratts or the Delanos they were sitting beside in cushioned chaises, it would be a fair-haired couple in golf outfits from Greenwich who looked just like them. My family took a lot of trips, but it was always to places like Lyford or Mill Reef or Bermuda or Caneel Bay—gated communities of privileged country clubbers exactly like us. I enjoyed those trips until middle school, when some part of me realized it was disturbing to travel two thousand miles to a place where everyone was wearing the same exact Roberta Freymann tunic. I found it horrifying, the idea that people can travel their whole lives without really *going* anywhere. It was around that time I decided I would be someone who really *went* places—exotic, uncultivated, uncomfortable places.

CJ wasn't like that before she met my father and became an Albright. She used to rough it in hostels as a teenager; she stayed in ashrams and teepees with Marilyn over the course of their third-world adventures. Marilyn was the kind of wealthy woman who understood that money couldn't buy experience; that, in fact, it often worked against it.

I brought the subject up to Georgia once. "Why don't CJ and Dad ever go anywhere cool?"

I could tell that she knew exactly what I meant but she'd just sighed and said, "Lucy, let them do their thing."

So I was sitting on the stoop of the football house, fuming after my phone call with CJ. The anger always hits me deep and hard and out of nowhere, like a migraine. I rarely feel actively angry about the Unforgivable Thing anymore—time has helped with that—but every once in a while something will set me off. I think this time it was the enthusiasm in CJ's voice as she was going on and on about the pros and cons of each Waspy destination. All I could see was my father's face upon receipt of the trip, thrilled and grateful for his wife's devotion. I told CJ I had to call her back. The tears were already falling by the time I made it out the back door and buried my head in my lap. I pulled out the cigarette I had stolen from a pack lying on a table inside the football house.

Stephen noticed me crying on the stoop. He was wearing a funny sweater with Rudolph on the front, and he came over and sat beside me. I didn't want to just sit there, so we went for a walk and he kept asking me to tell him what was the matter. He started talking about his mother's mood disorder and how it wrecked his family, and there was this empathetic quality in his voice, and suddenly I couldn't think of one good reason why I shouldn't tell somebody the real reason why I was crying, and then I was explaining the Unforgiveable Thing to Stephen DeMarco, a practical stranger, which shocked me even as the words spilled out.

I remember every detail of that day, the day of the Unforgivable Thing, all the smells and sounds and textures. They'll never go away. I was wearing Georgia's corduroy skirt, a white collared shirt, and my green Dansko clogs, all well within the parameters of the Friends Academy school dress code. That September in Nassau County it still felt like summer; the midday air was warm enough for swimming, and the maple tree in our front yard was green and brimming with life. Not a speck of fall was in sight, which is the worst time to go to school because you're as far from the promise of summer as you'll ever be. Ahead lie red leaves and pumpkins and homework and turkey and Christmas carols and snowplows and Valentines and mud and painted eggs and daffodil buds pushing their way up out of the thawing earth. And not that any of it's *bad*, but none of it's as good as summer, which is why I always feel a little down those first couple of weeks of September, especially when the weather's nice.

Georgia was at field hockey practice, and I would've been at soccer except that it got canceled because Coach Meyers had to take her five-year-old daughter to the emergency room after she fell off the swings at kindergarten recess. She got thirteen stitches above her left eyebrow.

Lydia called her mom to come pick us up, because we live down the street from each other. That was why I didn't bother calling CJ. I didn't even think she was home, because she taught double Pilates on Thursdays. By the time Mrs. Montgomery dropped me off, a wash of gray clouds had rolled over the sun, and the air smelled chalky, like it was going to rain. I was surprised to see CJ's black Lexus parked in the driveway.

The house appeared empty when I walked inside. I kicked off my shoes and called for CJ. The TV was on in the kitchen, playing a Tide laundry detergent commercial. Hickory lay sleeping on her bed. I knew something was wrong when I saw the half-unpacked grocery bags sitting on the counter. A new carton of milk was sitting out, and a brown paper package from the butcher. A quick stab of fear ran through me because it was so unlike CJ—she normally sprinted into the house to put away the dairy and produce after she'd been out doing errands.

Two near-empty glasses of white wine sat on the counter next to the milk, one of the rims smudged with pink lip gloss.

At this point I wasn't thinking entirely rationally; I wasn't running all possible scenarios through my head. I just wanted to find out where CJ was, because all signs told me she was in the house.

I ran up the stairs. There was a noise coming from the end of the hall, near my parents' room. I don't remember what I thought the noise was or what I expected to discover. I just kept moving forward, farther down the hall until I cracked open the door.

I would give anything to not have seen what I saw, to scrub the image from my memory. My mother's bare back, gleaming with sweat, her thighs hooked around a man with thick brown hair. His eyes were pinched closed as he grasped CJ's hips, but I would've recognized that face in a crowd of thousands. It was Gabe Petersen.

I backed down the hallway as quietly as I could, my feet silent on the soft Italian wool carpet, a force blocking the air from my lungs. My head felt like a tornado, too many reactions pooling at once. Gabe was my first thought. *My* Gabe. And then my father. Where was my dad? He was in London for a trial, and he wouldn't be back until the following night. He'd been gone for more than a week, and CJ was supposed to be cooking his favorite dinner, filet mignon. I thought of the wrapped brown package of meat, spoiling on the kitchen counter.

I felt a kind of sickness that I'd never known before, like someone was stabbing me in the gut with a thousand knives, over and over again. Half of me wanted to fling the bedroom door open and scream, demand an explanation, but the other half of me was so terrified that all I could think to do was run down the stairs and out the front door and down the driveway at lightning speed. It had started to rain hard, and I was barefoot, still in my skirt and polo shirt. I closed my eyes, but all I could see was the arch of CJ's back and her sweaty mop of hair and the white skin above Gabe's midthigh tan line, his perfect body on top of the white monogrammed duvet my father slept under every night, and I was crying so hard that when I opened my eyes again I could barely see, my hair soaking wet with rain.

I ran down the street with my head ducked, heading for Lydia's house, but stopped myself before I got there. I needed to tell Lydia—she had always been my rock, my other sister—but I couldn't. I couldn't tell anyone. I was suddenly terrified of what would happen if I said it out loud.

I didn't have anywhere to go and I was almost at the Montgomerys', so I snuck into their backyard and climbed up into the covered compartment of the swing set for shelter from the rain. I hugged my knees into my chest and wailed silently, praying no one had noticed me. I must've fallen asleep, and hours later when I woke up it was dark, and the rain had stopped, and I was shivering. As I crept down from the swing set and back along the road, different pieces of reality continued to shatter. I thought I would never get used to the shock; it flooded every cell of my body in excruciating waves.

Because it was *Gabe Petersen*, twenty-three-year-old Gabe Petersen, whom I loved unbearably. And it was *Mom*, my mother, the one who brought me warm milk and scratched my back when I was little and couldn't sleep; who read me *A Wrinkle in Time* and all the Narnia books and did all the characters' voices; who kissed me every time she saw me, even if I'd been in the other room for only ten minutes. *Why are you kissing me again, Mom?* I'd ask, annoyed, wiping off her slobber. *'Cause I love you, Sass!* she'd say always, picking me up in her arms and twirling us in circles.

My bare feet were freezing against the pavement as I walked home. I willed myself not to cry again, because it would be only a matter of minutes until I saw CJ. Every single thought, every feeling, every experience I'd ever had—all of it had been a lie.

My parents had always had the kind of relationship that made me confident they were lucky. I had noticed that the Montgomerys never kissed in public, and Mrs. Montgomery always went to bed much earlier than Mr. Montgomery. My parents did everything on the same schedule. Even if my dad had to work late and wouldn't be home until ten thirty, CJ waited for him to eat dinner. Sometimes they ate close to midnight, sharing a blanket on the couch. My mother swore on Hickory that they would never get divorced; that she loved my father as much as she loved Georgia and me, which, as it turned out, was a questionable amount of love.

When I reached our house, all the lights were on. I stared at the brightly illuminated windows, which normally looked cheerful and comforting in the dark. If I went inside, nothing would ever be the same. But I had nowhere else to go.

When I walked in the front door, a soaked, cold mess, CJ rushed into the foyer and pulled me into her, squeezing me tight, screaming at me for worrying her, asking frantically where I'd been. She was wearing her bathrobe and lots of her fragrant lotion. I fidgeted out of her grip. I didn't know what would happen if I looked at her face. I mumbled something about having gotten out of soccer practice late and walking home from school. CJ was still shouting questions at me as I dragged myself upstairs. I found Georgia in the playroom.

"Luce? What happened to you?" Georgia knew I had been crying. Georgia knows everything.

I looked at my sister. She was plopped on the red beanbag in front of the television, her bright eyes brimming with concern. The words were on the tip of my tongue; I could almost hear them escaping from my mouth in one quick breath. I felt how much better I'd feel if told her, if we could be in it together. Georgia was only eleven months older, my Irish twin, and she would know exactly what to do. But as I scanned her worried face I knew that I would never be able to tell her. There was no point in ruining her life, too. So I lied and said I'd had a fight with Lydia—the first of so many lies.

When my dad arrived home the next night, I watched from the top of the staircase as CJ handed him a cold gin and tonic and pressed her face into his neck. "Filet mignon *por vous ce soir*," she purred in broken French.

I ran to the bathroom and threw up. My parents thought I had the flu and let me go to sleep without questions. I put in my headphones and turned on Fleetwood Mac as loud as it would go. I wrapped myself up in Marilyn's sweater and decided that Marilyn would've hated CJ if she'd known who she really was. I had nightmares that woke me in a full sweat. They lasted for months.

Macy Petersen died in a car accident almost two years later, the summer after my sophomore year. She was driving Gabe's Jeep, alone, and slid off the road. I watched CJ bawl her eyes out. She tried to make me go to the funeral, but I said I was sick. I watched CJ doll herself up in a sleek black dress and Marilyn's pearls, with a fresh blowout and too much makeup, Georgia and my father in tow. I was devastated by what happened to Macy—everyone was—but there was no way I was going to go to the funeral and watch my mother flirt with her ex-lover, the brother of the dead girl, while my own father stood there like a clueless puppy.

When I finally finished telling Stephen about the Unforgivable Thing, what I loved was that he didn't take it too seriously. He didn't freak out like most people would've. He was perfectly nice about it—he just didn't dwell on it or look at me like what I'd said was inconceivable. He even made a couple of lighthearted jokes, but there was a genuine sense of compassion in the way he responded to me.

By the end of my conversation with Stephen the sickness in my stomach had subsided. I felt better than I had in ages. For so long, the

Unforgivable Thing had been a living part of me, something I felt I had to handle, an event I subconsciously weighed against each of my experiences. But talking to Stephen about it was the first time I realized that I was making it harder than it had to be. That maybe it didn't have to be something I had to bear. That CJ didn't have to be my problem. Maybe I still cared, but maybe I could also just forget about it.

I felt calm sitting next to Stephen on his couch, grateful for his sensitivity as the wine softened my limbs, but there was also something enthralling about being around him. Most boys, when they interact with you, seem sort of distracted or like they don't fully care about what you're saying. Parker was always like that—one eye on the TV or fumbling around with his phone. But when Stephen looked at me, he really saw me. He didn't look past me to the dozens of other things going on in his life. He listened, *really* listened, and I could see that it made him genuinely happy. Nobody listened like that.

A feeling of immense gratitude toward him warmed my chest. I wanted him to care about me, to protect me and be my friend, and his eyes told me that he would be.

"I'm so tired." I yawned.

"I can walk you home."

But the thought of going back to my empty dorm room depressed me. Maybe if Jackie was there it would've been different, but it was the weekend, and she would definitely be sleeping at Stuart's.

"Maybe I could stay here," I said. "Just to sleep."

"Sure. You want a T-shirt?"

"Thanks."

He handed me a New York Giants T-shirt. "Here you go."

"Eli Manning. Number ten." I smiled.

"I knew you'd like that one."

The shirt smelled good, like laundry soap. I climbed underneath his sheets, sleepy from the wine but mostly sober. I heard Stephen click off the light and climb into the bed next to me. I felt him face the other direction and I suddenly, desperately, wanted him to turn around. Even though we had kissed before, nothing about our interaction that night had felt sexual; it had just felt like friendship. I'd said I was staying over only to sleep, which *was* my intention. Stephen was probably just being respectful. Or maybe he didn't like me that way anymore. Maybe he was annoyed to have me there, taking up space in his bed.

I watched the back of his neck face away from me, the tender part between the collar of his T-shirt and hairline. The shift in my feelings for Stephen, the way I remember it, occurred that night while I was watching the back of his neck. The way the muscles slid as he breathed; how his hair seemed to perfectly part the concave hollow that formed.

I smelled his Old Spice. I wanted him to roll over and kiss me so badly that I couldn't sleep. The feeling swallowed me whole; I couldn't think about anything else. I became very aware of my tossing and turning under the sheets, the noise it made when I moved. At some point in the middle of the night, when I couldn't stand it anymore, I wrapped my arms around his torso and pulled him over to my side of the bed. He felt thick and warm.

When I woke up in the morning the room was filled with a lemon-colored light, and Stephen's arms were around me, the pads of his fingers pressing lightly against my stomach. I felt inexplicably complete and content. We started kissing easily, like waking up together was something we'd done a thousand times. He slid the Eli Manning shirt over my head, and it was something I wanted him to be doing—the way I'd felt when Gabe touched me that day in his car. I'd waited so long to feel that again, I thought it might not be possible. I was so relieved and surprised I wanted to laugh out loud. We got naked. His body hovered above mine, his green eyes heavy, full of hunger. The attraction was so palpable and strange; it scared and intoxicated me at once. Every part of my body trembled with lust.

"Are you sure you want to do this, Lucy?" His whisper was hot and damp in my ear. "Because we don't have to."

"Yes." I nodded into his shoulder. I'd only slept with one person, ever, but I needed more of whatever was happening. "But do you have a condom?"

He reached toward the nightstand and fumbled around until he found one. I watched him roll it on, felt him wedge my thighs farther apart with his knees. He buried his face in my collarbone and when I felt him inside me, I almost lost my breath.

I wasn't expecting to come—I never had from sex with Parker—but it happened anyway, his deep groans intensifying my own arousal, his final cry sending me over the edge. It felt so good that for minutes after I couldn't move or think or speak. I collapsed onto Stephen's chest, my heart pounding, and he ran the tips of his fingers up and down my spine.

"You are fucking incredible, Lucy."

I felt exhilarated and stunned. The sex was amazing, but that wasn't half of it. I liked him. I *liked* him. When had that happened? The best feelings are unexpected like that. I woke up and they were there, like snow.

12

STEPHEN

DECEMBER 2010

The problem with juggling girls on a small college campus, even for someone like me who is good at it, is the geographical parameters. There isn't a lot of space, and you never know who might be lurking in a window across the street or who might happen to walk by a specific place at an unfortunate time.

Keaton Banks, one of Diana's best friends, happened to be strolling along Carroll Street when she noticed Lucy and me leaving the dorm. I gave Lucy a quick kiss on the front stoop—rookie mistake, but Lucy is pretty, and it's hard not to want to kiss her all the time. Plus, I knew she was the kind of girl who expected a goodbye kiss from the guy she'd just fucked.

That evening, an outraged Diana stormed into my bedroom with that crazy look in her eyes like she wanted to castrate me. She screamed and screamed about what Keaton had told her. The poor guy in the single room next to mine—the number of times Diana has gone on a screaming rant in here, I didn't even want to know what he thought.

I took a beer out of the mini fridge and cracked it open. I refused to let her win this argument.

"Diana," I started calmly. "You and I are not together. You have made it very *clear* that you don't want to be with me." I sat down on one end of the couch, hoping she'd pipe down and take a seat herself.

But she remained standing, her hands flailing in front of her face. "Yes, because I don't trust you. But we're still sleeping together. And you keep telling me you want me back, and now you're sleeping with some *freshman*?"

"Diana, you and I have slept together three times since September, and always on your terms. I want to be with you. I keep on saying it, but if you're not willing to give me another chance, then I'm allowed to see other people. Christmas break starts in a couple of days. Why don't you take some time to think about it and we'll talk in January?"

"Oh, that would be convenient for you, wouldn't it?" she spat. "So you can keep screwing that little whore for another month. I know she's from Long Island, right near you. I know these things, Stephen. I'm not an idiot."

"Jesus Christ, Di. I'm not even going to be home for break. I have to go to fucking Florida with my family to see my grandfather."

Diana crossed her arms, still frowning. "Why? Is everything okay?"

"It's fine."

"How's your dad?"

"Depressed."

"And your mom?"

"I haven't talked to her in a while. Stop grilling me." I took a long sip of beer.

Diana finally sat down on the couch. "Your room is disgusting." She picked up a stale, half-eaten slice of pizza from the coffee table and tossed it into the overflowing trash bin.

I looked into her clear brown eyes. "You're not my girlfriend anymore. You don't have the right to lecture me about the messiness of my room."

Diana sighed. She was cracking her knuckles, the way she did when she was stressed.

"I want to be with you," she said finally. "Thinking about you and that girl is making me sick."

"So you want to be with me just so I'll stop fooling around with Lucy? That's mature."

"*Don't* say her name to me, Stephen. I'll barf on this table."

"Don't be so dramatic, Diana. Do you want a drink?"

Diana buried her head between her knees, ignoring my question. "You know I want to be with you," she mumbled. "But I'm terrified."

"I wouldn't cheat on you, again, Di. Never ever ever."

"How do I know that?"

"Because I *swear*. Isn't it clear how much I love you? I send you flowers and cards and nothing is good enough for you."

"*Flowers* and *cards* do not make up for the fact that you *slept* with someone else. You slept with Nicole right under my nose. I can't even think about it, it makes me so sick."

"What happened last spring was the biggest mistake of my life. It put everything in perspective. *You* are the one I love, Diana. I love you. *You*." Ah, the power of the l-word.

Diana finally picked her head up and looked at me. Teardrops clung to the bottom rims of her eyes. "I love you, too," she said. "But I'm not ready to get back together. I—I need more time."

"Time."

"Yeah."

"Fine. Take more fucking time."

"Just stop hooking up with her, okay? For my own peace of mind. And Jesus Christ, would you stop fucking Nicole Hart, too? God, I feel bad for that poor freshman. She probably thinks you actually like her."

"Diana—"

"Don't even *try* to tell me you're not sleeping with Nicole."

"I am not *sleeping* with Nicole. Jesus Christ, Diana."

"Fine, but you've *slept* with her this year."

"I'm sick of fighting with you. This is going in circles. We're not together. I'm allowed to hook up with other people." I reached for her hand, but she pulled it away.

"I want you to stop. If I have any hope of trusting you again, I need to know that you'll stop."

"You're being ridiculous. You can't fucking have it both ways."

"Say you'll think about it."

"Fine. I will." I tossed my hands up in surrender.

She lingered in the doorway, her hand trembling on the knob for a moment before she turned back around and kissed me hard, panicked. I could feel her indecision as we fucked on the bed, and I knew she was pissed at herself when it was over.

"This isn't happening again," she said, grabbing her clothes from the floor and pulling them on in a frenzy. "I swear to God it's not."

"You're the one calling all the shots here, Diana. You want to fuck, we fuck. You want to date, we date."

"You're sleeping with other people. I'm not going to date someone who *SLEEPS WITH OTHER PEOPLE.*" She was really screaming now.

"Can you keep your *voice* down, please? The walls in Copeland are not thick. And I will not *sleep with other people* if you commit to this," I hissed.

"How do I know *you* will actually commit to this? How do I know that? After what happened, I don't." The tears were running down her face again. I felt a massive headache coming on.

"I'm not having this conversation again. You either trust me or you don't, but I'm begging you to try. Please. Please, Diana." I knelt on the ground in front of her and wrapped my arms around her little legs, pressed my face into her leggings.

"I hate you for doing this to us." She pulled away. She grabbed her jacket, and I noticed that her shirt was inside out as she slammed the door, Evan's over-the-door coat hanger rattling in her wake.

My temples pounded. Sometimes I wondered why I even bothered to try to make it work with Diana. Perhaps the damage had been done. But the thought of losing her didn't sit well; the notion of getting through the rest of Baird without Diana, knowing she'd won, made my blood boil.

Lucy knocked on my door around ten. We already had plans to watch a movie, and despite my impending headache, it would've been rude to cancel. Lucy looked great in a fitted white sweater, her long chestnut hair all shiny and good-smelling.

I was tired from my evening with Diana, but Lucy plunked down onto my lap and I felt myself grow hard against her, the pain in my head dulling. I fidgeted with the button on her jeans.

"Let's watch the movie first," she whispered, but my hand was already down her pants, and I watched her neck fall back as it slid deeper.

"Hmm . . . if you want to watch the movie, then why are you so wet?" I pushed her down on the couch and pulled her pants all the way off. I pressed my mouth against the thin fabric of her tiny black thong, and that was the end of that conversation.

I watched Lucy come, closing her eyes and opening her mouth, digging her fingers into my back. As we lay there after, panting, I traced my fingers over her smooth, warm back and stared at her perfect ass.

"I could stare at you naked forever," I said.

"You know," she said, propping up on one elbow. "You're the first guy I've ever . . . come with . . . during sex."

"Are you serious?" I asked, though I wasn't surprised. Most guys don't know what the hell they're doing.

"Yes." She rested her head back down on my chest.

"Well, I'm honored, Luce. And for the record, you're the most beautiful girl I've ever had the pleasure of luring into my bed."

"You're so sweet," she said. "I'm sorry it took me so long to give you a real chance."

"It's no big deal. You're a freshman. I understand what it's like to want to play the field."

"No, Stephen. It's not like that."

I knew it wasn't *like that* for her. Girls like Lucy can probably count the number of sexual partners they've had on one hand. This was the only negative consequence of sex with Lucy—now that we were sleeping together and especially now that I was giving her all these eye-opening orgasms, she would expect me to be her boyfriend. This was impossible, of course, because it would require total severance from Diana.

At one point I did adore Diana, but the adoration stage never lasts long. What I've come to learn and what most people fail to understand is that love is a choice. If you assess the worth of your relationship solely in terms of your feelings it is likely to fail, or at least be extremely short-term. You cannot go on having these "feelings" for someone forever. With girls, the exciting part is winning their affection. That's the fun. Then you have to choose who you're going to love, backed by the reasons why. This may sound a bit calculated, but in all honesty I can't stand being single. I've always found life to run much more efficiently with a girlfriend.

It's been this way since my first relationship, my high school girl-friend, Jenna Landry. Jenna was the daughter of one of the chemistry teachers. She had thick hair like a horse's tail and a natural athleticism that propelled her onto the varsity track and volleyball teams. When I met Jenna, I'd had just enough practice with girls to know that if I played my cards right, I could make her mine. I've never been the guy girls drool over at first sight—I have my green eyes and a thick head of hair that grows too quickly, but amid the rest of the average Joe package those features are unexceptional, often lost.

But charm, that was something I could cultivate. It came naturally to me to flirt with the right amount of confidence, to know what others wanted to hear and express it with perceived candor. I was good at being charming, and it felt a hell of a lot more valid than being nice to look at. With limited trial and error, charm quickly became the quality I could rely on to get me into a girl's pants, to get me laid at summer camp by age fourteen, and then to get me Jenna.

Sexually Jenna was open and explorative; she let me take her virginity freshman spring, the night I told her I loved her on the couch in her basement. At first I spent time with Jenna just to avoid being at home with my depressed father, but then I learned the satisfaction that came with having a girlfriend—someone who was there for you, someone who was obligated to support you and provide consistent affection, someone to introduce to your family so they would think you were normal, like you were loved. Jenna and I broke up several times over the course of high school after various fights and squabbles, most of which she unreasonably deemed my fault. We broke up for good a week before we left for separate colleges, three weeks after the accident, two weeks before I met Diana Bunn.

The accident. I can't think about Jenna without thinking about the accident the fateful night of August 16, 2008, and it gets under my skin, badly, every time. I close my eyes and I still see the long, twisted piece of red hair, shiny, almost perfectly matching the color of the blood. The overpowering smell of Bubblicious bubble gum.

Too many people dwell on the past; it's better to pay attention to what's in front of you. In my bed in my dorm room, Lucy ran her hands through the hairs on my chest. I kissed her temple, proud of myself for successfully enticing a girl of her caliber. Wrigley didn't think I could do it, but he forgot just how good I am at this game.

There's something about Lucy. I'm going to keep fucking her for as long as possible. Which, with the correct approach, could be a very long time.

13

LUCY

This time it was Bree who shook the white powder out onto the mirror, which lay flat on Wrigley's kitchen table. Bree took out her credit card and buried it in the mound, attempting to sort the coke into neat, even lines, the way Pippa did. But Bree was a novice and so Pippa took over, but not in an authoritative way. That was what I liked about Pippa—she was bold but never commanding. She was just Pippa.

Bree and I had decided to try coke, not due to peer pressure, we promised each other, but out of curiosity. College was about experimenting—CJ had said so herself. I'd watched Pippa blow lines numerous times; Jackie, too; even Stephen now that we were spending more and more time together. They'd all pop up from inhaling their line with the same delighted, eager expression. Pippa said it wasn't anything like pot—a drug I'd never liked because it made me feel paranoid, stuck inside myself. Pippa said coke was just like drinking a lot of coffee. Plus, according to Pippa, it suppressed your appetite.

It was the night of the Wild West party, and we were pregaming at Wrigley's. I sat on Stephen's lap, his hands resting on my stomach, underneath my shirt. Pippa and Wrig were there, Bree, Jackie, and a few of Wrigley and Stephen's friends. Jackie always invited Stuart to come along when we went to Wrigley's pregames, but he never did. Stuart wasn't into drugs, and sometimes I didn't blame him for not wanting to be around Jackie when she was on them.

When it was my turn, Jackie slid the mirror in front of me.

"You don't have to, you know," Stephen whispered in my ear.

"I want to. Really, I want to try it."

Jackie handed me the tightly rolled twenty-dollar bill. I pinched it in my fingers. I wished everyone wasn't watching me. I held the bill in front of my right nostril, plugging my other nostril with my left forefinger. Then I inhaled sharply, the way Jackie had instructed. I didn't get the whole line, but I got most of it. Stephen licked his finger and swiped up the remaining powder.

"Show me your gums," he said, then wiped the extra coke all over them. "Yee-haw, cowgirl."

My mouth went numb in a surprisingly pleasant way. My brain felt light but sharp. I knew I'd be up all night.

"What d'you think of the coke?" he asked me later, when we were leaving Wrigley's to go to the Wild West party.

"It's fun." I nodded, unable to control the size of my smile.

"You're the cutest cowgirl in the history of cowgirls." He leaned down and kissed me, tipping my Western-style hat back. He tugged lightly at the braids on either side of my head, then ran his hands over the back of my jeans and pulled me close to him. "You're so tiny. You have the sexiest body."

Tiny—I cherished the word. The inside of my chest felt warm with praise. I'd lost twelve pounds since the beginning of the semester. I hadn't meant to initially—I'd just been trying to avoid the freshman fifteen—but once the weight started falling off, I couldn't stop. I wanted a gap in my thighs, the kind Bree had. Losing weight wasn't that hard. Four-mile run in the morning, hot vinyasa at YogaLab in the afternoon. I skipped breakfast and ate from the salad bar at the other two meals—lettuce and chickpeas with nonfat dressing, apples for snacks. I learned to appreciate the gnawing in my gut when I fell asleep at night. Food isn't actually that important, if you think about it. Physically, the human body can go weeks without it. Gandhi survived twenty-one days of complete starvation, and he's legendary.

14

STEPHEN

Manipulation is not a bad word. It's not a cynical mind-set. It's a proactive approach to exploiting opportunities. This was something I'd been thinking about ever since Wrigley's stupid little girlfriend, Pippa, cornered me in the library and told me that I was "manipulating Lucy" and warned me in a girlish whine to stay away from her. Good God. Freshman girls are so tightly wound up with hormones, you can't take them seriously. They genuinely believe that everything they say matters phenomenally. It's truly absurd. Girls in general are psychotic.

Pippa scrunched up her nose. "She *knows* that you slept with Nicole Hart on Sunday, right after she left your room. Do you realize how disgusting that is? You must have so many STDs."

"Whoa. Take it easy, Pippa." Pippa. What kind of a bullshit name is Pippa?

"I will not *take it easy*. Lucy is my best friend. And I *know* it's true. Don't even try to deny it."

Pippa stormed off before I could say another word. Good Lord. I come to the library for some peace and quiet so I can attempt to tackle my international-policy paper outline, and I'm harassed by hormonal freshman girls. The library used to be my safe haven.

I ducked into a desk behind the last row of shelves on the third floor to avoid further confrontation.

Well, Lucy knew. I suppose it was only a matter of time before Lucy's faultless image of me went to shit. In any case, I did need to stop fucking Nicole Hart. The consequences of that had proven more trouble than it's worth—Nicole's not even attractive. It's just the rush I'm addicted to. The sneaking around. The getting away with it. The getting away with *not* getting away with it. There's something else about cheating, too—it stabilizes me, evens me out. Monogamy isn't natural.

I wasn't even planning on seeing Nicole, to be honest. It was last Sunday; Lucy and I woke up, made coffee, watched the first half of the Giants game, and had sex. She always liked to have sex in the morning, which was absolutely fine by me. Sex with Lucy was the best part of Lucy.

After Lucy left, Nicole called to ask if she could swing by and pick up the blow she'd left in my room on Friday. She walked in ten minutes later. Nicole and I did not hook up *regularly*—we mainly just did drugs together—but she had a thing for me and was always down, even though she was sort of in Diana's circle and knew I would never actually date her. Nicole could be annoying and kind of just lurked around, but what did it matter? Sex was sex. We did a couple of lines and banged at the end of the bed, same place we did it on Friday afternoon. Luckily, Lucy found out only about the time in the morning. Luckily, Diana found out about zero times, even though screwing Nicole was well within my rights when it came to Diana and our nonexistent relationship.

Don't make the mistake of thinking I'm your average scumbag. It is not like that. I understand that by "moral" standards I am fucking up. It's not that I'm heartless; I just know this type of situation is fixable. People always say that you can't have your cake and eat it, too, but you can. I know what girls in Lucy's position want to hear, and I can provide that. More flattery doesn't make the girl feel better, just addicted, and then you've hooked her because she continues to be hungry for that certain category of feedback.

When I was eight, my brother, Luke, and I were playing basketball in my aunt and uncle's driveway, and I accidentally stepped on my cousin Christina's turtle and killed it. Its shell and guts were all crushed into the pavement. Christina was six and she cried for weeks—she loved that stupid turtle. She'd named it Marvin and put up such a fuss that her first-grade teacher had let her bring him into school every day. He'd sat in the corner in his crate while Christina drew with crayons or whatever the hell you do in first grade.

I remember my father sitting me down the day I killed Marvin and explaining that I needed to apologize even though it was an accident. He said he knew how bad I felt but that accidents happened and that I would feel better with time. I didn't understand what my father meant because I didn't feel bad about the situation at all. The only thing that bothered me was the prospect of Christina hating me, so I was very nice and apologetic to her in order to prevent that. I knew she was devastated, and I knew that Marvin was a smashed lump of turtle slime, but that didn't make *me* feel bad. It didn't make me feel anything.

That's just one example. Stuff like that used to happen throughout my childhood and into my teenage years—events or moments when I'd lack the specific emotional response expected of me. Time and time again, the empathetic reactions that seemed to be required never came—a lack of genuine grief at my grandmother's funeral, a lack of remorse when Jenna caught me making out with Mackenzie Mills in my buddy Carl's backyard, indifference as I watched my mom move out, my siblings sullen and teary-eyed. I learned about appropriate responses; I began simulating them when appropriate. And somewhere in that haze of it I came to the realization that I was different. I didn't want to hurt people, but I could, and when I did, there was something cathartic and liberating about it, especially because any collateral damage was almost always rectifiable. I know about guilt, and it doesn't apply to me—I don't carry the burden of it. It actually works to my advantage, most of the time.

I dialed Wrigley on my walk home from the library, the cold air whipping my face.

"What the fuck?" I snapped when he answered.

"What?"

I could picture the clueless look on Wrigley's face. The kid was actually dumb as rocks, which was why I wasn't legitimately angry.

"You told Pippa that I hooked up with Nicole. Remember that she and Lucy are, like, BFFs forever?"

"Oh, shit, yeah. I'm sorry, dude. It came out in the heat of the moment. Pippa and I were having some fight. I guess I was trying to hurt her and it slipped."

"Fix it, Wrig. Fix it."

"How?"

"Call Pippa and tell her what you just told me. You were angry and trying to hurt her. I did not fuck Nicole."

"But you did fuck Nicole."

"*Wrigley.*"

"I don't wanna call Pippa," Wrigley mumbled glumly. "We're over."

"Wrigley."

"Fine."

"Wrigley?"

"What, DeMarco?"

"Do it now."

15

LUCY

MARCH 2011

Carefully, I penciled eyeliner around my top and bottom lids, making sure to do it the way Pippa had shown me. I always took forever getting ready to hang out with Stephen. Jackie and Pippa watched me while they drank Coronas on Jackie's bed.

"You're really going to an Italian restaurant on a Saturday night?"

"He wants to take me there." I shrugged, unable to contain my smile. The fact that he took me out to dinner was so romantic, such a gesture. Even Stuart rarely took Jackie on dinner dates.

"But it's *Saturday* night," Pippa said. "Delta Gamma is having their big party."

Delta Gamma was the only semicool Baird sorority; the other few in existence were groups of feminist overachievers who organized charity events that no one ever went to. Greek life at Baird was a bust in general, aside from DG and a few of the frats.

"I know." I smoothed my hair. "We'll meet you there after."

"*We'll* meet you there after? So you're officially a *we* now?" Jackie frowned.

"I didn't say that." I crossed my arms, which prickled with goose bumps. I was always cold these days. I knew my arms looked too thin, and I could feel them judging me. I'd been on a yogurt kick—I'd read in a magazine that a woman lost ten pounds in two weeks by eating only nonfat Greek yogurt.

"I don't know, Luce. I don't trust him," Jackie said.

"Why? You barely know him."

"Well, the thing with Pippa in January. That was weird."

"What thing with Pippa in January?"

"I think she means when Wrigley told me that DeMarco hooked up with Nicole Hart," Pippa explained.

"Right." Jackie nodded. "That."

"That was months ago, and it wasn't even true. Wrigley called Pippa and admitted he lied. They were fighting."

"Yeah," Pippa said. "And Wrigley *is* a psychopath. He doesn't know what he's saying half the time."

"I know, I know." Jackie sighed, tucking a blond wisp behind her ear. "But what about that junior girl Diana? The one in Delta Gamma who Stephen used to date?"

"What about her? She's not in DG. She's just friends with those girls. Keaton Banks and them."

"You're right," Pippa said. "Plus, no way is Diana a DG. She's too . . . granola."

"What's 'granola'?" Jackie asked.

"You don't know what 'granola' is?"

"Jackie? What about her?" I repeated.

"Huh?"

"Diana. Why'd you bring her up? What about her?"

"Oh. I dunno. I just feel like I see her and Stephen talking at parties sometimes."

"Do you?" My stomach sank on instinct, though I was starting to feel like Jackie was looking for a problem simply because she didn't like Stephen.

"I do, too, sometimes," Pippa said. "I remember Wrigley saying they have a weird relationship."

"It's probably nothing," Jackie added quickly.

"What do you mean a *weird* relationship?"

"Who *knows*," Pippa sighed. "I wouldn't worry about it, Lucy. He obviously really likes you if he's taking you out to dinner on a Saturday night. Nobody at Baird goes on Saturday-night dinner dates."

"You don't like him, do you?" I glanced at Jackie.

"I never said that." I watched her open a new beer and reach into a bag of Cheetos. She ate anything she wanted. Everything was so easy for Jackie.

"I know you think I can do better," I said. "And maybe I can. I get that he's not the *hottest* guy at Baird. But I really don't care."

"Lucy, it's not about that. I couldn't care less what he looks like."

"So you admit it's about something, then?"

"Lucy . . . ," Jackie exhaled.

"Don't you want me to be happy?" I looked into her ocean-blue eyes.

"Of course I do. I'm sorry." The expression on her face told me she really was sorry.

My phone vibrated, and I grabbed it off the desk.

"I gotta go."

Pippa yawned. "Have fun. Be safe. Use a condom. Et cetera."

"Thanks, Pip."

"See you at the party later?"

"Yeah." I grabbed my jacket and ran out the door, suddenly too excited to really concentrate on being annoyed at Jackie.

Stephen was waiting for me outside the dorm. It was a hot night, the row of palm trees lining the walkway to Kaplan swaying gently in the warm breeze. He wore a white polo shirt and his New York Giants hat. I wrapped my arms around his neck and inhaled the familiar scent of his aftershave.

"Hi." I kissed him. I loved being able to kiss him after a day of thinking about kissing him.

"God I've missed you," he said close to my face, our eyes locking. "It's only been what—two days? Two days and I'm going crazy thinking about seeing you. Am I addicted to you, Lucy in the Sky with Diamonds?"

"If you're addicted to me, I'm addicted to you." I leaned my head against his chest, let him hold me close, absorbed with affection.

It was only a twenty-minute walk to the restaurant in Claremont, but it felt amazing to be off campus, alone with Stephen in a place that wasn't school.

The waitress sat us at a two-top, but Stephen asked if we could sit in a corner booth.

"So I can be closer to you," he whispered, sliding in next to me on the booth, his hand covering my thigh.

The restaurant, Giuliana's, had a modern vibe with dim lighting.

"Why Italian?" I asked.

"I dunno. It's romantic?" His lips curled. "And Giuliana's has the best pasta. I constantly crave Italian food, being Italian myself."

"Right," I nod. "DeMarco must be Italian."

"My dad isn't an immigrant or anything," Stephen explained, pressing a piece of warm bread into a plate of salted olive oil. "My great-grandfather was born in Sicily. His family came to New York when he was eight."

"Do you speak Italian?"

"Nope." Stephen chuckled. "I sort of remember my grandfather trying to teach us a few words, but it never stuck."

I took a piece of bread from the basket and let in soak in the plate of oil. I was letting myself eat whatever I wanted for the night. I was with Stephen, and I was happy. One carb-heavy meal wouldn't kill me.

"I'm glad we're here, Luce." Stephen reached for a second piece of bread.

"So am I. Although my friends were being annoying about it."

"Annoying how?"

"Mainly just Jackie. She says she doesn't trust you because she thinks you really did sleep with Nicole Hart."

"That's ridiculous." Stephen glanced away, and I regretted saying anything. I felt obnoxious for bringing up a subject we'd buried months ago.

"That's what I said," I offered, and the tension in my body eased when he reached across my lap and interlaced his fingers in mine.

"I just wanted to grab some wine and a bite with you on a Saturday night. I hope that's okay with Jackie."

By the end of dinner we'd finished a bottle of red, and Stephen's hands were fumbling with the button on my white jeans under the table.

"You should've worn a skirt, Luce," he breathed into my ear.

"I see why you wanted to sit at a booth." I pushed his hand away playfully. The waitress gave us a *Get a room* look as she dropped the check. I loved it. I wanted every stranger to envy our chemistry.

We climbed into a cab and I told the driver to take us to Delta Gamma on Logan Street.

Stephen turned to me. "I don't really want to go to that party."

"Why not?"

"I dunno. I just want to go somewhere and hang with you." He unzipped my jeans and slipped his hand underneath the elastic of my underwear. I glanced at the cabdriver, whose eyes were glued to the road.

"Is it because Diana is going to be there?" I couldn't help myself. I was a little drunk, and Jackie's voice echoed in my head.

"What?" Stephen removed his hand and stared at me blankly.

"Do you not want to show up to the party with me or something, because Diana will be there?"

"Why do you think she'll be there?" The flirtation had vanished from his grass-green eyes, and he looked at me coldly, in a way he hadn't before.

"Isn't she in DG?" I asked, knowing well that she wasn't. If I said I knew she hung out with a lot of DGs, I'd look like a stalker. I felt myself crossing a line.

"No, she's not. You're being ridiculous." He pulled away from me completely, and I wished desperately I'd said nothing. It was all Jackie's fault.

"I'm sorry. I don't know why I said that." I placed my hand on his knee and fought my way back toward being *Lucy in the Sky with Diamonds*, his girl, even though I knew exactly why I'd said what I did. It wasn't just because of Jackie. Stephen and I didn't show up at parties together. Maybe we did in larger groups, but never just the two of us. We'd never been visibly together in front of Diana.

Stephen placed his hand on top of mine, and I felt the stiffness loosen through my shoulders. He was probably just being sensitive toward Diana's feelings post-breakup. Of course he didn't go parading around with me in front of her and her friends.

"Lucy." He turned to me, a piece of silvery moonlight catching his face through the window. "Everyone knows about you and me. I'm not trying to hide anything. I just don't feel like going to a crowded keg party and standing around with a bunch of people when I could go be alone with you in a warm, comfy bed. That's all."

"I know. I'm sorry. That's what I want, too," I said, even though half of me wanted to waltz into the party on Stephen's arm in front of Diana and Jackie and everyone else. But I wasn't going to push it. I slid my hand under the waistband of his khakis to make him forget I'd picked such an absurd, girlish fight.

When we got back to Stephen's room, Evan was just leaving.

"You guys staying in tonight?" Evan asked. I barely knew Evan, even though he lived with Stephen. He had short, sand-colored hair and a kind face.

"We just got back from Giuliana's," Stephen said, irritation lining his voice. Stephen was always complaining about Evan, for whatever reason.

"Yum. Okay, well I'm gonna head to DG. I hear it's fun over there. Night, guys."

Evan left the room, and Stephen didn't say a word before shoving me down on the bed, harder than usual. He removed his own clothes before tearing off mine. His hands grabbed for me almost manically, cupping my breasts and running his tongue and lips over them, as though he couldn't do enough to them.

"Suck my dick. It feels so good when you suck it." He lay back on the bed. I was always happy to do it; it turned me on more than anything to know that I was getting him off, a feeling I'd never once had with Parker. I swallowed till his hardness touched the back of my throat and then swirled my tongue around the tip, the way Antonia had taught me in high school.

His groans intensified, and I cherished each one. He didn't come in my mouth—he rarely did—head was typically a prelude to sex. He flipped me over onto my hands and knees and fucked me from behind so hard I thought I might black out. He grabbed my hair with his fists and yanked it fiercely, and I felt that it was more than just the sex but that he was severely, wildly angry, at me or at something, and even though my hair felt like it was going to rip out of my head I didn't say anything because a part of me liked it—the part of me that was just as angry as he was really fucking liked it.

Afterward I lay on my stomach, my heart racing as he wiped the cum off my back with a paper towel.

"Go on birth control," he said, lying next to me, panting.

"Why?"

"Because I can't stand condoms, and I don't want to pull out every time. I want to come inside you. And we both know this isn't going to stop anytime soon."

"Okay," I whispered, even though I wouldn't go on birth control. I didn't need it. I'd stopped getting my period in December.

I nuzzled my face into his warm shoulder, relishing each second as he stroked my back with his fingertips. I would do anything for him.

16

STEPHEN

Diana found me upstairs at Hawaiian Luau, Baird's final rager of the year, held annually on the last Saturday before exams. Hawaiian Luau had always been a Chops party, before Chops got the boot my sophomore spring when some asshole overdosed on coke and blamed *Chops* for peer-pressuring him. The school caught wind and searched Slug, Chops's frat house, where they found fifteen grams, and that was it for Chops. Such a shame. Search any other house on or around Baird's campus and you are guaranteed to find some form of drugs, be it LSD, mushrooms, speed, narcotics, ecstasy—the list goes on. The administration is fucking delusional.

The hippies didn't go to Hawaiian Luau, but anyone on a sports team or in a frat did, anyone who took drugs and listened to LCD Soundsystem did.

Diana pushed the bedroom door open—without knocking, of course—and found me passing lines around with a late-night crew of like-minded amphetamine fiends.

"Stephen, do you have a sec?"

Everybody looked at me like *Oh shit, dude, your ex-girlfriend wants to talk to you, good luck*. But I could tell from Diana's face that she was in a good mood.

She led me down the hallway, to a quieter spot.

"Hi." She grinned. She looked pretty, with a pink flower tucked behind her ear and a Hawaiian lei around her neck. She wore a grass skirt and a white crop top that revealed her stomach. Diana has always had a nice stomach, but I flinched when I saw the exposed rectangle of skin. I guess a lot of girls look particularly good at Hawaiian Luau—there were lots of pictures being taken—but I was especially struck by Diana. Maybe it was her composed, tolerant smile. A look that said, for a change: *I don't want to kill you.*

"Hey, you." I'll never stop flirting with her.

"It's good to see you, Stephen."

"You're not gonna give me shit for doing blow?"

"It's your life." She shrugged.

I nodded, but half of me wanted her to launch into her usual lecture on the perils of cocaine—it kind of turns me on when Diana lectures me.

"It's been a while, Di. You look good."

"Thanks. I don't love that Hawaiian Luau is at Sigma Chi this year . . ." She twirled back and forth on her heel. Was she nervous?

"I know. It's not Chops."

"I heard you guys can live in Slug next year, though. Congrats."

"How'd you hear?"

"Everyone's talking about it."

"Yeah. But it'll just be Slug, no Chops affiliation whatsoever."

"Still, it's exciting."

I nodded. I was happy. After the administration seized Slug from its management company to do some sort of informal investigation, what had been Baird College's biggest party house remained uninhabited for a whole year. Now that the "investigation" was over, Slug was back on the off-campus housing market, and Wrig, Charlie, Evan, and I had snagged it.

"I'm pumped," I said.

"How'd you luck out?"

"It's not like anyone else is dying to live there," I laughed. "The place is in terrible shape."

"It's a dump. Do they know you're in Chops?"

"Of course not. And we're not in Chops. There is no Chops, Di." I winked.

"Just be careful."

"Thanks, Mom."

She cocked a grass-skirted hip, and I wanted to kiss her red mouth.

"It's been too long, Diana. I miss you."

"That's sorta why I wanted to talk to you." She stepped in closer toward me. I looked down at her sandal-clad feet. Her toenails were painted flamingo pink. "I've been doing some thinking."

"Thinking, huh?" I slumped against the wall. The blow hadn't given me much energy. It must've been the shitty stuff Wrigley got in LA.

"The thing is, I'm still in love with you," Diana said.

I grinned, the extent of my relief almost surprising me. I hadn't lost her. I'd been too quick to doubt myself. I'd never stopped having the upper hand. It was suddenly sort of funny hearing her make this grand declaration of love, as though she wanted it to appear as some sort of astonishing discovery. Of course Diana had never fallen out of love with me.

"Don't act all smug." Diana folded her arms. "You're in love with me, too."

"Am I?"

She stepped in closer and I could smell her lotion. "I know you've been with that freshman. Lucy. I know you have, even though I told you not to, and you know what? It's fine. I have to take responsibility for the position I put us in, too. I wasn't ready, and it wasn't fair of me to ask you to put your life on hold. But I'm ready now. That's what I'm telling you. I've given this a lot of thought, and I'm ready."

"Ready for what, Diana?" I was smiling. I knew I was driving her a little crazy with the brief, ambiguous answers, but I was drunker than I realized, and I wasn't sure exactly how I wanted to handle this. I'd been sleeping with Lucy for what felt like a long time now. Too long, maybe. I'd just left her downstairs at the party, where she was drinking jungle juice and wearing a grass skirt that looked a whole lot like Diana's.

Diana kissed me instead of answering my question, and it was a familiar kiss, even though it had been months since that kiss had happened. It was a kiss reminding me that Diana was the girlfriend and Lucy was the freshman I screwed, and that for whatever reason that's just how it was, and nothing was going to change it, not even time apart.

"I'm ready to get back together, is what I'm saying," Diana said when she pulled away from me. It was one of the things that had always drawn me to Diana—her unmerited confidence. She wasn't the prettiest girl in the room, but she acted like she could be. She wasn't scared of my opinion or anybody else's.

"Good." I nodded. I felt so fucked up suddenly. "You know that's what I've always wanted."

"So we'll have the summer to work it out. I know you'll be in Washington, DC, for the internship, right? Is that still happening?"

"Yeah."

"So I'll come visit you and we'll make it work. I know that's what I want now. I'm finally sure of it. Forgiveness has just taken me awhile, is all."

"That would be nice."

"You don't sound that happy."

"I am happy. *So* happy. I'm drunk, Di. I'm feeling wasted. I'm sorry. Why did you want to have this conversation tonight? Can't we discuss this when we're sober?"

"I'm not drunk."

"I don't believe you."

"I don't know." She threw up her hands. "I know it's not the ideal time to have this talk. I was going to call you tomorrow, but then I saw you here. With *her.*"

"Right." Lucy.

"She's pretty. I'm not sure how you pulled it off."

"She's not you, though."

"But she's too thin. It's kind of gross." Diana made a face.

"I know."

"I love you, Stephen."

"I love you always, Princess Diana. Let's get out of here. I'm too fucked up to be here."

"Okay." She placed her palms on my chest. "Shouldn't you talk to her first?"

"I'm not gonna talk to her tonight. It can wait," I yawned. "It's more casual than you think. I just wanna go home and be alone with you."

"Okay, but we're going to mine. I'm not sleeping in her sex sheets."

I didn't argue. I listened to Diana whine about how far the walk was to her house, and I watched her dig out her cell and call Safety Van to come and pick us up.

"It'll be here in five minutes," she whispered, pressing her mouth to my neck.

I had her back. I had Diana, just like that, after months of not having her and months of trying. She hadn't gotten away with ending the relationship on her terms. I felt both glad and strangely disappointed as I let her take my hand and lead me outside. I stared at her utterly familiar face, the pink flower hanging limply from her ear. She appeared less cute and seductive than she had during the beginning of our conversation. It's funny—when you get what you want, it almost automatically decreases in value.

17

LUCY

MAY 2011

He held my hand underneath the fake palm trees. Our bare feet stood on actual sand, which covered the entire first floor of Sigma Chi for Hawaiian Luau, the last party of the year. Instead of keg beer, the Solo cups were filled with jungle juice; instead of house music, Bob Marley pulsated through the speakers.

"You want another key bump?" His fingers brushed my bare stomach. I was wearing my black bikini top and a grass skirt over jean shorts, and I could feel the judgment from the junior girls who were friends with Diana. I could feel them hating me for looking this thin and flaunting it, because half of me hated myself for the same reason. Some dominant, semiconscious part of me had forced myself to go hungry, to whittle down to nothing, and now I couldn't stop. I wasn't even trying to hide it.

Stephen and I went into the bathroom and I let him feed the coke up my nose, even though I really didn't need more at all. Just an excuse to be alone with him. He hoisted me up on the sink and started to wedge my knees apart with his, and I wanted time to freeze because everything felt so perfect.

"We shouldn't . . . ," he whispered, when someone started banging on the door. There was a line outside the bathroom. There's always a line.

"We shouldn't," I agreed. My whole body had gone pleasantly numb.

"You're so beautiful, Lucy. Fuck." His fingers played with the edges of my underwear, and the knocking continued.

"Stephen . . ."

"Okay, okay. Fuck, Luce." He kissed my forehead. "I guess I'll have to wait till later."

He led me back out into the open rush of the party, and I swallowed the bitter drip of drugs down the back of my throat. Bob Marley had morphed into Calvin Harris, and the dance floor was beginning to fill.

"I'm gonna go mingle," Stephen whispered in my ear, our cue to separate. "I'll find you soon."

I wanted to stay by his side all night, but I knew I couldn't. It didn't work that way with him. His undivided attention wasn't a given, the way it had been with Parker. But that was a good thing—having someone's undivided attention is the worst, I had to remind myself.

I found my friends sitting on the makeshift bar, doing key bumps in plain sight. Everyone everywhere was doing coke. I watched Jackie do a bump right next to Stuart, who rolled his eyes.

"You could quit being a baby and *try* it, Stu," Jackie said too loudly, holding out the tiny clear bag. "Or you could just keep judging me all the fucking time."

I overheard Stuart say something about not dealing with her shit tonight. He slid off the bar and disappeared into the crowd. Even though I was wasted I could tell Jackie had taken it too far. Lately she'd been being a total bitch to Stuart when she was drunk, then sulking about it the next day when he was pissed at her.

I took Stuart's spot on the bar, propping myself between Jackie and Bree. I dangled my legs over the bar above the packed dance floor, relieved to be sitting. That key bump was my third, or maybe fourth, and it had gone straight to my head. Bree handed me her cup of jungle juice and I took a sip. On coke nights I never ate, so I could afford to have some sugary jungle juice. With all the sugar I barely tasted the alcohol.

"What was that all about?" I glanced at Jackie.

"Stuart acting like my fucking father again. I don't want to get into it." She knew I was going to tell her she should apologize, and she turned to talk to the girl on her other side—a tennis teammate—before I could respond.

Bree leaned her head against my shoulder. "I can't believe this is the last party. I'm sad."

"It's not the last party, B. We'll be back."

"Yeah, but still."

"Are you going to miss Walter?" I grinned. Bree had finally lost her v-card to a sophomore named Walter. They were semidating.

"*No.*" She elbowed me in the ribs. "I just don't really want to be *home* for three months."

"I know what you mean," I said, even though, for once in my life, I was almost looking forward to being home. Stephen would be home in Bayville for the month of June—only twenty minutes from Cold Spring Harbor— before he started his internship in Washington, DC. He was going to take me out on his friend's boat on Long Island Sound, and he'd mentioned that I should visit him in DC over the Fourth of July. We'd started making real plans, like a real couple. I smiled just thinking about it.

"Where's your lover?" Bree asked, reading my mind.

"Mingling."

Out of the corner of my eye I spotted Diana standing in line for jungle juice. I noticed her at every party and absorbed every detail of her, from her curly hair to her slim calves to the self-important air with which she carried herself. I was fixated on her, on trying to pin down exactly what it was about her that had drawn him in. She was wearing eye makeup and a grass skirt and a white crop top. I watched her talking to someone else in line, her arms crossed above her stomach. Her bare abs both- ered me—her stomach was slimmer and more toned than I'd expected. Even though Jackie and Pippa thought Diana was only average looking, I knew she was pretty—she had to be pretty. She had big brown eyes and that athletic-but-cute look working for her, and she just seemed fearless, like she didn't give a shit. I'd caught her staring at me too many times, shamelessly staring, her hatred transparent and justified. If I were her, I'd hate me, too.

I watched Stephen emerge from the kitchen and maneuver his way through the crowd, brushing past Diana in the drink line, subtly but un- mistakably grazing her lower back with his hand. My stomach lurched, and I blinked, and then Stephen was rounding the stairs with Wrigley, and Diana was refilling her red plastic cup. I was drunk and maybe the back grazing had been a figment of my imagination. Or maybe it hadn't. Maybe Stephen thought Diana was everything, and she sort of *was* beautiful and captivating, and of course he was still in love with her. Or maybe the back grazing had been a casual, inadvertent movement due to the overcrowded party. I scanned the room, and people seemed to be bumping into one another all over the place.

I watched Stephen disappear at the top of the stairs, and when I looked at Diana I saw that her eyes were following him, too, and I hated that we were both watching him. I hated that I shared that with her.

Someone was passing a handle of Fireball across the bar, and when it was my turn I chugged it, because Fireball was too easy to drink, and then someone was taking pictures of us all sitting with our legs dangling off the bar, and I tried to suck in my stomach and crossed my fingers that my thighs wouldn't look fat, pressed together in shorts, because whoever was taking the pictures would definitely post them on Facebook. And then the Fireball made its way down the bar and back again and down and back and then senior girls kicked us off because the bar top was their domain, and then someone started a game of jungle juice flip cup.

Time was passing and I was feeling wholly fucked up. I waited for Stephen to reappear, but he wasn't reappearing.

"Have you seen Stephen?" I asked anyone at the flip-cup table who was listening, which turned out to be no one. I looked at my watch and it was two in the morning and I shamelessly abandoned the flip-cup game, scanning the downstairs rooms for him in his bright red Hawaiian button-down, my insides knotted. But everyone seemed to be wearing bright, tropical colors and he was nowhere, and then in my drunken blunder I remembered that he had gone upstairs.

"Hey, Lucy." Topher Rigby stopped me at the base of the staircase and offered to refill my drink. Jackie and Topher had grown up together in Connecticut and she'd told me eighty times that he liked me, but he was *way* too short, and besides, I was with Stephen. It annoyed me how Jackie was always telling me to go for Topher when *clearly* I was with Stephen.

Topher grabbed my empty cup before I could answer. He started talking about lacrosse. Topher was always bragging about being on the "lax" team, probably to compensate for his, literal, shortcomings. I watched him as he talked, the top of his frizzy dark hair barely clearing my forehead. His face was decent; if he were taller he might've been hot.

"I gotta go," I said, cutting him off. "Good to see ya, Topher."

I practically sprinted up the stairs. I was on a mission. I placed my jungle juice down on the ground because I knew if I had another sip, I'd be sick.

I checked the bedrooms until I found one with people in it, and there was Wrigley's blond head bent over a textbook covered with coke. I scanned the rest of the room—if it contained Wrigley and blow it would contain Stephen. But my eyes found every face and none of them belonged to him. I did a double take, squinted harder. And Wrigley was asking me if I wanted a line and I was shaking my head, asking him if he'd seen Stephen, and he was shrugging.

"He was in here earlier."

I flew back into the hallway and felt all those Fireball pulls and jungle juices hit me, absorbing into nothing in my empty stomach, and for a moment I wished to God I could let myself eat something because then maybe I wouldn't get so sickeningly *drunk* on top of coked out, and I drifted farther down the hall, determined, and stopped in my tracks when I turned the corner, because there he was in his red button-down at the end of the hall. His arms were wrapped around the waist of a curly-haired girl in a crop top and a grass skirt. He was holding her too close, and then he was kissing her. In the same perfect way he'd kissed me, hours earlier.

My vision went foggy like it had when I was eight and I fell out of the big hickory tree in our backyard. I'd landed hard on my back, in one even thump, and for a full minute I'd stared up at the blue sky through the branches and hadn't been able to breathe. Georgia, who was still in the tree, had started screaming, and CJ sprinted out of the house in her bathrobe. She'd yelled for my father to call an ambulance, but then a miraculous burst of air had whooshed into my lungs while CJ knelt next to me, her hands squeezing mine, her tears splashing my forehead.

All my life I've felt like a gutsy person—someone with a reasonable amount of *guts*—but when I opened my mouth to say something to Stephen, to yell, to object, nothing came out. My vocal cords were tied up like the end of a balloon. And then I was tiptoeing backward down the hallway and down the stairs, my heart frozen inside my chest, and the déjà vu hit me like an oncoming train: I was watching CJ straddle Gabe Petersen and his hands pressed to the curve of her sweaty back, and I felt so immobilized by pain, the cut deep in my gut and the knife twisting, my feet backtracking silently along the carpet and down the stairs, except these stairs weren't covered in overpriced Italian wool, they were creaky hardwood, and my bare feet were slipping over the steps and I knew I was falling before I felt myself sliding, my body thumping over each step like a bumpy ski run until I landed in a crumpled mess at the base. I heard the volume in the room drop, I felt people staring at me, and I didn't think I would be able to stand.

And then some guy's arm was hoisting me up—Stuart's, I think—and Pippa was saying, "I've got her, thanks," and adjusting my stupid bikini top.

"Lucy, where are your shoes?"

I didn't know, and it didn't matter. I knew I would be sick. I tried to tell Pippa about Stephen and Diana, though I knew I wasn't making much sense.

"I'm taking you home. We're going home and we can talk about this there."

"I'm gonna be sick, Pip."

"It's okay. Let's just get home first."

I shook my head, my legs wobbly under me. I couldn't stop seeing Stephen and Diana's kiss, just moments before, and I really was going to be so sick. . . .

Pippa held my hair while I puked into the bushes outside Sigma Chi.

"Do you feel better?" she asked afterward.

I nodded. "I think so."

"I called Safety Van. It'll be here soon."

"But we're close to the dorm."

"You can barely walk, Lucy. And I ordered pizza."

"I'm not hungry."

"The only thing that just came out of you was jungle juice. You are eating some motherfucking food."

"I just can't believe it, Pip."

"What can't you believe?"

"Stephen and Diana."

"They were actually kissing?"

"Yeah."

"Shit."

"Yeah."

"Maybe he was really drunk. Like out-of-his-mind drunk."

"Maybe. What am I gonna do?"

"I don't know. We'll figure it out." Pippa handed me a bottle of water. She looked especially pretty in a flowy white dress, her dark hair loose down her back. She was such a good friend; it made me feel worse.

"You don't have to leave the party, Pip. Stay. I'll be fine."

"Don't be ridiculous, I'm taking you home. It's late anyway. And Wrigley is wasted and like, trying to bitch me out."

I stared down at the uneven cracks in the pavement and felt the coke wearing off, felt a massive headache looming as the serotonin drained from my synapses.

It seemed like hours later when Safety Van finally pulled up in front of Sigma Chi. Pippa and I got in the back seat. The smell of pine-scented air freshener was making me nauseated all over again. Suddenly, the side door flung open.

It happened so fast, and I was too numb to react. Stephen and Diana climbed inside Safety Van and sat down in the middle row, in front of Pippa and me.

"Corner of Logan and Grove, please," Diana said in her voice, which I didn't recognize, because I'd never heard her speak.

I opened my mouth to say something, but my vocal cords had hardened again, and no sound came out. Safety Van started moving.

The way Pippa's temples were pulsing I could tell she was going to do something—she had a bad temper when it came to this kind of stuff.

"Are you *fucking* kidding me?" Pippa's voice was so loud, she was almost yelling.

The driver glanced at us in the rearview mirror. Diana shot Pippa a glare, but Stephen kept his head forward. I held my breath, too stunned to move a muscle. How was this possible? Not two hours earlier Stephen and I had been in the bathroom together. He'd put a key up my nose and his tongue in my mouth and his hand—the same hand that was in this van—inside me. Not fifteen hours before that I'd lounged in Stephen's bed after morning sex, our bare legs intertwined under the sheets while he'd told me about his friend Carl's boat, the *Kiss Me Kate*, a center console anchored in Long Island Sound. *Carl never uses his boat; I know where he keeps the keys. I'll take you out for a spin and a waterski and some East Coast beer—first weekend we're both back in Strong Island, it's on.*

Safety Van stopped in front of Diana's house. She slid the door open and climbed out first, her tawny nest of hair flashing in front of my face. As Stephen climbed out behind her, Pippa leaned forward over the seat and started punching his back with everything she had. She shoved his head into the passenger seat and clawed at his neck. "Fuck you. *Fuck you!*" she screamed. "You fucking creep."

The driver was yelling at Pippa to calm the hell down. Stephen said nothing, averting his eyes as he ducked Pippa's punches and climbed out of the van.

You better wear your black bikini, but I'm serious, Luce, it's a date. The first of many summer dates, I hope.

I looped my index finger through the strap of my black bikini, which I'd worn to Hawaiian Luau for Stephen. A lot can change in fifteen hours, I learned that night. I watched him follow Diana into her house, closing the door behind him.

18

STEPHEN

My aunt Amy—my father's sister—insisted on throwing an unnecessarily extravagant lunch for my father's fifty-eighth birthday. It wasn't like it was his sixtieth or some big Hallmark occasion, but according to Amy we all needed to make a very big effort because "your dad is having a rough time," even though it's been a damn decade since the divorce and continuing to enable my father's grief is wildly counterproductive and downright pathetic. But I've learned it's safer to keep such opinions to myself when it comes to my family, so I didn't make a peep when Amy announced she'd invited twenty-five people to *our* house for lunch, without bothering to ask my father beforehand, when her own house is ten minutes down the road.

I'd been living with my cousin Vivian—Amy's daughter—and her fiancé, Rod, in Washington, DC, for the summer, sticking it out at my internship at Steptoe & Johnson that I'd gotten via Vivian via the help of Rod's lawyer friend at the firm. It was bitch work, but Steptoe was résumé gold.

So Rod, Vivian, and I barreled up to Long Island from DC for the weekend in absurd traffic, and I spent the entire time listening to them discuss their wedding registry. Six hours of hearing about different types of candlesticks was enough to make me want to jump out of Rod's Mitsubishi. It was so late by the time they dropped me off at home in Bayville and I'd absorbed so much information about china patterns that I could barely keep my eyes open.

When I woke up the next morning it was that perfect, sun-drenched kind of summer morning where before you even open your eyes you see red glow, and you hear birds singing, and you know it's going to be nice weather that day. I lay awake for a while propped up on pillows and had a look around my childhood bedroom. Everything was exactly the same as it had been since I was nine: the gold plastic soccer trophies on top of the dusty wooden bookshelf, the blue-and-white-striped New York Yankees curtains, and the framed poster of Eli Manning above my headboard. I told my dad he could get rid of it all, to turn my room into a gym or an office or something of some use, but he refused, and so it still looks like a prepubescent sports-obsessed kid lives here. I think it makes him happy to try and freeze time, to pretend that the three of us are still tucked in our beds, that my mother is still downstairs in the den blasting jazz, applying to be a contestant on *Jeopardy!* and drinking Tanqueray, ignoring him. Having that woman in this house made him feel complete, even though he was all the more unhappy for it. It's funny how so many people end up finding such comfort, even contentment, in their misery.

I finally got out of bed, took a lukewarm shower, and trotted into the kitchen to find my father bent over the stove, sizzling strips of bacon that made the whole downstairs smell sensational. My dad is a wide, sturdy man. *Big-boned*, my mother would say when she was feeling manic and honest, usually curling her lips in my direction and adding, *like you, Stephen.*

Aunt Amy was in the kitchen, too, already starting on lunch. I hugged both of them and wished my father a happy birthday, then poured myself a cup of coffee and walked out onto the back porch, warm rays of sunlight hitting my face.

Skipper, our old golden retriever, sniffed around my ankles.

"Go on, Skip." I shooed the dog away. I don't like dogs all that much, to be honest, and I don't see why people go so crazy over them. Skipper is more of an attention-seeking nuisance than anything else.

I turned my face back toward the sun. God, it was warm out. I suddenly craved a spin in Carl's boat, like the good old days when we'd take the *Kiss Me Kate* out on the sound, have a few beers.

Lucy popped into my head then, probably because I have this fantasy of having sex with her on a boat. I'm not sure why; I think it's because she's the kind of girl who would look very sexy on a boat.

Lucy's hometown, Cold Spring Harbor, is only twenty minutes from my house in Bayville. I wondered if she was home. I thought about texting her, saying something about this nice weather, maybe adding a flattering comment. Maybe something about the boat. Lucy was a sucker for the flattering comments. But I hadn't talked to her since Hawaiian Luau, since the unfortunate Safety Van incident, and for all I knew she could hate my guts. I didn't need to be stirring things up with her over the summer—better to wait until school started to evaluate the damage.

I sipped my coffee, always black, and gazed up at the cloudless sky. My train of thought was disrupted by the sound of Luke's voice as he walked through the front door with his bombshell girlfriend, Kathleen.

"Wanna take Carl's boat out?" I asked my little sister, Sadie, who lay on the chaise next to mine.

"There isn't time!" Amy yelled from inside—she's like God; she hears fucking everything.

"It's eleven thirty," I called back.

"The guests will be here in two hours, Stephen. You can make yourself useful by helping in the kitchen, not taking Carl's boat out for a joyride."

Aunt Amy can be a real cunt when she's stressed, and it's only gotten worse since my mom went off the deep end. There was absolutely no reason for her to invite two dozen people to her brother's fifty-eighth birthday, when what my father actually needs is to get laid.

Apparently the fact that this month marks ten years since my mother left is something we are all supposed to be very sensitive toward, according to Amy, though I don't see how drawing *attention* to the fact that my father is still miserable helps in the slightest.

My mother was never any good at being a parent—her symptoms were always prevalent. A few years before she was even diagnosed, she "accidentally" left one-year-old Luke at the playground in Bayville. Just left him there. My mom got in her car and took off down the street because she swore she saw some childhood friend who'd supposedly died years earlier. She was gone twenty-four hours. Some lady found Luke sitting in his stroller in the park and called the police.

My father knew what he was getting into when they decided to try for a third kid, and I don't feel sorry for him. The crazy shit kept happening. I don't know if it would've been different if my mom had taken her meds, but she didn't—she claimed they made her feel "off." When she disappeared with Sadie for a week, something in my father snapped, and he finally listened to everyone who'd been telling him to file for divorce. But ever since then he's lived in a fantasy world, one where my mother is going to morph back into the nonbipolar green-eyed secretary he fell for in 1982 and return our college savings, and every night when reality reminds him that this won't ever happen, that my mother is a clinical madwoman with no interest in managing her illness, and that he's overweight, past middle age, and stuck working his dead-end accounting job, he slides a little deeper into his depression. With that in mind, family functions are often a drag. I'd better start drinking.

I finished the last of my coffee in one gulp and walked inside to say hello to Luke and Kath. I've known Kathleen for five years—that's how long she's been dating my brother. It's absurd; he's never cheated on her.

Kath kissed me on both cheeks—she thinks she's French or something—and I tried not to stare down her low-cut top.

I mixed myself a strong Bloody Mary before Aunt Amy forced me to arrange a bunch of tiny cucumber sandwiches that Kathleen had brought on a serving plate. I don't understand the point of those things—they're like air. I could eat a hundred and still be starving. I poured more vodka into the remnants of my Bloody and made another while Amy wasn't looking.

By two o'clock almost everyone had arrived. Most were relatives, some were still happily married Nassau County couples, and some were Aunt Amy's divorced friends, whose kids were likely spending the weekend with their ex-husbands and new, younger stepmoms. These are the women Amy secretly hopes will hit it off with my father, and it's easy to pick them out—they are late-fifties, sad-looking and washed-out; they're wearing unflattering tent dresses and have stopped bothering to dye their frizzy, graying poofs of hair. It's no wonder their husbands would rather fuck a hot thirty-five-year-old than pop Viagra and close their eyes. Even though my mom is crazy she's better looking than any of these grandmas, and I knew my father wouldn't be interested.

We all squeezed into a long, perfectly set table that Amy had rented for the patio. I decided to switch to red wine. Even on the hottest days of summer, I'm a red guy.

Sadie had made these dumb place cards on which she'd pasted various photographs of my father, and she'd wedged me between one of the divorcées and my uncle Daniel, Amy's husband who always wants to have tediously long conversations about topics like the Civil War and why he sent his kids to charter schools.

Luke and Kathleen sat across from me, under the shade of a leafy maple while I was sweating my balls off in the sun. Luke always makes it very clear that Kathleen needs to be seated next to him at family functions. He wants to make sure she feels comfortable. It's so bizarre— he's fucking hot-glued to that girl. He can't make a single decision that doesn't involve her. If you asked him how he wants his eggs cooked, he would probably need to ask Kathleen. He told me last summer that he wants to marry her. When I asked him how he was sure he said, verbatim, "Because I know I would die for her," as if that were a perfectly normal thing to say. I'm all for having a girlfriend, but why would anyone in his or her right mind ever *die* for someone else? I would no more die for a girlfriend than sleep with the divorced grandma to my left. I know if I told Luke that he'd just clap me on the back and say, "Stephen, you just haven't met the right girl yet." To which I'd have to smile graciously and answer, "Yeah, you're right, thanks, Luke."

The truth is, I'll *never* feel about a girl the way Luke feels about Kathleen. Even with whomever I end up marrying. I bet half the people out there are like me, faking the whole love thing. But Luke's not. I *know* Luke's not faking it, and it's both freaky and sad. It's easy to find the emotional themes of a person's life in the convictions they hold most blindly. Luke is the kind of guy who judges himself based on his feelings and what those feelings mean to him. His sense of self-worth comes from the validation of what he believes to be principled choices. He accepted a mediocre job in bond trading right out of college, a job he'll probably stay in for the rest of his life while Kathleen waters the plants. They'll have a few kids, and he'll wipe their asses and clean SpaghettiOs off the floor. He won't live a bigger life than that.

While we all sat waiting to eat, I took the opportunity to observe

Luke and Kathleen across from me, because God knows they barely knew anyone else was even in the room. It's helpful for me to observe the way couples interact with each other.

They'd each had a couple of glasses of wine before we sat down, and the two of them were all *over* each other at the table. Luke's hand rested on the back of Kathleen's thin neck, underneath her hair, while Kathleen nuzzled her nose and mouth around Luke's ear, one hand on his thigh. *Hand on back of neck—noted. I like that, Luke. Classy yet sexy. Understated yet affectionate. You two are clearly close. You love each other dearly and deeply.*

Kathleen is raven-haired and petite and wowza beautiful—the kind of beautiful that is almost unfair. It's pathetic that some people get by on their looks and think they're happy because of who they are, when they're really only happy because people tell them they look like supermodels. Everybody wants to look like a supermodel.

People are always telling Luke he hit the jackpot with Kathleen, which I guess is true. Luke is a good-looking guy, though. He's better looking than me. He's in better shape, too.

Eventually Kathleen took a break from licking Luke's neck and turned toward me, saving me from an awful conversation with Uncle Daniel about the Battle of Fredericksburg. I wasn't kidding—he is always bringing up the fucking Civil War.

"Excuse me," I told Daniel. "Kathleen?"

"Stevie, I want to know about your love life. Are you still dating . . . Diana, is it?" She batted her eyelashes. Kathleen is the kind of woman who knows she's hot and goes out of her way to make sure everyone else knows it, too, even her boyfriend's little brother.

"Diana, yes," I replied. "We're together, basically."

"Basically?" Kathleen always pries.

"I mean, we got back together a little over a month ago, but we had a rocky year. It's one of those relationships, you know, where we both love each other but something always seems to get in the way." I gave Kathleen a sad smile.

"Like *what* gets in the way, Stevie?" she asked, looking legitimately intrigued. I have asked her not to call me Stevie about eighty times.

"I'm not sure. It's complicated."

"But you love her."

I felt my throat tighten and go dry; the wine residue around the back suddenly made me very thirsty. What business of Kathleen's was my love life?

"Yes, of course. I love her so much."

Kathleen beamed like I'd just told *her* I loved her.

"Then do whatever it takes to make it work," she said, her dark eyes shiny. She squeezed my brother's hand and looked at him as if they were Romeo and Juliet, the trope for true love.

"I'm sure as hell going to try." I shifted in my seat and took another sip of wine.

"Good." She smiled, brushing a wave of black hair off her tan, defined collarbone.

"You two seem so happy. It's inspiring." I said it to feed her ego and, in turn, heighten her affection for me. There's no harm in having Kathleen think I'm the greatest.

"Your brother is just so sweet, Lukey."

Luke gave me an appreciative grin.

Thankfully we were interrupted by my grandfather, who can barely walk and had flown up from his retirement community in *Florida* so as not to miss my father's fucking fifty-eighth birthday party. He cleared his throat to say grace, even though this wasn't a remotely religious event. After the old man finished reciting the Lord's Prayer and blessing about fifty "absent friends" by name (aka my grandmother and a bunch of dead old geezers who no one had heard of), we were free to eat.

I love eating the way I love sex. Even when I'm satisfied, I almost can't stand when it's over. My satisfaction isn't satisfying. It's an endless, insufferable cycle, and I crave it any way and always. Sometimes when I eat I get so immersed in eating that I forget my own name, lost in the pleasure. And with eating, there's the added benefit of not having to appease anyone's emotions in the aftermath.

It was a typical DeMarco family-style Italian meal, and I'll give it to Amy—the woman can cook. I helped myself to generous servings of the good stuff: spaghetti Bolognese, braciola, meatball lasagna, eggplant parm, caprese salad, and Amy's famous buttery garlic bread. Kathleen went crazy over her cucumber sandwiches—by far the least appealing dish on the table—probably because they each contained about one calorie.

We all sang "Happy Birthday" to my father, and Luke cut the double chocolate cake, homemade by one of the divorcées. It was quite a feast, combined with all the wine, and afterward I was so full I could barely move.

As with postsex, I tend to feel a bit thwarted postmeal. I sipped my red, and, glancing around at the different people at the table, began to feel a bit funny. I get this same glum, slightly anxious feeling every so often, so I'm able to sense it coming on; it's a kind of uncomfortable uneasiness with roots that are impossible to place. Today I felt especially bothered by the continuous sight of Luke and Kathleen in front of me. I glanced farther down the table at Vivian and Rod, their hands interlaced on the table, dumb grins plastered on both their faces. Vivian and Rod are another couple who've been together forever.

Rod taught Vivian, Luke, and me how to surf out in Westhampton eight years ago—my grandfather has a place near the ocean, where we grew up going in the summers. It's a simple beach house, the kind of place where there are never enough beds, where aunts and uncles and cousins and friends are all packed in together, and someone always ends up sleeping on the couch or an air mattress and sometimes there's even a tent or two pitched out back. I was thirteen the first summer Rod came out to the beach with Viv. I remembered him standing next to me in the water while I lay on the surfboard, holding it steady while slices of ocean washed over its smooth, fiberglass surface. If a surfable wave would come along he'd say, "Okay, this is the one. Ready to paddle, Stephen?" and push me into the wave seconds before it broke, yelling, "Paddle, paddle, paddle!" after me. We'd do that until I'd finally catch one, long after Luke and Viv had caught many.

The thought that my cousin had been with the same guy for more than eight years made the jittery feeling stirring in the base of my stomach intensify. They kept their hands interlaced on the table while Vivian chatted with my aunt Barbara to her right, and Rod talked to Christina—his soon to be sister-in-law—across from him. It was a default position, so clearly instinctual, the way their fingers just rested on each other's, and I thought, *This must be what people talk about when they talk about intimacy.*

I really did not feel too well then. The nerves had spread from my stomach up to my head, and in addition to feeling anxious I sensed my mind slipping into a dark space. A languid tunnel. The room around me was growing hazy and distant. I wished all these people would just leave.

The worst of it came next, the image of the glossy red hair sliding its way into the center of my mind, the way it does. The hair, so red, burnished, vivid as anything, matted against the black leather seat of the Jeep. Her car. My pants unzipped. The blood around her mouth. The pearly white tooth lying on her lap, buried among the shards of glass. "Zombie" by the Cranberries lingering on the radio. The mechanical chewing inside my mouth. The sweet, Bubblicious bubblegum smell. I don't like thinking about the accident, but once the memory takes hold of my mind, it won't let go.

I needed some air. I took a long sip of cold water and hoped the funny gloomy feeling would leave sooner rather than later. It always left eventually, but sometimes there would be hours of this, like someone knocking repeatedly on a door inside my head, asking a question I will never be able to answer because I don't know what the question is.

For a moment I thought about going upstairs and calling Diana, thought maybe that would make me feel better. She was finally my girlfriend again. But I knew calling Diana wouldn't make me feel anything at all.

Then my eyes settled on my father, the birthday boy seated at the head of the long, lively table. A million conversations bubbled around him, laughs breaking loose, dishes passing, forks clinking. He wore a badly wrinkled shirt, his dusty gray hair thinning near the crown of his head. A sad, sole red balloon was tied to the back of his chair. The piece of cake in front of him remained uneaten. He pretended to listen to a conversation but spoke to no one, his mouth a tight line, his eyes vacant and lost. I breathed relief. For some reason, the sight of him made me feel a little bit better.

19
LUCY
JULY 2011

CJ was waiting for me in the parking lot of the Cold Spring Harbor train station, perched in her giant black Lexus, wearing giant black sunglasses, drinking a giant black iced coffee. I'd just spent a night in the city with Lydia and Helen and the rest of our Tory Burch–clad friends from high school for Kelsey Nelson's birthday party at Dorrian's. I can't really stand Dorrian's, but everyone always wants to go there.

"Dad and I used to go to Dorrian's!" CJ exclaimed on the car ride home.

Of course they did. Dorrian's is the preppiest bar on the Upper East Side. I grunted a response, too hungover to fathom my dad and CJ gallivanting around Manhattan in their twenties.

"Was it fun, Luce?"

"Meh."

"Was Parker there?"

"Yep."

"And how was that?"

"Pretty sure he still hates me."

"Well, you didn't exactly handle that situation well, Lucy. He was very upset. I talked to his mother all about it."

"Well, he brought his new girlfriend to the party, so I think he's doing fine." I leaned my head against the window.

"New *girlfriend*? From Bowdoin? I didn't know he had a girlfriend."

"Neither did I."

"Oh, honey. That must've been awkward."

"Not really, CJ. I don't care who Parker dates."

"Well, you must *care*, kind of."

"I don't."

"What was she like?"

"I dunno. Blond. Short. Very CK Bradley."

Parker's new girlfriend couldn't have been more typical, with shoulder-length highlighted blond hair, clearly flat-ironed, and rosacea that she tried to conceal with too much foundation. She'd been wearing big fake pearls and a bright pink Diane von Furstenberg wrap dress. Everything about her was unoriginal and preppy and posed. She glared at me while she discussed boring people from Trinity with Helen, clinging to Parker's arm like a Seeing Eye dog. The only thing Parker said to me all night was that I looked like I'd lost too much weight, and Lydia and Helen nodded in agreement.

"So it wasn't a fun night? You didn't have fun at all?" CJ rapped her fingernails on the steering wheel.

"It was *fine*, CJ. I dunno." The night had been boring. The whole summer had been boring, actually. I should've listened to my parents and gotten an internship instead of manning the front desk at CJ's Pilates studio and thinking about Stephen, and wondering about Stephen and how he was and why he hadn't called and if he was sorry.

"Well," CJ placed her empty plastic cup in the center console. "Georgia is home! And she's brought her boyfriend."

"I know."

"His name is Elliot and he rows crew at Yale."

"I know that, too. I read the family group texts."

"Well, you don't need to be snide, Lucy. He's great. Aren't you excited to meet him?"

"Sure."

"Why are you in a bad mood?" She glanced over at me. "I know I keep saying it but you look *so* thin." She squeezed the top of my arm. "Did you eat anything last night?"

"Yes. Lydia and I got pizza before the party."

"Did you *eat* the pizza?" CJ sounded exactly like Jackie.

"*Yes*, CJ. Can we just listen to the radio?"

I cranked up the volume and stared out the window at the familiar East Coast landscape; the hilly mounds framing the highway, the huge trees lush with green leafy branches that made the Lexus feel encapsulated. On the West Coast everything seemed to stretch farther; there was space and sky and room to actually breathe. I closed my eyes until I heard the familiar sound of CJ's tires crunching over the gravel.

Outside, the Long Island air was hot and humid; I could almost feel the moisture seeping into my lungs. CJ slid her hand into the loose waistband of my jean shorts as we walked inside.

"See? Your clothes don't even fit. How much weight have you lost?"

"Just a few pounds. These shorts were big to begin with." I wriggled out of her grip. I knew she didn't believe me, but I went inside before she could say anything else. My dad was rinsing dishes in the kitchen.

"Daddy!" I wrapped my arms around his neck, and the familiar smell of his Noxzema made tears sting the corners of my eyes as he gave me his signature butterfly kiss.

Georgia sat at the kitchen table playing cards with Elliot. She grinned her easy, wide Georgia smile. As always, she looked beautiful in that effortless way. Her shoulder-length blond hair fell in a curtain around her heart-shaped face. A few tiny freckles sprinkled her enviable nose, which sloped at the end, the way I'd always wished mine would. She looked more and more like CJ's doppelgänger.

Georgia stood and her eyes met mine, inches from my face. The sight of them punctured my insides—the same cerulean-blue Georgia eyes I'd known all my life. I thought back to six years ago, when we were thirteen and fourteen, having sleepovers at the Montgomerys' and making Fluffernutter sandwiches in the middle of the night. It was hard to believe we were the same set of sisters.

We hugged, which didn't come naturally anymore, at least not for me.

"Your hair is getting so long." She picked up the ends.

"I know. I should cut it."

"How was the city?"

"Fun," I lied.

"This is Elliot," Georgia said, a rosy flush spreading over her collarbone. "Elliot, this is my sister, Lucy."

Elliot gave me a firm handshake and an obnoxious Ivy League grin. "Lucy, it's wonderful to meet you. Georgia has great things to say about you."

I forced a smile and scanned him. He wasn't tall—maybe five ten on a good day—with a sandy-blond crew cut and a boyish face. He had on a salmon-colored polo shirt and khaki pants, and I noticed he wore one of those gold rings that are from those exclusive societies they have at the Ivies.

"I like your ring," I lied. The way Elliot looked at me, I knew he knew I was being sarcastic.

"Thank you. It's our crew team's ring."

"Oh, right. CJ mentioned you do crew."

He squinted, perplexed. Georgia jumped in. "Mom, she means. Lucy calls Mom CJ. It's a thing." She shrugged and gazed at me innocently.

"I *row* crew," Elliot corrected.

"I'm going to take a shower." I already wanted to punch both of them. I knew I was being kind of rude. Normally I hated being rude—it made me feel small and weedy—but the spite felt good. I wanted Georgia to know I thought her boyfriend was lame without having to say it.

"Nice to meet you, Lucy." When Elliot smiled, his oversize front teeth made him look like a chipmunk.

"Make it quick!" CJ called after me as I ran upstairs. "Dad's making your favorite—soft-shells."

I almost got excited before I remembered I wasn't eating fried food. I was only eating vegetables and protein until I got down to 110. I had just eight more pounds to go, but the smaller you get, the harder it is to lose weight. I could do it, though. Come sophomore year I would be skinnier than ever and tan from August beach days at my grandparents' house on Cape Cod. And Stephen would be forced to look at me.

I turned on the shower and let the hot water rinse my shoulders, washing off the grime of the city. I put on a pair of leggings and a baggy sweater, so CJ couldn't comment on the size of my arms again. My weight was none of her business.

Everyone was already sitting at the dining room table when I came back downstairs.

My dad spotted me in the doorway and grinned. "Guess what's for dinner, Sass? I made soft-shells for you and Georgia Peach."

"They're amazing," Georgia said, already digging into her second one. Georgia was thin—she would always be thin—but thin wasn't thin enough anymore. I knew I weighed less than her now. Georgia ate whatever she wanted, like we both used to. We used to make peanut butter and honey sandwiches after school—two each—and eat them in front of episodes of *Seventh Heaven* before dinner. Our metabolisms were like sharks'.

"You know what?" I said, the lie forming in my twisted brain. "This is the worst news, but I found out this semester I'm allergic to shellfish. They were doing free allergy testing at the health center. Apparently it makes me lethargic." I served some salad onto one of the familiar blue china plates, along with a few roasted potatoes that I'd be sure not to touch. Potatoes are full of starch—empty carbs.

"That's terrible." My dad frowned. "You live for seafood."

"I can have some seafood, just not shellfish."

CJ peered at me, two slits of aqua between black mascara. "That doesn't sound right. I'll make you an appointment with Dr. Williamson. Those school nurses don't know shit."

Georgia flinched. Elliot widened his dopey eyes.

"Well, I've stopped eating shellfish and I have much more energy, so maybe they do know shit."

Sometimes I can't help acting like the worst daughter ever. Even my dad looked at me with disappointment written all over his face. If only I could tell them, I thought for the billionth time.

But I couldn't. I'd played it out in my head endlessly, how I would do it, what I would say. I'd tell CJ first. I'd sit her down, maybe in the living room, and I'd say the words. Tell her what I saw her doing that day. Who I saw her screwing in my father's bed. But after the part where I tell her, the hypothetical scene stops rolling. Mentally, I cannot make it continue. I cannot see CJ's response. Like death, it's an incomprehensible outcome. Human nature does not allow me to go there.

I picked at the salad, chewing each spinach leaf individually. My stomach growled and my hangover stabbed at my brain. Elliot started talking about his beloved crew team and explained how he and Georgia had met at one of his races. She had been running a Habitat for Humanity bake sale on the riverbank. The story was so cliché it made me want to puke. I twirled my fork around and was barely paying attention until I heard Elliot address me.

"Are you dating anyone, Lucy?"

"Why?" I asked. "I mean, not at the moment."

"Lucy used to date Parker Lines in high school," Georgia said. "Don't you know the Lineses from Maine, Ell? Luce, doesn't Parker's family go to Northeast Harbor?"

"Yeah."

"I've definitely heard the name," Elliot chirped brightly. "All boys in the family, right?"

"Four brothers."

"Lucy saw Parker last night," CJ commented knowingly, clutching her goblet of chardonnay. "He has a new girlfriend."

"Already?" My dad looked up from his plate.

"It's been more than a year," I said. "I don't care."

"You know, I really think you two can find a way to be friendly. Maybe we should all do lunch at Cove Club. I'll call Patricia."

"Please don't call Patricia." I sighed. CJ loves the Lineses because Mr. Lines is a VP at Morgan Stanley. They donated the new turf playing field at Friends Academy.

"Any new love interests out in California?" Elliot asked out of nowhere, his buck teeth sticking out like a beaver's. "Mountain-men, explorer types? I'm sure it's a very different dating pool out there."

"Not really," I replied tartly. I felt CJ's eyes on me like a hawk.

"There was some guy who kept calling her over Christmas break," CJ told Elliot. "*And* spring break, come to think of it. But maybe that fizzled. I receive limited information. Luce?"

My stomach dropped at the insinuation of Stephen, erasing my appetite, though I would've rather been hungry than sad.

"Well," Elliot started, turning toward me. "I have tons of single friends interning in Manhattan this summer. If you're interested." He smiled a chipmunk grin.

"Lucy will meet someone," Georgia said. "It's only her freshman year." She gave me a look that told me she was sorry for Elliot's nosiness. I didn't know why she was still so nice to me when I acted the way I did. It was what I loved about Georgia even when I tried my hardest to dislike her—her incontestable goodness. There weren't a lot of people in the world who were that purely *good*, without pride or expectation or even awareness of their goodness. I used to be more like that. Not Georgia good, but better than I'd become.

The fact that I still loved Georgia for her goodness made me think that there might be hope for me, that I wasn't lost to cynicism, that maybe one day, in a different situation, I'd be able to emulate the same selfless grace. Just not in this house, not with CJ across from me, the three-carat diamond on her ring finger burning my corneas.

That was why Georgia should've been the one to see what I saw that afternoon. Not because I wished that pain on her—I didn't, I never could—but because she would've handled it the right way. She has more compassion than I do; she's more levelheaded. She wouldn't have let it ruin everything.

———————

Six weeks later, the morning before I flew back to California, CJ made me step on the scale in her bathroom. I pressed my bare feet into the cold plastic and the little red line ticked up, teetering a couple notches above the 115 mark. 117. Ugh. *How?*

CJ sat down on the side of the porcelain tub. Her face scrunched like it did when she was about to cry.

"Lucy—" Her voice wavered. "You've got to gain some weight back. Promise me."

"I've gained four pounds since the beginning of the summer. You've been force-feeding me carbs."

"Four pounds isn't enough. You still look unhealthy. I think you should see a nutritionist when you get back to Baird."

"That's absurd. You're overreacting."

"Overreacting? You've lost twenty pounds since last September! And you were tiny to begin with."

"I was not *tiny*," I said accidentally, and I could see the concern intensifying on my mother's face. "I'll gain some more weight back," I added quickly.

"Do you still have your period?"

"Of course." A fresh lie.

"I'm worried you have an eating disorder."

"That's absurd."

"You're five foot seven, which with your weight means your BMI is eighteen. Eighteen is a disturbingly low BMI."

"How would you even know that?"

"I'm in the health industry."

"You teach *Pilates*."

"*Lucy!*" CJ's blue eyes were watery and fixed, suddenly scary with rage. She stood. "I am so *fucking* sick of your attitude. All summer long you've been acting like an entitled brat. Is this how you act around your friends?"

CJ rambled on about my behavior, and I stared at the smooth white tiles on my parents' bathroom floor. I looked at them for so long that my vision blurred. I wished they would suck me right into their sea of muddled whiteness.

The words coming out of CJ's mouth were calling me spoiled and ungrateful and apathetic, and for once, I knew she was right.

I had nothing to say in response. I watched the white tiles some more. I closed my eyes and Stephen flooded the blackness behind them, like he had all summer. I felt his hands pressed against my hips in the bathroom at Hawaiian Luau.

You're so beautiful, Lucy. Fuck.

I can't wait to take you out on the boat this summer. You're gonna love it.

I'm gonna go mingle. I'll find you soon.

And then his lips pressed to Diana's, right in front of me. Their hands interlaced in Safety Van, like another reality. Like I'd dreamed the whole thing.

Why, why, *why* did he fill up my whole head? My whole body? All the time. To the brim. A person like that. Why? It was over, anyway. Even if I chose to decide that he wasn't a manipulative jerk, it wasn't like he was banging down my door with apologies. I hadn't heard a peep from him. I was beyond pathetic.

I heard CJ walk out of the bathroom, her voice trailing. She was still yelling that she was absolutely going to make sure I saw a nutritionist at school, as though she had any authority over my life in California. After she left I closed the door, took off all my clothes, and examined myself in the full-length mirror. My body was a sliver of what it had been. I could see the bones in my shoulders and through my chest. I'd gone down a whole cup size and was borrowing A bras from Bree, who, despite her nonexistent figure, ate whatever she wanted. My skin was golden brown from lying on the beach in Chatham for the whole month of August; the tan lines ran right above my nipples. My brown hair was streaked with lighter pieces from the sun. I was skinny but I wasn't gross-skinny. I looked good. I looked better than Diana. He would have to notice.

En route to LaGuardia CJ sped down the Long Island Expressway and rambled on about her cousin Linda's terrible battle with anorexia.

"It's something she never got over, Lucy. To this day she won't use anything but skim milk in her coffee. Not even two percent, not a droplet. That's how *messed up* she is in here." CJ tapped her head with her pointer finger.

She pulled the Lexus curbside at the terminal and helped me haul my bags out of the trunk. She squeezed me hard.

"I love you, Sass." When she let go, her eyes were wet.

I felt tears rise in the back of my own throat, and I pushed my sunglasses down. "Bye. See you in November."

"Please eat well. Lots of protein and *carbs*. And call me when you land in LA."

I rolled my suitcase through the sliding glass doors and down the shiny black ceramic flooring toward the check-in kiosks. The airport smelled of stale, overused air. I glanced over my shoulder when I reached the end of the United line and could still see CJ through the windows, standing on the sidewalk in a stream of sunlight, watching me, her hands clasped together in front of her chest.

20

STEPHEN

I was sweating bullets as I flipped through chapter five of the *LSAT Logic Games Bible*: "Grouping Linear/Combination Games," while I waited for Diana on the back patio of Giuliana's. There were just seven weeks until the LSAT and I couldn't afford to lose a minute of studying. I'd already torn through two other LSAT prep books over the summer—I was going to be the most prepared bastard at the test.

"Law school?" the short Asian waiter inquired as he filled up my water glass.

"That's the plan. Can I get a Scotch and soda on the rocks?" Diana was *always* late.

"I hear it's tough to get in. Good luck, bro." What kind of Asian says, "bro"?

"Thanks. Can I get that Scotch and soda, please?"

"*Sorry* I'm late!" Diana's face was sun-kissed from her summer on Lake Winnebago, where she'd taught canoeing. Pieces of her caramel hair had lightened from the sun, and her tanned skin made her brown eyes pop.

"I'll have a glass of merlot. And he'll have a Scotch and soda on the rocks." Diana smiled, the whites of her eyes shining.

"Already ordered one, baby." I reached for her hand. I loved this—Diana and me back together at Baird, having a little date night in town, hearing her recite my drink order like old times.

"I love that you picked Giuliana's, Stephen. You remember we came here on one of our first dates." She tilted her pretty head.

"Of course I remember. I think about that night all the time."

"Close that book. You've been studying too much." She circled my palm with her thumb.

"I know, but the test is soon, Di. It's an overwhelming amount of information."

"You're gonna be so good." She shimmied out of her cardigan. It was a steamy September night and I would've much preferred the air-conditioned comfort of indoor seating, but Diana loves the damn patio at Giuliana's.

"I'm just glad I'll have you by my side." I studied the smooth, bare skin above her tank top line. "I think this is gonna be a good year for us, Di."

"Let's hope it's nothing like last year." She retrieved her hand and looked at me sharply. I felt a fight brewing if I wasn't careful. With Diana, it was always something.

"Princess Diana." I met her gaze. "Stop. Let's not dwell on the past. I love you."

"I know."

"Say you love me, too."

"You know I do."

"I want to hear you say it."

"I love you, too."

I reached across the table for her hand again as the waiter set our drinks down.

"Let's try not to fight, okay? Let's just try to just appreciate each other."

"Okay. You're right."

"To the first Saturday night of senior year." I raised my glass, desperately in need of a sip. "And to new beginnings." I placed a small white box on the table in front of her.

Diana tried hard not to smile as she opened the box. She examined the necklace, silver with a small turquoise stone. It was a regift, an old birthday present someone must've given my mother years ago. I found it in the basement, tags on and still in its box, in a large bin of stuff my mom left behind when she moved out. Diana loves turquoise jewelry, so I snagged it.

"Stephen! It's beautiful." She fingered the silver-set stone. "What's the occasion?"

"No occasion. Just wanted to do something nice for you."

"Thank you," she said, glowing. "This looks like real turquoise. It looks expensive. Where'd you find it?"

"At a boutique in DC," I lied.

"I just love it. Did Vivian help you?"

"No way. I know your taste. Here. Try it on." I shifted my chair closer to Diana's and fastened the necklace, watching the pale hairs rise along the back of her neck.

"It's perfect," I said, centering the turquoise stone on her collarbone.

"You shouldn't have."

"I'm glad you like it."

"I don't like it. I *love* it."

"Well, I don't like you. I *love* you." It was an in-joke between Diana and me that originated freshman year, the first time I told her I loved her, one January morning before class.

We'd woken up angry at each other after some stupid fight about my having flirted with another girl at a party, a ridiculous accusation on Diana's part.

"Sometimes I feel like you don't even like me," she'd huffed, stealing the covers, which isn't easy on a twin bed.

"I don't like you!" I'd yelled. I was annoyed and hungover and tired and I half meant what I said but added, "I love you," anyway.

"What?" Diana propped up on one elbow.

"I don't like you. I love you, Princess Diana."

And she'd loved me, too, of course. And she still did. Her reference to our ancient inside joke, that early intimate moment, assured me that she loved me more than ever.

After dinner, as we walked north through the town of Claremont, toward campus, I felt the promise of the new school year in the still-summer air—the capacity of what it would hold.

"I think I should go home," Diana said, gesturing toward her new house on the corner of Cutler and Hutchins.

"Home? It's Saturday night. The first Saturday night back. You know we're having a party at Slug."

"I know I'm being lame, but I'm honestly so exhausted, Stephen. Red wine was a bad idea in this heat. And I *really* have to be productive tomorrow and get a jump start on my thesis outline. Besides, Keaton and most of the girls won't be back for a couple more days. Just go have fun with your friends. I'll be boring and tired the whole time."

"Aw, Di." I circled her waist with my arms. "You sure?"

She nodded, midyawn. "Have a beer for me?"

"Sure thing." A beer? I'd have four shots, two lines, and a good portion of the keg for her. I was suddenly glad that Diana was staying in for the night. This was our first rager of the year, and Diana didn't like it when I did drugs and got too wasted.

"Come get in bed with me later?" She touched the turquoise stone on her necklace.

"Duh."

"Not too late. Promise?"

"Promise. That necklace looks mighty pretty on you."

"I'll see you later." She wrapped her arms around my neck. "Don't have too much fun without me."

"Never do." I lightly smacked her ass as she skipped away, and she turned around and blew me a kiss. Diana and I were golden.

Back at Slug, our first party was going strong. The window AC unit was on full blast, and the downstairs was packed to the brim with faces, old and new. It was too crowded, actually, because by the time you reach senior year, you realize parties where you are unable to move are not actually fun. Still, the fact that so many people were stoked on the return of Slug—*my* house—had my blood flowing.

I looked for her instantly. Since the moment I'd left Diana at her house, since before that even—since I got back to Baird—Lucy was all I could think about, really. She was back on campus—I'd seen some Facebook photo of Lucy and Pippa and their posse at some dinner, with the caption "We're so #sophomoric."

It was too packed and dark to see well, so I ran upstairs and found Wrigley and Charlie in the shelter of Wrigley's bedroom, in front of a coffee table piled with blow.

"This is kind of absurd." I locked the door. "You can't move down there."

"Isn't it awesome? Like the good old Slug days. We're back, bitches." Wrigley howled with intoxicated, coked-out laughter.

"Where've you been, dude?" Charlie asked.

"Dinner with Diana."

"Dinner with Diana," Wrigley repeated. "How'd that go?"

"It was good, actually. We're in a good place."

"Well, that's great, Stephen." Wrigley scooted over and handed me the rolled-up twenty. "Diana is a good girl."

"She is," I nodded, snorting my line.

"She here?"

"She's tired. Staying in."

"Ah."

I sank back into the pillows, my coke buzz settling in blissfully. It was going to be a great fucking year.

An hour later I was fucked up on Scotch but clearheaded from the coke when I ventured back downstairs. It was still crowded, and Nicole Hart sort of cornered me and started telling me about her summer, and I was *very* glad that Diana hadn't come.

And then I saw her, a glimpse of the side of her face past Nicole's shoulder as Nicole blabbered on about Nantucket or Sun Valley or God knows where. I excused myself from the conversation and tried to push through the crowd, but it was too jam-packed and Drake was blasting and suddenly people were pushing, and getting across to where Lucy stood was hopeless. I went into the kitchen and found Charlie making nachos.

I was feeling fucked up as shit but poured just two more fingers of Scotch into an empty glass. The back door was open, and people were finally starting to stumble out, thank God. It was three in the morning. I watched a group of girls stagger across the porch. Lucy was among them. My Lucy, because I'd know those twiggy legs from a mile away. Long and bare and golden brown. I walked toward the door, my eyes working their way up to the top of her. She was tan and wore a fitted white dress and colorful bracelets on her stick-thin arms. God she looked good. Too skinny, maybe. I staggered out onto the porch just as she reached the bottom of the stairs. Her arms were crossed. She appeared to be waiting for her friend, the equally thin, blond one, who was talking to Evan.

"Lucy." I held up my hand, an easy wave.

Her eyes met mine, but she didn't say anything. She didn't smile, but she didn't glare, either. She looked good enough to devour, and in the span of ten seconds I thought of the sex in all its glorious formations—Lucy on her back, Lucy on her hands and knees, my fingers as far inside Lucy as they ever could be while her ocean eyes locked mine, short of breath, same as now. There was that stir between my legs. I wanted to touch her.

Lucy held my gaze long enough for me to know that if I wanted to cheat on Diana, I probably could. She finally looked away. I watched her pull her friend from Evan and I watched them cross the street, probably heading to Adler, the main sophomore dorm. *#Sophomoric.*

I inhaled Charlie's nachos before dragging myself upstairs, an inebriated zombie. I forgot that I was supposed to get in bed with Diana after the party and I was too zonked to hear my phone ring. I almost had a heart attack when Diana stormed in at seven the next morning, her eyes searching the room for signs of betrayal.

There was no one else, clearly there was no one else, I told her, half asleep and still drunk and so incredibly relieved that I hadn't done anything stupid. But I hadn't gone over to Diana's like I'd promised and I hadn't answered my phone and there were still "trust issues," and the slam of my bedroom door told me this was going to be another fight.

21

LUCY

OCTOBER 2011

"Lay-gup! Lay-gup! Lay-gup!" My YogaLab instructor's Latin twang echoed through the studio. *Leg up, leg up, leg up!*

I lifted my leg up. My glutes burned with pain, but YogaLab's yoga tone class was more of a workout than hot vinyasa, so I'd started going every day, sometimes with Jackie or Pippa, but usually alone. Bree never exercised—her metabolism continued to mystify me. The instructor switched us to lunges with weights, and I braced myself for the discomfort. My biceps were already trembling.

After class finished, I showered and weighed myself in the locker room. I'd been eating less than seven hundred calories a day to lose the weight CJ made me gain over the summer, but I was still at 116. How was it possible?

I walked back toward campus to Adler Quad, where my friends were sprawled out on a blanket next to a palm tree, sharing a joint. The whole image was so characteristically *Baird*—I had to smile.

"How was your workout?" Jackie asked, munching on a bag of Doritos.

"It felt good."

I knew what she was thinking. *Why do you work out so much? Why do you eat salad every single meal? Who are you trying to impress?* But Jackie had already made those kinds of comments enough, and I had learned to ignore them. She offered me a Dorito and I took two, out of pride, crunching the salty, empty calories in my mouth. They tasted delicious, of course, but the thought of the harm they could impose on my yoga-toned, broccoli-fueled body made them, as always, not worth it.

I plopped down onto the blanket and tilted my face out of the shade of the leafy palm, toward the sun. Proximity to Adler Quad was probably the best perk to living in Adler, the sophomore dorm where the four of us shared one of the coveted suites—an apartment-style setup with our own hallway, two bedrooms, a bathroom, and a small living area.

As usual Adler Quad was bright green and buzzing with Baird's diverse student body—the intellectuals smoking hand-rolled cigarettes, the Delta Gamma girls sunbathing, the bros playing Frisbee golf, the hippies slacklining between palm trees, the art majors painting, the music junkies in guitar circles, and the others, like us, who fit somewhere in between two or three of the defined social circles. This was the scene at Baird most weekdays after class for those who didn't rush straight to the library. The sunshine often felt endless in California, eighty-degree weather always beckoning us outdoors. I gazed toward the opposite side of the quad, where Slug guys were playing badminton, like they did most afternoons.

Jackie passed me the joint and I inhaled, careful not to overdo it. Too much weed made me anxious and immobile. And hungry.

"Evan Donovan is so attractive," Bree was saying, stretched out on her stomach in the waning sunlight, her hands propping her chin. "Don't you guys think?"

"Meh." Pippa sucked the joint. "Not my type."

"He's too scrawny," I said.

"That's because you like Stephen and Stephen is *fat*," Pippa said.

"I don't like Stephen, and he's not *fat*."

"He's *large*," Jackie said.

"Actually, I see what you mean about Evan, Bree," Pippa said, glancing in the direction of the badminton game. "He's definitely your type."

"What does *that* mean?"

"It just means that you two would be cute together!"

"Well, he has a girlfriend, so it's hopeless." Bree took the joint from Jackie.

"Maybe they'll break up."

"Meh. Doubt it."

"What about *Walter*?" Pippa nudged Bree's bony ribs. "The infamous v-card stealer."

"*Never* again," Bree said, and we all laughed. After a month of hooking up, Walter had written Bree an incredibly cheesy sonnet declaring his love for her, and she'd run for the hills.

The sun sank lower in the sky, and the Slug guys finished their badminton game. I watched them grab their backpacks and walk across the quad, back toward their house. Wrigley saw us and waved, but Stephen didn't look over. Maybe he hadn't seen us. I watched him cross Carroll Street, his white T-shirt stretching the span of his back. The dip at the base of his neck glistened in the melting sunlight.

I could feel my friends looking at me, feeling sorry for me. I didn't want their pity, and the weed was making me feel worse—more analytical than usual.

"He could at least say hi," Bree muttered.

"It's fine. He knows he's not exactly my favorite person."

"Still."

"Whatever." I shrugged. "He's with Diana now."

Except for that first Slug party, Stephen and Diana were together everywhere—walking across campus hand in hand, eating in the dining hall, teaming up for games of beer pong, kissing against the deck of the houseboat on Lake Mead (I hadn't wanted to go to Mead this year, but my friends had insisted). The sight of the two of them never failed to make my insides lurch, never failed to make my head foggy with anger and lust and jealousy and frustration and sadness all mixed into one heavy dose of agonizing nostalgia.

You're so beautiful, Lucy. Fuck.

I can't wait to take you out on the boat this summer. You're gonna love it. I'm gonna go mingle. I'll find you soon.

One second I'd had him, the next he was gone. It only takes a moment for something perfect to erase itself—a flight of stairs that leads to something unimaginable and irreversible; Stephen's mouth pressed to Diana's, Gabe's hands holding CJ's hips. A perception shatters and an imaginary line is drawn, separating the way it was from the way it is.

"He's back with Diana now and yet he refuses to give you any kind of explanation after the shit he pulled at Hawaiian Luau last year? I hate boys." Pippa stubbed the roach.

"It's so true," Jackie agreed. "I hate how guys just never take responsibility for the things they've done. They never feel like they have to own up to anything."

"Not all guys," Bree offered.

"Well, guys like Stephen. Dicks like Stephen."

"You just need to hook up with someone else, Luce," Pippa said. "It will make you feel a million times better."

"I know, I know." I hugged my knees into my chest. "But like, who?"

"There are tons of guys," Bree said. "What about Stuart's friend Clay?"

"He's hooking up with that freshman," Jackie said.

"What freshman?" Pippa pressed.

"Some Delta."

"Ugh. Fuckin DGs."

"What about Kevin Bianco?"

"Um, Kevin Bianco is one of the guys who gangbanged that girl while one of them was filming it," Jackie said.

"That was him? *Ew*. Oh my God. Never mind."

"That junior guy Riley? The super tall one on the soccer team?"

"Girlfriend."

"Hmmm. Wes Davenport?"

"I'm pretty sure Wes Davenport is gay," Bree pointed.

"*I* know," Jackie said, grinning ear to ear. "Topher Rigby. He's so cute and he already likes Lucy."

"Topher Rigby is shorter than me," I said. "I've told you this."

"Yeah." Pippa winced. "Topher is midgetish."

"He's not a midget, Pippa," Jackie said. "He's basically Lucy's same height."

"That's a deal breaker," Pippa said. "She would never be able to wear heels."

"So don't wear *heels* for a couple of months and have a fling with him. I love Topher! We were, like, in the same playgroup as babies. He's so cute and hilarious and he'd be *so* nice to you. And maybe you'll end up liking him."

"I guess that's true," Pippa said. "Maybe he's good in bed to compensate for his height. Like a Napoleon complex."

"A Napoleon complex is when a man acts aggressive and arrogant because he's insecure about being short," Bree explained. "It has nothing to do with being good in bed."

"Thank you, encyclopedia Bree," Pippa rolled her eyes and turned to me. "Lucy, my dear. You are a very beautiful girl and despite this conversation there are lots of boys at this godforsaken school who would *love* to get into your tiny little yoga pants."

"Let's go in," Bree said. "I need to shower."

"Same," Jackie said. "Let's go in and shower and make drinks and do something fun tonight. Something different. No Slug boys."

"Amen. Slug boys are the worst." Pippa stood and swept the grass off her jeans.

"I should really do my Latin reading," Bree said.

"I'm supposed to work on this piece for *The Lantern*," I said.

"Do it in the morning," Pippa said. "I'll wake up early with you guys. I have to do my effing calculus."

Six hours, five vodka sodas, and one generous line of blow later, I found myself in Topher Rigby's dorm room. Jackie had texted Topher to come meet us at whatever random, midweek party we'd gone to, and he'd shown up in a clean polo shirt and with a freshly shaven face. Jackie was right—Topher *did* have a handsome face, and the more I drank the taller he became, and by the end of the night I was basically hanging on to his arm as we continued an in-depth conversation about *Breaking Bad*, and the next thing I knew we were in his room, which smelled faintly of Axe.

Topher's single in Adler was covered in lacrosse posters and lacrosse trophies and photographs of his Wilton High School lacrosse team and several five-by-seven close-ups of himself *laxing in action*.

"So you play lacrosse?" It was a dumb, easy joke, but Topher laughed too loudly and poked my side, and my subconscious sober self debated running out the door.

"You're funny." Topher sat down on the bed. "I can't believe Lucy Albright is in my room on a Wednesday night."

I really couldn't stand any of this—I didn't know if it was his height and poufy black hair that were bothering me, or just the fact that he wasn't Stephen. I knew if I didn't sit down on the bed I was going to

leave, maybe run down the street to the 7-Eleven for an emergency bag
of Smartfood popcorn.

"You can sit down," he said.

I sat.

He leaned over and kissed me, his mouth opening slowly against
mine, his tongue sluggishly sliding in. I waited for him to throw me
down on the bed with his lacrosse biceps and really make out with me,
but the kiss remained vertical, gentle, dispassionate.

After a while my neck started to hurt from kissing in such a locked,
upright position, so I lay back against the pillows, which Topher took
as an invitation to slide his hand up my shirt. He touched my breasts
carefully, like they were ancient artifacts. His hand reached for the button of my jeans and it felt like hours before he'd successfully unzipped
them and pulled them down around my knees. When he placed his
hand inside my underwear I wasn't turned on and he didn't know what
he was doing and all I could think about was Stephen, and I wanted Topher's hands to be Stephen's hands, and I missed Stephen so badly that
tears glazed my eyes while Topher dedicated his fingers to all the wrong
places. I was sober enough to know the hookup was bad, drunk enough
to stay as long as I did, even if it was just so I could tell Jackie I'd tried.
I'd put myself out there.

"Kiss me harder," I said finally, after it felt like he'd been kissing me at
the speed of a turtle for about an hour.

"Huh?" Topher lifted his head and gave me a funny look. His dark
hair was tousled and thick.

"I just feel like you're kissing me really softly." I regretted saying anything, but I'd already dug the hole.

"Uh. Okay." He sort of laughed but I could tell he was confused, or in-
sulted, or both.

"Forget it." I sat up and yanked my clothes back on. "I should go."

"You can sleep here," he said. "We can just talk or put on a movie. Or
Breaking Bad?"

"Thanks, but my room is so close." I slid into my sandals, and when
he stood to kiss me goodbye, I hovered a good two inches over him.

"Sorry," I said. "I'm just tired."

"No worries," he said, even though he probably thought I was nuts.

He asked for my number anyway, and I gave it to him because there was no other option.

I hated myself as I walked back toward our suite at the west end of Adler, Stephen filling every corner of my head, the hallway lights still fluorescent at 2:00 a.m. Months had gone by without a word from him—*months*—and now he was with Diana. And what exactly was I hoping for?

Maybe he missed me. That first night at Slug I'd caught him staring at me, unmistakably staring at me. Then he'd waved—that had to have meant something. But even if he did miss me he wasn't *saying* he missed me, and even in the hypothetical scenario in which he was saying he missed me, how could I give him the time of day after what he'd done? It was a pointless question with the wrong answer, and the only thing that made sense was that I knew I had fallen in love with him—it was what had made these past months so horrific. People always talk about realizing they're in love during the happy moments, but I think you realize it in the bad ones. The ones that knock you off center, scaring you when they prove that no matter what kind of logic is in your head, it's what's in your heart that determines fucking everything.

22

STEPHEN

NOVEMBER 2011

Have you ever been cited, arrested, charged with, indicted, convicted or tried for, or pleaded guilty to, the commission of any felony or misdemeanor or the violation of any law (without the record later being sealed or expunged)? If yes, please describe. Include a statement of the charge(s), the disposition thereof, and the underlying facts.

I stared at the question for the umpteenth time, a line of sweat dampening my forehead.

The early-decision deadline for my application to Columbia Law School was approaching fast. Only eight more days.

If yes, please describe.

Fuck fuck fuck fuck fuck.

I couldn't help but laugh at my ironic misfortune. My "misdemeanor" wasn't even related to the night of the accident. My "misdemeanor" was the DUI I received six weeks before the accident. What can I say? It was an unlucky summer for driving.

The night of the DUI happened two months after my eighteenth birthday, and it was on my fucking record, and the record had not been later sealed or expunged.

I'd been drinking at Carl's with some guys—Carl's parents were always out of town and we used to get shitfaced in his garage all the time. On my way home I called Macy Petersen, because by that point cheating on Jenna had become routine, and Macy was the sexy, soft-spoken girl whose body had begun to preoccupy my thoughts. She was a couple of years younger, went to private school at Portledge, and we met at a party one weekend shortly before my high school graduation. It was too easy to hide our relationship that summer; Jenna was preoccupied training for Emory's volleyball team, and I snuck off with Macy as much as I could. Macy let me fuck her however I wanted. The way she came with me, you could tell her boyfriend didn't know what he was doing. We drove around and screwed in the car or on the golf course, wherever we felt like going.

"I'm coming over," I told her on the phone that night. "Sneak out to the barn."

Macy's parents lived on this huge estate in Oyster Bay with a barn slash guesthouse where Macy and I would meet up late at night. I used to park on the road near the end of her driveway and walk up to the barn in the dark, unnoticed.

But this time I didn't make it there. I was used to driving drunk—it wasn't my choice mode of transportation, but I'd been in enough situations where it had occurred, and I considered myself to be a relatively cautious, alert driver when under the influence. So when the red and blue lights flashed in my rearview mirror it caught me off guard. I pulled over, paralyzed with fear.

The fucked part is, I wasn't speeding or swerving—it was a broken headlight on my dad's goddamn Subaru. So the cop came to the window and was telling me about the broken light, but she could smell the Dewar's on me—those bastards have bloodhound noses. Officer *Gonzalez*—I'll never forget her name. She looked like a big Mexican lesbian feminist who probably despised men.

And that was that. The Breathalyzer showed a .09 percent blood-alcohol level and I was done. A $500 fine, license suspended for a year, thirty days of community service, and a scarlet *F* scorched onto my record.

My dad yelled at me in the car on the way home from the police station that night, and all I could think was how I wasn't that drunk and my driving had been *fine* and this was all his fucking fault for being too depressed and spaced-out to notice the broken headlight.

Everything leads back to the DUI in the world of the law, because there is always a box on every godforsaken form that asks about your criminal history and whether you've ever been charged with a *misdemeanor*, and I always have to check that box simply because I got unlucky.

But I choose to look on the bright side because six weeks later, on August 16, the night of the accident, the world was on my side. The trouble I *could've* landed myself in, should an Officer Gonzalez type have been in the right place at the right time *that* night, would've made the DUI look like a parking ticket. If you think I don't count my lucky stars, you're very wrong.

I stared at the application again.

If yes, please describe. Include a statement of the charge(s), the disposition thereof, and the underlying facts.

I was about to begin "describing," when Diana barged into my bedroom.

"You're not dressed? We're going to be so late." She was out of breath, flustered in a silvery flapper dress and matching headband, circa the 1920s.

"Oh, shit. The *Gatsby* party. What time is it?"

"*Ten*, Stephen. What have you been doing?"

"My Columbia application. Sorry. I took an Adderall and was just plowing through. Lost track of time."

"It's fine. Just hurry. Everyone left two hours ago and I was *waiting* for you but you didn't answer your effing phone."

"Sorry, sorry. I've been so focused and my phone's been on silent." I snatched it from the end of my bed. "Aha! Princess Diana, four missed calls. Hmm. Stage-five clinger?"

"I'm your girlfriend," she said, circling her arms around my neck. "I'm allowed to call you as many times as I want. Now get dressed." She kissed me.

"What am I supposed to wear?"

"A suit? This!" Diana pulled a black tux out of my closet.

"*Hell* no. That thing cuts off my circulation."

"Well maybe you should stop drinking so much beer." She poked me in the stomach. "Why do you even have this?"

"It's for Vivian and Rod's wedding. I need to get it tailored but I haven't had time."

"Just put it on and let's go."

"*Fine.*" It kind of turned me on when Diana got all bossy. "You look gorgeous by the way," I told her, even though she looked sort of ridiculous in her sparkly getup. If Diana Bunn had existed in another decade, it certainly would not have been the 1920s.

Half an hour later we walked into Kappa Sig on Perry Street. The fraternity hosted the *Great Gatsby* theme party every year, and it was always fun because there was a list, which meant the party didn't overcrowd. Diana and I crossed our names off at check-in in the foyer, which was littered with thick peeling paint chips. All of Baird's frat houses are such shitholes.

There were trays of martinis in little plastic martini glasses, and jazzy Roaring Twenties music blared from a real record player—Duke Ellington, Eddie Condon, Louis Armstrong—the shit my mom used to play. Diana skipped off when she saw her friends, and that was one good thing about Diana—she never clung to me at parties.

I reached for a second martini and looked around the semicrowded room, allowing the combination of melodious jazz and strong gin to warm my chest.

There was Nicole Hart looking even more ridiculous than Diana; Meagan Lewis, a girl I fucked a couple of times freshman year while Diana and I were fighting; Evan and his boring girlfriend locked in a slow dance; Pippa McAllister, Wrigley's bratty ex-girlfriend, talking to a girl in a short, black sequined dress and black high heels propping up a pair of legs so long and perfectly slim that they could only belong to Lucy. Her face made a quarter turn, one half of her red-lipsticked mouth sliding into a smile at someone's joke. And if anyone belonged in another decade it was Lucy in the 1920s, because her little black dress was so textbook and her made-up face so classically beautiful, I could've sworn I'd stepped into a party at Jay Gatsby's own mansion.

I grabbed a third martini.

"You have the longest legs I've ever seen," I said, suddenly standing next to her, breathing in the sugary scent of her. Her hair was pulled up into a twisted chestnut bun, and I watched her neck curve like a swan's as it made its way toward the source of the flattering comment.

"Lucy." We locked eyes, color flushing her cheeks, and I realized that it had been way too long since we'd last spoken, and I didn't know how she was going to react.

"Hey." Her voice was smaller than it should've been in that outfit.

I could feel Pippa's giant eyes lasering into me, but I ignored them.

"How are you?"

"I'm good," she said, twisting on the long stem of one of her heels. A familiar Duke Ellington song filled the room.

"Do you like the music?"

"Jazz. It's okay."

"'In a Sentimental Mood.' Duke Ellington. Great composition. But it's from the thirties, not the twenties. I won't tell anyone."

"You know jazz?" A mix of cynicism and surprise infused her voice.

"Some. My mother used to listen to jazz. She'd turn the volume loud and dance with my father in the kitchen. Before things got . . . worse. It was a long time ago." I held Lucy's gaze.

"And you remember the names of the songs?"

"Some of 'em, yeah. I have a good memory."

Lucy was looking at me like she wanted to say something, her lips parted, but then she closed them and said nothing. Pippa had wandered off, thankfully.

"You've been good?" she asked finally, even though I didn't mind the silence. I liked just looking at her and was grateful she hadn't run off after Pippa.

"Yeah. Busy. I have my thesis due this winter and law school applications. It's been hectic, actually."

She nodded, and over her bare shoulder I caught Diana staring at me from across the room, frowning, her arms folded.

"Lucy," I said, turning back to face her. "I want to say that I'm sorry. It's really overdue, but I'm really fucking sorry. Okay?"

"You're a little late on that one." Lucy shrugged, her eyes sad under all the dark makeup.

I sort of liked that she wasn't afraid to show me her brokenness. She didn't bury it with pride or shame like a lot of people, and God, there is something so attractive about a broken person. I took in the details of her face and I wanted so badly to kiss her. If Diana hadn't been staring straight at us, I might've done it.

"Diana and I . . . we just have a history is all," I said. "I have to see this thing through, I guess. It has nothing to do with you." It was the truth, and I suddenly wanted to be honest with Lucy—honesty made people feel cared for and valued.

"Whatever, Stephen. It doesn't matter now." She sipped her martini.

"Yeah," I said, noting the contradiction in her words, because to Lucy, it did matter. The way she was looking at me, the sadness and lust transparent behind her deep blue irises, her facial muscles practically twitching with want, told me she wasn't remotely over it, that it mattered a whole fucking lot, that she would take this conversation to bed with her and think about it tomorrow and the next day and the day after that, deciphering its meaning, the way girls do. She wasn't seeing anyone—social media and the incestuous Baird College gossip circle told me as much.

"Thanks for apologizing," she said eventually.

"It's good to see you," I said, locking her gaze for as long as I could before she turned and walked away, expensive perfume in her wake.

"What the *fuck*?" Diana sneered when I found her in the kitchen, pouring more gin into her glass.

"Calm down, Diana," I whispered, grabbing the gin from her and topping off my own drink. "I wasn't doing anything wrong. I literally ran right into her and she started asking me about my thesis."

"*Why* was she asking you about your *thesis*?"

"I don't *know*, Diana. Why don't you ask her?" I knew very well that Diana would never approach Lucy. She had no problem yelling at me, but she despised female confrontation.

"Ugh. She's just so skinny and, like, thinks she runs the sophomore class. I can't believe you slept with her."

"She doesn't think she runs the sophomore class, Diana."

"Why are you defending her?"

"I'm not *defending* her. I just don't think she thinks she runs the sophomore class. She's probably a lot different than you think." I pinched my sinuses, regretting my position in this unnecessary argument.

"Stephen." Diana looked up at me, her eyes shimmering with bizarre silver makeup. "I love you, and I want this to work." Her whisper was slow in my ear: "But if you ever touch that girl again, I'll kill you."

PART
THREE

23

LUCY

AUGUST 2017

Bree and Evan's rehearsal dinner is held at the Parsonage Club, a country club in Tewksbury where the Donovans are members. The dining room is enormous, with high ceilings and wide French doors opening to a terrace overlooking the rolling green hills of the eighteenth hole.

After a long day of last-minute errands followed by two rehearsals at the church, my stomach is growling for dinner, and I scarf down chicken piccata, wild rice, and a sourdough roll before I have time to feel bad about it. Whatever. I'm going to need the strength.

Bree squeezes my shoulder on her way back to her table.

"I told you he wouldn't be here," she whispers.

"What'd she say?" Pippa asks, her mouth half full of chicken.

"Nothing." I take a sip of champagne. My phone dings in my purse—it's a text from Melissa.

> MELISSA (WORK): Why is the Departures article still live? I told you to take care of it. TAKE CARE OF IT. I talked to Harry and he agrees, obviously.

"Fuck," I mumble. I consider calling Harry, but it might not be worth it.

"What's wrong?" Jackie asks.

"Just my psycho boss." I tell her about the *Departures* fiasco.

Another new text flashes on the screen.

> DANE: Crushing the dinner babe? Bet ur the hottest bridesmaid. Send me a nudie? Your beautiful butt in a tiny thong? :-)

"Oh my God," Jackie says, nearly choking on her wine leaning over me, reading the text. "Is this seriously the guy you're seeing?"

"It's not funny. All Dane does is ask me for pictures of my ass," I say, which only makes Jackie laugh harder.

"Jackie! I actually need your advice."

"Okay, okay, sorry. Well, you like him, right?"

"I mean, I do. He's so . . . hot. One of the hottest guys I've been with."

"Hotter than Billy?"

"Different."

"So the problem is . . . ?"

"I don't know how much we have in common . . . intellectually."

"Elaborate."

"We don't have very intellectual conversations. Half the time I don't understand what he's talking about. He's obsessed with skateboarding and Ariana Grande, and you know the Instagram handle Butt-Snorkeler?"

"ButtSnorkeler . . . no. Maybe?"

"Well, he's obsessed. It's like this collection of butt pictures that he always shows me. I don't know what I'm doing."

"Having fun?"

"Sure. But that's unsustainable."

"Why does it have to be sustainable?"

"I dunno. Maybe you're right. I just feel like at a certain point these things are a waste of time. Bree's getting *married*. Georgia is probably going to get engaged to Lars soon."

"At least it's not Elliot."

"Thank *God* it's not Elliot. But now she's got it all figured out, and me? I'm sleeping with someone who won't even pay me back for his fourteen-dollar pad thai. He owes me at least three hundred dollars."

"What?"

"We went to Montauk for a weekend in early June and he just never paid me back for his half of the hotel room, not to mention dinner at the Surf Lodge, or the wine and beer from the liquor store. I've bugged him about it a million times. He's always like, 'Oh yeah, of course, babe, I'll Venmo you,' but he never *does* it. Dane doesn't *do* anything he says he's going to do."

"Lucy." Jackie sips her champagne. "The money thing is an absolute deal breaker. June was nearly three months ago."

"I know."

"A guy should never make a girl pay for a *hotel room*. What a loser."

"I assume Travis pays for everything?"

Travis is Jackie's new boyfriend in LA. He does marketing for the Lakers and threw her a surprise twenty-fifth birthday party. Jackie always finds the best boyfriends.

"Mostly." Her smile is irrepressible, and I can tell how much she likes him.

I glance over at Pippa, who is deep in conversation with the guy to her right, one of Evan's attractive groomsmen.

"It's not really Dane that's the issue," I sigh. "I mean, I could end things with Dane and the problem still wouldn't be fixed."

"The problem being . . . ?"

"New York in general," I say honestly. "I've recently realized that."

"Really?" Jackie places her chin in her hand and leans forward with wide eyes. It's something I love about her—when she listens, she really listens. Jackie and I can talk for hours.

"You know the LCD Soundsystem song 'New York, I Love You But You're Bringing Me Down'? Joan Didion's essay 'Goodbye to All That'? I'm relating to those at the moment."

"The Mary Schmich quote: 'Live in New York City once, but leave before it makes you hard. . . .'"

"Exactly. People in New York are so angry."

"It's true." Jackie nods. "What is all the anger *about*?"

"Lack of sky? Twenty-dollar cocktails?"

"Shoe-box apartments?"

"But I love the city."

"I love it, too," Jackie agrees. "We grew up right there."

"I love running in Central Park, and I love all the seasons and the way the cabs smell."

"No cabs, Lucy! Subway!"

"I've been horrible at that. And my job is a disaster," I go on, sipping more champagne. "My boss hates me. And my salary sucks. And *Bree* moved out." I glance over at Bree at the next table. She's wearing a pale green silk dress and the diamond earrings Evan gave her as a wedding present, just this afternoon. Her face is in the crook of Evan's neck, and she's smiling up at him, one of those ginormous, goofy smiles that didn't appear on Bree's face until she started dating Evan.

"You definitely need a change," Jackie says, snapping me back to our conversation. "New York sucks the life out of everybody eventually. Move to Santa Monica. Hang with Pip and me."

"Maybe." I smile at the thought of living in California again.

"You would *love* our neighborhood, Luce. There are so many cute little shops and cafés, and we're two blocks from the ocean. You could just write and go running on the beach and reset."

"Sometimes I think about going back to school and trying to be a journalist, for real this time. No more sales."

"I think that would be great. It's what you've always wanted. I hear USC has a great journalism program." Jackie raises her eyebrows. "Just sayin'."

"Back to la-la land." I match her grin. "I don't hate this idea."

"Um, it would make my *year* if you moved to LA. Not to be selfish, but I really miss you. You know how much I love Pippa, but we can't *talk* the way you and I can."

"I know. Speaking of which, sorry I just talked your ear off complaining. I just needed to vent. Thanks for listening."

"Don't apologize." Jackie grins. "So are you gonna send Dane a nudie?"

"God, no. I did send him one the other week, but boobs only. No face."

"Smart thinkin', Luce," Jackie says sarcastically, because she would never be dumb enough to send nudes.

"It's all Stephen's fault. He's the one who made me feel like sending naked pictures was sexy, and personal. Sending them to Dane I just feel like some kind of porn service."

"You sent Stephen more than just boobs," Jackie points.

"I was an idiot when I was nineteen." A waiter whisks away our plates and almost immediately plops down dessert—carrot cake with cream cheese frosting. I dip my fork into the end with all the icing.

"And twenty, and twenty-one, and twenty-two?"

"Touché."

"I'm stuffed." Jackie leans back in her chair and pushes away her dessert.

Why am I still hungry after a huge dinner? That's the problem—once I let myself start eating, I can't stop. I let the thought slide, devouring my slice of cake and allowing the waiter to top off my Veuve.

"Are you nervous to see him?"

"Stephen?"

"Who else?"

"I was," I say, remembering my near panic attack on the train that morning. "The whole wedding was making me nervous because whenever I thought about Bree and Evan, I couldn't help but think about Stephen and me. But now that I'm here and it's actually happening, it's okay. It's been a while."

"I guess it has." Jackie sighs. "And you haven't seen him since that Baird Christmas party in the city?"

"Nope. *God* that was an awful night. Bree made me go with her, and he was the last person I expected to see—Stephen hates alumni shit like that. But of course there he was, with fucking *Jillian*."

"Jesus."

"I don't really miss him at all anymore. But I do hate that he has another new girlfriend."

"Of course he has another new girlfriend, Lucy. He's a serial dater. He can't be alone. We know this."

"I know, I know. Still."

"Well, at least *Jillian* won't be joining him at the wedding," Jackie says. "No plus-ones unless the couple is married or engaged. No ring, no bring." She wiggled her naked finger in the air.

"Thank God. I would die."

Suddenly the sound of a clinking glass fills the room, and everyone looks up at Mr. Donovan, Evan's father, who is kicking off the toasts. He stands and says a lot of nice stuff about Bree and how happy she's made his son, and he toasts Bree's parents, cheery but oblivious Midwesterners who have no idea their only daughter is wearing Tiffany diamonds that cost more than the average car.

Next up is Evan, standing tall and handsome in front of the open double doors, the orange sun nudging the horizon behind him.

"I'll keep this short and sweet, because you already know why we're here," he says, raising his glass and gazing down at Bree. "Bree, you continue to take my breath away. I'm in awe of your grace, your kindness, your intelligence, and your beauty, equally radiant inside and out. When I first fell in love with you, I used to feel so frustrated that I hadn't found you sooner. You were right there at Baird, right in front of me for two years. Right there!" There is light laughter from the audience. "But one of the many important lessons you've taught me is that things happen when they're supposed to happen, and you can't rush them. So even though, in my opinion, it wasn't soon enough, not a day goes by that I don't feel so incredibly lucky to have found you when I did. Thank you for planning this perfect wedding all the way through." Evan raises his glass to the audience. "And of course, a huge thanks to my incredible parents for helping with the planning as well, and to Lauren, our tireless wedding planner." I glance over at Lauren, who looks like she's about to collapse with appreciation. "And thank you to all of *you* for being here. Your love and support means everything. And last, to the Bensons: Cindy, Gordon, Gordie, and Ian—my wonderful soon-to-be in-laws, thank you for being here and for letting me share my life with your daughter, your sister, who I love more every day. I can't wait for tomorrow. I don't think I'm going to be able to sleep." Evan's smile is exploding from his face, and the audience giggles and *awww*s as he leans down to kiss a beaming Bree.

"Aw fuck," Pippa says. "Literally no one is ever going to say that to me."

"He wasn't even reading off of anything," Jackie notes, wide-eyed.

I glance over at Evan and Bree and am suddenly dizzy, and I don't understand how any of this happened. It seems like just the other day that Stephen and I were lying on the beige couch in the apartment on a lazy Sunday, my head in his lap, while Bree peppered Stephen with questions about Evan, who had just moved to Manhattan.

"You know I've always had a crush on him," she admitted, because Bree is shamelessly honest like that.

Then Stephen had told Bree that Evan was single, and I'd bugged him nonstop to set them up, because the four of us going on double dates seemed like the best idea ever. So Stephen did set them up, and the four of us went to Schiller's on the Lower East Side, and it was the only double date we ever went on, and not because Bree and Evan didn't hit it off—they did. And here we are, almost three quick years later, watching them vow to love each other for the rest of their lives.

Fewer than twenty-four hours to go. I know I'm being pathetic and probably narcissistic, and I hate myself for it. I don't want any of this to be about Stephen, but somehow it is. Who is he now? I don't know if he passed the bar exam, but probably. He's smart. He's with Jillian. I wonder what'll run through his head when he sees me. What will he say to me? Will he be clean-shaven, or sporting a hint of stubble? Clean-shaven, probably, if he works in an office. It's been ages since I've thought about him in this kind of detail, but the fact that I'm seeing him tomorrow allows me to go there. It's that inkling of possibility that spreads from my unconsciousness up into my consciousness, and even though I know that it's wrong and I know now that I have the willpower to *understand* that it's wrong and actively *not* want him . . . I still let myself wonder.

Stephen DeMarco came back into my life on the second Friday in January of my sophomore year. I remember the exact date because it was Friday the thirteenth.

It was eleven o'clock and I was already in bed. I had been at a party earlier in the evening where Jackie was trying to set me up with one of Stuart's friends, Cameron-something, but talking to Cameron-something had felt like chewing wood. After one lukewarm Miller Light I'd beelined for the exit. Jackie would be pissed and give me shit for Irish-exiting again, but I didn't care. In recent months, trying to get drunk and socialize had become intolerable, like a chore.

Besides, tonight everyone was going to end up at a Slug party, and I avoided going there. Seeing *him* entwined with Diana made me sick to my stomach, and alcohol only made it worse. I could feel myself sinking into a dark, uncharted place, and it was just easier to deal with my pathetic problems from the solitude of my own bed.

My phone chimed on the nightstand.

JACKIE: Where'd you go?

I powered off my phone, still sober enough to get ahead on my twentieth-century American lit reading. We were rereading *The Catcher in the Rye*, and I was at the part where Holden recalls James Castle committing suicide by jumping out the window at Elkton Hills. I always hated that part, because it reminded me of a girl in high school who killed herself in her garage. Her name was Suzanne Heath, and she was in my freshmen year English class. She never said much, but I sat right next to her and noticed that she always got A's on her papers. She was dead by the end of the year. She killed herself in her garage using carbon monoxide poisoning one night in May while her parents were out. Thinking of Suzanne made me think of Macy Petersen, because even though Macy's death was an accident, she was the only other person my age I knew who'd died.

The thing that has always unnerved me most about Macy Petersen's death is that the last time I saw her was the night she died. At that point I hardly ever ran into Macy anymore, except every now and then at Cove Club. I'd been out with Antonia at a random house party in Lattingtown or maybe Bayville—I don't know exactly where, but I remember it was out of our typical bubble, toward the part of Nassau County that CJ deemed "trashy." It was a Saturday night near the end of the summer, and I was especially sickened by CJ, by the mere sight of her and my father going through old photo albums on the couch. I was drinking vodka from a water bottle in my bedroom and trying to shut my brain off, and I wanted to go somewhere—anywhere—so Antonia said we could go to a party with her brother and his girlfriend. I snuck out the back door after my parents went to sleep and waited for Antonia's brother's car at the end of my driveway.

I don't remember many specifics from the night—I got too drunk at a lot of high school parties in the years that followed the Unforgivable Thing. But I do remember my interaction with Macy almost vividly, a pocket of clarity amid the muddled blackness. Maybe it's because I learned of her death the next day that I even remember talking to her at all—maybe memory works like that. I had been standing out by a fire pit and I must've had the spins or been falling, because the next thing I knew Macy Petersen was there, and she was holding my arm and walking me inside. She took me into the bathroom and made me pull the trigger.

"Just get it all out," she said as she held my hair away from the toilet. "You'll feel better."

Afterward she handed me a glass of water and I asked what she was doing there, because it was late, and Macy wasn't the kind of girl who snuck out at night, and there was no way she didn't have a curfew. Mrs. Petersen was even stricter than CJ.

"*Don't* tell anyone," Macy said, crossing her long arms. "Because I just broke up with my boyfriend and I know it's too soon, but I really like this other guy, and I'm sort of here with him. Well, not really. I'm just giving him a ride home, because I was babysitting nearby and he lives around here. But anyway, I came inside for a sec and I saw you on the terrace and you looked wasted. Like you might be sick kind of wasted."

"Oh, jeez. Was it bad?"

"You were just stumbling. Nothing embarrassing."

"I feel a lot better now." I stared up at her from the bathroom floor and thought how beautiful and graceful she was, how her hair reminded me of the Little Mermaid's. I remember thinking how *nice* Macy was and wanting to tell her about CJ and Gabe, but I knew it was unnecessary, and that it wouldn't make any sense at all. "Thanks, Macy," I managed instead. "Sorry you had to watch me puke. That couldn't have been pretty."

"Not a big deal." She was putting on mascara in front of the mirror.

"So who's the guy you're with now?" I asked.

"He's no one you know," she said quickly. "He's this older guy, from Bayville. And I'm not *with* him—it's not like that. I shouldn't have said anything. I'd really rather keep it quiet, for now. Since Zach and I just broke up."

"I won't tell anyone."

"The other issue is, this guy, he sort of has a girlfriend." Macy's round eyes landed on mine in the mirror. "He says they're breaking up and that he's not into her, but we're keeping it really quiet for now. I was still with Zach when I met him, too. It's shitty, I know. I wish I didn't like him so much. I feel like a slut."

"You're the furthest thing from a slut, Macy."

"I should go." Macy tossed her mascara in her purse and helped me up off the floor, hugging me goodbye. "You're okay getting home?"

"Yeah. My friend Antonia's brother drove us." Back on my feet I felt dizzy again. I picked up the beer I'd been drinking earlier.

"Don't drink anymore, Lucy," Macy said, unwrapping a piece of bubblegum.

"I know, you're right. You take it."

"Can't," she said from the doorway, her eyes glinting, the palest blue. "I'm driving, remember?" She popped the gum into her mouth and disappeared.

My mind spiraled into thoughts of Macy and that forever-ago night, and I missed her in a strange, distant way, because I never really knew her all that well except when we were little kids, and it had always struck me as eerie and sort of tragic that the most intimate moment we ever had was that night, minutes before she got in her car. I even felt like I'd played a role in Macy's death in an odd way, though Lydia told me that was ridiculous. I don't know. It just always seemed so senseless to me that Macy went and drove her car off the road, right after she dropped off that guy she liked so much. Sober as a judge. Just so fucking unfair. Maybe if Macy hadn't died we would've become friends. Maybe I would've even told her about Gabe and CJ, eventually.

I was deep in thought when the door creaked open, light spilling in from the hallway of the suite. My heart quickened when I saw the shape of a male figure in the doorway, and then I figured maybe it was Stuart, maybe he and Jackie were home early and had decided to sleep in her room for a change.

"Lucy?" The voice was hoarse and low.

"Yeah?"

"Can we talk for a minute?"

I closed *Catcher* and sat up straighter, nerves prickling my spine.

"Who is that?"

The door opened farther and light filtered over the figure's face, which is when I saw that it was Stephen.

"Lucy?"

"Are you drunk?" I became very aware of the fact that I was wearing my matching snowflake pajama set that my grandmother had given me for Christmas. CJ's mom always buys tacky stuff, but the pajamas were warm.

"Can we talk for a minute?" He flicked on the overhead light. He was wearing a Baird College T-shirt and dark stubble covered his cheeks, his weak chin.

"How come?" Nerves were awakening all over my body.

"Nice jammies," he said. "Isn't it a little warm for flannel?"

"It got cold tonight."

"Cold enough for flannel?"

"I wasn't expecting company."

"Or you would've worn something sexy?"

My stomach flipped. I couldn't believe that he was in my room. "Why are you here?"

"How are you, Lucy in the Sky with Diamonds?" When he used the nickname, it felt like the greatest thing that had ever happened. His mouth curled itself into a slight smile. I noticed a faded ski-goggle tan around his eyes—probably from a ski weekend at Bear Mountain, an hour and a half east of Claremont. A lot of Baird kids skied at Bear Mountain, and I knew through the grapevine that Keaton Banks—Diana's friend—was always inviting their senior crew to her family's condo in Big Bear Lake.

"Are you drunk?" I repeated.

"Not really." He sat down at the end of my bed. "*Catcher in the Rye*, huh? That book is overrated, in my opinion. A guy wanders around New York City doing nothing for three days? Cool story, Hansel."

"It's one of my favorites."

"I like the digs," Stephen said, looking around. "Adler's sweet. I lived here my sophomore year, too."

"How did you know I live here?"

"Most sophomores live in Adler."

"You know what I mean. Here. This room."

"Pippa told me."

"She wouldn't do that."

"Well, she didn't give me directions or anything. But she was talking about how you guys live in the same suite on the third floor of Adler, and there are only two suites on each floor. So, you know. Process of elimination."

He was still grinning, his eyes fixed on mine. He smelled like beer and his usual Old Spice. I didn't know what to do with my hands, so I just stuck them underneath the covers.

"So you just barge into people's dorm rooms in the middle of the night?"

"Only some people's."

"Creepy."

"Why didn't you come to our party tonight? Your friends were there. I haven't seen you at Slug in ages."

"Because I have work." I picked up *Catcher.*

"Lame. It's Friday. You can SparkNotes that shit."

"I'm actually trying to do well in this class."

"Oh, right, because it's English. And you want to get accepted on the French Riviera trip. Miss travel-journalist-in-training. Tough business to crack, but I have faith in you."

"Why are you here?"

"Who sleeps in the other bed?" he asked, ignoring my question.

"Jackie."

"Ah. The blonde who hates me. So how'd you guys land a suite? These are coveted."

"I dunno. We had good numbers in the housing lottery. Seriously, what are you doing here? It's almost midnight." I regretted the question immediately, because I didn't want him to leave.

"I just wanted to talk to you for a minute. Is that okay?"

I nodded, relieved that he wouldn't be leaving. I felt so weak, like his presence had slowed every cell in my body.

"Not in here," I said.

I climbed out of bed, grabbed my bathrobe and led him to the living area. It was small, but we'd managed to squeeze in a couch, one arm-chair, a coffee table, and Pippa's TV.

"Cute robe," he said.

"Stop making fun of everything I'm wearing." I sat down on the couch.

"I said it was cute, Luce."

I felt my face flush. I loved that he was still calling me Luce.

"What is it you want to talk about?" I folded my arms.

He sat on the other end of the couch and took his time observing the walls, which we'd decorated with Bree's old tapestries from boarding school.

"I wanted to say that I've been thinking about you," he said finally, his grass-green eyes landing on mine. "A lot."

"You have?" I was too excited to care that I'd let such a pathetic response slip. He and Diana had finally broken up. I knew it. After his apology at the *Gatsby* party with its flirtatious undertones, I knew he would come back to me.

"I do, Lucy in the Sky with Diamonds."

"But I thought you were with Diana."

"Yes. I suppose I am."

"Oh." My gut tightened, disappointment quickly pooling where the hope had been.

"I fucked it all up. I'm a royal jackass."

"I don't understand what you're trying to say."

He shifted on the couch. He placed his ankle on top of his knee, which was awkward because he wasn't very flexible. He placed it back down on the floor.

"I still have feelings for you, Lucy. I wanted to make it work with Diana but it just isn't working. I miss you."

I miss you. He missed me. He was still with Diana, but he missed me. I relished the words. They were all I had wanted to hear for months.

"But you're still with her. You just said it."

"Graduation is right around the corner." He shrugged. "We may as well wait till then to break up."

"It's not really right around the corner. It's in five months."

"Right." He looked down at the carpet.

"Do whatever you want." I shifted my gaze to the window, to the inky-black sky. There are certain rules you learn to abide by, certain games you learn to play when dealing with guys like Stephen, guys who never want things too easily. I remembered that things worked better between Stephen and me when I gave him something to push against.

"I didn't mean it to come out like that," he said. "I sound like an asshole."

"What else is new?"

"Come *on*, Lucy."

"What? What are you trying to say?"

"I meant that Diana will make my life a living hell if I break up with her now. We have the same group of friends. It's hard to explain."

"No, I get it." I did get it. Parker's friends, some of whom had been my good friends, more or less stopped talking to me after I dumped him the night of spring formal.

"You are so beautiful. It gets me every time I see you." He pinched my chin with his thumb and forefinger.

I knew I should tell him to stop, to get up and leave, but I couldn't. My head felt as heavy as a rock. It felt so good to be close to him again, I could hardly think.

"Are you going out to Bear Mountain next weekend?" he asked. "I'll be there. It'll be mostly dudes. But sophomore girls can come." He grinned.

"Maybe," I said, already filling with excitement. A bunch of Chops guys were staying at a kid named Jared's house near Bear Mountain for a ski-slash-party weekend, and Pippa and Jackie had been talking about going. It suddenly seemed like the best idea.

"Although," I added, remembering Keaton's condo, "I'd rather not hang around your posse of senior girls."

"The senior girls to which you refer will not be in attendance next weekend." Stephen winked. "I would tell you otherwise."

I nodded, a mysterious force lurching low in my gut. Subconscious acknowledgment of self-betrayal, maybe.

"I miss you a lot." Stephen's small green eyes latched to mine.

"I miss you, too." Saying it back was like dipping into a warm bath.

"I don't know exactly what it is, Luce. We just always . . . got each other. Emotionally. And physically." One side of his mouth curved. He slid closer to me on the couch.

I listened to him shit-talk his relationship with Diana a bit longer. He said that he loved her but that he wasn't *in love with her*, that he didn't think he ever had been. I watched him while he spoke. His face possessed that self-assured smugness that people like Jackie loathed, but that for some reason I'd never been able to. I knew he thought I was gullible and easy—it wasn't like I didn't know that. And I *was* both of those things, or at least I'd driven myself to be them. I didn't have to accept what he offered, but I did, because I had known from the moment he opened my bedroom door that night that I was going to let him sleep with me, regardless of the circumstances. There was no way out. I'd imagined this scenario in my head a million times. There wasn't anything I wanted more. I didn't know if I was addicted to the pain or if love *was* pain that you had to push through in order to access something greater, a final result you didn't understand but stored your faith in.

There are girls, like Georgia, who never let stuff like this happen to them. It's only when you do let this stuff happen to you that you realize your morals and actions are not as aligned as you'd hoped. Maybe things would have been different if I hadn't seen CJ and Gabe that day, but I did, and I know what I know. Lust and love erase ethical parameters, and that's just the way it is.

We went back to his house to do it. I couldn't risk the girls coming home, and there was no chance of Diana walking in at Slug—she was away at Keaton's ski condo for the weekend. I changed out of my snowflake pajamas into normal clothes beforehand, his hands already all over me as I undressed and redressed, his beery breath heavy in my ear. We snuck in the side entrance of Slug, since the party was still in full force. His room was messy and smelled like sweat. I watched his face go slack as he slid himself inside me. On top of him, I savored each grunt below me, each hungry thrust, feeling satiated with something for the first time in longer than I could remember. I didn't even come—I was too distracted by the excitement and relief of being with him again. He shut his eyes in bliss and groaned as he came, gripping my hips. There was almost nothing I loved more than watching him get off. I found it so privately empowering, the knowledge that his paramount pleasure was mine alone. It was the same feeling I got when I made it a whole day without food and woke up the next morning to the churning in my gut.

Stephen had to get up early for a meeting with his adviser.

"I'll see you soon." He leaned down to kiss me goodbye, his three-day stubble scratchy against my chin. "And I'll be thinking about you naked all day."

I murmured a goodbye, already miserable that he was leaving.

"Oh and, Luce?" he called from the doorway. "I hate to say this, but maybe use the side staircase when you leave. You know, be stealthy.

Charlie and Wrig are cool, but if Evan sees you, well, the kid has a giant moral compass up his ass."

I nodded, absorbing the implications of what he'd just said but knowing that it would be unfair for me to react. I knew what I was doing. I had conceded to my part in this, and the way I felt now was infinitely better than sitting alone in bed or pretending to have fun at parties or tolerating Topher Rigby's clammy, inexperienced fingers on all the wrong parts of me.

"I'll text you when I get back," he added, before closing the door behind him. He was going out to Bear Mountain later that day to meet Diana and their crew.

I didn't bother trying to go back to sleep after he left—I knew I didn't belong in Stephen's bedroom anymore. On the way out I saw a red bra on the floor that was undoubtedly Diana's. I picked it up and held it inside my coat down the side staircase and out the door until I was far enough from Slug, then threw it in the nearest trash.

24

STEPHEN

I stared at the piece of paper in front of me.

> Thank you for your interest in and application to the University of Virginia School of Law. After careful consideration of your application and all supporting documents, regrettably, we are unable to offer you admission.

I felt the shock of another rejection letter press my chest more heavily this time, because UVA was the last school I would hear from. It followed rejections from Stanford, Harvard, Berkeley, Yale, Penn, and Northwestern, after my initial rejection from Columbia early-decision back in December. The career counselor had told me I was crazy not to apply to safety schools, but screw her. Not only did I receive an A on my thesis "International Regulation in the Financial Services Sector: Systemic Risk and the Search for Precision," but my LSAT scores were in the ninety-fifth percentile, and I deserved Ivy League. It was the *fucking DUI* that was fucking me in the ass.

I ripped the letter into pieces and stood, livid. There wasn't any point in going to a mediocre law school, I reminded myself, but I could've added Wash U or Notre Dame or BU to the list—somewhere one tier down but still top thirty. Regardless, I'd assumed Northwestern would be a shoo-in.

I debated punching the wall, but collapsed back onto my bed instead. I watched the ceiling fan spin around and around and around, circling stale air through the room. I tried to hold my vision to a single moving blade until I grew dizzy. The thought continued to slam the center of my mind: I hadn't gotten into law school. I hadn't gotten into law school, and I was entirely, royally fucked. It was far too late to apply for paralegal jobs; every half-decent law firm had filled those positions months ago.

I picked up my cell and called Luke, a semblance of a plan forming in some crevice of my mind.

"Hi." Luke picked up on the first ring. He probably doesn't receive many phone calls except for Kathleen.

"I've had a change of heart, Luke," I said. "I'm going to wait a year on law school. I need to make some money first. I need a job."

Luke's bond-trading gig was kind of lame, but he'd made decent connections in the financial world, and there were always firms looking for hungry suckers right out of college.

"Huh? I thought you were set on getting a law degree. I know Columbia's out, but what about the other schools? Have you heard back?"

"Not yet," I lied. "But I've realized I have all these fucking student loans from Baird to pay off and I really don't need *more* loans piling up right away. You make decent money, right? Can you talk to your boss, see if he knows anybody hiring? Not at your company, but maybe he has connections. I'm a poli sci major with an econ minor, top of my class. Tell him that."

After we hung up, Luke connected me with his boss, who was very quick on email and responded that he knew someone who knew someone who was desperate for an equity research analyst at a boutique brokerage firm in the financial district, a place called BR3 Group. I sent over my documents, and the CEO, a guy named Doug Richter, called me less than an hour later.

"Those are some impressive LSAT scores, Stephen DeMarco," he said through the phone. "You sure you're not interested in law school?"

"That was my original objective, but I've come to my senses," I lied, still anxious. "At the end of the day I have a mind for finance, and that's where I want to be. I'm an economics minor at Baird. I graduate next month. My GPA is shaping up to be a three point eight."

"Yes, I see," Doug said. "I'm looking at your transcript right here. Smart kid."

"Thank you, sir."

"Why do you want to do equity research?"

"Because I'm curious, I'm mathematically minded, and I'm great with people. And because of money, of course. I'm driven by money, and I know I can make it—for myself and for your firm, Mr. Richter."

"That's exactly what I like to hear, DeMarco. I'll forward your information to my hiring manager. We'll be in touch."

"I do appreciate it, Mr. Richter."

"Please, call me Doug. Take care, DeMarco."

I thanked him and hung up the phone. I hate it when people say *take care*. What does that even mean? Take care of what?

I took a deep breath and tried to stay positive. If I could get this job—or a job like it—I'd be okay. I could work for a year and reapply to law schools—*second-tier* law schools if I had to. Officer Motherfucking Gonzalez wasn't going to stop me from being a lawyer—a dirt-rich lawyer who'd make Luke's trading salary look like a subpar bonus. I didn't *need* a degree from a top-tier institution in order to be successful. Fuck Columbia and Stanford and Harvard and Penn and Northwestern and UVA and all the rich, hypocritical pricks on the admission councils who probably drove their vintage Corvettes drunk twice a week.

I sat on my bed staring at my laptop screen and waited for something to happen—an email offer from the hiring manager at BR3 Group, perhaps. I was still unable to shake my aggravation. I needed a distraction, and I knew exactly what that distraction would be. I took out my phone and texted Lucy.

STEPHEN: What are you doing, pretty girl?

She probably received it right away, but she waited about thirty minutes to answer. Girls always make a point of waiting a certain amount of time to text you back, as if it matters.

LUCY: Just got out of class, meeting with my adviser soon, then library. You?
STEPHEN: Just hanging in my room. Wanna head here first? I miss those sexy little Lucy legs.
LUCY: Fineeee. Give me 20 ☺

Diana had driven to Long Beach to have lunch with her aunt, so it was a perfect afternoon for Lucy time. Lucy and I had started sleeping together on the sly three months earlier. It didn't happen too frequently, because I spent so much time with Diana, but ever since the night it started again, I couldn't stop.

She pushed open my bedroom door half an hour later.

"Can you lock it?" I asked.

She bolted the door, not before rolling her eyes. I stood and picked her up, tossing her weightless body down on the mattress.

"I'm getting sick of using the side staircase," she said while I tried to kiss her. "I feel like a prostitute."

"You're not a prostitute." I lay on the bed next to her, my hand resting on her stomach. Lucy wasn't very good at the whole sporadic, casual-hookup thing—I could tell our dynamic bothered her but also that she wasn't planning on ending things, either. Still, she picked little fights and made constant jabs at me about my continuing to date Diana. Of course it was all *my* fault, even though she understood the terms of our relationship and, one way or another, had accepted them.

"Luce." I tucked a piece of hair behind her ear. "You know it isn't always going to be like this."

"You must think I'm an idiot."

"I do not think you're an idiot."

"And what about your friends? If Evan saw me coming up those stairs—"

"He wouldn't."

"What if he did?"

"I'd make something up. Don't worry about it."

She sighed and blinked at me with her dark blue eyes. No makeup.

"I like it when you don't wear makeup."

"I have a meeting with my adviser in thirty minutes." She pinched my earlobe between her thumb and forefinger.

"Better hurry and get these clothes off you, then." I ran my hands up her inner thighs, over her cropped leggings. "You have the hottest body."

"Stephen. Tell me something honestly."

"Anything."

"You say things won't always be like this, but do you mean it? If you don't, you don't. But I want to know." She bit her lip, waiting.

"I do mean it," I said honestly. There was no way Diana and I were staying together after graduation. We'd discussed it. She was moving back to Milwaukee for a summer internship and then Saint Louis for grad school in the fall, and in truth I can't stand the Midwest—it's full of overly cheery people, ineffectual job markets, and the salaries are comic. "Actually, Luce," I continued, planting light kisses along her neck. "There's a good chance I'll be in New York this summer."

"Why? Columbia?" Her eyes widened. "I thought you didn't get in."

"I didn't. I've actually decided to defer law school for another year and work a job in finance. And most of the companies where I've applied are in New York."

"Wow," she said. "What about the other law schools? Have you heard back?"

"Not yet, but I've already made up my mind. I've just realized that it would be good to get some actual work experience under my belt before I start school again. Plus, I really need to make some money and start paying off my students loans." I'd mentally rehearsed my answer to that question, since everyone would ask.

"That does sound smart, Stephen," she said. Lucy thinks I walk on water.

"Which means," I went on. "That we can hang out this summer. If you're going to be back east, that is."

"Oh, really?" She grinned sardonically. "You know, you say these things, but they're just words. It's easy for you to say them without meaning them."

"Lucy." I sat up and stared at her clothed body stretched out on my bed. I was starting to get annoyed. I remembered the rejection letters and felt the anger bubbling inside my chest again. I fought it down, focusing my attention on the exposed sliver of Lucy's abdomen. "I'm having a graduation party at my house in Bayville on June fourteenth. Just something small, but you should come." I could tell she was trying not to look too excited, but the smile crept through her lips.

"What about Diana?"

"Diana and I are going our separate ways after graduation."

"Interesting." She rolled her eyes again.

"Stop rolling your eyes at me. Things *are* going to change after I graduate. I'm not lying."

"Stop telling me what to do."

"Lucy in the Sky with Diamonds." I placed my knees on either side of her hips and pinned her shoulders to the mattress. This was the way we could be together only in private, and I knew she savored each moment. "I know you want to pick a fight with me right now, but you only have twenty-five minutes until your meeting, and I really hate it when you're in my bed with your clothes on. I've been hard for over half an hour thinking about you coming over. So can you please shut up so that I can fuck you?"

Her eyes went shiny with lust, and she did shut up, and I peeled her clothes off in less than ten seconds. Out of the corner of my eye I saw pieces of the UVA letter poking out of the trash can and I fucked her harder, furious. Doubt and anxiety clouded my head, and I just wanted to fill it up with something else. I grabbed her hair in my hands and she dug the heels of her feet into my back. We often ended up fucking like this—angry. She was almost always angry with me, and this time it was Officer Fucking Gonzalez who'd ignited my fury. Because what if I didn't get the analyst job at BR3 Group, and what if I couldn't get a job at all, and what would I do then? The panic sequestered me, but then the sensation was so perfectly tight, and the pleasure concentrated toward the tip and I wouldn't let it happen, I would follow up with Doug Richter tomorrow and tell him I'd fly to New York the next weekend for an interview if that's what it took, and *God* it felt so good. I'd do anything. *Anything.* I felt full and warm and golden inside Lucy, and my LSAT scores were off the charts, and I would be fine. Fine. Completely, completely fine. I lay back on the bed and let Lucy slide on top of me and oh, the feeling. I felt her pulse on top of me, felt her spine arch under my fingertips and in those last seconds the explosive awareness of what was coming filled every part of my body. I closed my eyes and thought blissfully of nothing, trancelike, the feeling filling me and then emptying out into a hot, heavenly stream, leaving me breathless, until I realized I'd come inside her.

"Fuck," I said. "I didn't pull out."

"Shit," she said, standing and pulling on her clothes. "I'm going to be late for my meeting."

"Told you, you shouldn't have done so much talking."

She flashed me a look.

"Lucy, I'm not trying to be an asshole but can you get Plan B? I'll pay you back."

"Don't worry about it," she said, reaching for the door.

"So you'll get it?" I pressed. "You can't risk this kind of stuff."

"I said I'll get it."

"Thanks, Luce. We're having the Eighties party here tonight. Maybe I'll see you later."

"Maybe."

"What?" I could tell she was pissed, or annoyed, or something.

"Where's Diana? I might as well ask."

"On her way back from Long Beach," I answered flatly.

"Got it."

"I get it," I added. "If you don't want to come tonight."

"I'll try to stop by for a sec." She turned away from me.

"I don't even get a kiss goodbye?"

"I'm really going to be late. See ya," she said, closing the door behind her.

I listened to her trot down the back staircase and waited for the sound of the back door shutting before opening up my laptop to check my email. Still nothing from Doug Richter or anyone at his firm. I gritted my teeth and waited, the anxiety settling back in.

25

LUCY

APRIL 2012

Mr. Levy called me into his office one Friday afternoon in April. Mr. Levy was my adviser, and he also taught Toni Morrison: An Immersion, which I was taking for my cultural diversity credit.

His office was located on the third floor of Foster Hall, the humanities building, north-facing with windows overlooking the San Gabriel mountains.

"Have a seat, Lucy," he said.

I sat down in the hard wooden chair, already feeling a little sore from my sex with Stephen that afternoon. It had been almost two weeks since we'd had sex before that, and I hated that it would probably be a couple more until we did it again. I hated that he had all the control.

"Do you know why I called you in here?" Mr. Levy scratched his salt-and-pepper beard.

My stomach wobbled. I knew I wasn't doing great in the stupid Toni Morrison class, but I didn't think I was actually failing.

"I know my last paper wasn't the best," I said. "I was going to talk to you about it. If I could just have a couple of days to rewrite it—"

"Lucy, Lucy." Mr. Levy held up his hand and smiled. "Your paper was fine! Not the best essay you've written, but that's not why I called you in here."

"Oh."

"Overall you've received excellent grades during your first two years at Baird. Lit theory brought you down a bit, and your Toni Morrison grade will probably fall below your average, but you still have one of the highest GPAs of any English major or minor in your class. You're just above a three point seven."

"That's good news." I tried to smile but my mouth wouldn't move.

"It's *great* news. The English department is thrilled to be able to offer you a spot in Writers on the Riviera next month. You're one of the twelve students accepted. Congratulations, my dear!" Mr. Levy beamed. His chronic enthusiasm could be exhausting.

"Wow." My voice came out scratchy and hoarse.

"The committee *loved* your personal share about wanting to be a travel writer—how you grew up reading the travel sections of your mother's magazines in the bathtub. It was so different! Most students write about a passion for Hemingway or *Gatsby*, you know, something that could be in line with a potential thesis, which is all well and good but gets repetitive. We found yours very refreshing. And I love that you're interested in journalism. Perhaps you could do a piece for *The Lantern* while you're over in France."

I nodded and forced a smile, unable to speak. I avoided mentioning to Mr. Levy that my stint at *The Lantern* was likely over—I hadn't written for the paper in months. I hadn't picked up any assignments since October, come to think of it, and staff writers were expected to contribute at least two stories a month.

"You're happy, I hope?" Mr. Levy probed. "I know you've been excited about the possibility of taking this course. It's an exceptionally phenomenal experience. Robin Murphy is fantastic—I believe you've had class with her, yes? Anyway, I'll give you all the paperwork—just look it over, sign where I've highlighted, and return it to me by the end of the week. Then the department will begin getting flights booked, and, voilà. I'm *thrilled* for you, Lucy. You've worked hard for this."

I remembered my prior passion for Writers on the Riviera, and I did my best to look pleased. The truth was I'd forgotten about the program and the application I'd completed last fall and the fact that the English department informed the accepted students in April. My mind felt like sludge, like a big piece of it had dropped right out from under me, and I couldn't see straight.

"What are the dates again?"

"You'll leave on the fifteenth of May, right after the semester ends, and return the twentieth of June." Mr. Levy smiled again. He never stopped smiling. When I smiled that much, my mouth hurt.

"Do I have time to decide?" I asked. "About going on the trip, I mean."

"Oh, I thought you'd be sold." Mr. Levy's brow creased with confusion.

"I am, I mean—I just have to talk to my parents and run it by them. I'm sure it'll be fine. Thank you. It's a big honor."

"Of course. Run it by your folks and let me know by the end of the week. But Lucy, take my word for it—this is an opportunity you want to take."

I left Foster and walked back toward my dorm the long way, around campus instead of cutting across the quad. I took my phone out and stared at it, remembering the feeling I'd gotten when he'd texted me to come over just a couple of hours earlier—the warm rush to my chest, the excitement blocking all of my other sensations, particularly the in-evitability of *this* sensation, the sad, solitary aftermath of our half an hour in bed together. I wished so badly that he would text me and tell me to come back over. A fresh round of lust welled from deep down, al-most unbearable. I wished everything were different.

But things *would* be different. It was only a matter of time, and I could make it just a couple more months.

June 14. June 14. June 14. The date repeated inside my head—Stephen's graduation party in Long Island, which he'd invited me to, at his *house* in Bayville. No more Diana—just Stephen and me. Back in New York. A fresh start.

It was hot out, and I noticed a couple of freshman girls in bathing suits lying on Adler Quad. I'd been in such a funk lately that I'd almost forgotten summer was coming, but I was suddenly excited. June 14.

But then I remembered Writers on the Riviera in the South of France and my meeting with Mr. Levy that had happened ten minutes ago, and I realized I was supposed to be excited for the trip, even though it fell over the fourteenth of June.

No. I couldn't go to France. I couldn't miss Stephen's party on June 14. I'd go to France another time, on my own agenda.

My dad and CJ would be ecstatic if they knew I'd gotten into

Writers on the Riviera; obviously I couldn't tell them. I'd been rav-
ing about the course for years, and if I said I didn't want to go, they'd
know something was seriously wrong with me.

Walking past Slug, I felt the usual pangs of anxiety. A part of me
wanted to run inside and yell at the top of my lungs: *I HAD SEX WITH
STEPHEN DEMARCO IN THIS HOUSE AN HOUR AGO! I'VE BEEN HAV-
ING SEX WITH STEPHEN DEMARCO IN THIS HOUSE SINCE JANU-
ARY. SOMETIMES WE DO IT AT MY PLACE OR IN HIS CAR OR IN THE
SHOWER IF NO ONE'S HOME, BUT IT'S MOSTLY RIGHT HERE IN HIS
ROOM. DID YA KNOW THAT, DIANA?*

Except I didn't have half the guts to do that and it would only ruin
everything, so I hurried by the house, squinting in the hot sun, wishing
I'd remembered sunglasses. I walked for much longer than I intended.
I walked all the way down Carroll Street, into town, before I turned
around, and it was dusk by the time I got back to Adler, the purple sky
blending into pinks and blues behind the mountain. Showering made
me feel calmer. I put on boxers and a T-shirt and climbed into bed with
my stupid Toni Morrison book *Beloved*. I didn't think Toni Morrison was
anything special, but everyone else seemed to.

A while later I heard the door to the suite open, followed by voices in
the living area. They were back from our friend Ella's birthday dinner.
Ella was a year older, a junior on Jackie's tennis team. I'd used my Toni
Morrison paper as an excuse to get out of the dinner, even though it
wasn't due for another week. I braced myself for conversation. Lately I'd
been wishing I lived in a single. Living with three other people—even
my best friends—was exhausting.

Jackie opened the door to our double, frowning when she saw me.
"*Bed* already? It's not even nine."

"It's the Eighties party!" Pippa delved through Jackie's closet, pulling out options and piling them on the floor. Bree was fidgeting with
the speakers in the other room, and soon Michael Jackson flooded the
suite, erasing any hope of finishing my reading, which I couldn't focus
on anyway.

Jackie grabbed something neon pink from her dresser and looked at
me. "You *are* coming, right?"

Of course Slug was hosting the Eighties party. My stomach twisted into a knot at the thought of walking into that house, seeing him and Diana all over each other and knowing he'd been inside me that afternoon.

"I'm so exhausted," I said lamely. "And I really messed up my last paper. I need to do better on this one."

"Whatever." Jackie looked so annoyed that for a second I thought she was going to hit me. She spun toward the door before jolting back around. "So it's because of Stephen, just to clarify?"

"No—"

"So basically, you just go and fuck him whenever he texts you and then you don't go to his parties so you don't have to see him with his girlfriend?"

"Jackie—"

"Because that's just ridiculous," she continued, teetering in her stance. "Why do you even like him? He's like, a con artist or something. How do you not see that? What's *happened* to you? You're like a different person than you were. All you do is work out and sit around and pretend to do homework and feel sorry for yourself."

She stumbled through the living area and crossed into Bree and Pippa's room.

"She had about six margaritas at dinner." Pippa sat on the edge of my bed.

"It's fine." I closed *Beloved*. I wished I could disappear.

"But you should come, Luce," Pippa said. "It's gonna be fun. I know you hate seeing DeMarco at Slug parties but *fuck* that kid. He's a dick. And his girlfriend is a bitch, and she dresses like a lesbian."

"It's not about him, really. I honestly do have all this work. I'm sorry I'm being lame, Pip."

No way was I telling them about my afternoon at Stephen's. I usually admitted it when I hooked up with him—when I disappeared during a party or wandered into the suite in the morning with knotty hair wearing the previous night's clothes. I'd promised myself I wasn't going to become the kind of girl who lied to her friends about boys—but something about the way Jackie had just looked at me felt worse than usual, and I just couldn't tell them.

Pippa acted disappointed, but she quickly moved on to picking out an outfit, and I could almost feel her exhilaration. She was hooking up with someone new who she "really, really liked," a junior named Nick, and he would be at the party. She was telling me the details of their most recent text conversation, and I half listened.

"I'll close this so you can focus," Pippa said when she was done raiding Jackie's closet.

I pretended to read while I listened to them pregame in the other room. I heard the boys come in; I heard Jackie yell "*Stuuuu!*" and pictured her sinking down onto Stuart's lap on the couch, drunk and thrilled that he was there. Someone was probably cutting up lines on the big mirror. The music switched from Michael Jackson to Pretty Lights, and I heard everyone do a round of shots, and when they left I put on Marilyn's sweater, turned off the lights, and lay in the dark. I stuck my headphones in and turned on Fleetwood Mac. I played "Gypsy" as loud as it would go.

Lightning strikes . . . maybe once, maybe twice.

I closed my eyes and let the darkness consume me. The images all blurred in my mind again: Stephen's emerald eyes locked to mine and CJ's voice reading me bedtime stories and Gabe's hands pressed to CJ's sweat-slicked back and filet mignon lying on the counter and Gabe's lips against mine and the way Stephen fucks me and Mr. Levy's enthusiasm and the trip to France that I would never go on and the smell of Stephen's aftershave and the dip in the back of his neck and his arms around Diana's waist and June 14 and Jackie's judgmental glower and the glittery look in Macy's eyes the night she crashed her car and Georgia and me in matching pajamas and my father kissing CJ over the kitchen sink, her hands held hostage, wet with dish soap. All of it fighting for right and wrong; all of it so unclear that I wanted to laugh at the same time the hot tears rolled down my cheeks in the dark as the next track on the playlist began, and Stevie Nicks sang on.

Tell me lies, tell me sweet little lies.

26

STEPHEN

MAY 2012

I had to decline Diana's invitation to her family's cabin on Lake Winnebago the week after graduation. Doug Richter turned out to be my savior—BR3 Group hired me as an equity research analyst to start May 30, with a salary of $60K. Relatively shitty compensation, but it was a job, and my relief was palpable.

Saying goodbye to Diana was semiawkward, because her parents were right there, and I had to leave for the airport in order to make my flight home.

It was the day after our own graduation, and I'd just finished a picnic lunch on Adler Quad with the Bunns. My dad and siblings had left the night before, so lunch was just the Bunns and me.

"I'm really sorry I can't make it to Winnebago," I was saying to Mrs. Bunn on the grassy quad, the almost-summer sun strong on our faces.

"Oh don't you worry about it, Stephen. We'll miss you but it's just *so* impressive that you've gotten yourself a job, the economy being what it is."

I nodded. People were always blaming everything on the economy. Why's it so hard to get a job? The economy. Where's my holiday bonus? The economy is bad this year. Why am I paying $6 for a container of yogurt? Because of the economy. Why won't my wife suck my dick? The economy sucks.

"Thank you. I sure will miss this one, though." I squeezed Diana lightly on the shoulder. Mrs. Bunn beamed. The woman had always worshipped me.

"Well, I'll let you two say goodbye. Diana, we'll be at the hotel." Mrs.

Bunn gave me a big fat kiss on the cheek and Mr. Bunn shook my hand. I high-fived her younger brothers.

"I can't believe you have to go right this second, Stephen." Diana's expression fell.

"I know. But my flight's at five thirty."

"This all just . . . came to an end so fast, I guess."

"School?"

"School. Graduation. Us." She looked up at me, her eyes caramel saucers.

"I know." I nodded.

"I mean, did we think this through? We've just . . . come so far. Maybe I could try New York."

"Di, you've already been accepted at Wash U in Saint Louis. You're set on getting your master's."

"I know, but I'm sure there are lots of great programs for social work in New York."

"Di, I love the idea, but we've had this conversation. Wash U has one of the best programs in the country, plus you hate New York. You don't even like visiting. Imagine how much you'd hate *living* there."

"But, I just—" Her face collapsed, and I braced myself for the tears. "I just want to be with you. Don't you want to be with me?"

"Of course I want to be with you." It was a half-lie. I reached for her hand, felt her tenseness diminish in my grip. I'm good at reading people. I saw Diana's future in her unplucked eyebrows and knotty hair, in the way she kicked back with the boys with her brazen, wide-mouthed laugh, pretty enough, but oblivious to anything that was wrong with her. It had made her intimidating as a Baird senior; it would make her marginal and even confusing in a city like New York. Diana would move back to the Midwest. She'd get her master's in Saint Louis, and after grad school she'd migrate to another city, like Chicago or perhaps back home to Milwaukee—somewhere west of Cincinnati, close enough to her family. She'd buy $4 pints of locally brewed beer with her social worker's salary and spend her life merely existing on the perimeter of the financial and cultural world, and that would be enough for her.

"I mean, I'm not saying I'm going to move to New York tomorrow,"

Diana continued. "I'm already enrolled in classes at Wash U this fall, and I have my summer internship in Milwaukee starting the first week in June. I'm just saying . . ."

"What?" I stepped in closer toward her.

"I just . . . I love you, Stephen."

"I love you, too, Princess Diana."

"So do you want to try to stay together or what? Just say something." She sounded annoyed suddenly.

"Why are you mad?"

"I'm not. I just think we need to be really honest right now."

"So let's be honest." I took her hands in mine and looked into her wet eyes.

"Maybe we should leave things open-ended and not make any rash decisions, at least for the summer? I'll come visit in August after my internship ends, before I move down to Saint Louis. And then we can reevaluate."

I considered this. It wasn't the worst idea. It would be nice to know that I could see Diana at the end of the summer before saying goodbye forever. Plus, it wasn't like she'd *be* in New York holding me back from anything or anyone. Diana was right; it wasn't *mandatory* to make any final declarations that very second.

"I wouldn't have it any other way," I said, leaning down to kiss her.

Two weeks later I began my job on Liberty Street in downtown New York. I love Manhattan, right down to the pavement, the sheer tonnage of the structures that comprise it. Every scent and noise of the city evokes power and propulsion, the religion of its trade.

BR3 Group's offices were cramped and disorganized. My cubicle was barely that—it was more like a tiny desk with walls, smashed in a row of other cubes just like it. My boss was an overweight forty-something moron named Gary Kubina who'd been made a VP at BR3 Group without having spent a day in graduate school. He had graying temples and a framed Pace University Bachelor of Business

Administration diploma hanging on the wall of his office that made me cringe every time I saw it.

I moved into Luke's spare bedroom in Chelsea in an apartment he also shared with his buddy Geoff. I wasn't too keen on sharing an apartment with my brother; he's really very anal, especially with Kathleen around all the livelong day. But his place was affordable and not a terrible commute from work.

On Friday after my first full week at the office, I got home and ended up drinking a six-pack and watching *Family Guy* by myself. Geoff worked brutal hours for a hedge fund and was never home, and Luke and Kathleen had gone to Bed Bath & Beyond to look at curtain rods—I'm not joking.

I felt lonely as shit, actually. I needed to reconnect with my friends from high school; I hadn't been great at keeping in touch during college. Some of them were coming to my graduation party, but that wasn't for another couple of weeks. I tried calling Carl, but it rang and went to voice mail.

I turned off *Family Guy* and took a shower. I tried whacking off, but my head was all fuzzy from the beers. After toweling off I climbed into bed and took out my phone. I hadn't talked to Lucy since I'd been back in New York, and I realized I didn't even know if she had definitely come back east for the summer. I *had* invited her to my graduation party, which I doubted she'd forgotten. I typed a new text.

> STEPHEN: Luce, you back in New York? Hoping you can still make it to my grad party on the 14th . . . but I don't think I can wait another two weeks to see you. If you're around, dinner this weekend? It's been way too long.

I waited, already imagining Lucy's sexy bare body on top of mine. But she didn't respond all night, and I fell asleep with my phone in my hand. She hadn't replied by the time I woke up the next morning, either. It started to make me a little nervous—and I hated to feel nervous because of Lucy—but I told myself it was only a matter of time before she answered. I knew the way her mind worked; it was led by the mental weight of her emotions. The heart. Lucy had fallen for me; I'd watched her sacrifice so much of herself on my behalf, even though I'd never given her what I knew she wanted.

But that was about to change. It was summer in New York, Baird College was old news, and it was time to reward Lucy for waiting so patiently.

27
LUCY
JUNE 2012

I lay by the Montgomerys' pool on the first day of June, listening to Helen and Lydia gossip about some scandal at Trinity. I wished Helen would leave so I could be alone with Lydia, but despite their clashing personalities she and Lydia had grown even closer over the first two years of college, because Lydia was dating a Trinity golf player and their lives had become intertwined in the NESCAC bubble.

I'd already been back in Long Island for two weeks without a word from Stephen, and despite the ever-widening pit in my stomach, I was channeling all my willpower into not texting him, because if things were really going to change, then *he* needed to be the one to change them. That's what Lydia said, at least, and she was usually sensible about those matters.

I'd pulled every string my parents had to get myself an internship at *Vanity Fair* so that I actually had something to do for the summer, but it didn't start for another three weeks and I was going out of my mind with boredom and frustration, staring at my cell phone as if it might sprout wings and fly.

I almost texted him so many times, the message perfectly crafted, my thumb hovering over the send button. But I willed myself to wait, or to take his silence at face value. He'd said things were going to change. If he hadn't meant it then why would I want to be with a manipulative liar? That was Lydia's argument, and I forced myself to get behind it.

So when my phone chimed that day in June and I looked down to see that the name on the screen read *Stephen*, the relief that flooded my body was so immeasurably wonderful that I felt I had floated up into the air on a pillow of clouds. I relaxed into the Montgomerys' plush poolside chaise and felt an easy smile spread across my cheeks—the kind of smile I'd forgotten because it had been so long.

> STEPHEN: Luce, you back in New York? Hoping you can still make it to my grad party on the 14th . . . but I don't think I can wait another two weeks to see you. If you're around, dinner this weekend? It's been way too long.

My heart fluttered inside my chest with the alleviating knowledge that everything was going to be okay. Stephen hadn't forgotten about inviting me to his grad party. Stephen hadn't forgotten me.

"What are you smiling about?" Helen peered over at me from her chaise.

I showed them the text. One good thing about Helen and Lydia was that they didn't give me a hard time about Stephen the way that Jackie and my friends from Baird did. They didn't know him, and they didn't know all the things that had happened in detail, so it was easy for them to be more forgiving, but still—it was nice to be able to show friends his text messages without receiving looks that were equal in judgment and pity.

"Okay," Helen said, sitting up straighter. "This is positive, but you have to wait at *least* twenty-four hours to respond." She adjusted her Ray-Bans.

"Agree," Lydia said, her mouth full of Lay's potato chips. She'd gained at least ten pounds since the start of college, but it didn't seem to bother her. "And if you do get dinner with him, you *have* to address the past and make sure that your relationship is actually going to evolve going forward. Because if it's not, what's the point?"

"I agree. But why do I have to wait *twenty-four* hours to respond?"

"Because, Lucy," Helen explained using her *I'm in Ivy Society so I know everything* voice. "He's been MIA for, what, a month now? It's just good sense to keep boys on their toes, otherwise he'll think you're desperate."

"I slept with him in secret for four months while he had a girlfriend. I think he's seen my desperate side." I gazed at the Montgomerys' turquoise swimming pool, which glistened in the sun.

"True." Helen lay back on her chaise and examined her manicured nails. "That was sort of pathetic of you."

"But we've all been there, Helen," Lydia said. "Remember when you chased Connor Steadman around for a *year* while he was obsessed with Emily Novak?"

"You don't need any more of those chips," Helen scowled, grabbing the bag from Lydia and taking her own handful. I stared at Helen's flabby upper arms and thought about telling her she didn't need any more chips, either.

"I think our point is," Lydia continued, her expression semiwounded from Helen's harsh comment. "This could be your fresh start with him, Luce. Let him see you for what you really are—a smart, funny, gorgeous, skinny, amazing girl, and not his always-available mistress."

Skinny. I smiled at Lydia, who, like Georgia, like Bree, was unconditionally kind.

"Speaking of skinny." Helen threw the bag of chips onto my lap. "You finish these. I feel like a beluga whale next to you, and I *really* don't need these—I had a bagel for breakfast."

"It was scooped out," Lydia said.

"True." Helen crossed her arms, frowning. Helen is the kind of girl who orders scooped-out bagels and then complains that she's not losing weight. She doesn't understand that you don't get skinny by ordering scooped-out bagels. You order no bagels.

Helen kept at me. "I mean really, Lucy. You've always been thin, but this is slightly horrifying."

"What she means is"—Lydia frowned at Helen—"are you sure you don't have a problem? It's okay if you do. A lot of girls at Amherst have eating issues."

"Oh my God, everyone in Ivy is ano," Helen said. "I've tried the not-eating thing, but I just can't do it. If I skip breakfast and lunch I pound, like, six sandwiches for dinner. Is it the coke, Lucy? Tell me honestly."

"No! I'm not *addicted* to cocaine, Helen. I'll only do it on the weekends."

"But every weekend, right? Like every Friday and Saturday? I'm not *judging* you. I practically do it every weekend at this point. It's like, seeping out the walls at Ivy."

"It's around most weekends, I guess. Although I didn't really go out much last semester," I said honestly, very conscious of Lydia, who had only tried cocaine once that I knew of.

I glanced down at my phone, the rush of Stephen's text message coursing a new wave of excitement through me.

"Don't respond yet," Helen said, watching me.

"Twenty-four hours." I nodded.

I unrolled the bag of Lay's and selected three of the smallest chips, even though my stomach growled from the five ounces of plain yogurt I'd eaten for breakfast hours earlier after my five-mile run, and I wanted to inhale the entire package.

Bailing on France turned out to be the smartest decision I ever made, I thought six days later as I got dressed for dinner with Stephen, even though CJ had threatened to call the school on account of my rejection from Writers on the Riviera (I'd made the mistake of telling her my GPA).

I was in a trance as I blew-dry my hair, thinking about Stephen. I was already imagining our dinner—a busy restaurant, a bottle of red, the flirty, possessive way he'd engage with me. What it would be like to kiss him again. I pictured the details of his face as I slipped into a pale yellow Ella Moss dress—the outfit I'd chosen on Monday when (after twenty-four hours of waiting) I'd texted Stephen back and he'd called me to make dinner plans. I was so excited I'd barely slept all week, and I'd spent the days sunbathing with Lydia by her pool, getting as tan as possible.

Stephen suggested we do dinner near his house in Bayville, because he was going to be home from the city for the weekend anyway, and there was a restaurant he wanted *us* to try. He insisted on picking me up in Cold Spring Harbor, and though I did everything in my power to get CJ out of the house, she refused. I'd told her I was going to dinner with a friend, but CJ always figures everything out.

"The one you liked freshman year? The one you were *involved* with? He's older, isn't he?" She was watching me put on makeup in my bathroom, standing with her arms folded, her blond bob fresh with $500 Serge Normant highlights. The way she spent my dad's money was nauseating.

"He's a little older. Not much."

"Is he the one from *Bayville*?" CJ was always saying that Bayville was absurdly tacky.

"Yes, CJ."

"Jeez, you're so *tan*," she said, staring at me. "Is that just from this week at the Montgomerys'? Did you even wear sunblock?"

The doorbell rang and CJ ran out of the bathroom and down the stairs to answer it before I could finish applying mascara.

I heard CJ answer the door. I pictured her examining Stephen from head to toe. I felt her judgment leaching into my subconscious. Stephen was the anti-Parker, and CJ thought Parker was the reincarnation of Jesus.

I looked in the mirror one more time and decided I looked pretty enough. I was practically sick I was so nervous-excited. My whole body prickled as I skipped downstairs.

Stephen DeMarco is standing in my front doorway, talking to my mother.

"Lucy in the Sky with Diamonds." The words stopped my breath. His demeanor toward me didn't shift in the presence of CJ, which made me smile. She cocked her head at him, sort of glaring.

"It's a nickname I have for Lucy," he explained.

"The Beatles song. I know it." She looked unimpressed.

He looked nice in a white oxford button-down and green shorts that matched his eyes, his face clean-shaven. Unusually preppy for Stephen, but I could tell by the twitch in her cheek that CJ didn't approve—I knew her facial expressions by heart. She was polite anyway, because WASPs are always polite, and even though CJ isn't a born WASP she won't let you forget that she's married to one of the Waspiest ones.

"It's nice to meet you, Stephen." She flashed a white-toothed smile. Dentist-bleached.

I watched them shake hands. His eye contact was excellent, as always.

"You have a beautiful house, Mrs. Albright. I love the limestone." Wow. CJ is obsessed with the fact that our house is limestone.

"Thank you." Her smile was plastic, regardless. I knew she really didn't like him. Whatever.

"Bye, CJ," I said, cutting the encounter before CJ could find another way to elusively reproach Stephen.

"Have fun, guys."

I made sure to avoid eye contact with CJ as she closed the front door. Finally, I was alone with Stephen. He looked at me, with the eyes, and I thought he was going to lean down and kiss me on the cheek, but he didn't. He opened the passenger door for me. He seemed a little nervous, too. Maybe it was because, now that we were outside of Baird's walls, our dynamic was different. He could no longer rely on the private world we'd created inside his bedroom at Slug. We were out in the open again.

"You look really good," he said as he pulled his Ford Explorer out of the driveway.

I suppressed my smile. I couldn't believe I was actually in the car with him, driving down the Long Island Expressway.

He sped west on the highway, windows down. My hair whipped around my face. I felt like I'd escaped from a cage and was soaring free.

"You didn't have to pick me up," I said. "I could've driven to Bayville."

"No sweat. I like driving."

He held the steering wheel with one hand, but he didn't reach for my hand with his idle one. I suddenly wondered if I had misinterpreted this whole evening—maybe Stephen was just trying to be friendly. Maybe he felt bad about what had happened at school and wanted to apologize in person. The thought made me nervous, but then the car slowed to a stop and he turned to smile at me. We were parked in a driveway.

"I have a surprise for you. We're not going to the restaurant for dinner."

"Where are we going?"

"It wouldn't be a surprise if I told you. But we have to make a quick stop here. I forgot something." He opened his door and climbed out of the car. "Come on."

"Where are we?" I squinted in the fading light.

"My house. I have to grab something, but come inside. You can meet my dad."

Meet his dad.

Summer crickets chirped loudly as we tiptoed up the slate steps. The white-shingled house wasn't big, but it was homey. A small foyer led back to the kitchen, where framed family photographs littered the walls in even arrangements. Stacks of overflowing papers piled the countertops. Alphabet magnets and more photographs cluttered the refrigerator. CJ thought it looked messy when people stuck stuff all over their refrigerator, and our own kitchen was sterile, like something out of a catalog. The DeMarcos' kitchen felt lived in.

Stephen's father was rinsing dishes.

"Dad, this is Lucy." Stephen patted his father on the shoulder.

Mr. DeMarco turned off the faucet and grabbed a dish towel before shaking my hand. He looked a lot like Stephen except heavier-set, and not as tall.

"You'll have to excuse me," he said. "I'm a mess, and so is my house."

"I love your house," I offered.

"Well, it's normally in better shape, but my daughter had friends over last night and didn't clean up. That's what my kids do now, trash my house and drink my beer."

"Not me," Stephen said.

"Oh, sure." Mr. DeMarco smiled softly. A golden retriever sprang around his feet. He tossed a piece of raw carrot on the floor, and the dog ground it up with his molars.

"That's Skipper," Mr. DeMarco said when I rubbed the dog's ears. "So you guys are headed out?"

"Yup," Stephen said. "We're going to get some dinner."

"That's fun." When Mr. DeMarco smiled, his eyes glazed over absently.

"I'm going to grab something from the garage. Luce, meet me in the car?"

I nodded. "It was nice to meet you, Mr. DeMarco."

"You too, Lucy."

Outside, the dusky air covered me in a velvety breeze. An afternoon rainstorm had burned off the excess heat, but it was still warm enough that I didn't need a sweater over my dress. I'd forgotten how much I loved June—June is the best month. It's the promise, I think, of what the summer can bring.

Stephen emerged from the garage with a tank of gasoline and two paper bags.

"Okay, what's happening here? Are you going to murder me and burn the evidence?" Being around him made me feel my sense of humor again.

"Goddammit, what gave me away?"

"Tell me the surprise."

"It's a *surprise*. C'mon."

Stephen drove us through town, where the streetlights danced in yellow ribbons on the pavement. We headed toward the water, past a sign marked GOOSE POINT MARINA—PRIVATE. The air was thick and pungent, scented with heavy aromas of motor oil and salt. I followed him out of the car, along the shore, and down to the end of a wide white dock. The moon shimmered over the glossy black water.

A bearded man sat slumped in a dinghy marked *Launch*, reading a book with a flashlight.

"Hey, man." Stephen waved. "Can we get a lift out? Last name's Hardman. It's the center console *Kiss Me Kate*."

"We're going on your boat?" I asked.

"I've told you about Carl's boat, haven't I?" he whispered. "It's practically mine; he never uses it. I've always wanted to take you out on the old girl."

His eyes rested softly on mine. He was so adorable I thought I might burst with affection. Every time another swell of happiness surged through me I reminded myself that I was supposed to hate him for the way he'd treated me, that any self-respecting girl would instinctively loathe him. Except I didn't hate him at all. I loved him, I knew now more than ever, and it wasn't a choice. It was just the truth.

Stephen pressed his palm against the small of my back as the dinghy sped out into the black night of the Long Island Sound, the engine buzzing like a hornet, blasts of warm wind gulping past our faces. His hand was low enough on my back for me to know that this night was about more than him feeling sorry. He hadn't brought me out here to apologize.

The harbormaster dropped us at the mooring, speeding back toward shore in his dinghy. It was dark except for the moon and stars, and quiet except for the water lapping. Stephen and I were completely alone. We had never been this alone.

"Why *Kiss Me Kate*?"

"Carl's grandparents gave him the boat for his middle school graduation—his grandparents live on Centre Island and are crazy loaded—and Carl had a ginormous crush on this girl Ashley who played Kate in *Kiss Me Kate,* the eighth-grade play that year," Stephen explained as he unscrewed the red plastic tub of gasoline and poured it into the tank. "So that's what he named it, to impress her. Kid's a moron."

"So it worked?"

"Absolutely not. He barely knew Ashley, and when she found out about the boat I think she was more freaked out than anything else." Stephen shook his head, chuckling. "Poor Carl."

Stephen put the engine in gear and salt water sprayed my bare legs as the *Kiss Me Kate* zoomed through the sea. The lights of the houses along the shoreline shrank and the stars popped brighter as we made our way farther out into the sound. When he brought the center console to a halt, there were no other boats or moorings in sight. The sky full of stars formed a huge dome around us.

"So, almost birthday girl, what do you think of your surprise?" Stephen scooted close to me on the white leather bench, which was damp with salty spray.

"What?" I couldn't not laugh, my heart dancing inside my chest. My twentieth birthday was in four days, the tenth of June, and I'd barely been thinking it. I was secretly dreading it, hoping it would pass quickly and quietly. "How do you know my birthday?"

"I know lots of things." His eyes scorched mine. "Oh, I almost forgot." He unwrapped the paper bag and pulled out two slices of pizza wrapped in aluminum foil, and a Ziploc bag of weed. "Beats sitting in a restaurant, right?"

"This is incredible." I couldn't stop my smile. "I'm relieved you're not trying to murder me."

"You never know. The night is still young."

He handed me one of the pieces of pizza, which was still warm. I hadn't eaten all day and was too jittery to be hungry, but I forced it down. I didn't want Stephen to think I was one of those girls who didn't eat, even though that's who I'd become. One of those skinny bitches Lydia and I used to shit-talk as we stuffed our faces with chips and *queso* at the food court at the mall. *Queso!* Instead of salsa! Can you imagine?

I hadn't eaten pizza in months, and I'd almost forgotten how good it tasted. I savored each bite of oily cheese and bread and fresh tomato sauce, momentarily forgetting the existence of calories. Stephen opened the bag of weed, and I watched carefully as he rolled a joint. He did it firmly, licking the edge of the milky-white paper before sealing it closed. I'd never been able to roll a decent joint, though Pippa had tried to teach me several times. Stephen's eyes glittered green as he flicked the lighter in one quick motion. The end of the joint burned and coiled.

When he passed it to me I inhaled more than I meant to and that easy, sodden stoned feeling hit me at once. My body felt glued to the cushion seat of the boat.

I looked up at the stars and couldn't take my eyes away. "The stars are so beautiful."

"You know what else is so beautiful?"

I laughed, and when I peeled my eyes down he was staring at me.

"Good one," I said.

"It's only the truth."

I rolled my eyes, radiating inside.

"Lucy in the Sky with Diamonds." He spread his hands out in a panorama across the sky. "Just like you."

I felt paralyzed with bliss. Time had stopped. The pain had been worth it. All of it, for this.

"How's being home?" he asked. "How are things with CJ? She does seem a little prickly. Or maybe she just didn't like me."

"It wasn't you," I lied.

"So things aren't better?"

"Not really. They're fine. The same as usual." I was too stoned to form better answers. I couldn't stop staring at the stars. I wished I knew more about the constellations. Georgia knew basically all of them.

"What about you?" I asked. "Tell me about your job. I didn't even know you'd gotten one."

"Yeah." He paused. "I know we didn't . . . spend much time together before graduation. Things got hectic. I'm sorry about that. But the job was kind of last-minute. It's a trading job at this smaller company downtown."

"That sounds cool."

"It should be okay. I need to make money."

"So you already have an apartment?"

"I moved in with my brother," he said. "But he's *always* with his girl-friend, so I'm either alone or third-wheeling."

"Is that why you came out here for the weekend?"

"Nah. I just wanted to get some fresh air and help my dad plan some stuff for the grad party next weekend. You're coming, right?"

"Stephen," I started, nervous to ignite the conversation Lydia and Helen had insisted was imperative we have, especially now that I was stoned. "We need to talk."

"About what?" He inched closer to me on the leather bench. I kept my eyes forward but could feel his breath on the side of my face.

"The elephant in the room."

"We're not in a room. We're on a boat. Are there still elephants on the boat?"

"Yes, and they are going to sink it."

Stephen laughed wholeheartedly, which warmed the space behind my rib cage.

"Fine, Lucy. Have it your way. Let's talk about what an ass I am."

I knew he would say something defensive; he had to have some sort of plan for how this would all go, how he envisioned *us* proceeding outside the walls of Baird. He wasn't spontaneous, not really, not like I'd thought in the beginning. His impulsiveness was feigned; it masked a deeper set of intentions. I'd spent months thinking about the way he operated, running a fine-tooth comb through the tangled mess of my feelings and his actions and claims. I understood that each of his choices was driven by an objective or a desire. His moves were calcu-lated, slightly impetuous but always weighed against the consequences.

"I know I did a lot of fucked-up shit," he said finally. "A lot."

"Yeah, well. I know I'm not blameless. It was my choice to keep sleep-ing with you. I knew you were with Diana."

"So you're letting me off the hook?"

"What hook? There was never a hook with us."

"Maybe that's true. I've just always been so attracted to you." He sighed, blowing a stream of smoke into the air.

"I know. I was so attracted to you, too. It was ridiculous."

"It was a little ridiculous." He laughed. "I don't know what it is about you. About you and me."

You and me.

"That school is a shit show," he continued. "It wasn't always good for me. I think I had to graduate for my own sanity. I'll miss it like hell, but I couldn't do another year."

"I know what you mean. It's not a lifestyle."

"No way. It's fun as fuck, but, at a certain point . . ."

"It becomes unsustainable."

"Yeah," he said. "It changed me. All the messed-up shit . . . A lot of people probably look back and laugh about their college years and what they did, think of it as this *stuff* they got out of their systems, but I'm not proud of it. It's one of the reasons I wanted to see you. There are things I need to tell you."

I leaned back into the seat, suctioned, feeling too high. I wanted to sober up so I could appreciate this night in all its perfection.

"Yeah?" I laughed. "I'm high. But tell me."

"I'm high, too." He smiled, laughing, his eyes shiny. "But I mean every word of this, okay? For the record. Don't listen to me when I'm drunk, but when I'm stoned I actually make more sense."

"Okay. Tell me."

The *Kiss Me Kate* bobbed in the water. I was so happy I thought my joy might lift me right up out of the seat and fly me over Long Island Sound.

"Lucy." Stephen took my hand in his. "I really liked you. Remember how many times I asked you out when I first met you?"

"I remember. A few times." I smiled, stoned.

"I just . . . I had this relationship with Diana that I *thought* was over, and then it just wasn't. Me going back to her wasn't about you. I want you to know that. We'd just been together for so long. And all my friends and all her friends were always telling us we needed to 'work it out, work it out, work it out,' and I felt like I was *supposed* to work it out with her. I dunno. But I want you to know that we broke up after graduation. For good."

My fingers were getting too hot; I removed my hand from his.

"Luce." I could feel his eyes on me, but I suddenly couldn't bring myself to look at him. I stared ahead at the dark sea. I knew what was going to happen, and in my blazed, paranoid state of mind, the part of me that wasn't overjoyed was afraid. I just needed to not be high.

"I didn't know if I would come tonight," I said. "I almost canceled." It was such a bad lie I wanted to laugh out loud.

"Look at me," he said.

"I can't."

"Look at me."

"Just give me a second."

Stephen took my chin in his hand and turned it to face him. My spine went to hot glue.

"Lucy." His mouth was centimeters from my face. "I miss you, and I really fucking mean that. I'm so sorry about everything. Can we give this another shot? Can you do that?"

There it was. Everything I had wanted to hear, lying on a silver platter. I sensed the hope that would spring back into my system as soon as the weed wore off, the possibilities of the months ahead, the attraction I could surrender to completely without feeling horrible and weak, the happiness I could have.

"Can I tell you the truth, Stephen?" Aside from making me paranoid, pot turns me into someone who needs to tell the whole stupid truth.

"Of course."

"Sleeping with you at school was so hard for me. Sleeping with you and then seeing you with her. It killed me."

"I know."

"Do you?"

"Yes, I do. Because I know you, and I know that you wouldn't have done that unless you really cared about it. About me. But what I'm trying to get you to understand is that I cared about you, too. I *care* about you. I just had the Diana shit to deal with and I'm sorry. I'll keep apologizing if you want me to."

"The Diana shit. That's nice. I'm sure she'd appreciate that."

"Oh, come on. You sound like her, you know."

"Don't downplay your relationship with Diana because you want me." I stood, feeling oddly strong. Like I could say anything and not lose him.

"I'm not. I want you because I want you. It's a separate thing." He stood, too, his eyes locking mine from above. "I think—I've always thought—that I could love you, Lucy. That I could love you more than I ever loved Diana. Maybe our timing has just been fucked."

I froze in my stance, the words branded into the foundation of each emerging thought: *that I could love you . . .*

His eyes were heavy on mine in the darkness. The breeze smelled like weed and brine and gasoline. The physical act of wanting him caused my chest to tilt forward, toward him, a magnetic current pulling me there.

He was a good four or five inches taller than me. I studied the contours of his face in the dark, the way his hair grew in wavy pieces, well below his ears. He was handsome, I could never say he wasn't.

"You need a haircut," I said.

"You in the black bikini at Lake Mead," he started, ignoring me. "The first time we met. Do you know how often I think about that day? I remember you exactly. You had this funny expression on your face, like you thought I must be kidding, trying to talk to you."

Consciousness was pulling me back into myself. With my next exhale the air tilted, and I felt one notch closer to the sober ground.

He stepped forward and kissed me, holding the sides of my face, and as I parted my mouth to let him I let the happiness flood in, too, and I felt whole again.

We had sex on the seat of the *Kiss Me Kate*, because we always had sex, no matter where we were. It was something I loved about him—his relentless attraction to me was absurd and intoxicating.

Afterward I curled my fingers through the hair at the base of his neck, just above the dip, his big palms spread over my bare back. I would've stayed like that forever.

"I got you something for your birthday," he whispered. I slid off him and he reached down beside the seat and handed me the other paper bag.

The brown paper crinkled as I peeled it back. Inside was the Beatles' "Lucy in the Sky with Diamonds" poster, the edges frayed. The purple and orange image was of a girl (Lucy), with long hair morphing into an image of the four Beatles.

"Where did you get this?"

"A flea market in Brooklyn. It's a cool spot; you'd like it. We'll go sometime."

I ran my fingers over the imperfect surface of the poster. I looked up at him, elation filling every inch of me.

"It's perfect. Thank you."

He kissed me again, his hair tickling my cheeks. He pulled me back onto his lap. His body was thick and familiar, but I would never get tired of it. I wanted him even when I had him. Too much wasn't enough. We had sex again, on the seat of the bobbing boat, under the stars, leather and salt and sweat brewing around us in the night.

28

STEPHEN

AUGUST 2012

I'd forgotten that August in Manhattan is sweltering as hell. It felt like a bonfire under my ass at all times; the heat literally rose up through my body. I'm a fairly sweaty person to begin with, but in August in New York in a suit, I may as well be a fucking snowman melting into the sidewalk—and having gone to college in Southern California, that's saying something. The air-conditioning at work was motivation enough to get out of bed in the morning. Luke broke our AC unit and fled to Kathleen's for arctic shelter—the bastard.

When Lucy slept over the other night she didn't complain, but she probably liked the heat wave since she weighs about ten pounds and is always cold. I, on the other hand, had trouble staying hard because I was so goddamn uncomfortable. It was like trying to fuck someone in a sauna. But then I fixed my eyes on Lucy on top of me, and I can always come with Lucy.

She was leaving to go back to Baird soon and was worried we weren't spending enough time together—the quintessential girl worry. But Diana was supposed to arrive this weekend for the visit we'd planned at the beginning of the summer. I hadn't seen her since the day after graduation, and though we weren't technically together, the weekend was already scheduled. We had dinner reservations and her mom had even bought us tickets to see *Wicked* on Broadway—backing out of the Diana weekend was not an option. Plus, I was sort of excited to see her. Despite her disconnect from my new life in New York and the city in general, Diana knew me better than almost anyone; her familiarity was a comfort I missed.

I spun around in my swivel desk chair. Another monotonous Monday in the cubicle. The overcast sky drizzled humid rain outside, which

I couldn't see from my desk but knew from my walk to work that morning. I'm always the moron who forgets an umbrella and has to buy a five-dollar shit one from a Chinese man on the corner. Rain was a good sign, though. I hoped it would break the heat.

I squinted at the half-finished report. Boredom encumbered me. My eyes ached from staring at numbers on the computer screen. I glanced down at my cell. Lucy probably thought I was an asshole after our conversation. It wasn't that I *didn't* want to see her before she left for California. Lucy and Diana and work ran in parallel universes; I simply didn't have enough time for all of them, so I skipped between them, like three treadmills running side by side, giving each what I could when I could. I picked up my office phone. She liked it when I called from work—she said she liked picturing me at a desk in a crisp suit performing grown-up research analyst tasks.

Her voice was scratchy. "Mm hey."

"Were you asleep?"

"I just got up."

"It's past ten."

"So? I'm having coffee in bed."

"Get going, lazy girl. Don't you have *Vanity Fair* today?"

"My internship ended last week, remember? Stop lecturing me."

"What are you wearing?"

"*Stephen.*" Lucy consistently feigned frustration with me, but I knew she liked the honed attention with its sensual nuances. I pictured her in an oversize T-shirt and underwear, her chopstick legs stretched out long under tangled sheets. Her lip dipping into hot coffee.

"Well, sorry for bothering you, Luce. I'll leave you be."

"Mm . . . don't go yet."

"Why? You want something?"

"What are *you* wearing?"

"A suit that is basically soaking wet because of how much I'm sweating." I waited for her laugh, which came earnestly.

"Well, let's do something this weekend. I'll come in on Friday. We can go hear Lydia's boyfriend's band in the West Village."

Lucy was always trying to get me to spend time with her friends, but around them I just felt uncomfortable. Like an outsider who didn't own enough Vineyard Vines.

"The Trinity golf player is in a *band*?"

"Or we can just hang at yours," she sighed. "I'll cook."

"You don't cook."

"Fine, we'll go out."

"Can you come in before Friday? I think I have to work this weekend."

"I'm babysitting all week."

"Babysitting for who?"

"Some friend of a friend of CJ's who's in town for the week. Her kids. I already said I'd do it and I don't have a night off until Friday. You have to work Friday *night*?"

Friday night. Diana would land at six with her neon green L.L.Bean duffel and she would stay until Sunday evening. Two nights. Diana jokes and Diana hair in my drain and Diana cuddles and easy Diana talks and Diana sex.

"Well, yeah," I said. "I have that big report due. I told you."

"Why are you being a dick?"

"I'm not being a dick."

She mumbled something.

"I'll call you later. We'll figure something out. Finish your coffee, sleepyhead." I hung up the phone, pinching my sinuses at the predicament.

I'd genuinely enjoyed Lucy's company all summer. We'd become a sort of couple, oddly enough. She stayed at my place some weeknights after her internship, and most Fridays and Saturdays. We'd have long, lazy weekend dinners followed by hours in bed. Twice I took her out to the beach house in Westhampton, on rare weekends when the occupancy was low.

Lucy and I squabbled so that we could fix it; the fights she picked weren't as dramatic as Diana's, but she liked to pick them so that she could nestle into my lap once they were resolved. Her marred interior required fresh rounds of validation. Our cat-and-mouse game was a routine we'd locked down, and the chemistry ensued.

She was a beautiful thing to have on my arm, everyone thought so, including Lucy. She undoubtedly understood the caliber of her attractiveness, evident in the skimpy clothes she often wore and the pouts she gave waiters after asking too many questions about the menu. Her behavior sometimes reminded me of Kathleen's; it was the universal way of the pretty girl, and I'd started to find it bothersome.

The workday dragged on. Right when I thought I could leave work at a reasonable hour Gary poked his big sweaty face inside my cubicle.

"How's that report coming along, DeMarco? I'll need a copy on my desk before you leave today. Coolio?"

Gary was always saying moronic things like *coolio* and chuckling to himself.

I nodded and flashed him the fakest grin, suppressing the urge to add that it would've been helpful to have known the deadline earlier. Sometimes there's just no fucking point.

The report took me five more hours to finish and when I finally left work at eleven I had two missed calls from Diana. I texted her saying that I would call when I got home. It was still too damn hot to take the subway, so I sprang for a cab. The lights were still on in the Fairway next to my apartment, so I bought a premade lasagna, the frozen kind you heat up. Maybe Luke would be hungry. He'd texted me earlier saying that he would be home that night and not doing Kathleen's laundry for a change. He said he had news.

Unfortunately Kathleen was there when I opened the door; I could smell her perfume before I even stepped into the room—she bathed herself in the stuff. As usual, the apartment felt like a furnace. The love-birds sat side by side on the couch, drinking rosé and watching that movie where Diane Lane wanders around vineyards in Tuscany alone and cries a lot. Luke paused the film when I entered the room, and the two of them looked at me with wild, elated expressions, as if they were on ecstasy at a rave and not sitting on the couch watching a low-rate romantic comedy produced for middle-aged divorced women.

"What?" I muttered. I didn't intend to sound grumpy, but it had been a long motherfucking day and I was not in the mood for some Kathleen spiel about how she'd discovered a recipe for low-fat artichoke dip or had bought Luke a $500 jacket half off.

I'd barely set my briefcase down when Kathleen flung out her skinny little arm, her hand weighed down by something glistening on her finger.

My stomach cramped. *No.*

"We're engaged!" Kathleen squealed. Next to her, Luke beamed like a moron.

I wanted to turn around and run out the door, but I was forced to put on my happy face. "Wow! Kath! Luke!" I leaned down and kissed her on the cheek, nearly gagging on a whiff of perfume in the process. "Congratulations, guys. Tell me how it happened."

Kathleen didn't spare a detail as she swung her dark glossy ponytail from me to Luke. I poured myself a strong drink and stuck the lasagna in the freezer; I was barely hungry anymore in light of this disturbing information. I understand why people get married—I'm not at all against marriage. I plan to get married in five or six years, certainly. What bothered me about Luke and Kathleen, though, was the way they preached their unique *need* for each other, as though they'd both be miserable in their lives if they hadn't happened to meet. Because they "complete each other." The reality is, you just need someone to team up with. Marriage is a business deal, essentially. You save money on things like taxes and health insurance, you obtain a sense of security and social normality, and, of course, every man needs a woman to carry his children. I'll probably just marry whoever I'm dating when I'm twenty-seven or twenty-eight and call it a day—it doesn't really *matter* who the chick is, if you think about it. It's just about taking that next step in your own life. There's no way I'm gonna be some loner who's still single when he's thirty.

I drank my Scotch too quickly as I half listened to Kathleen blabber on and on about how she'd suspected Luke had bought a ring for numerous reasons, but how he'd done such a great job of hiding it from her, and how earlier that day when they'd met for lunch at her favorite restaurant, he'd knelt down and popped the question.

"He was going to do it over the weekend, but he said he couldn't wait!" Kathleen shrieked, gazing down at the rock on her left hand.

Luke interlocked his fingers in hers and smiled. "It's true. I couldn't wait another second. *And* I wanted to make Monday better."

I thought I might hurl. I excused myself to my room and said that I had to make a phone call, which was true.

I turned the fan in my room on full blast and stuck my face directly in front of the cold air. Diana picked up on the second ring.

"Finally."

The familiar sound of her voice was a comfort. I glanced at my alarm clock. It was almost midnight, which meant it was just before eleven in Milwaukee. Diana was probably reading in bed. I pictured her in boxers and an old tee, a glass of seltzer fizzing on her bedside table.

"Sorry. Work was busy as hell and then right when I got home Luke told me he's engaged."

"Whoa. To Kathleen?"

"Who else."

"That's crazy."

"I know."

"You don't sound happy."

"I'm just tired."

"I'm sorry. Bad day at work?"

"Not the best. How are you? I'm excited to see you."

"I'm good . . ." Her voice was distracted, far away.

"Glad to hear."

"Stephen, I actually need to talk to you about something."

"Okay, what's up?" I walked over to the only window in my bedroom and pulled the curtain aside, before remembering that the view was a close-up of the adjacent building's brick wall. Fucking New York City.

Diana was quiet on the other end of the line.

"Di?" I pressed. It was late. I didn't have time for an emotional, drawn-out conversation. I just wanted to pass out.

"I can't come visit you this weekend. I canceled my trip."

Built-up frustration from the day teetered. "Um, *why*? What's wrong?"

"I'm seeing someone here."

"Excuse me?" Anger seized me, instant fumes rising, pummeling up through my chest.

"Look, Stephen, we're not together. I know you've been sleeping with Lucy all summer, so don't act so surprised that I haven't been sitting around waiting for you. We never said we wouldn't hook up with other people." She sounded frank. The lack of sensitivity in her voice was concerning.

"Yes, we never said we wouldn't *hook up* with other people. Not *date* other people."

"You're so full of shit. I know you're dating Lucy. Katie Kopecky saw you two out in the Hamptons together."

"Who the fuck is Katie Kopecky?"

"She was in our *class* at Baird, Stephen. She's from New York City."

"Diana," I exhaled, trying to wrap my head around the words coming out of her mouth. "Lucy is about to go back to school. It was just a summer fling."

"Whatever. I honestly don't care what you do anymore, that's what I'm trying to say. I've developed feelings for someone else. It just sort of happened. He's not like you."

"And what the fuck is *that* supposed to mean?"

"It means I can trust him." I had never heard her voice sound so icy.

Half of me cared. Half of me genuinely cared, genuinely wanted to hang up the phone, take a cab to LaGuardia, buy a one-way ticket to Milwaukee, show up at Diana's door and fight for her. I thought of her knobby knees, her pale breasts, and the way she looked at me with that distinct expression that was at once girlish and sexy. She was mine, and I didn't want some dirty bastard getting his hands on her.

But I didn't know her new address in Milwaukee, and I was suddenly so exhausted that my eyelids drooped as though they held weights. I had to be up for work in six hours. And this other half of me really didn't care at all. It was just about winning, and you have to pick your battles.

I had always known Diana and I weren't going to end up together. I knew this. So maybe it would be better this way. Diana and I would end for good, Lucy would go back to school in a week, and I would find a new girlfriend, a New York girlfriend. Something new.

"Hello?! Stephen?!" Diana's voice blared through the phone, jolting me awake.

My eyes popped open. "Sorry. I'm just thinking."

"I'm so sorry to do this." She sighed, and I could tell she had started crying.

"It's okay. I understand."

"You could take some of the responsibility for this, you know."

"I do. I understand that my actions have impacted the dynamic of our relationship."

"You sound like a robot. Do you even care?"

"*Yes*, I care. Jesus Christ, Diana, you're the one who's ending this. You think it's easy for me to hear that you're with another guy? Have a little heart."

"I'm so sorry, Stephen," she whispered, the octaves of her voice breaking. Then she really started bawling. The never-ending river of tears.

"Just tell me who he is."

"You don't know him." She sniffled.

"No shit. I don't know anyone in Milwaukee."

"We met through mutual friends. He's also in social work. He's actually going to be in my same program at Wash U."

"So you're moving to Saint Louis together?"

"Not *together* exactly, but . . ." Her voice trailed.

"Well, that's wonderful."

"Oh, Stephen." Diana broke into what sounded like a fresh batch of tears.

The image of some random dude fucking Diana partly outraged me and partly turned me on. I felt a flutter in between my legs.

"I need to go to sleep, Diana."

"Stephen, please. Please don't hate me."

"I don't hate you. I'm just tired. It's past midnight here and I have to be up at six."

"You can still have the *Wicked* tickets, of course. My mom is going to send them to you."

"That's ridiculous. Just tell her to return them."

"They're nonrefundable, is the thing."

"Oh."

"I'll always love you, Stephen," she said before we hung up. "I just can't be with you anymore."

I texted Lucy that I would be available to spend the weekend with her after all, and that I'd managed to snag two tickets to the Saturday matinee of *Wicked*, if she'd like to join me. I plugged in my phone to charge overnight. I still had a boner, so I summoned the energy to jerk off—it always calms me down.

29

LUCY

AUGUST 2012

CJ made pizza the night before I left to go back to Baird; I caught the scent of fresh dough and tomatoes when I walked in the door. I'd just come from spending my last weekend in the city with Stephen. My eyes were red from crying on the train.

"You have *got* to finish packing, Lucy," CJ nagged. "I told you to pack before you went to the city. We're leaving for LaGuardia at six tomorrow morning."

"I know. I'm almost done."

I sat down in one of the beige armchairs in the family room off the kitchen and took in the familiar details of my house: the peach-colored curtains, the sterling silver–framed photographs, the white cashmere blanket that CJ had carefully folded over the back of the couch. I closed my eyes, which burned with exhaustion. Traces of the morning's hangover tugged at the back of my brain.

CJ kissed me on the forehead and scrunched up her nose. "You smell like a distillery. Have you been drinking?"

"Not since last night."

"Well, I'm making pizza for dinner. The best hangover cure."

Stephen and I had eaten at Motorino the night before, after he'd taken me to see *Wicked* on Broadway, and pizza was the last thing I wanted, but I felt too guilty to object. There was something about the way CJ stood there in her frayed Berkeley T-shirt and leggings that made me feel sad and sorry about something. Charcoal circles ringed her clear blue eyes. Grayish roots were visible at the top of her short blond hair. I studied her face; fine lines seemed to smudge what were once sharper, more defined features. My parents still had their good looks but had begun to appear weather-beaten, like old jackets marked by winters of wear.

My dad turned on a Frank Sinatra album, and an old rendition of "The Way You Look Tonight" filled the room.

"Oh, Ben!" CJ smiled at my father. "Our wedding song."

"Did you know you have the most wonderful mother in the world?" he asked, wrapping his arms around CJ's middle. She laughed and they slipped into a slow dance, looping and twirling around the kitchen. At six two, my dad stood a good eight inches taller than her. During the slow parts he leaned down and buried his face in her hair.

I thought I might be sick. I wished Georgia were home, but she'd already gone back to Yale.

The pizza tasted strange, like the tomato sauce was sour. CJ has never been the greatest cook. She peppered me with questions about Baird and the classes I'd signed up for for junior year, and who was going abroad and who wasn't.

After dinner I was finally able to escape to my bedroom, where I replayed the conversation in my head. We'd been lying in his bed that morning drinking coffee, our legs tangled underneath the covers.

"Sooo, I'll see you over Thanksgiving?" I knew I was being the quintessential clingy girl, trying to pinpoint our status. Stephen was being aggravatingly cryptic.

"I'll be here. You have an open invitation to my bedroom."

I struggled with this response, trying to mold it into some sort of definitive answer.

"So are you going to hook up with other people?" *God*, I was pathetic.

"That's not going to be my focus," he said, staring at something on his laptop.

"What does that mean?"

"It means exactly what it's supposed to mean."

"So you might hook up with other people." I felt like a bothersome child. When he wasn't all over me, I sometimes got the feeling that all I did was irritate him.

"Lucy." He closed his computer and finally looked at me. "You're going back to school. You have two more whole years at Baird. And I'm in New York now."

"I know." My stomach plummeted. I hated that I was making him tell me something that I didn't even want to hear.

"So I don't know what's going to happen," he said. "Let's just try to talk when we can. If I get to a point where I'm feeling like I want to hook up with someone, I'll tell you."

"Gee, thanks."

"*What? What* is it that you want me to say, Lucy? Look, I have to concentrate on work and applying to law school. I'm sorry, but that has to be my priority. I'm really not looking to go hook up with a bunch of random chicks in the city. But I also can't exactly get myself into a long-distance relationship right now."

I didn't know what I'd expected him to say. The back of my throat felt tight and I sensed the tears collecting behind my eyes. I hated how fragile and powerless I felt. I really, really didn't want him to see me cry.

"Lucy . . ." he pulled me onto his chest and ran his hands through my hair, the way he did. *Two more whole years at Baird.* I couldn't stand it. I didn't want two more years at Baird, not if it meant losing Stephen.

We had sex one more time, in the late-morning light; I swallowed back tears as he pulled my face toward his, our foreheads pressed together, our eyes locked, as in sync as we had been. It lasted longer than it ever had—a drawn-out, sad goodbye.

Afterward I'd packed up my weekend bag and he'd walked me to the subway, a noticeable nip in the late August air. Fall loomed. The end of summer always pierced something inside me—but this year was worse than ever. Stephen wrapped his arms around me outside the Twenty-Third Street station.

"That was amazing sex before," he whispered in my ear.

I nodded, unable to speak. I felt like I might break into a million pieces if he let go of me.

"I'll miss you," he'd said. "Maybe I can try to come visit one weekend, if work isn't too crazy. Otherwise, see you over Thanksgiving?"

I'd nodded, a little hope filling the pit in my stomach.

"Luce. Say something."

"Goodbye," was all I could manage. I kissed him and ran down into the subway, swiping my MetroCard and barging through the turnstile before I could change my mind and do something crazy, like run back up the stairs and chase him down the street and tell him I wanted to drop out of college and stay in New York.

In my bedroom I forced myself to finish packing and then took a long shower, wrapped myself in a towel, and collapsed onto my bed. I sank back into my pillows and pictured Stephen's face: his intense, inquisitive green eyes, small but distinct mouth, the scruff on the side of his jawline. I already missed him more than I could stand. The summer had been a dream, from that first night on the *Kiss Me Kate*. I couldn't believe it was over. I would be back in California the next day. Pippa and Bree were spending first semester abroad in Madrid, so Jackie and I were moving into a house off campus—just the two of us. I wished I'd had the foresight to apply for study abroad programs, but I hadn't. I supposed I'd been counting on Writers on the Riviera in France to be my overseas experience, or perhaps it was really just the lack of motivation that was progressively becoming an issue.

I wanted to feel remotely excited about going back to school, about unpacking and decorating the house with Jackie, but I was dreading all of it. I could already feel the bleakness of the months ahead, the same bleakness I'd felt before the summer. The perfect, perfect summer, that was over.

I heard CJ's distinct footsteps move up the staircase and prayed she wouldn't come into my room, but the door creaked open. Hickory followed, leaping up onto my bed and curling into a blond ball. I rubbed her velvety ears. CJ placed a mug of steaming chai on my bedside table, the scents of vanilla and cardamom filling my nostrils.

"Thanks, Seej."

"I thought maybe you wanted some help packing." She didn't sound as wound up as before, thank God.

"I'm almost finished, but thanks."

"Are you excited to go back?" She sat down on the edge of my bed and smoothed my forehead with her hand, which was warm from the chai.

"I guess."

"How was the weekend? Did you say goodbye to him?"

"Yeah." My voice cracked, the tears pooling in my eyes. There is something about hearing my mother's voice when I'm sad that will always make me cry. "I don't know what's going to happen."

"Luce." She brushed my cheek with her warm hand. "It's going to be okay. I know it's the hardest thing, but you have to trust that whatever is meant to be, will be. Time tells all."

"I know."

"Is there something you're not telling me?"

"What do you mean?"

"I don't know. I just—I got a vibe from him, if I'm being honest. I can't put my finger on it but—"

"CJ. Stop."

"He doesn't appreciate you."

"You don't even know him. You met him for five seconds."

"It's a gut feeling."

"Please just leave my room, CJ."

"Sass." CJ's voice was hushed but clear. "I'm always here, you know. If you ever need me. I'm right here."

I kept my eyes shut; hot, silent tears slid down my cheeks. CJ squeezed my hand, and when I finally opened my eyes, I saw that she was crying, too.

"What happened to us?" she whispered, her voice cracking, and I tried to answer but when I opened my mouth no sound came out, and CJ was already standing and straightening my duvet, and then she left the room.

30

STEPHEN

OCTOBER 2012

With Lucy back at school again, and Diana and me definitely over, and work sucking the life out of me, and the days growing shorter, I was beginning to go a little crazy. What I needed was to find a new girlfriend, and fast.

New York was a stale, lonely place to be single, especially with the onset of winter and my law school applications looming. So when Carl invited me to a dinner party that his girlfriend was throwing because they needed more dudes, I gladly obliged.

Carl's girlfriend was this tall, horsey-looking chick named Beth. I thought she was a wet blanket and wasn't sure exactly what Carl saw in her, but then again Carl looks like Seth Rogen and he doesn't have good game when it comes to women.

I guessed that Beth didn't have very many friends, because the party was small. We gathered around the living room with our drinks like a bunch of boring yuppies while Beth passed around hors d'oeuvres.

When the doorbell rang, Beth rushed to answer it with such urgency you'd think the president was arriving. A girl entered the room, her cheeks flushed pink from the cold. I heard her apologize to Beth for being late and mutter something about a crazy cabdriver. I watched the girl take off her coat and set down the bottle of wine she'd brought. Someone handed her a glass from one of the already-opened bottles.

"This is Alice," Carl said when she sat down next to me in the only free chair. "She knows Beth through . . . work?"

Alice nodded, and I shook her hand while inconspicuously checking her out. She was cute. Her blond hair was clearly highlighted—I could see the darker roots coming in—and it fell in silky wisps past her shoulders. She was wearing lots of eye makeup and a fitted maroon dress, her substantial tits spilling out of the low-cut scoop neck.

Beth had cooked some kind of Middle Eastern meal, and Alice munched on a bite of lentil salad. I poured myself more wine and turned toward her, and we proceeded to have the standard introductory conversation that everyone in New York in their twenties has upon meeting someone new. What do you do for work? Where are you from? Where did you go to school? Who are our mutual friends?

After several minutes I learned that Alice also graduated last May and had started her job in insurance in June. She grew up outside of Pittsburgh and had attended Penn State, where she was very involved in her sorority. She had one of those bubbly personalities that rose quickly to the surface and allowed for easy, sinuous repartee. I identified her as a girly girl from a close-knit family who'd lived an uncomplicated life thus far, and saw New York City as one long opportunity to turn her narrative into a Nora Ephron film. I could tell she was the type of girl who'd get upset if she got a little muddy.

The bottle of wine in front of us was soon empty, and Alice asked if I wanted more. I said that I did, and she rose to go retrieve the bottle she brought from the kitchen, which gave me the chance to fully check her out. She was shorter than I'd realized, and flaunted incredible curves. As she strolled back toward the table with a bottle of pinot noir, I found myself imagining her naked.

I was starting to feel a little uneasy at the party for some reason, and I was glad when she sat back down next to me. I watched as she expertly uncorked the bottle.

"I was a waitress for, like, three summers," she explained. Her smile revealed a large set of gums and teeth that protruded a bit, but it didn't take away from her cuteness.

"So where do you live in the city?" I prodded.

She poured the wine, and it *clunk clunk clunked* through the nose of the bottle and into our glasses.

"Hell's Kitchen, with my best friend from college." *Just north of me, one stop on the express train. Easy.*

"I live on Twenty-Second and Eighth," I offered. "Not far."

She asked about my job and my plans to go to law school. There was an underlying desperation in her voice when she asked me questions, as though it were an interview of sorts. I recognized the subtle, frazzled notes behind the intention: the girl who wants a boyfriend.

Our conversation flowed throughout dinner. Alice was easy to flirt with in the way that she was receptive to all my jokes, tossing her head back in a throaty, committed laugh.

We hit a couple of midtown bars after Beth's—the kind of bars where the atmosphere is sterile and depressing and they play Journey songs. Carl kept buying tequila shots, and after taking back three or four I lost track of Alice, my mind a dull blur of booze; a thick, sour taste coated my tongue. By the end of the evening she was nowhere in sight, and Carl and Beth offered to drop me off in a cab on their way home.

I was so fucked up I nearly forgot to ask Beth for Alice's number. The thought flung back into my head just after I'd exited the taxi, and I rapped on the closed window. I had no idea what time it was but Twenty-Second Street was coated in the tangible gray haze that heralds dawn. Carl and I had done some coke earlier in Beth's bathroom, and then again in the bathroom of one of the bars.

Beth lowered the window and an annoyed expression swept over her horsey face.

"Beth, I forgot to ask you, would it be cool if I called Alice sometime and asked her out? Is she seeing anyone?"

Beth shrugged. "You can call her. She doesn't have a boyfriend."

"Great. Could I get her number?"

"Sure, hang on—"

"I'll text it to you, bud," Carl interrupted, as if to say, get the hell out of here so I can go home and fuck my ugly girlfriend.

I watched the cab speed down the street, the red brake lights flashing in the smoky grayness before the car hooked a right onto Twenty-Third Street. I was still wired from the coke but felt the anxious onset of depression creeping in at the back of my brain, like a leech.

Inside, I drew the curtains closed and climbed into bed. My mind reeled in the darkness. It was unclear if I slept, but if I did, it was only for an hour or two. When full morning light crept through the drapes I rose to make coffee, my mind static and blank.

I drank a whole pot and watched *Family Guy* until midmorning when Carl texted me Alice's number and I felt my juices start to flow again. I decided to give her a call. Calling a girl is always more genuine than texting her, at least in the beginning. Alice answered on the third ring and seemed excited to hear from me. We chatted a bit about the previous evening. I asked if she wanted to have dinner, and we set up a date for that Wednesday.

I hung up the phone and it occurred to me that I had never before been on a real date. Sure, I'd been out to eat with girls I'd dated in high school and college, but I'd never been to dinner with a girl where the notion of sex afterward wasn't a guarantee. I would certainly be required to pay for the meal, and I'd need to pick the restaurant.

I felt slightly unsettled Wednesday evening when I left work and caught the subway up to Hell's Kitchen, to an Italian restaurant near Alice's apartment where I'd made a reservation. The sun hung low in the sky, the October air crisp.

I arrived a few minutes before seven and ordered a Scotch and soda at the bar while I waited. Alice pranced in ten minutes later, looking made-up and polished in a slinky black top that revealed a sliver of pale cleavage.

"You look gorgeous." I kissed her on the cheek.

"Thanks. Sorry I'm a little late. I live four blocks away, so I have no excuse."

As the waitress led us to our table, I was suddenly filled with the stimulating realization that I could be anyone. For the first time in over four years I was not a physical representation of my past; there was no neon highlighter underscoring my faults and blunders. Alice had no predetermined sentiments about my personality or the choices I'd made.

The waitress came over and recited a long list of specials. We ordered a bottle of pinot noir.

"I'm glad you suggested dinner." Alice smiled and shifted in her seat across from me, providing a more generous view of the tops of her buoyant breasts.

There was a fixed anxiety behind her eyes that told me she counted on this night going well. She didn't seem like the type of girl who dated much, not because she wasn't cute but because she belonged to the heavily populated category of desperate, available, decently attractive twentysomething girls in New York City. These girls weren't beautiful enough to be picky; they were always on the hunt for a decent man, always semiconscious of their ticking biological clocks.

Alice ordered the salmon, I the T-bone steak. I watched her adjust her bra strap (black) and wondered how long it had been since she'd had sex.

We fell into a fluid conversation, especially once the wine hit. Alice's voice spun off in a girly twang, her long fingernails were painted a shiny plum color, and shimmery makeup smudged the skin around her eyes. She was the kind of girl Diana and her friends at Baird would have hated—they would have called her "tacky" or "basic." But I felt almost enchanted watching her from across the table. She was just what I needed—something fresh.

We ordered cocktails after the wine was finished, and I could tell she was getting drunk, the way her cheeks had reddened. She leaned forward on the table, pressing her weight into one elbow. I watched a piece of her yellow hair slip into the crevice of her chest.

"I'm having fun, Stephen."

"I find you incredibly attractive, Alice." I watched her exterior collapse from the compliment, an uncontainable smile breaking over her face.

When the check appeared on the table, I pulled out my wallet.

"Are you sure? We can split it." It was a half offer, the way she glanced away when she said it.

"No way. This is a date." I grinned, conscious of the fact that I was checking her boxes.

"You're sweet."

"I'm going to use the bathroom."

"Sure," she said. "I'll meet you outside."

I signed the bill and found the restroom. I pissed in a stall and did a small key bump of coke. Just a nudge; I felt tired from all the red wine and the dealer Carl had hooked me up with really did provide a nice product. My phone vibrated in my pocket and the screen flashed a text from Lucy.

LUCY: How are you?

Fuck. I'd been bad about keeping up with Lucy since the summer. It wasn't something I'd necessarily intended, but staying in touch with her was beginning to feel like a chore. I tapped out a quick response.

STEPHEN: Hey you. I've been meaning to call you. Work has been nuts. Let's catch up this weekend.

I found Alice outside, smoking a cigarette. She looked sophisticated standing in heels, tendrils of smoke curling around her face, and I was suddenly overcome by the same feeling I'd had the night I first realized I liked Diana in our freshman dorm at Charlie's pregame. I'd felt the impulse and the right to claim her—the simple clarity that she should be mine.

"My place isn't far from here," Alice said, stubbing her cig.

"Really?" I feigned surprise, though I had chosen the restaurant for that very reason. "I'll walk you home, then."

A short few blocks and we stood in front of her building on the corner of Fifty-Fourth and Ninth. I hovered over her; she was super short, even in heels.

"I would invite you in, but, you know . . ."

"But . . . ?"

"I barely know you." She giggled, shifting her weight onto one hip.

"Alice, I get it. You're not that kind of girl. If you did let me up, I'd sort of be forced to think less of you."

"Exactly."

"Can I kiss you?" I stared into her dark eyes and slowly leaned down, pressing my mouth against hers. Her lips were soft and supple. I pushed her against the side of the apartment building with some force.

"I should go." Alice pulled away after several minutes of intense kissing, her face flushed.

"Damn. Okay."

"Thanks for dinner, Stephen."

"You're welcome, Alice in Wonderland. Go get some sleep. I'll talk to you soon."

"Alice in Wonderland?"

"I dunno," I laughed. "It fits you." On the assumption that the date would go well, I'd come prepared with a nickname.

"You're too funny." She laughed easily, leaning in for another kiss.

The next morning I googled the address to Alice's office and had flowers delivered to her desk. I chose red carnations, which she'd mentioned at dinner she loved and had carried as a bridesmaid in her cousin's wedding the month before.

I included a note, too, which the congenial Pakistani man at Ava's Florist Shop transcribed for me: *Alice in Wonderland, I hope you have a wonderful day. I'm very glad I met you.*

31

LUCY

FEBRUARY 2013

There was a disturbance in the air. It had been there for months, but now it was almost tangible, like a film coating the atmosphere.

"You're coming," Jackie said.

I watched a blade of sunshine slide across the wooden floor of the small house Jackie and I shared on Carroll Street. I sat on the couch and listened to her get dressed, a tight knot fixed at the base of my stomach. A resistance. Something imperceptible dragged at me, a line hooked below. My mind wouldn't move.

"I don't really want to day drink."

"It's Sunday funday. Ella got a keg." Jackie always wanted to hang out at Ella's now.

I stared at my hands.

"Lucy, come *on*. I need you. Do I look like I've been crying?" She smoothed her tangled hair away from her face.

Jackie had been crying all morning. Stuart had broken up with her a month earlier. Their fighting had gotten worse; he'd finally declared he wanted to experience college without a girlfriend, but we all knew the truth. Jackie had taken Stuart for granted, and he was tired of putting up with her Jackieness.

"A little. Splash some water on your face."

"I just miss him so much." She sank down next to me and pressed her forehead to my shoulder. "If I have to see him today, with that sophomore *whore* . . ."

"Natalie?"

"*Don't* say her name."

I brushed fresh tears off her cheeks with my thumbs and looked into her desolate blue eyes. "Well, if there's anyone who's an intimidating ex-girlfriend, it's you. Plus, why would she be there? She's not going to show up at a random senior party."

"That's true I guess." Jackie let out an exasperated sigh. "But if she does show up with him, I'm making Ella kick her out."

"Jack, don't worry. They're not going to show up at a party together. Natalie is nothing to him, I promise."

"How do you know?"

"Because. I've been that girl, remember?"

"Lucy, don't do that to yourself. Stephen did care about you in his own fucked-up way. He's just a *dick*. He screws over every girl. Come on. Let's just go *try* to have a fun day."

"I wanted to go to yoga today."

Jackie rolled her eyes. "You go to yoga *every* day."

"Well, *also* I have calculus homework."

"Why are you taking calculus?"

"Math credit."

"Oh, that reminds me. You know how I'm taking Intro to Shake-speare? For my humanities credit?"

"Yeah."

"Well, our teacher went on maternity leave, so Mr. Levy is taking over starting tomorrow. What do you think of him?"

"Mr. Levy? I had him for Intro to Shakespeare, actually. He's nice. He's my adviser."

"I know, that's why I'm asking. Didn't you say he's kind of a drag?"

"He's not a drag, he's just dorky. But nice. You'll like him. And I still have all my notes from Intro to Shakespeare, if you want them."

"That'd be great." Jackie looked at her watch. "All right. Let's not waste the day. You never do anything anymore."

"You don't have to criticize me because I don't feel like getting drunk all the time."

"I'm not criticizing you for not getting drunk. It's called *socializing*."

"I socialize."

"Not anymore. You didn't even come out last night."

"*Fine*. I'll go."

"Yay! We'll have fun, I promise."

"Let me get dressed."

"Please don't take forever."

"I *won't*."

I changed into jeans and a black tank top, swiped some mascara on my lashes and let my hair down. It was getting longer. I examined myself in the full-length mirror on the back of my bedroom door. I hadn't done cardio in three days *and* had accidentally eaten some of Jackie's pizza the night before. The tank top made my arms look big. I changed into a white shirt with sleeves.

Jackie hadn't moved from the couch, where she sat aimlessly staring into space. She was a mess, and rightfully so. I on the other hand had expended my pity card after finding out about Stephen's new girlfriend in November. It had been more than three months since I was destroyed by someone I'd barely been dating. It had been one month since Jackie was dumped by her devoted boyfriend of two and a half years. Jackie was the one who got to be sad. My grief was unmerited, and I did my best to keep it private.

Her name was Alice Edwards, and she had straightened, fake-blond hair, Facebook told me a few days after I found out. Pippa had wedged between Jackie and me on the couch and flipped her laptop open, claiming that the only logical thing to do was properly stalk the girl. Jackie and Pip agreed that her gums were uncharacteristically large and her roots outrageous. Even Stuart got involved (*Luce, she's nothing; you're a babe*). In one photo they were standing in some bar holding fruity cocktails. She was wearing a sleeveless dress that revealed arms on the flabby side. At least I was skinnier than her—it was the only thing that made me feel remotely better.

Finding out about Alice had been my own fault, when I'd stupidly called Stephen over Thanksgiving break. I didn't even know what I wanted to say. His phone calls had mostly stopped by that point, which should've told me everything, but instead his silence was undermined by the parting words I'd memorized: *Maybe I can try to come visit one weekend, if work isn't too crazy. Otherwise I'll see you over Thanksgiving?*

My hands shook as I dialed his number. I asked him if he wanted to get dinner on Long Island.

"I'd love to catch up, but I should tell you that I've started seeing someone, Luce. I'm sorry. I guess this was bound to happen, us seeing other people." His voice contained its usual, unaffected charm. I went into my bathroom and threw up, coffee and skim milk—it was all that was in my stomach.

The fall had been a blur of angst, a collection of anxious days. I had not been seeing other people, even though I should've been. I just couldn't bring myself to do it. Some boys hit on me, but none of them were Stephen DeMarco.

"Do I look okay?" Jackie asked. She hadn't bothered adjusting her appearance. Her bun was uneven and last night's makeup was slightly smudged from crying. As usual, she looked like a gorgeous wreck.

"You look beautiful."

We walked to Ella's. It was a balmy afternoon, and people were out in the backyard, music blaring through the speakers. The sun sat high in the cloudless sky, splitting down in sharp rays. Jackie filled two red Solo cups with foamy beer and handed one to me. Beer was almost never worth the calories. I already wanted to leave.

Ella came over and attacked Jackie with a ferocious hug, like they hadn't seen each other in years. It sort of bothered me how close Jackie and Ella had become. The captain of the girls' tennis team, Ella was boisterous and loud; around her I could never seem to get a word in. She only paid attention to me because I was Jackie's roommate.

"Lucy!" Ella said, turning to hug me with half the enthusiasm. "Guess what? Billy's here. He asked if you were coming."

"*Yes*." Jackie nudged me. "Do it."

My eyes scanned the party for Billy Boyd, a junior and the head of BORP—Baird Outdoor Recreation Project—a student-run group that led outdoor trips, like camping in Joshua Tree and surfing in Santa Barbara and climbing Mount Baldy. Billy was friends with Ella because Ella was friends with everyone heavily involved in Baird extracurriculars, and I knew via Ella via Jackie that he had a crush on me. We'd made out drunkenly at the Eighties party in January.

"He's super cute," I said.

"And I hear he's a great kisser," Ella continued. "Is it true?"

"Really great." I nodded, even though all I remembered about my kiss with Billy was being momentarily pressed against him under a black light on the dance floor of Kappa Sig before running home and gorging on microwaved popcorn. Melted butter.

"We should do shots," Ella decided, so Jackie and I followed her inside. We found Pippa and Bree in the kitchen, and Ella poured tequila into five glasses while she confessed an explicit, embarrassing sex story involving her boyfriend, a senior named Owen. I lost track of the story but everyone was laughing, and Ella was pouring another round, so I downed my shot, the sour liquor burning my throat, my eyes watering. I must've been wincing, because Ella handed me a lime wedge.

"Are you okay?" she asked, the pitch of her voice rising as though she were speaking to a toddler.

"Fine," I answered, deciding once and for all that I was not a fan of Ella, with her showy stories and thick ponytail and motherly concern.

"Bree. Pipsqueak. Tell me *all* about Madrid." Ella quickly returned her attention back to the group. "You haven't properly filled me in."

I already knew every detail of Bree's and Pippa's semester abroad in Spain, so I slipped back outside when Pippa started recounting her romance with Eduardo, a thirty-year-old Spanish businessman with a bottomless bank account and a second home on the coast of Majorca. He took Pippa and Bree to Ibiza on his yacht.

Out in the backyard the sun blazed down stronger than before. I leaned against the side of the garage under the partial shade of a palm tree, feeling tipsy.

Someone's arm brushed the side of mine, and I turned to see Billy next to me. I remembered the first time I'd laid eyes on Billy Boyd, freshman fall. He was in my orientation group the first week of school. I remember we were all sitting in a big circle and I kept staring at his particularly silky head of hair and wondering what type of shampoo he used. He had big hazel eyes and I remember thinking he was attractive but that there was also an edge to him that I liked—something in the mud caked around his ankles and his dented Nalgene covered in bumper stickers. When it was his turn to recite his earliest memory he smiled, and dimples appeared on both cheeks.

I knew I should've gone for someone like Billy back then instead of whoring myself out to Stephen. I supposed now was my chance.

"Hey, Lucy." His voice was faintly raspy. I wondered if he was sick. A wave of light brown hair fell across his forehead, and he pushed it back with his whole hand. His coppery eyes matched his Carhartt shorts.

I returned the smile and tried to appear more sober than I felt. "Long time no see, Billy Boyd."

"Seriously. Where have you been hiding?"

I had been a drunk psycho the night I made out with Billy—definitely drunker than he'd been.

I shrugged. "I haven't gone out much this semester."

"How come?"

"I don't know. I can't drink the way I used to be able to. My hangovers have gone from zero to sixty."

"Ripping shots in the middle of the day?" Billy laughed. "Definitely seems like you can't drink."

"So you were spying on me?"

"I saw you in the kitchen," he said. "You're hard to miss, you know."

"Well, Ella offered us those shots. And she's the host." I hated the way I sounded trying to flirt.

"Oh. Then you had to take them." Billy pulled sunglasses down over his eyes. I watched his Adam's apple slide back and forth as he took a long sip of beer. I couldn't remember ever noticing Stephen's Adam's apple. I wondered if he had one. Did all men have them? I would look it up later.

Billy drained his cup and drew his eyes back to mine. Billy was very good-looking, but he didn't make me feel anything.

"I didn't know you were friends with Ella," I said dumbly, not knowing what to contribute to the conversation.

"Ella's been on a few trips with us."

"With BORP, you mean?"

"Yeah. You should come sometime. We're going up to Death Valley in a couple of weeks. Have you been?"

"No. I hear it's beautiful."

"It's incredible. I'll send you the info, if you want. Bring your friends. Change it up."

"Maybe I will. I've been meaning to do more of that stuff."

"'That stuff' as in, camping and mountain biking?"

"Right—have adventures, et cetera. Get off the beaten path. Actually taking advantage of living in California, instead of just ripping tequila shots." I had a feeling I'd said the right thing, and my shoulders relaxed a little. Billy laughed.

"I wasn't making fun of you," he said.

"Remember when we made out?" I asked. The second shot of tequila was rushing to my head, and I felt a boost of confidence. I hadn't flirted in ages, and Billy had a crush on me.

"*Duh*. It was only the highlight of my life." He smiled. Those *dimples*. Maybe I could feel something.

"Ha-ha."

"But in all seriousness, yes, I do remember when we made out, Lucy."

"Me, too."

"You do? I had you pinned as blackout."

"Well, I wasn't sober. But neither were you."

"I was more sober than you."

"I need a refill." I shook my empty cup. I was sick of beer, but if I was going to keep drinking, I might as well get drunk.

"The keg's done," Billy said. "But I'm about to head back to my place and my roommates just got some thirties. Do you and your friends wanna come over and play flip cup?"

"Now?"

"Why not?"

"Sure. I'll go find them."

"What's your number?" Billy pulled his iPhone out of his pocket.

"I'll text you the address," he said after I told him, grinning as he turned to leave.

I wandered inside, where I was supposed to be looking for my friends and inviting them to Billy's. A clock was ticking in the corner of whatever room I was in. *Tick-tock, tick-tock*; slow and very fast at once, something uncanny. My flirtatious mood flipped and there was that sudden disturbance in the air again; it was almost everywhere now, as unmistakable as the smell of smoke. I suddenly had the overwhelming feeling that something terrible was going to happen, or had already happened, or was in the process of happening. Heat was rising off my chest, and whatever attraction and hope I'd just seen in Billy had already evaporated, leaving me right where I'd been before, drowning in the center of my own misery. *Why why why* did this continue to happen to me? I felt so awful and afraid. I couldn't stand to be at the party another second.

I stumbled out the front door while no one was looking. When I got home my phone buzzed, a text from a random number that I took to be Billy's.

See you soon, address is 404 Hutchins.

Wrigley's old house. My insides lurched. I deleted Billy's message. I knew I would never text him. I would never go on his camping trip to Death Valley or have the delirious desire to be close to him. Two shots of tequila and a beer on an empty stomach told me what I already knew: I just wanted Stephen. In every crevice of my head and heart I wanted Stephen. It didn't matter that I couldn't have him. There was still no room for anybody else.

I found the rest of Jackie's pizza in our fridge and ate every bit of it cold, right out of the box. I shoved two whole sleeves of Ritz crackers down my throat.

Afterward there were crumbs all over me and I went into the bathroom to take a shower. I took off my clothes and inspected myself in the mirror. I felt so stuffed with food it repulsed me; my stomach protruded like a pregnant person's, a hard ball of beer and carbs and cheese.

I turned on the shower and waited for the sound of the rushing water to drain out all other noise, just in case Jackie came home. I locked the door and knelt in front of the toilet, bending my head over the bowl, tears spilling out of my eyes. I stuck my middle and index finger down my throat, scratching at the back until I felt the vomit rise up. I did it over and over again, until I was puking only liquid, sure all the food was out.

In the shower I turned the water as hot as it would go and rubbed my skin with soap until it squeaked clean. I brushed my teeth and climbed underneath my sheets. It was only seven o'clock. I took my vibrator from the zippered pouch in my nightstand and placed it between my legs. I closed my eyes and turned up the speed. I thought of Stephen, imagined me fucking Stephen and how good it felt for him to fuck me, because that was the only way I could come. Coming was maybe the only escape from my contaminated mind, and I did it again and again and again, until I was raw and had exhausted everything.

When I finally slept I slipped into a vivid dream. It was the middle of July and I was aboard the *Kiss Me Kate* with Stephen, the sun baking our skin, the salt water spraying us as the boat zipped around Long Island Sound. He wore a navy-blue captain's hat like the one from Lake Mead, and he picked me up and I wrapped my legs around his waist, my fingers resting in the crook at the base of his neck. We kissed and kissed, sliding down onto the seat of the *Kiss Me Kate*. I felt his tongue inside my mouth; I tasted him, warm and real.

I woke up in a cold sweat in the dark. The clock read midnight. When I remembered my pain I felt it all over again. I saw Stephen's translucent green eyes and heard his voice on the boat the summer before: *I want you because I want you. It's a separate thing. I think—I've always thought— that I could love you, Lucy. . . .*

But he didn't love me. It hadn't happened. Something wasn't enough. I spiraled into myself, desperately racking my brain for what had gone wrong, for what I could've done to make things different.

Jackie didn't come home all night, and she wasn't in the house the next morning when I left for calculus. She finally walked through the door midafternoon, long after classes had been dismissed for the day.

"Where have you been? I called you." I sat at the coffee table in front of my impossible calculus homework, still depleted and hungover from the day before.

When she didn't answer, I stood and walked into the kitchen where she was filling a glass with tap water.

"Where did you sleep last night? Did you hook up with someone?"

Jackie's mouth formed a thin, tight line, and her eyes narrowed, settling starkly on my own.

"Jackie, what's going on?" I folded my arms, my stomach pooling with dread, because even though I didn't have a clue why she was upset, I didn't think I could deal with a conflict that turned Jackie's eyes that angry. "Is this about yesterday? I'm sorry I left the party early, I'd just had too much to drink and I wasn't feeling it with Bill—"

"Intro to Shakespeare was interesting," she interrupted, placing her glass down on the counter.

"Huh?"

"Mr. Levy is a nice man."

"Yeah. He is."

"Uh-huh. I happened to mention that my roommate Lucy Albright is one of his advisees, and guess what he told me?" she asked, but then I already knew.

"Jackie—"

"He speaks very highly of you," she went on. "He told me you're one of his smartest advisees. He also told me how disappointed he was that you *decided not to go to France*, given that you were one of the few students *admitted* into Writers on the Riviera."

"Jackie—" The tears caught in my throat; they stung my eyes as I fought them back.

"You told me—you told everyone—that you didn't get accepted and that you were *devastated*. You want to tell me what the hell is going on?"

There were tears in Jackie's eyes, too, and I loathed myself.

"Jackie, I'm sorry I didn't tell you the truth. I'm really sorry. I just—" I searched my numb head for a defense or an explanation but my mind had gone static, and accessing a deeper well of myself was suddenly impossible. I could think of nothing but the fact that I didn't regret giving up France for my summer with Stephen, not for a second, and even though I wished I could, and knew I'd be a better person if I did, I couldn't help but feel an unshakable pride in the certainty of my decision, and there was a weak comfort in that.

"It's not just that you lied." Jackie swiped a tear off her cheek. "You were *dying* to go on that trip. I don't understand, Lucy. What's *happened* to you? You're like a shred of yourself. I don't know who you are anymore. I really don't." The anger in her voice had softened into an unbearable sadness.

Jackie was looking at me the same way Lydia had looked at me in my bedroom in Cold Spring Harbor over Christmas when she'd caught me googling the calories in creamed spinach. Tears had glazed Lydia's soft brown eyes.

"You're just so thin."

"I haven't lost any more weight," I'd said, which was true.

"I know, you've looked like this for a couple of years now," Lydia said, her familiar face afraid. "But you're so thin that it scares me sometimes. You don't look okay." I'd seen Lydia cry a million times, but somehow this was worse than any of them. "I mean, don't get me wrong, Lucy. You're stunning. You're the skinniest, prettiest person I know. But are you okay? I mean, *really*, are you okay?"

I hadn't known what to say to that and I hadn't wanted to lie to Lydia, my oldest friend, my other sister, and I had been hungry for so long that I'd grown accustomed to the light-headed feeling that followed me around and seemed to stunt my thought processes.

It was the same feeling I felt in front of Jackie now. Was that it? Was I simply so hungry that I'd stopped being able to think? I tried to speak, but an invisible weight crushed my sternum. I wanted desperately to explain, but there was no explanation. I was a tin can, hollow and empty of everything.

32
STEPHEN
FEBRUARY 2013

"Happy birthday, Stephen!" My father opened the front door and greeted me with a slow, strained hug.

"This is Alice," I said. "Alice, this is my father."

Alice beamed and they shook hands.

The twenty-fourth of February, my twenty-third birthday, fell on a drab winter Sunday, and I decided it was the right time to bring Alice home to meet my family. Luke and Sadie would both be there, and of course Kathleen had to come along. Alice and I had been out the night before and had gotten a later train out of the city than planned. My head still throbbed from the hangover.

Luke and Kath were already at the house; since they went to bed at ten o'clock on Saturday nights they'd gotten an earlier start. I glanced at myself in the hallway mirror and noticed how tired I looked. Tea-colored bags hung under my eyes and I hadn't shaved since Wednesday.

"*Love* your earrings, Alice," Kathleen said, sucking up as usual. Kathleen looked sensational in a pair of fitted dark jeans and a silky orange top. Her legs were slim but strong, and I couldn't help but discreetly check out her perfect ass. I couldn't believe she was going to be my sister-in-law. Was it inappropriate to half detest/half want to fuck your sister-in-law?

Luke stood there like a moronic yuppie in khakis and a belt with fucking *whales* on it. He never used to wear preppy shit like that, but now Kathleen dresses him up like her own little Ken doll. I'd become extremely tired of being around them and their increasingly obnoxious

J.Crew-ness. I was very much looking forward to August, when our lease would be up and the lovebirds would finally get their own place.

"Birthday boy!" Kathleen exclaimed, practically strangling me. "Congratulations! I heard about NYU."

I smiled, thanking her, gagging on her perfume. I'd been accepted to New York University's School of Law the week before, which was a relief, though it wasn't Harvard or Yale or Columbia. Officer Gonzalez and the DUI still had me fucked, because the Ivy Leagues had proven out of the question. But it wasn't the worst way to get fucked, and I had to be grateful. I thought of the silken red hair, skin white as snow, the motionless eyes, too much blood, the sound of *Zombie zombie zombie* . . . and I was grateful. I was.

"If you want my *real* opinion, I was actually surprised you decided to stick with the law school route," Kathleen continued, even though no one had asked for her real opinion. "I figured once you started the finance job you'd just sort of stay on that track. Like Luke."

Ha. Because I'm exactly like your run-of-the-mill, risk-averse fiancé Luke.

"Well, that was never my plan," I tried to say as nicely as possible, because Luke was watching. "My plan was always to reapply to law schools. The only reason I took a year off to work was to make some extra money, pay off some of my loans." *And I wouldn't stay in that fucking middlebrow financial research shit job for another month if it meant a lifetime of on-the-sly blow jobs from you, Kathleen.*

"That makes total sense, Stevie," Kathleen beamed. "And it's so cool to see you following your passion. We're all *so* proud of you."

Luckily Luke changed the subject when he asked Alice how her job was going, and I escaped to the kitchen to help my father with the drinks.

"Congratulations on NYU, Stephen. I'm proud of you."

"Thanks, Dad."

"Did Mom call you today?" He glanced at me, and I noticed the deep lines that ran across his forehead, and a sharper crinkling around his eyes. His hair was grayer and thinner than I remembered. He looked exhausted and old as fuck.

"No," I said, stirring a gin and tonic for Alice while Skipper started to lick the backs of my legs. "Go *on*, Skip."

"Well, it's not even six." My dad sighed. "Maybe she'll call tonight."

"I wouldn't count on it."

"Oh, Stephen." His expression fell, even sadder. "I'm sorry."

"About what?"

"About Mom."

"Dad, it's fine. Honestly." I wished he could understand that I didn't give a flying fuck whether my nutcase mother called on my birthday.

"Are you sure you don't want to talk to someone? A therapist? You know Luke talked to somebody a couple years ago."

"*No*, Dad. Mom's been forgetting my birthday for years. It's old fucking news. It doesn't upset me."

"All right."

"Honestly, I'm fine."

"Okay. Well, Alice seems like a nice girl."

"She's really great." I stirred my Scotch and soda, roused at the idea of a cold alcoholic beverage.

"I'm glad you're happy." He pulled a rack of garlic bread from the oven, and the familiar buttery scent filled my nostrils.

"Thanks, Dad."

"How's Diana doing? Have you two kept in touch?"

"Diana? I dunno. I haven't talked to her in months."

"Oh."

"I should give her a call," I added, because my father stood there expressionless.

"And what about Lucy? The girl you were seeing last summer?"

"What about her? It was casual."

"But you liked her, right?"

"Dad," I sighed. "Lucy is still at Baird. She's only a junior. It was never that serious. Why don't we go into the living room and you can get to know *Alice*? My girlfriend? That's why I brought her here."

"Okay." My dad licked a spray of lime juice off his thumb. "Help me carry these drinks."

We all sat around the living room. The last rays of sunlight spilled in through the bay windows and illuminated the stone-colored upholstery on the couch and chairs, the glass bowl full of fake apples, the intricate colored pattern of the Oriental rug.

"So, Alice, Stephen tells me you work in insurance." My father took a sip of his Stella. I could almost feel the effort in his question, the exertion he was putting into being cheerful.

Alice nodded and they proceeded to have the world's most boring conversation about insurance, with occasional chime-ins from Kathleen and Luke, who were nestled against each other on the love seat like mating lions. Sadie didn't say much, because what have you got to say about insurance when you're sixteen?

"I'm *thrilled* I got a job in New York and not Pittsburgh," Alice went on. "Pittsburgh is just such a buzzkill in comparison. I mean, the city of Pittsburgh itself is fine. It's clean. But in terms of job prospects and restaurants and *everything*, there's nowhere like NYC." Alice was always pronouncing the acronym like that: *en-why-cee*. It was something I found obnoxious and certainly called attention to the fact that she was not a native New Yorker.

"So did you interview for a lot of jobs in Pittsburgh?" my father asked.

"Some. But I knew I wanted to be in New York, so I interviewed everywhere I could. And when I got the job offer in *en-why-cee*, I accepted right away. Even though I didn't—don't—necessarily want to be in insurance forever." Alice folded her hands on her lap, her face a little flushed. She seemed nervous.

"You know, I was in the same boat right after I graduated," Kathleen said, flipping her shiny raven hair to one side. "I thought I wanted to be a teacher, but then I got a job in consulting, and I was so freaked out about being unemployed that I took it. And now I've been in consulting for four years and *love* it. And then I have other friends who worked in one industry for a year, then switched to something totally different. So my two cents? Don't worry about your first job impacting your entire career. You never know where your path will lead you."

"Yeah, I've heard people say that." Alice gave Kathleen an appreciative smile. "That's a real relief to hear."

I took a large swig of Scotch. The problem facing Kathleen and Alice, and even Luke, is that they aren't career-oriented people. They've never known what they want professionally, so they've weaved together convenient stories in order to make themselves feel better about their lack of incentive. Someone holds a gun to your head and asks you: "What do you want to be?" *That*, the first thing that pops into your head, is what you should be. You just fucking make it happen. If you want to be a doctor, go to med school. You want to be a writer, write something. If you want to make movies, go to Hollywood and pursue it. Just *do* something about it. Like me, for instance. From a young age I knew I wanted to be a lawyer. So I'm *pursuing* it. It's not a walk in the park. I haven't loved spending the last two autumns slaving away on law school applications and working a bullshit humdrum job in the interim; it wasn't *easy* receiving rejection letters, repeatedly. But it's all been a sacrifice for a larger ambition, an ultimate purpose.

Kathleen's theory was extremely typical. She *thought* she was happy working in consulting, but in reality her happiness was constructed based off the life she'd built around that job. Did she stroll to work each morning with passion and hunger and dynamite firing up inside her bones? Hell no. Kathleen probably sat at her desk every day and, like most people in the world, waited for it to end. It's always boggled my mind the way the majority of individuals sit around waiting for the next event, then the next—subconsciously waiting for life to end. Kathleen would get off work and march off to some spin class where she'd sweat for an hour, probably enjoying it much less than she'd admit. After spinning she'd trod on home, where she'd make dinner and drink wine with Luke, and *that* was why she believed she was happy—the day's result, that two- to three-hour period when she could relax and spend time with her fiancé was, in her diluted mind, worth the insipid sludge of the rest of her life. Kathleen should've been a teacher, if that was her real ambition. Or maybe she has no ambition, which is the reality for a lot of people. Alice included, as far as I can tell.

"Shall we eat?" my father asked finally, standing. "I'm not the world's best cook but I did make Stephen's favorite, roast beef. Tofu for Kath, of course."

Of course Kathleen was a fucking vegetarian.

"Aw, John, you didn't have to! I'm totally fine with all the sides."

"I'm glad to do it. You're my future daughter-in-law, after all."

Kathleen smiled her gorgeous face off.

We went into the kitchen to serve plates and I mixed another round of drinks for Alice and me, pouring extra Scotch in mine.

My father disappeared into the bathroom, probably to self-medicate.

The others seated themselves in the dining room, leaving Alice and me alone in the kitchen. She nuzzled up to me.

"How am I doing?" she asked.

"You're doing great."

"Your dad is sweet."

"He's a wreck."

"Huh?"

"He's very depressed." I was feeling honest and a little drunk already. Hair of the dog.

"Do you think so?"

"Yes."

"'Cause of your mom?"

"Mainly. But let's talk about it later."

"I'm sorry, baby." She pressed her face into my chest and I felt the heat of her breath through my cotton shirt, suddenly turned on.

After dinner there was chocolate cake with buttercream frosting from my favorite bakery in Bayville. Everybody sang "Happy Birthday" while I sat there like a smiling fool.

We helped with the dishes, and then Luke, Kathleen, Alice, and I caught the 9:36 train back into Manhattan. When we reached Penn Station, the lovebirds took a cab over to Kathleen's place in Murray Hill, and Alice and I rode the subway two stops down to my apartment.

We walked in the door and I barely said a word before I peeled off her clothes, threw her down on my bed, and fucked her hard from behind. I'd been waiting to do it all night. Afterward Alice curled up next to me, her arm resting across my chest as my orgasm subsided, my heart still hammering inside my chest.

"I love you," I said out loud, into the darkness. It felt like the right time to say such a thing. She said it back, like I knew she would, and I wondered for a moment what it would be like to say it and *feel* it, the way Luke and Kathleen did, and Alice did, and Diana did. Even if it was just some fake feeling, I still wanted to know how "I love you" could be more than just spoken words to someone whose company you enjoyed a decent amount. The question rattled around inside my head, a curiosity that wouldn't quite settle as I closed my eyes and waited for sleep.

33

LUCY

JUNE 2013

"Daddy and I are leaving in ten minutes," CJ shouted over the running water. She was scrubbing dishes at the kitchen sink so hard they squeaked.

"'Kay." I poured myself a cup of coffee, unresponsive at seven thirty in the morning, especially since I'd hardly slept. Georgia was steeping a bag of Earl Grey because she was one of those people who drank *tea* instead of coffee.

"And we won't be home until later tonight," CJ blabbered on, like I cared. "I'm teaching back-to-back privates all morning and then thank *God* I have a cut and color in the city—Serge is going to keel over when he sees these roots—then a late lunch with your grandmother, and then Daddy and I have Rand Petersen's birthday party at Cove Club—"

"Mr. Petersen?" I interrupted, inadvertently spitting coffee back into my mug.

"Yes. Remember Macy's father? Oh, poor Macy." CJ's face fell. "She'd be your age now. Such a sweet girl. That long red hair of hers, I'll never forget it."

"You're going to Mr. Petersen's birthday party?" I couldn't help myself now. I felt Georgia's eyes on me.

"Yes. They've invited a lot of people. Should be a great time as long as I can get Serge to deal with my hair first." CJ shouted upstairs, "Ben, hurry *up*! You're going to miss the train!"

"Do you think their older kids will be there? Eleanor and Gabe?"

"I would assume? It's their father's sixtieth. Gabe lives in the city—I know that much—so I'd be shocked if he missed it. Not sure where Eleanor is these days."

"How do you know where Gabe lives?" I couldn't stop. A pit of doom pooled in my stomach.

"Well, I ran into Teresa Petersen the other day and she was telling me all about Gabe's job. He does marketing for *BuzzFeed*. Isn't that cool?"

"Is Dad going with you tonight?"

"To the party? Yes. What's the big *deal*, Lucy?" CJ held my gaze for a moment, and I scanned her aqua eyes for the slightest trace of guilt or suspicion, but there was nothing. She sighed and began wiping down the countertops, and it was evident that to CJ, her secret was still very much a secret.

"Luce." CJ wrung the sponge. "You know you have your appointment with Dr. Wattenbarger today at three fifteen."

"His name is Dr. *Wattenbarger*?"

"Yes. He's very well regarded."

"That sounds like a made-up name."

"It's not a made-up name, Sass," CJ said. "It's German."

"Why do you still call me that?" I glared at my mother on instinct; I watched something in her expression retract.

"I think Wattenbarger is an Austrian name," Georgia said.

"How do you even *know* that, Georgia?" I turned toward my sister.

"Look," CJ started. "Regardless of his heritage, Barry Wattenbarger is a brilliant doctor. Maura Littlehale said he singlehandedly saved her marriage. So, Lucy, you know you have to leave work early today, right? You told them? You have to get a train out of the city by at least two, and I was thinking Georgia could drive you."

"Why? I can drive myself."

"I don't know if it's a good idea, you driving in this condition."

"Are you joking?"

"Mom," Georgia said from the kitchen table. She was still in her pajamas and blinked her sleepy blue eyes, identical to CJ's in color. "Let Lucy drive herself to her own therapy appointment. Jesus."

It was one of the most defiant things I'd ever heard Georgia say to CJ, or maybe to anyone.

"Fine," CJ said, surrendering easily to Georgia as always. She turned off the faucet and removed her gloves. "You can take Dad's Audi. Keys are in the visor. Georgia, if you need a car—"

"I don't. Thanks, Mom."

"Ugh, these *roots*." CJ pulled at her hair in the hallway mirror. I wanted to smack her. "All right. Bye. Love you guys. I'm on my cell if you need me." She yelled for my dad again; he shouted goodbye, and I heard them shut the front door.

"So CJ told you." I watched Georgia pour herself a bowl of Honey Bunches of Oats. Whole milk.

"About your appointment?" Georgia asked. "I overheard her talking to Dad. Who cares? I know plenty of kids at Yale who see therapists."

"I'm seeing a psychiatrist."

"The only difference is that psychiatrists can prescribe medicine."

"Yeah. CJ thinks I'm crazy."

"No, she doesn't. You're not crazy."

"Whatever. Maybe I am."

I went upstairs and got dressed—a boring navy-blue shift dress for my "internship," which was volunteering for Bill de Blasio's campaign for mayor, because I'd been too sullen and out of it to remember to apply for summer internships, and my dad knew de Blasio from Columbia. It was a last-minute "favor"—I hated being the kind of girl who was eligible to receive last-minute favors. I should've worked for something and I didn't. Georgia was going to Switzerland for July and half of August on a competitive medical internship.

I gathered my workbag together and watched CJ's Lexus worm down the driveway and out of sight.

What happened next was involuntary. It wasn't because CJ had made me an appointment with a psychiatrist—I hadn't objected to that, because I knew I was losing it. I'd left Baird at the end of junior year a complete mess. Mr. Levy said I had no choice but to renounce my journalism minor—I still had several all-college requirements to fulfill, and along with the remaining mandatory courses for the English major, my senior year schedule was already chock-full. I remained on shaky terms with Jackie, who still hadn't forgiven me for lying to her about Writers on the Riviera, even after I admitted the truth to Pippa and Bree and apologized profusely to all of them for lying. I couldn't bring myself to tell them the real reason I hadn't gone to France, and every time I thought about those three magical months—Stephen and the *Kiss Me Kate* and Westhampton and the city and long dinners and his apartment and consuming sex—everything inside me hurt so badly that I almost couldn't breathe, much less defend my decision. I despised that it was summer again; it was just a reminder that it wasn't going to be anything like last year. I knew I was supposed to feel happy, but the summer just seemed like something great that would happen to everybody else. The last thing I wanted to do was ride the Long Island Railroad into Penn Station and slug through tedious days at campaign headquarters while Stephen breathed and walked and existed in the very same city. The hole in my heart engulfed me.

So in the end it wasn't the appointment with Dr. Wattenbarger that sent me into CJ's walk-in closet on a mission that morning. No, it was the image of my mother walking into Gabe's father's sixtieth-birthday party with my dad on her arm that threw me over the edge; envisioning her flaunting her Pilates figure in some fitted, expensive cocktail dress with her freshly blown-out head of lemon-blond hair. And Gabe would be there—of course he'd be there—and CJ would wink at him and flirt with him and God knows what else while my father stood around chatting with dull members of Cove. I hated her so much I could barely stand it. Aside from missing Stephen, my hatred for CJ was the only thing I could truly feel.

I made sure Georgia was still in the kitchen as I tiptoed through the master bedroom. The air-conditioning felt cooler in my parents' room, and the white monogrammed duvet cover was smoothed perfectly over the king-size sleigh bed. There wasn't a ruffle in the pillowcases. I felt empowered and almost possessed making my way across the taupe carpet toward CJ's walk-in closet. The oversize teak jewelry box sat on the floor next to Stuart Weitzman boots and strappy Jimmy Choos. I opened the box to make sure it was the right one. Hickory, curled in a yellow ball in the corner of the room, lifted her head and I met her gaze, silently willing her to understand before I lugged the jewelry box down the stairs and out to my dad's Audi.

It was too heavy to carry on the train, and besides, I was already moving forward with a momentum that might've decelerated if I were to have switched modes of transportation. An irrevocable force had taken over; I no longer occupied my own mind. I maneuvered the Audi out of the driveway and onto the road, and as I sped through the Cold Spring Harbor streets I felt as though I were not really driving but dissolving into the rush of green trees that whooshed by, like a fresh stroke of paint.

The roads were strangely empty and I made it into lower Manhattan in fifty minutes. I parked in a garage on Houston and walked east toward the pawnshop I'd found on Google Maps, Sal's, lugging the teak box with me in the breaking summer heat. It was just before nine and the shop wasn't open yet, so I bought a cart coffee and waited on the stoop. Delancey Street was grimy and smelled like piss. It seemed to be getting hotter by the minute, and I was relieved when the owner finally appeared and unlocked the iron-chained gate masking the door.

He peered at me underneath bushy black eyebrows as I followed him into the shop. I set the box on the floor.

"I am Sal. What could I do for you?" he asked in an indiscernible foreign accent, unlocking the register. His cheeks were pockmarked and rough, and he gritted his teeth while he studied me.

"I have some things I'd like to sell." One by one I removed the pieces of Marilyn's jewelry collection from the box. The ivory-and-gold-twisted bracelet; topaz studs; feathered earrings; the Indian kamarbands CJ let me borrow when I was Jasmine for Halloween in fourth grade; the freshwater pearls CJ wore to dinner parties; the diamond-encrusted emerald earrings; the funky, bright-colored market beads that Georgia and I used to play dress-up in. Tokens from the world, the first fuel for my dreams. I watched the heaping pile in front of Sal. I felt nothing.

Sal touched Marilyn's jewelry with his wide, hairy fingers.

"A lot of dis ees junk." He picked up a strand of mala beads, then a chunky coral necklace that was clearly plastic.

"Right," I said. "But some of it's real. Some of it should be worth a lot."

He nodded, studying the emerald earrings.

"Dis ees your jewelry, honey?"

"It was my mother's. She passed away."

"Some of eet ees very nice," he said, dividing the loot into two piles. "I take none of that." He motioned toward the costume jewelry and cheaper stuff.

"I geev you a price for thees." He gestured to the other pile—the precious gems and semiprecious stones, the pieces CJ cherished and saved for only dressy events.

He wrote a number on a piece of paper and handed it to me.

"That's fine," I said. I didn't know how much everything was actually worth, but Sal's price was more than I'd anticipated. A lot more.

"Cash weel be good?"

"Yes," I said, suddenly shaken for the first time all day, because I had never seen anything close to that sum of money in cash form, and I wasn't sure what I was going to do with it.

Sal disappeared into the back and emerged five minutes later. He handed me a paper bag.

"All of eet ees there. Count eef you like."

I peered into the bag at the crisp stacks of bills. It reminded me of something out of a movie.

"I believe you. Thanks." I scraped the rest of Marilyn's collection—the "junk"—into the box, which was much lighter without the heavier jewels.

I stepped back out into the intensifying heat and walked east, toward the river. My mind was thick with something slow and heavy like tar; it swirled with the vivid images of CJ and Gabe Petersen that would never stop haunting me, and my feet pedaling backward and the smell of rain on the pavement and every microscopic never-ending detail of *that day*—and then it was the tender spot on the back of Stephen's neck and his bottle-green eyes, and then Marilyn's wide smile and Marilyn sleeping in huts with AIDS patients in Africa and her jewelry sitting in the dark backroom of Sal's horrible shop, gone forever, like Macy and her Little Mermaid hair, and everything else that would never return.

I didn't stop walking until I had crossed one of the small bridges over the whooshing FDR traffic and arrived at the edge of the East River. The morning sun glittered over the water in front of Brooklyn as the sharp smell of salt rolled in. Runners in neon shorts flashed by, all too in-the-zone to notice me unlatch the clasp on the beautiful teak box and empty the remainder of Marilyn's jewelry from the world—the junk Sal wouldn't take—over the railing and into the murky, dark water below. I dropped the box in after everything else and watched it float for a moment, bobbing lightly in the sun, before disappearing under the oily surface.

As I watched pieces of Marilyn's life sink into the East River I felt that I was sinking, too, as though the most vital, densest sections of my brain had plummeted out from under me into the water, dragging the rest of my body down with them. The sadness inside me had morphed into something else, something that swapped between numbness and terror. It was the only thing left. I had disappeared from my own being.

In the spaces between the emptiness, random memories pooled: CJ's voice saying *Up and at 'em* every morning for thirteen years, followed by the sound of the shades snapping up; Georgia and me in red soccer jerseys. sucking orange slices at halftime; the sound of my father's *G-* and *L*-shaped pancakes sizzling on the griddle; the smell of dirt and pine on his skin after he finished splitting wood in the backyard; the four of us taking Hickory for walks in Caumsett; Georgia and I stretched out on beach towels on the Cape; wobbling on my dad's strong shoulders in the ocean and jumping off into the salty sea; maple-sugar snow in blue bowls; the feel of CJ's thumb and forefinger gently pinching my earlobe—*I made these ears, Sass.*

I felt far too sad to show up at my internship, sadder than I had all my life. Back on Delancey, I hailed a cab and told the driver to take me to the only place I could think to go, Saint Thomas Church on Fifty-Third and Fifth.

Joining the Episcopal Church had been my parents' compromise. My father was a born Catholic. CJ had grown up without religion and said that the Catholic Church put an especially bad taste in her mouth. But Marilyn had been Episcopalian, and my father promised it was the most lenient form of Christianity out there, so CJ obliged and Georgia and I attended just enough Sunday school and Confirmation classes to pass for practicing members of the Episcopalian faith. My parents used to take us to Saint Thomas, my father's favorite Episcopalian church in the city, for nighttime mass the week before Christmas. CJ, Georgia, and I would take the train in from Cold Spring Harbor and meet my father after work. We bundled in layers—Georgia and me in matching peacoats and CJ in her elegant, cream-colored wool. I never got particularly excited about church, but I loved going to Saint Thomas, the four of us squeezed into a pew under the ninety-five-foot-high Gothic ceilings. The altar was grandly decorated with poinsettias and other

Christmassy flower arrangements, and the readings were always wonderful, but the *best* was the music—glorious, holy Christmas melodies that filled every inch of the magnificent church, the sound of the organ reverberating all the way up the stone walls into the rib-vaulted ceiling. Sometimes there would be tears in my father's eyes, and then in CJ's, because whenever he cried her own tears followed, involuntarily. Back then there wasn't a doubt in my mind that she loved him more than anything.

After mass we always went downtown to dinner at Balthazar, my father's favorite French restaurant. Georgia and I would play hangman with crayons on the white paper tablecloth and we always ordered steak frites and Shirley Temples with extra maraschino cherries. But I hadn't eaten at Balthazar in years, and I couldn't remember when it had stopped or why we didn't go to Saint Thomas at Christmas anymore. All I knew was that the tradition was over, just a memory, and thinking about it made me feel strange and old.

At Fifty-Third and Fifth, I paid for the cab and stepped back into the blazing heat. The midtown block was quiet for a Friday morning. I walked inside the church, inhaling something familiar, and a schedule told me that the next service started soon, at half past ten.

I took a stack of envelopes from the lobby, then made my way into the enormous chapel and sat down at one end of a pew near the back and waited. I knelt on the floor and pressed my palms together. I hadn't been inside a church since Easter—we really only went on Christmas Eve and Easter now—and despite being confirmed I had never felt wildly religious in the first place, but I decided I should pray anyway. The guilt that was frozen somewhere inside me knew that I had just committed the worst sin of my life, made worse by the fact that doing it had been easy and seamless and disappointingly unsatisfying.

But the hard kneeler hurt my knees, and I couldn't remember how to pray, so I sat up, pulled out Sal's paper bag and got to work. By the time good, God-loving people of Manhattan had begun to fill in the seats around me I had already placed twenty hundred-dollar bills in each of the ten offering envelopes, totaling the twenty thousand dollars I'd received from Sal that morning in exchange for Marilyn's irreplaceable possessions.

The reverend began the service, proceeding through the opening hymn, then the lesson and the gospel and the epistle, and then a reading of Psalm 23, which I remembered was my father's favorite as the words were spoken:

The Lord is my shepherd; I shall not want.
He maketh me to lie down in green pastures: he leadeth me be-
side the still waters
He restoreth my soul: he leadeth me in the paths of righteousness
for his name's sake . . .

I held the Holy Bible in my hands and felt something move through me, like grace, and maybe I was feeling God, or maybe I was just one of those people who mistook emotion in a church for God; I didn't know for sure. I just knew in that moment that I needed to get better, and that nobody was going to do it for me, and when the big silver plate passed my pew during the offertory I placed my ten envelopes among the rest, and the usher met my eyes with curiosity but not conclusion, and I nodded, signaling him to continue forward, and the offertory hymn boomed through the chapel, loud and great, and for the first time all morning I was finally crying, thick tears sliding down my cheeks in unrelenting sheets. I buried my face in my lap, and I didn't care if anyone around me saw, because you were allowed to cry in a church, and for the first time in a long time I felt the temporary respite of not being judged, not by anybody and not by myself, and I let myself feel it, and it felt so good that I cried more healing tears into my hands until the music stopped and the minister said a prayer to close the offertory.

I slipped out of Saint Thomas before Communion, before anything about the money could be remotely suspected. I walked all the way down to the garage on Houston, fifty-three blocks to clear my head, the tears streaming intermittently. I got the Audi and got out of the city as fast as I could, blasting Stevie Nicks on the way home, already feeling just the tiniest bit clearer. I drove straight to Dr. Wattenbarger's office in Cold Spring Harbor, an hour early for my appointment, finally ready to talk.

34

STEPHEN

NOVEMBER 2013

Several months into our relationship Alice began to bother me in an array of ways. For example, the other morning I was taking a shower and noticed an enormous clump of her hair clogging the drain. It had stopped up the whole shower—I was standing in half a foot of bathwater and had to manually pull gobs of her hair out of the drain with my fingers. It was disgusting.

My first semester of law school was bombarding me with work, and the other night Alice came over while I was trying to finish the outline for my civil-procedure class. She snuggled up against me on the couch, crinkling the notes I had neatly spread out around me in a systematic order. I asked her to please move over, and she looked at me like I'd just kicked her in the face. That's the problem with girls like Alice—they're like dogs, so insecure they need your fucking affection all the livelong day.

My feelings of annoyance were a side product of being in a relationship, as I'd learned over the years. Boredom followed by exceeding boredom. Life morphs into a monotonous slide show, each day identical to the one before it.

It had been this way for a month or two, the back-and-forth battle in my head over my need for Alice and my desire to get rid of her. Generally I liked having her around. But then there were days, more frequent lately, when all I wanted was to be alone, and Alice would call and whine that we should order dinner and that I didn't spend enough time with her. So then we'd order takeout, and when it arrived she'd complain about the food but devour it nonetheless, her upper arms looking flabbier than they had when we'd first started dating. I wondered why she didn't join a gym.

It was at such times that I became most interested in having sex with someone else. The thought would enter my mind slowly, like a slug, and lodge itself there for the foreseeable future.

I'd only cheated on her once, in Miami in August, the weekend of Luke's bachelor party. Everyone was shitfaced and I ended up doing lines with a girl named Gabrielle or Gabi or something, who I met in one of the clubs. She was the type Luke had written off as "super trashy," but I didn't think she was bad. Bleached hair, a skinny body. A blurred image came to mind when I tried to picture her that night on the hotel bed. Mostly I just felt like having sex with a girl who wasn't Alice, not even because I was *mad* at Alice or even irritated at her. We'd been on great terms that weekend, actually, because I remember talking to her in the bathroom of Gabrielle's hotel room and telling her how much I missed her, and then after we hung up I walked out into the room and fucked Gabrielle until five o'clock in the morning. The precise reason eluded me. All I knew was that I felt a hell of a lot better after I did it, like I'd shaken something from my system that had been eating me alive for months.

The next morning I'd tiptoed into the hotel room I was sharing with Luke, but he was already awake, sitting in bed talking to his beloved bride on the telephone. Of course Luke would spend his bachelor party on the fucking phone with his fiancée; the antithesis of the very essence of a bachelor party. I didn't know why I'd bothered to plan the event for him in the first place.

"You sleep with that chick?" Luke murmured after he hung up with Kathleen. "No judgment," he added, frowning.

"No way. We were doing lines and I fell asleep."

"Isn't cocaine a bit outdated? And isn't that sentence an oxymoron?"

I closed my eyes and the sockets burned with exhaustion. "Don't be an ass, Luke. I'm hungover as hell."

"I'm not judging you, Stephen. I know you and Alice aren't super serious."

If there was one way Luke knew how to get under my skin it lay in his ability to backhandedly put me down. Luke was well aware that I viewed my relationship with Alice as a serious one. His justification of what he assumed to be my infidelity was only achieved by trivializing my relationship. My perceived failure was another pat on the back for Luke, the ultimate committed fiancé and embodiment of loyalty; the only *real* man in the DeMarco family.

I grabbed a half-empty Poland Spring bottle off the nightstand and chugged what was left.

"As a matter of fact, Alice and I are serious," I informed Luke, my head pounding. "We're probably going to move in together."

"Are you kidding me?" Luke stared at me with his mouth open.

"Nope."

It had been Alice's idea, which she'd brought up over brunch earlier in the summer. I'd been complaining about how expensive going out to meals was, which turned into a conversation about the expensive nature of New York in general, and how it had only become worse now that I was an unemployed law school student. We were squeezed into a booth at Freemans, and Alice rubbed my back and told me about her grandfather's apartment, a rent-controlled one-bedroom in Kips Bay. She explained how her grandfather, who lived in Myrtle Beach full-time, had given Alice permission to use the apartment once the current renter moved out in January. He would only charge her a fraction of the rent—a thousand bucks a month at most.

"Anyway," Alice had said that morning. "I know it's barely been a year, so maybe I'm getting ahead of us, but I was thinking . . ."

I reached for her hand. "You were thinking?"

Her face relaxed into a smile. "I was thinking that maybe, if it feels right, we could live there together. Rent would only be five hundred each—we could both save *so* much money. And you're only subletting right now, so it's not like you'd have to worry about getting out of a lease. Plus, it would be a way to guarantee that we'd still see each other all the time. You know what they say about what happens to couples when one person starts law school."

I nodded. I had already heard the stories from some of my classmates; there was no denying it, law school ruined relationships, especially the first year. The 1Ls who were serious about getting good grades didn't have time for their significant others on top of a heavy workload.

"That's definitely something to think about," I said, the seed planted in my mind, my eyes scorching Alice's. I watched joy flood through her and knew that she truly loved me. People who are harder to access pose a challenge, and the challenge makes them easier to love. By not always yielding answers but deliberately hinting at them, I challenged Alice's score with herself, her own assessments and convictions. I had driven her to love me; I'd watched her love for me take shape with my own eyes.

Why shouldn't I move in with Alice? She was, for the most part, a great girlfriend. Being with Alice often felt like it had with Diana during the good old days, before she found out about the cheating, before Lucy came into the picture.

The fall blew by. On Thanksgiving I took stock of the state of my life. Though I was thrilled to be done with my shithole days at BR3 Group, the first three months of law school had been the most demanding of my academic career. We'd given up our lease when Luke moved in with Kathleen and Geoff got a one bedroom closer to his office, and I was subletting a studio on Waverly near NYU. It was overpriced but temporary—Alice's offer had proven too good to pass up, and we were moving in together after New Year's. Luke had gotten married in September, although that seemed to change nothing except for Kathleen's last name. Now that Vivian and Luke were both married, my nosy relatives spent Thanksgiving dinner probing me about my love life.

"So, Stephen, are you next?" they cooed.

"Time will tell," I replied. "But I'm going to visit my girlfriend in Pittsburgh tomorrow, and we're moving in together in January." I liked the way it sounded; I watched my relatives nod in approval and knew I'd said the right thing.

Alice had bought me the plane ticket to Pittsburgh for our one-year anniversary—she wanted me to meet her family and see her childhood home. She picked me up at the airport, standing outside despite the cold, wearing an oversize gray wool coat that made her look older than she was. Seeing her made me think of Lucy for some reason, and I wondered where in the world Lucy was, right that minute.

The Edwardses' house wasn't a mansion, but it wasn't small, either. Alice mixed us whiskey gingers in the kitchen before giving me a tour. The glass chandelier hanging in the foyer and the faux zebra carpet lining the upstairs hallways told me both that her father did well in banking and also that the Edwardses were a bit nouveau riche.

In Alice's bedroom I studied the framed photographs, each one

tucked neatly into a polished frame—Alice skiing, Alice in a balle-
rina outfit, Alice and her brother, Duncan, at Disney World, standing between Mickey and Minnie. Alice's hair had once been a darker,
indistinct shade of dishwater blond, and I suddenly understood the urgency behind her periodic trips to the salon. As Alice discovered more
in her room to show me, I placed my arms around her middle and felt
that familiar pull from below, the never-ending desire for sex.

"Alice in Wonderland, can we?" I whispered into her apple-
shampooed tresses. I hadn't had sex in a week, and my body was tense
and tender all over.

"Not *now*, Stephen. My parents are downstairs waiting for us. Later."

We gathered around the dining room table for dinner. The Edwardses were extremely average people. Mrs. Edwards did most of the
talking, while her husband and son concentrated on their steaks.

Midmeal I excused myself to the bathroom; the whiskey was running through me. On the way I nearly tripped over a dog lying in the
entrance to the dining room, the Edwardses' old collie.

"Aw, don't mind Nellie, she doesn't move around much," said Mrs.
Edwards sadly. "She has cancer; we found out recently."

"I'm so sorry. I didn't know." I glanced at Alice, whose bottom lip
trembled.

The dog looked up at me expectantly with shiny black eyes like marbles, and I had the sudden urge to kick the dumb creature in its face.

On the bathroom wall was a framed picture of Alice and Duncan as
children in matching overalls and turtlenecks, sitting side by side on
the front porch of what I took to be this house. It struck me how typical
everyone turned out to be, how rare it was for somebody to make a life
that had more to show than an old photograph of kids on the wall. All
people ended up caring about was some stupid dog or some ugly painting their kid made in art class. And the thing that really got me was that
people were *satisfied* with this outcome, even *happy* that they turned
out like every other schmuck on the block who assembles a swing set
and thinks it's extraordinary.

Mrs. Edwards had immaculately laid out printed-paper napkins in a
bamboo box on the back of the toilet next to a basket of potpourri—like
everything else in the house the arrangement felt forced. What exactly

was I *doing* here, in this bullshit average house in Pennsyl-fucking-vania? I felt displaced and recognized the pang in the base of my stomach, a distaste and longing for the same intangible thing.

After dinner I told Alice I needed some fresh air, so we went out to the front porch and sat on the steps. I inhaled the cool, late autumn air. Alice lit a cigarette.

"Do your parents care that you smoke?"

"It's not their favorite thing." She shrugged. "Are you okay?"

"Yeah."

"You sure?"

"Just a little headache."

"I'm sorry, baby."

She pressed her cheek against my arm and proceeded to ramble on with stories of the dog Nellie, how sad she was about Nellie and why, and I did my best to provide consoling answers. Even after we thanked her parents for dinner and went upstairs and fucked in the shower, I hardly felt any better. I watched the backs of Alice's short legs through the water and all I saw were Lucy's legs, svelte and impossibly long. The way they curved into her beautiful ass. Her perfect body. I came hard thinking about Lucy and it was over too quickly, disappointingly so. I stared at Alice's naked, wet figure.

That night I lay in the guestroom bed alone (the Edwardses were not kosher with premarital sleepovers) and decided that I needed to text Lucy, even though it had been a very long time. I couldn't remember why we'd stopped communicating in the first place—just because there was a geographic distance between us it didn't mean we shouldn't *talk*. It suddenly seemed right that I should say hello, check in and see how her senior year was going.

I snatched my cell off the nightstand.

> STEPHEN: Hey Luce, it's been a while. How are you? Happy Thanksgiving.

I sent the text and waited, my eyelids drooping.

She hadn't answered by midnight so I switched the light off, exhausted. But once I shut my eyes, sleep wouldn't come. I tossed and turned through the night, a series of random, relentless thoughts crowding my head. I was still awake when a grayish-yellow light peeked through the curtains and slid its way along the carpet, and I felt doomed at the prospect of getting through a full day with the Edwardses without a wink of sleep. I rolled over and checked my phone again. I wanted an answer, just to know she was there on the other end. But Lucy hadn't texted me back.

I managed to drift off somewhere around dawn, and when I woke it was half past nine and Alice was shaking me, telling me to come downstairs for blueberry pancakes.

I dressed and checked my phone one more time, craving affirmation that she still wanted to talk to me, a want so prevailing I couldn't ignore it. But there was no text from Lucy, and she didn't respond all day, or the next day, or the next, or the day after that. She didn't respond at all.

35

LUCY

JANUARY 2014

"You seem better," Jackie said as we walked to the house party down the street from us. "Even better than first semester, I mean." The sun hid behind a thick wash of clouds, but the air was warm.

"I do feel better," I agreed. "I feel like my old self again. Aside from the fact that I've totally screwed up my old self's career plans."

"What do you mean? Not minoring in journalism?"

"Given that I've only taken *two* journalism courses during my entire four years here, no. I was so out of it I didn't even take the right classes. How did that *happen*? I could've done more writing for *The Lantern*, but I didn't. And now I can't exactly go and try to be a journalist without any formal education in journalism. I won't even be able to get hired as an intern."

"You could go back to school. Get a master's in journalism. Right?"

"I guess. I just feel like I've played my cards all wrong."

"You can't think like that, Luce."

"I know, I know. I should schedule a call with Dr. Wattenbarger and ask him about it. He's very wise."

"I mean, I wish *I* could talk to your therapist. I'm the one freaking out about Stuart every five minutes."

"Breakups are hard."

"It's been a whole year, though."

"I know. Baird is just too small, that's the problem."

"Yeah, like right now, case and point. The party has to be at *Stuart's* house. And I want to go because it's where all our friends are going, and I can't *not* go because that would be so dramatic."

"Exactly. How are you supposed to get over Stuart when you constantly have to run into him? If we weren't at Baird, if we were out in the real world, he'd be old news." I linked my arm through Jackie's. I was grateful to hear her confirm what I'd been feeling myself—*even better.* All around me the world seemed bright and sunny and fresh. Baird was humming with students excited to be back from Christmas break, and the air stirred with a sense of anticipation that invigorated me from the inside out. *God it was* nice *to be wearing shorts and a tank in January,* I thought, smiling up at the exotic, slender-stemmed palm trees lining Carroll Street, with their beautiful, intricate fanning green leaves that I felt I hadn't truly noticed until now.

During the first fifteen minutes of my first appointment with Dr. Wattenbarger back in June, he'd diagnosed me with clinical depression.

"You are depressed, Lucy," he'd said, smiling at me with whimsical gray eyes, as if this were excellent news.

"Right. That makes sense."

"*Clinically* depressed. I knew it the moment you walked into my office," he'd continued brightly, running a hand through his thick silver hair. "I've been doing this a long time. I can see it in your face, in your movements, in the way you speak. This is positive."

"How is this positive?" Of course CJ would send me to some crazy doctor who thinks depression is fantastic.

"Because it means I can help you. You have a chemical imbalance in your brain—it's what's giving you these intense feelings of despair. It's what is causing you to feel like you're moving through molasses. But I can prescribe you an antidepressant that will make you feel much better. Fast."

"What do you mean, a chemical imbalance?"

"Think of it like an infection. Like strep throat. If you had strep, you'd be given antibiotics. Depression is like an infection in your brain, but it's chemical. Your neurotransmitter levels are low. Neurotransmitters are the chemicals that relay messages from neuron to neuron, and right now yours are firing too slowly, which is why you feel this sense of lethargy and dejection."

I watched Dr. Wattenbarger write me a prescription for Prozac as he continued to explain about depression and how it affects one in ten people in America.

"It's probably genetic," he said. "But it's hard to tell, because about two-thirds of people with depression are left undiagnosed. Especially older people who've developed an aversion toward therapy."

I'd nodded, figuring I'd gotten it from CJ's side of the family. CJ's mother is a complete nutcase, always miserable and complaining about everything and yelling at my grandfather even though he's 80 percent deaf.

"It's important that we combine the Prozac with regular therapy, though," Dr. Wattenbarger said. "While depression *is* rooted in a chemical imbalance, there are external factors that can facilitate the condition."

"External factors?"

"Yes. 'Triggers,' I like to say. That's where the therapy is effective. We do the work to figure out what's going on with you, what kind of struggles you might be dealing with in your day-to-day life that may have helped trigger the depression."

I nodded again.

"So you'll come see me once a week," he instructed. "And you'll fill this prescription and take one pill daily with breakfast." Breakfast. I would have to eat breakfast.

CJ had been right about Dr. Wattenbarger after all—he was a good psychiatrist, because the Prozac worked fast. After a few days it was as if something had shaken loose deep within me and lifted up and out of me. I felt lighter. I started to notice things, as if a fog was breaking or a windshield was defrosting or my eyes were acclimating to the dark. Life became clearer and clearer, until suddenly, I could see everything.

I went to Dr. Wattenbarger's office once a week for the rest of the summer. The more I saw him, the more comfortable I felt with him, and the more I confessed. I'd gone to him with the intention of talking about the Unforgivable Thing, but the Prozac made me feel so much better so quickly that even though I knew I should still tell him it seemed unnecessary, and the few times I did open my mouth to say the words, nothing came except for air, and Dr. Wattenbarger looked at me with his curious gray eyes.

Dr. Wattenbarger and I discussed Georgia and my dad and my grandparents and Gabe and Parker and Lydia and my friends from school and *parts* of CJ, and even a little about my "eating issue," as he called it. And we usually ended up discussing Stephen. Dr. Wattenbarger said that Stephen wasn't necessarily the reason I'd become depressed, but that my feelings for him (in effect, the feelings he gave me) had been a source of relief for me, therefore Stephen himself could be deemed a "trigger."

When it came to talking about Stephen I spared few details, because the more I heard the truth out loud the more sense it all made.

"What's he like?" Dr. Wattenbarger had asked that very first day.

In my foggy mind a clear image of Stephen had appeared—I could always picture him lucidly—and an invisible clamp seized my chest.

"It's hard to explain him."

"Try."

I fought the barricade across my collarbone, until I found words, and they spilled out.

"He's tall. He has dark hair, and these intense green eyes. He's easy to talk to. He always knows what to say. He can have a conversation with anybody. He's funny. I'm always laughing when I'm with him. *Genuinely* laughing, not pretending. He's smart. He knows exactly what he wants, and he goes for it. And he gets me. He gets parts of me that other people don't. He can make me feel so good about myself, better than I've ever felt about myself, like a million bucks. He's different, but good different. And there's this *thing* between us, it's like chemistry but more tangible. I've never met anybody who makes me feel that. Not even close."

"But there's a problem?" Dr. Wattenbarger's expression grew thoughtful.

"Yes."

"What is it?"

"Everything else," I'd said, hitting on something, proceeding to tell him about the unabashed cheating and lying, the flipside of the irresistible charmer I held on a pedestal.

"You have to be careful with charm," Dr. Wattenbarger had said. "You know what they say—charm is the ability to make someone think that both of you are quite wonderful."

After a few sessions, Dr. Wattenbarger told me that Stephen's motivations were consistent with *sociopathic* and *narcissistic* behaviors.

"Like Patrick Bateman in *American Psycho*?"

"Not exactly," Dr. Wattenbarger replied. "There's a spectrum, Lucy. Serial killers like Patrick Bateman are on one end. Stephen is probably closer to the other, less extreme end."

We'd looked up both terms in his giant psychiatric glossary.

SOCIOPATH—A person with antisocial personality disorder, the most widely recognized personality disorder. Antisocial personality disorder is a chronic mental condition in which a person's way of thinking, perceiving situations, and relating to others are dysfunctional and destructive. People with the disorder typically have no regard for right and wrong and often disregard the rights, wishes, and feelings of others. A sociopath is often well-liked because of his or her charm and high charisma, but he or she does not usually care about other people. Though some sociopaths become murderers, most reveal their sociopathy through less extreme means.*

*Harvard Medical School estimates that as many as 4 percent of the population are conscienceless sociopaths who have no empathy or affectionate feelings for humans or animals. Males are three times more likely to be sociopaths than females.

NARCISSIST—A person with narcissistic personality disorder, a mental disorder in which people have an inflated sense of their own importance, a deep need for admiration, and a lack of empathy for others. Behind this mask of ultraconfidence lies a fragile self-esteem that's vulnerable to the slightest criticism. It is estimated that this condition affects 1 percent of the population, with rates greater for men.

"A lot of people cheat and lie, though," I'd proposed to Dr. Wattenbarger during a later session, thinking of CJ.

"Do you think that?"

"I think it happens more than it should."

"Maybe so. But you can't attribute every cheating episode in history to sociopathic behavior. It could be an isolated event or have some kind of context. Chronic unfaithfulness is a different story. When you lie and cheat consistently, as it seems Stephen does, well, that isn't human nature. There's no *guilt* in that kind of behavior, see? Someone who causes harm to others without *guilt*—that's a sociopath in action."

"Yeah. I guess." *Like me*, I couldn't help but think, since the absence of guilt had been a notable void since the day I'd sold half of Marilyn's jewelry and tossed the rest in the East River. I kept waiting to regret what I'd done, to feel some sense of remorse as I'd witnessed CJ in hysterical tears on the phone with the police and as I'd watched her fire Gloria, our housekeeper of ten years. I was shocked at myself and slightly horrified, sure, but I didn't feel guilty. Instead, I felt strangely liberated. I felt no shame for what I'd done, which, in Dr. Wattenbarger's eyes, would've made me a sociopath, too.

"Just avoid him, Lucy," Dr. Wattenbarger said during our last session of the summer. "Promise me that you will cut all contact."

"I will. I haven't talked to him in months. And he doesn't even go to Baird anymore."

"I know. But if he calls you, if he texts you. He *will* try to contact you. People like Stephen, they don't change. He will always come back for more. He won't give it up until he has to."

And Dr. Wattenbarger had been right. Stephen did contact me, once, in November, late at night.

> STEPHEN: Hey Luce, it's been a while. How are you? Happy Thanksgiving.

I hadn't answered. I'd wanted to, a million times, desperately, but I fought against it. I didn't let myself stop hearing Dr. Wattenbarger's calm, knowing voice: *People like Stephen, they don't change. He will always come back for more. He won't give it up until he has to.*

He won't give it up until he has to. What did that mean? When would he have to?

"Lucy?" Jackie's voice interrupted my thoughts of Dr. Wattenbarger and therapy and Stephen being a sociopath. *Stephen is a sociopath.* The thought had never quite settled. If I let myself, I could miss Stephen all the way down to the tips of my toes. I could fight to reason all of it in my head.

"Huh?" I turned to Jackie.

"You're spacing out. What were you thinking about?"

"I was just thinking that I'm sorry," I said honestly, because apologizing to Jackie was something I'd been meaning to do.

"Sorry? For what?"

"I don't think I've been a very good friend to you. At points throughout college, I mean."

"If you're talking about the France trip, I told you, I'm over it. I get that you were going through some shit."

"It's not just that. Sophomore and junior year in general. I just wasn't at my best, and sometimes I don't even know why you guys stuck by me."

"Luce, you were never a bad friend. I think that's what makes you such a good friend—you don't even realize it. It's just who you are. Even at your lowest points, you've always just accepted me, way more than a lot of other people ever have. With the way I acted with Stuart and everything. God, I was a real psycho. No wonder he dumped me."

"Jackie." I squeezed her hand. "You're not a psycho."

"I might be."

"We all might be. I love you."

"I love you, too. C'mon. We're here."

We hurried up the creaky porch steps and inside 622 Carroll, where we were greeted by Topher Rigby, who'd ended up being one of Stuart's housemates.

"*Hello*, ladies."

Jackie and I both towered over Topher. We said hello and made our way across the wood floor of the foyer, which was sticky with a layer of dried beer.

"Now every time I see Topher I think about him trying to finger you sophomore year," Jackie whispered in my ear.

"Ew, don't bring that up," I said. "Makes my skin crawl."

"He just had zero idea what to do at all? Like, what was he actually *doing* with his hand?"

"Jesus, *stop*." I cringed as we walked into the living room, which had no furniture except for a Ping-Pong table in the corner.

Like most Baird party houses, 622 Carroll was a shithole, and, as usual, it was packed. Stuart was playing beer pong and glanced over when he noticed Jackie. He always seemed to notice her right away. I watched them make eye contact and wave.

"Ugh, he looks so good," she pouted.

Stuart did look good, and I pulled Jackie into the kitchen, which was crammed with people pushing their way toward the keg.

"We should've brought beer," I said. "This is going to be impossible."

"Lucy. Jackie," said a voice behind me. "Take these."

I turned around to meet a pair of familiar coppery eyes, flecks of amber glistening in the irises—it was Billy Boyd. He handed us two cold cans of PBR. When he smiled, those heart-wrenching dimples appeared on either cheek.

"Billy!" Jackie exclaimed. "You're a lifesaver."

"I'm heading out back," he shouted over the hum of the crowd. "It's too packed in here."

"What's out back?" I knew very well what was out back—another beer pong table, a fire pit, and some yard space; it was a stupid question that told me I might, maybe, like him.

"Room to breathe," Billy replied. "You guys want to come?"

"You two go." Jackie eyed me intuitively. "I'm gonna say hi to Stuart."

Billy was already making his way outside, and I seemed to have no choice now but to follow him.

"How've you been, Billy?" I cracked open the beer. I didn't know if he'd wanted me to come outside with him, or if he'd asked out of politeness.

"Oh, you know. Good." He grinned with half his mouth, and my attraction to him was so surprising and strong that I had to bite my lip to keep from laughing.

"I saw you in yoga the other day," he continued.

"You did? I don't think I saw you. I didn't know you did yoga." I sipped my beer and tried to keep cool. I'd always been terrible at flirting.

"Yup. You're not the only one."

"So you must've been at YogaLab. That's the only place I practice."

"Yeah. But I don't love YogaLab. It's too corporate."

"It's not corporate!"

"They have studios all over the country, Lucy."

The way he said *Lucy* made my spine prickle. I studied the definition of his biceps as they moved underneath the sleeves of his white cotton T-shirt, golden brown from days spent surfing and rock climbing with BORP.

"I actually liked it when I went the other day," Billy went on. "But have you taken Heather's class? She's awesome."

"Every guy is obsessed with Heather."

"*Obsessed* is a strong word."

"Oh, come on. She's basically a model. You know she's so pretty."

"She's pretty." Billy said. "Not as pretty as you."

I was trying not to smile too hard, but I couldn't help it, the corners of my mouth poking my cheeks. Behind Billy, dense clouds were finally beginning to break over the mountains. The sun sank low in the sky, casting a tangerine glow over the horizon.

"It's a good sunset," I said.

He glanced up. "I want to show you something."

"What is it?"

"It's a surprise."

He led the way inside the house. We wormed through the crowded kitchen and up the back staircase. On the second floor was a bay window that opened onto the roof. Billy unclasped it and squeezed himself through.

I'd been on the roof of 622 before, with Stuart and Topher and their friends, but I followed Billy, who'd already hoisted himself up onto a higher level.

"Come here." He held out his arm and hoisted me up in one quick motion.

"Wow." I stood straight, my breath catching in my chest as I took in the view. "I've never been all the way up here."

Baird stretched around us, from Adler Quad past Swanson Chapel and all the way to the athletic fields at the perimeter of campus. The white-peaked San Gabriel Mountains rose on one side, and toward the other I could see beyond the freeway, and the western end of Claremont spilled on for miles, toward Los Angeles. The bottom of the sun nudged the earth, a fiery glow torching the horizon and rinsing up through the sky in a wash of sherbet hues.

"It's peaceful up here." Billy sat down on the roof. I sat beside him, the warm air like a coat of velvet against my bare arms.

"It's beautiful."

"Are you hot?" he asked. "We can go back in."

"No." I shook my head. "This is perfect."

Billy wedged closer toward me, and I felt my heartbeat quicken behind my chest as the side of his arm brushed mine.

"How do you know about this spot?" I asked him. "I didn't even know you could get up to this level of the roof."

"I don't remember. I discovered it freshman year with some buddies, I think."

Billy and I watched the rest of the sun sink below the earth, and I felt like I was meeting him for the first time. He didn't bring up anything about last year and how I'd been weird about things, and I was glad because I didn't want to think about the murky state of my mind then or why I'd resisted him; I just wanted to put the past in the past and leave it there. At some point he leaned down and I knew he was going to kiss me, and when he did I felt safe, like a ship coming into its harbor.

36

STEPHEN

The wheels of the train growled and steamrolled under me as I sped out of Manhattan on an LIRR car packed with tired commuters in suits. Most of them, at least the ones visible to me, had their eyes closed. An overweight woman across the aisle wearing an ugly flowered blouse noisily slurped a cup of gross-looking Chinese soup. Peach-colored lipstick smudged the rim of the white Styrofoam.

I closed my eyes and let the week drain from me like slush. It was only Thursday, but it had been a long, hellish week. I inhaled the musty scent of something ancient and boring, like ink. Like some jackass doing the *New York Times* crossword puzzle every damn day for fifty years on this stinking seat. God the train is depressing. I thought about how all these people zipping out of the city would zip right back in tomorrow to spend another day exactly like this one.

Thankfully I would not be one of them. I was taking the day off because Sadie and I were flying out to California tonight for a long weekend. Sadie would be applying to colleges soon, and Baird was on her list.

My father had gladly obliged when I'd offered to take Sadie to visit Baird. I was looking forward to a few days away from the cluttered filth of Manhattan, the stresses of law school, and my increasingly annoying girlfriend. Alice and I had moved in together in January, and it wasn't all I'd had it stacked up to be. Financially I felt more secure, but Alice's grandfather's apartment was much smaller than I'd realized, and the two of us were basically squatting on top of each other, fighting for half a foot of space. I just needed a break.

I'd also been bothered by Lucy's continuous radio silence—she'd been ignoring me for months. I actually couldn't stop thinking about her, and I didn't like it one bit. I felt a strange sort of desperation to see her again, and not just because Alice was getting on my nerves. There was something about Lucy; whatever I'd had with her felt unsustainable but at the same time unfinished. Maybe it always would.

Visiting Baird was the perfect excuse to see Lucy. She could ignore my calls and texts from afar, but she wouldn't be able to avoid me on such a small campus. As the train roared east I looked out the window at the blur of bare trees and back parking lots, and somewhere in the bleakness I saw Lucy's creamy thighs, her slender arms moving down the length of my body. The idea of having sex with her this weekend had become mind-consuming, and the more I thought about it the more I knew I needed to make it happen. Sex with Alice had become routine, and was difficult to appreciate unless we went at least a week without seeing each other, which rarely happened. Imagine watching *Top Gun* every night of your life—it's good, great even, but you know exactly what's coming and over time, with repetition, it loses its appeal.

I closed my eyes and imagined Lucy's face. It had been so long, I almost couldn't conjure its clear image. In my head was a feeling, more than a picture. A mistake I had made. A two-thousand-mile barrier to something I had never seen through.

My phone buzzed. One new text.

ALICE: I miss you already.

I responded that I missed her, too. She always had a hissy fit if I didn't respond to her texts in a timely manner.

I opened a new message window and tapped out another text to Lucy.

STEPHEN: I know you want nothing to do with me but I need to talk to you. I'm taking Sadie out to visit Baird this weekend. I'm getting on a plane to LAX tonight. I'll be on campus tomorrow. I miss you.

Sadie picked me up at the train station. I climbed into the Explorer and immediately turned down the Kesha song blaring from the speakers.

"I will never get used to the fact that you can legally drive a car," I said. "Nor will I feel safe as your passenger."

"I'm a better driver than you, idiot." She shot me her classic Sadie expression, which told me my joke was less annoying than boring.

"How's school, Sade?"

"Ugh, kinda stressful. Dad is all over me about the SATs."

We stopped at a red light and Sadie turned to me, her eyes clear. A wriggled line appeared over her brow and I could tell that she was truly frazzled. I felt sorry for her, for thinking that her life in high school was something to stress over. Life only got a hell of a lot harder.

"But I'm *so* excited to see Baird," Sadie continued. "I really think I'd love being on the West Coast, like you did. Anyway, how are you? How's school?"

"Still busting my balls. But I only have two and a half more years of hell."

"Hey, Eeyore." Sadie punched my shoulder. "Snap out of it. You've wanted to go to law school for, like, forever."

"I know."

"Are you regretting it?"

"No, of course not. I'm just in a bit of a funk."

"How's Alice?"

"Oh, you know."

"What's the problem?"

"Nothing."

"Doesn't sound like nothing."

The truth was, my issues with Alice couldn't be summed up into any kind of cohesive reasoning. There was no one glaring thing wrong; it was a general dissatisfaction that I had been too busy to seriously consider.

"I need a little break from her, I guess," I told my sister, though I knew my irritation was equally due to the fact that I couldn't stop feeling hot and bothered by thoughts of Lucy.

Two hours later our plane sat on the runway at LaGuardia. Sadie was already asleep, her head wedged against my shoulder. I'd always been jealous of her ability to pass out instantly in any setting.

I shifted in my seat, a dull pain already forming in my low back. Once we got up in the air and the flight attendant came around I would order a Scotch or two. That would help.

The captain's voice emerged from the loudspeaker, announcing that we were next in line for departure on the runway and that all electronic devices needed to be shut off.

I felt the plane's engine fire up below. Gravity absorbed my body into the seat as the wheels flew forward. I loved the feeling of taking off in an airplane; the way you got suctioned backward, surrendering all control. The engine ripped and roared and the wheels glided smoothly as I relaxed into the magnificent surge, and suddenly we were floating in the air, among the clouds, and all was calm.

As a kid I had a phobia of airplanes. I didn't trust them. I'd never been on one before, and my parents booked a trip to Cancún for spring break when I was in third grade. I made a big stink and refused to go because I thought airplanes were bullshit, that there was no way a giant, heavy metal contraption could stay suspended in the sky carrying hundreds of people across countries and oceans. My mother yelled at me and said I was ungrateful, and that most children didn't get to go on nice vacations to Cancún, so I had better suck it up (as it turned out, Cancún was a dump).

I decided to find the answer, the concrete logic behind the miracle of flight. I read about the Wright brothers, the mechanical engineering of the airplane and the physics behind it, the dorsal fin, laminar flow, loop antenna, drag, upwash, torque, accelerated stall. Once I understood the science of it, I was no longer scared of flying.

I hated the notion that anything was insubstantial; my need for things to be tangible and concrete was an urge that came deep from within. There was never a time when I believed in Santa Claus or the Easter Bunny; I was simply not ignorant enough. There were answers and why shouldn't answers be known? Why should we drift aimlessly through an atmosphere of questions and emotions and fragile faiths, when it's the hard numbers and mathematical truths that keep the earth spinning on its axis?

So many people are petrified of science, of its harshness, but I take solace in it. It is the only truth we have. One plus one equals two. The world is so fucking simple when you break it down.

37

LUCY

I woke up to a pang in my chest, a gong striking my clavicle. My mouth felt like sandpaper, and my skin was clammy and cold. I huddled under my quilt, the crisp egg-yolk light streaming through the blinds.

I wanted everything to be normal, unobstructed, but something in the air had turned overnight. Billy was already sitting up on the edge of the bed, putting on his Chacos. I stretched my neck to look at the alarm clock, which read 7:45.

"Why are you up?" I asked him. Billy's broad back faced away from me, and I placed my hand on the center of it, over his soft gray T-shirt.

"I have that test today, remember? I'm meeting Greg for breakfast to go over some stuff before." He turned around and kissed me quickly on the forehead, then leaped up and grabbed his backpack off my desk chair.

"I'll call you later," he said.

"Good luck."

"Oh, what time do you want to leave today?"

"Huh?" My mind was a blurry bees' nest and it took me a minute to remember what he was talking about. "Oh, for Bear Mountain?"

"Yeah, where else?"

"Around one thirty? After lunch?"

"Okay." He smiled. "Bye."

After he left I curled into the fetal position underneath the covers. Half of me wished Billy was still in the bed with me, and the other half was relieved to be alone so I could think.

Billy had become familiar; I'd gotten used to waking up with him in the mornings, the clean soapy smell of his skin, his spine-tingling dimples and the way his body felt. He took me camping with the BORP, which wasn't really my thing, but I was making an effort. Jackie said it was important to make an effort in relationships. I was trying to listen to her; I figured I was terrible at relationships, considering mine had all turned into small disasters.

I couldn't fall back asleep, and at eight fifteen I gave up and sat up in bed. My class didn't start until nine thirty. I peered through the blinds at the blistering sun, as one persistent thought wobbled through me unsteadily.

Stephen is in California. Stephen is coming to Baird today.

I plucked my phone off the nightstand and reread his latest text for the billionth time:

> STEPHEN: I know you want nothing to do with me but I need to talk to you. I'm taking Sadie out to visit Baird this weekend. I'm getting on a plane to LAX tonight. I'll be on campus tomorrow. I miss you.

I clambered out of bed and into the kitchen to start some coffee. I washed my face in the bathroom while it percolated.

The smell of caffeine calmed me, and I poured a large mug that I brought back to bed. I wanted to talk to Jackie, but she didn't have class on Fridays and would kill me if I woke her this early. I stood in the center of my room and sipped the hot coffee, trying hard to clear my mind. It wasn't like I had to see him, just because he wanted to see me. It wasn't like I owed him that. I'd done a fine job of ignoring him all these months; I could easily ignore him for another weekend.

I pressed my hands around the warm mug, just as the doorbell rang. Nobody ever rang our front door; friends knew to go through the back.

When I opened the door to the sight of Stephen my body froze, my breath snagged in my chest.

"Well," he said. "If the mountain won't come to Muhammad . . ." His green eyes narrowed in the shallow sunlight. The tips of his ears were pink. *Stephen's* ears.

Without asking, he let himself inside.

"Fuck, that's some strong sun." Beads of sweat gathered at his temples. "I think I got burned just walking over here."

As I fully took in the sight of him, Stephen, back at Baird, inside my house, I could barely stand, my legs were shaking so badly. Sometimes I felt afraid of my heart, the way it started and stopped.

"I didn't say you could come in." My voice felt smaller than it had in months. I was wearing a pair of Billy's boxers and a worn-in T-shirt without a bra. I folded my arms over my chest.

"Lucy," Stephen said softly. He stepped toward me, and then his arms were around me. His T-shirt was warm and damp with sweat against my cheek.

I pulled away. I had to sit. I walked into my room and put on Marilyn's cashmere sweater for armor. I sat down on the edge of my bed. Stephen sat beside me.

"Luce . . ."

"Stephen." I didn't know what to do. I knew if Pippa or Jackie were in my shoes they would kick him out, but I wasn't Pippa or Jackie. I wasn't going to kick him out.

"I'm sorry to barge in on you like this. But I did try to call and text. . . ."

"I know. I should've gotten back to you. I've been busy."

"Busy, huh?"

"I'm going to be late for class." I stood. His presence on my bed made it feel foreign, like it wasn't where I'd slept every night for the past seven months.

"What class?"

"Comparative literature."

"Yikes."

"It's not so bad."

"This is a nice room, Lucy in the Sky with Diamonds."

"Don't call me that."

"Why not?" His facial expression turned amused.

"It's not like we're friends."

"No, I suppose we're not." His eyes met mine. "It's really good to see you."

His olive skin was paler than I remembered, but his features were still the same; the thick eyebrows, the small bow-shaped mouth. As usual his dark glossy head of hair was in need of a trim.

"This isn't the best time," I said. "I have to get dressed. I have to pick something up from the mailroom before class."

"Can I watch you get dressed?" He grinned. I wanted to punch him for the sleazy comment at the same time that I felt a familiar stitch of affection for him, for his uncompromising commitment to our chemistry. The lust pulled from deep below.

"That was a joke. Relax." He lay back into the pillows on my bed.

"How did you know where I live?"

"Jared told me." Jared was a guy in the class above mine, a former Chops member. He still lived on campus finishing up his degree.

"Oh."

"Sadie and I are staying with Jared. We're going out to his place in Big Bear Lake tonight."

"You're going to Big Bear Lake?" Panic shriveled my insides.

"Yup, this afternoon after Sadie finishes her visit. You've been to Jared's place, right? It's sweet. And Jared says there's a fun concert this weekend. Wrigley and some alums are meeting us there."

"Yeah, Paper Diamond is playing. I'm going."

"Really?" Stephen's eyes widened. "Awesome. Where are you staying?"

"We rented a condo near the venue." I stared at him, aware of the danger surrounding the fact that my panic was quickly melting into excitement. A layer of fizz on my skin.

"Cool." His eyes locked mine. "Is it going to be a problem for you if I'm there?"

"No," I lied. "Why would it be?"

"Just making sure. It would be nice to spend some time with you this weekend."

I swallowed at the sight of him lying comfortably on my bed, his hands interlaced complacently across his chest, and I felt the forces of hatred and love clawing inside me, fighting each other for permission.

"I really do need to get ready for class. And you need to leave. If Jackie wakes up and finds you here . . ."

"No questions asked." He stood. "Can't risk a Jackie run-in before coffee."

"I made coffee. It's in the kitchen if you want some," I offered for no apparent reason. "There are to-go cups in the cabinet."

"Coffee would save me right now. You're the best, Luce. I'll call you when I get to Bear later? How about you answer for a change?"

"I'll try." I smiled, not unaware of the subdued frustration my lack of response had caused him. I was proud of myself for having been so unavailable.

After he left I got dressed and walked east across campus, toward Foster Hall. I passed Adler Quad and the old badminton net and was overcome by the feeling that everything was at once completely differ-ent and entirely the same. I was caught somewhere between relief and horror, between anger and affection, the binaries slicing each other, my heart left hanging on a string. The fact that I would still be so insanely attracted to Stephen shouldn't have been a surprise, but somehow it was, burning my insides, fogging my head, unraveling everything I had spent months mending and patching and restoring.

And I felt more excited than I had in all those months—that was the worst part. The hours I'd spent divulging my soul in Dr. Wattenbarger's office last summer felt far away and unimportant. Thoughts of Stephen sailed me through Mr. Sterling's two-hour lecture on postmodernism. *He's here. He's on campus again. He's going to Bear Mountain this weekend. He wants to spend time with me.*

I was delirious and idiotic and naive and irresponsible and self-destructive, and I knew all of that. But none of it weighed anything against what I actually felt. Do you follow your head or your heart? Which do you do? Your heart, always. Right? I didn't think I would ever stop believing that. I was old enough to know that it was a rare feeling to like someone the maximum amount. Anybody would've been lucky to feel the way I did.

38

STEPHEN

Jared told me where she lived, in the little green house with the white shutters on Carroll Street. There is a fine line between being romantic and being creepy, but romantic is usually a safe bet if the girl (A) has or has had strong feelings for you, and (B) is emotionally fragile. With Lucy it was both, and I knew that she'd interpret a spontaneous knock on her door as pure romance.

She looked good, healthy, better than I remembered, even in boxers and an old tee. Not as bone-thin. I could see her nipples through the cotton, and I had to look away for my own sanity.

When my buddy Jared told me Lucy and her friends were going to Bear Mountain for the Paper Diamond show, I told him to count Sadie and me in. Jared is like Wrigley—he doesn't judge. He's a good kid. His dad's a big-shot producer in LA, and their place in Big Bear Lake is enormous. His parents were never even there. I knew it wouldn't be a problem.

After Sadie toured the campus and visited an art history class, we headed to Bear Mountain in Jared's truck. Wrigley was living in Venice; I called him from the road and told him to get his ass out to the mountains.

Jared's massive house was right on the lake, at the end of a long, winding driveway. The fresh air smelled of pine trees and wood smoke. Inside, Jared gave Sadie and me one of the bedrooms upstairs.

Wrigley arrived from LA after we finished dinner. I was so glad to see his stupid face that I nearly pounced on the kid—I'd missed that asshole more than any of the other guys I'd hung around with in college. Wrigley and I understood each other; we always had. That night the crew staying at Jared's lounged in front of the fire playing drinking

games. Something about being on the lake and in the mountains puri-
fied my mind, and I felt better than I had in weeks.

I didn't see Lucy until the following day. Pippa McAllister had rented
a condo right in Big Bear Village near the concert venue, so Wrigley and
I stopped by to pregame. Lucy had actually answered my text and told
me to come—a positive sign.

Wrig and I had started drinking at brunch, and by the time we got
to Pippa's around four I was decently buzzed. Floor-to-ceiling glass windows overlooked the mountain, which made the condo feel airy and
more spacious that it actually was. Music thumped from the speakers
propped on the mantel, and a cracked door led to a balcony where people were passing a joint. The place was crowded; I dug my eyes into the
mass of faces and looked for her. I spotted her slim legs dangling from
the countertop, legs I'd memorized. I lifted my eyes to see her profile in
laughter, her neck stretched back, shiny brown hair spilling down over
a cream-colored sweater. Wrigley passed me a beer and I pressed my
fingers hard around the chilled can.

"C'mon, Sade, let's go say hi to Lucy."

"Lucy?"

"You remember Lucy? From a couple of summers ago?"

"Is she the skinny brunette? I lose track of your girlfriends." Sadie
rolled her eyes.

I bumped through bodies and faces I didn't recognize, younger kids I
didn't know, and made my way over to her.

"Hey."

"Hey." Her dark blue eyes were shining.

"Did you ski today?"

"Nah," she said. "The snow sucks."

"Bear's never the greatest in March," I nodded.

"Hi," chirped Sadie.

"Hi, Sadie!" Lucy replied enthusiastically, clearly having not forgotten Sadie. "How was your visit at Baird?" Lucy was nice to nearly everyone, which could get annoying.

Sadie and Lucy delved into a conversation about the art history class
Sadie had visited the day before. I pretended to listen while I watched
her; the side of her face when she smiled, the creases that sharpened at

the corners of her eyes, her dark eyelashes. She was wearing makeup. She looked insane. Jackie, who she'd been talking to before we walked over, shot me a death stare before darting away.

"Do you want a drink?" Lucy was saying. "I'll make you guys a drink. I need another, too."

Her jeans were frayed at the knee, and I studied the patch of skin visible through the rip. It was too much. A chill rose up my spine. Standing so close to her, I recognized the smell of her. I wanted to get drunker. I shook the can of beer in my hand, and it was almost empty.

"Yeah, make us whatever you're drinking."

"Whiskey ginger?"

"Perfect."

A part of me wished I could just get it over with, just go off alone with her somewhere and fuck her, I mean really fuck her good and hard a couple of times, and then go get on with my life. It was how Lucy had always made me feel—distracted. Unbearably so. There were long periods of time during which I hardly thought of her, until out of nowhere, for one reason or another, she'd pop into my mind. And then the idea of her would take hold and absorb aimless pockets of time—on the subway, in the shower, riding the elevator, lying in bed at night. Unsolicited pestering. Lucy was an itch, a song stuck in your head or a movie you need to rewatch or a food you suddenly crave. But I couldn't push her away, because she wasn't *there* in the first place.

"Here you go." She handed us each a tumbler of whiskey and ginger ale poured over ice. I took a sip and it was cold and not too sweet. Just right.

The three of us chatted for a while and when our drinks were empty, Lucy mixed another round. Then a tall guy who looked like he'd stepped out of a fly-fishing catalog called Lucy's name, and she hopped down from the counter.

"I'll be back."

I watched her walk over to the tall guy and he put his hand on her shoulder and leaned in too close to her. I looked down at my drink and it was empty again. I glanced at Sadie; I hoped she wasn't getting too drunk.

"Are you okay, Sade?"

"Yes, *why*?"

"Just making sure. Maybe don't drink anymore for a bit."

"Lucy is *so* nice," she purred, stumbling a little.

"She is."

"She's *so* pretty."

"She is." My eyes floated over to where Lucy had been standing, but she was walking up the stairs and fly fisherman was following her. I took the bottle of Jameson off the counter and poured the last of it in my cup.

"You're flirting with her," Sadie cooed.

"Not really."

"Are you and Alice in a fight or something?"

"No," I told Sadie. "Let's go find Wrigley."

I wasn't sure how much time passed, but the sun had dunked behind the mountains and lights were popping on inside the condo. Wrigley had quickly become the king of the party, despite knowing hardly anyone. He dumped a pile of coke on the coffee table and cut lines with his credit card. Lined up they looked like little white caterpillars.

"No drugs, Sadie," I whispered to my sister. "And don't tell Dad you saw any of this, okay?"

"I'm not an infant, Stephen." Sadie rolled her eyes.

Lucy reappeared from upstairs. "Hey, Luce, want a line?" Wrigley asked her.

"Sure." I watched her take the rolled-up twenty from Wrig and tighten it between her fingers. She plugged a nostril, leaned over the glass table and inhaled.

"Hey," I said behind her, into her hair.

When she turned around she was grinning. She seemed older suddenly, in a good way. Mature. Confident.

"Oh, hey." Her eyes landed softly on mine.

"Lucy," someone called from the doorway. "C'mon, we're leaving."

It was the fly fisherman with a disapproving frown on his face. He ran a hand through his mop of brown hair.

"I'm gonna head to the show," Lucy whispered, just to me. "See you there?"

"Sure."

I watched her slide her arms into a long faux-fur coat. I watched the fly fisherman cover her head in a hat with a big white pom-pom attached to it. I watched them leave, watched the door click shut behind them. The room was foggy and loud. I wished they'd turn down the fucking music. Something inside me felt desperately unhinged.

Wrigley asked me if I wanted a pill of ecstasy.

"What the hell." I held out my palm. "When in Big Bear."

When Sadie wasn't looking we swallowed the small blue pills.

"Lucy looks good," Wrigley said.

"Right." I'd always been sick of people telling me that, as if I were somehow the partial owner of that information.

"Are you guys gonna bang?" Wrigley's eyes grew wide.

"I shouldn't." I shrugged.

"How's, err, Alice, is it?"

"She's fine." I really didn't feel like talking about Alice. She'd called twice today, and I had yet to call her back.

Wrigley could read something amiss in me, the way he'd always been able to.

"DeMarco, these pills are magic. Don't worry, brother. In twenty minutes you'll be soaring."

He was right. Twenty minutes later when we left the condo to walk over to the concert venue—a spot in town called the Goldmine—I felt blissfully calm as an electrifying euphoria hit my brain. I felt indescribably better. I fucking love drugs.

Paper Diamond was wompy electronic music, which I didn't typically enjoy, but while rolling on ecstasy the sound was vibrant and incredible. Wrigley bought us cold beers and I'd never tasted anything so good. The Goldmine was crowded and alive, neon lights bouncing through the audience like colorful jet streams. I felt phenomenal.

I texted Lucy.

STEPHEN: Come stand with me.

She replied almost instantly.

LUCY: Where are you?
STEPHEN: Front right of stage.
LUCY: Give me five.

Minutes later she appeared, dreamlike effervescence shrouding her like a halo. Light blue glitter shimmered on her cheeks.

"Where'd the glitter come from?" I put my arms around her and pulled her close. I kissed the top of her head. I didn't care if Sadie or Wrigley or anyone saw.

Lucy melted in my arms. I stood behind her and pressed my hands against her stomach, felt the small, contracting muscles of her abdomen through her shirt. Her hair smelled like flowers and we swayed to the music.

"I need you, Luce," I whispered in her ear.

"I thought you had a girlfriend?" She turned to face me, the whites of her eyes shining in the semidark.

"I don't care."

"You don't care?"

"She's not you."

It was too easy to say the right thing. I leaned down and kissed her; I thought I might inhale her.

"I shouldn't do this, Stephen."

"Because of that guy?"

"Partly." Her face was so beautiful I almost couldn't look at her.

"God, I've missed you. You're so fucking beautiful, do you know that?"

I kissed her and she kissed me back, pressing her fingers into the back of my neck, her tongue gliding into my mouth. I spun her back toward the stage and wrapped my arms around her warm middle, down the front of her jeans into her underwear, shielded by her long jacket. I pressed two fingers against her, making the circles I knew she loved. It didn't take long, just a few easy minutes until her back arched and I felt her, the shudder coursing through. Lights exploded from the stage, every beat of sound pulsing with the beat of my heart, and the world fell away.

After the show we took a taxi to Jared's, the decision that she would come back with me unspoken. Sadie leaned against my shoulder, her eyelids drooping. Lucy fumbled around with her cell. An incoming call from Billy Boyd flashed on the screen, and she put the phone in her pocket.

Back at Jared's I took Sadie upstairs to our bedroom. She was already under the covers when I turned off the light.

"I hope you had a good time, Sade."

"Mmm. So fun," she slurred. "You're the best."

Lucy waited for me at the bottom of the staircase. It was already three in the morning. It seemed to have gotten very late very quickly and unnoticeably, the way it does when you're on drugs. The house hummed with the stillness of the late hour. I'd stopped rolling from the E but still felt mellow and gratified. Some of the guys were having a nightcap in the living room, but I just wanted to be alone with her. I interlaced our fingers and led her down the hall. We poked our heads into the bedrooms but all of them were taken, so we walked upstairs and checked there. But every room was occupied, either by people passed out or luggage marking claimed territory.

"Shit," I said. "I didn't realize there were so many people staying here."

"We could take a shower." Lucy stepped in close to me and I felt the blood rush between my legs.

"I really just wanna lie down in a bed with you," I breathed.

"Me, too. You're so sexy." She pressed her mouth to my neck.

"Come here." I led her down the hallway and creaked open the door to the bedroom I was sharing with Sadie. "There's an extra bed in here."

"Stephen, no." She gestured to my sister, who was zonked out in the other twin bed, still in her clothes from the day.

"Sadie's passed out. She sleeps through anything. Seriously. We'll be so quiet." I pressed my hips against hers. "C'mon, Luce. I can't wait any longer."

Her moan sufficed as consent. I shut the door and we found each other in the darkness. I peeled off her clothes. I held my breath as she unbuckled my belt. Her smooth skin against my own was like ecstasy all over again, and I couldn't contain myself. I pushed her back against the pillows and pressed myself all the way inside her.

I came as quietly as I possibly could, which wasn't easy. It felt so euphoric I wanted to howl to the heavens, to whatever divine force had brought sex with Lucy back to me.

Afterward she lay across my chest, panting. I ran my fingers through her hair. As my orgasm faded I started to feel the returning, rattling pangs of reality: the death hangover that would engulf me in the morning, the brutal trip to the airport and flight back to New York, a pestering phone call from my father about how it all went, an angry call from Alice about my poor communication over the weekend.

I glanced over at Sadie, still a snoring lump on the other bed.

"I miss you, Luce," I said softly.

"I miss you, too. You started school, huh?"

"Yeah. It's a lot of work."

A few moments of silence passed until Lucy spoke again.

"What's your girlfriend like?"

"What do you mean?"

"I just want to know."

"She's nice," I sighed. "But it's been tough. We moved in together, actually. It's not the best situation."

"You moved *in* together?" Lucy's hushed voice rose an octave, and I already regretted saying anything.

"Shh. Yeah. In January."

"Jesus."

"I'm starting to realize it was a mistake."

"A mistake? How do you accidentally sign a lease?"

"Why are you mad about this?" I asked, though I knew. I shouldn't have asked.

"I'm not mad. I just can't believe you're talking shit about a girl you willingly moved in with."

"You know what?" I whispered, annoyed. "People do make mistakes, okay? I'm in law school, broke as shit, and Alice's grandfather is letting us live in his empty apartment for chump change. I thought it was the right thing to do, but it wasn't. Throw me a fucking bone."

I could see the glare on her face even in the near dark. She lay back down and pulled the covers over her, turning away from me.

"I'm sorry, Luce. I'm just tired."

"You're right, though," she said quietly. "You can live wherever you want. I don't know why I was surprised."

God I hate when girls are passive-aggressive, which they are constantly. It always requires some kind of emotional coddling.

"Lucy, want to know the truth? When you left New York to come back here, I was crushed. But I couldn't have done the distance. Not with work, not with the LSATs. Then I met Alice and we fell into this relationship. Just because I met her . . . it wasn't the end of us. You and me, I mean. It was never supposed to be the end of us."

"You always talk about things as if it's all a matter of convenience."

Pearl-colored moonlight shone through the window. I sensed the onset of dawn lurking behind the gray darkness.

"Are you seeing that guy?" I asked. "The one at the condo today?"

"Yeah. I doubt he'll talk to me after this, though."

"You could just lie."

"Why? 'Cause that's what you do?"

"Come on, Lucy. I just want you to be happy."

"No, you don't."

"Why would you say that?"

"Why do you want to fuck me so badly? What's the point?"

"Why'd you fuck me? Why'd you spend the whole night with me instead of with your boyfriend? You didn't have to do that."

"You are such an asshole."

We weren't even whispering anymore. She started climbing out of the bed, but I pressed her shoulders down.

"I'm sorry, Luce. I shouldn't have said that, I'm just panicked. I miss you. I don't know what to do."

"You talk about it like she doesn't exist."

"I'm sorry. I'm just not in love with her. Come on, I don't want to fight."

Lucy stopped trying to wriggle out of my grip.

"Stephen."

"Are you gonna move back to New York?" I asked her. "After graduation?"

"I don't know."

"You don't know? What about journalism school?"

"I didn't apply. I wouldn't have gotten in, anyway. I barely took any journalism courses."

"I thought it was your minor?"

"I fucked up my minor."

"Oh."

"Jackie wants me to move to LA with her."

"Don't move to LA."

"Why?"

"Aren't you sick of California by now? Besides, LA doesn't suit you. You're a New Yorker."

"Maybe LA suits me better."

"No way."

"New York isn't out of the question."

"Good. I need you to come back, Luce."

"Why? So I can be your slutty mistress when your live-in girlfriend is off doing errands?"

"I'm moving out of there by June, whether or not you come back. I've already decided."

She was quiet for a moment. "For real, Stephen?"

"Yes. And I don't want her the way I want you. You could never be my slutty mistress." I swept my eyes down and studied her naked body, the curves of her breasts. "Your boobs have gotten bigger."

"A little, yeah."

"I like it."

"Thanks."

"Lucy in the Sky with Diamonds?"

"Yes, Stephen DeMarco?"

"You mean a lot to me. Don't forget it." I traced my fingers along her spine. I could feel how tired we both were.

"You mean a lot to me, too," she whispered. "More than you know."

Somewhere in the stirring dawn, midconversation, we fell asleep.

PART
FOUR

39

LUCY

AUGUST 2017

I haven't been to enough weddings to know whether I'm the kind of person who cries at weddings, but there are tears in my eyes as I watch Bree, calm and collected, in the moments before she walks down the aisle. The sun is shining streams of light through the church windows and it's a perfect summer day, not a cloud in the bluebird sky. I watch Pippa, the maid of honor, carefully smooth Bree's veil and train around her feet. Bree smiles at us and nods.

Bree and Evan chose to have Pachelbel's Canon in D play during the processional instead of "Here Comes the Bride." It is so much more beautiful and classic; the delicate melody of the piano and violins creates a pure, holy sound that fills the nave of the church. The bridesmaids pair off with the groomsmen and begin the walk down the aisle. I'm the second to last, before Pippa and the best man. Evan's only groomsman from Baird, Charlie Rosen, is my partner for the processional, and he hooks his elbow in mine like we'd practiced. The butterflies in my stomach whirl like crazy. I know he's out there.

I turn back to Bree one last time. "You look perfect," I say.

"We're up, Lucy." Charlie tugs my arm and my lilac satin dress suddenly feels too tight, but I take a deep breath and put one foot forward. Pachelbel floods my eardrums as we proceed down the aisle. *Slow and steady, slow and steady.* My whole body feels numb and hot, even though the church is air-conditioned, and I keep my eyes straight ahead at Evan and the priest and the rest of the wedding party. The aisle feels much, much longer than it did during the rehearsal.

Charlie and I part ways at the altar and I take my place standing next to Jackie before allowing myself to look out at the audience. There are 250 people packed into the church, but I only see one, and I see him right away because he's the one person looking straight at me, his emerald gaze unwavering. He sits close to the front, in the fourth row, and there is a girl next to him who I recognize immediately because I've looked at her Facebook pictures countless times, and I've cried in front of those pictures and I still look at those pictures—infrequently, but I do. I recognize her heart-shaped face and wispy bangs and broad shoulders, and one of her hands is resting on his leg, and before I can even begin to wonder *why* she is here when no one else was allowed to bring a plus-one, she lifts her other hand to shield a yawn and I see the diamond on her left ring finger, glinting in a narrow beam of light.

I feel gutted, like I have so many times before involving him, stunned in a way that makes my legs want to collapse underneath me. Except I can't let my legs collapse because in this moment I am a bridesmaid on the altar at the wedding of one of my best friends, and Bree's father is walking her down the aisle and I have to hold it together. Because if there's one thing I've come to understand over the past few years, it's that life is a lot bigger than my individual issues, and there is something selfish about indulging in your own problems, especially on a day like today that is 100 percent about Bree. Still, I'm grateful when Jackie takes my hand and squeezes it, because she sees the ring, too, and she sees that even though everybody else has turned to watch the bride, Stephen is still looking straight at me.

After graduation I moved back to New York because I couldn't not. Because the words *I need you to come back, Luce* and *It was never supposed to be the end of us* played on repeat in my head every second of every day.

"I really wish you'd stay in Cali with us," Jackie said as she watched me pack. She sat on the edge of my bare mattress with her hair tied back by an old red bandanna, one she'd bought in town freshman year before the Wild West party. The sight of the bandanna—the memory of that night, so long ago now—made my eyes well with tears. Jackie was moving to LA with Pippa in a week. Bree already had a job in New York City and if I got one soon enough, we were going to move in together.

"I'll just see how the summer goes," I said. "If I don't get a job by August, maybe I'll move back out here." It was half true.

"It's because of him, isn't it?" Jackie blinked at me.

"What do you mean?"

"'Cause of Stephen. You think it's going to work out. You think he's going to leave his girlfriend and the two of you will live happily ever after."

Jackie's reproaches never failed to sting, but I was used to them. Her bitterness toward me wasn't constant but it was residual, a lingering effect of my having slept with Stephen in Big Bear Lake. Pippa was more understanding—"chemistry is annoying, it happens"—but even though Jackie claimed to be over it I knew she couldn't stand what I'd done. Initially she said she was upset because I'd betrayed Billy—I'd told him the truth about sneaking off with Stephen in Big Bear, and I didn't object or fight back when he told me, rather rationally, that he no longer wanted anything to do with me.

Still, I knew Jackie was angry at me and I knew it was about more than just Billy, and I'd pressed her, until one night she caved.

"I just can't believe you'd give up everything you worked so hard to move past. Everything your therapist said . . . all that stuff *you* agreed with. How can you not see it? You think he's going to make you happy, but he's not. *Players only love you when they're playing.* Stevie knows best, right?"

"He isn't the reason I was depressed, Jack," I told her. "Depression is a chemical imbalance. It's genetic."

"You don't understand what I'm trying to say," Jackie had muttered. "It's pointless. You're just going to have to figure it out for yourself."

I didn't talk to her about Stephen after that, didn't tell her about our conversation in bed the night of Paper Diamond or that we'd been talking ever since, or that he begged me to send him naked pictures because he wasn't turned on by Alice, or that he'd promised to end it with Alice and move out of their apartment by the end of June. But I could tell Jackie knew what I was up to; she knew when I stared at my phone for too long, smiling at something on the screen. The thing she didn't understand was that Stephen and I had had terrible timing at Baird. There wasn't any reason that under the right circumstances, things wouldn't be great. What we had wasn't some trivial flirtation that could be summed up in a Fleetwood Mac lyric. But I didn't bother explaining that to Jackie, because a lot of times people on the outside of situations can't understand anything.

I flew back east and applied to every job under the sun. A job in New York was my ticket to an apartment in New York, and an apartment in New York was my ticket to Stephen—well, closer to Stephen. Bree had had her position at J.P. Morgan lined up since the previous summer, but my parents were adamant that I couldn't look for an apartment with her until I found a job. *We're not going to fund your life while you skitter around Manhattan, Lucy,* were CJ's exact words as my dad sat there nodding, because agreeing with CJ was all he knew how to do.

My dad said his friend at the *New York Times* could probably get me a last-minute internship, but unpaid, so I declined. Holding out for a job in journalism—the career my parents assumed I still wanted—wasn't worth it. I didn't really care what I did, so long as it was semirelevant to my major and paid enough for me to fund my own life in the city. I just wanted to get hired as quickly as possible, so I cast my net wide, drafting endless cover letters and tailoring my résumé accordingly.

Of course it was CJ who ended up landing me a job, because of course it was CJ who knew the trendy, Botoxed women who had connections at English degree–populated conglomerates like Edelman and Hearst and Condé Nast.

"Francesca can get you an interview at a company called *The Suitest,*" CJ told me, examining her champagne pink nails, freshly manicured. Francesca was CJ's most Botoxed Pilates student. She came to the house for private classes. Her lips looked like they'd been injected with Jell-O.

"It's some kind of online publication that covers hotels," CJ went on. "And Francesca's ex-ex-husband Harry is the director of sales. So the job is ad sales *but* it's the travel industry, so I figured you might be interested. I bet you'd get it—Francesca knows how smart you are, and she and Harry are on fabulous terms, despite the fact that she caught him having an affair with his *male* personal trainer."

Francesca's ex-ex-husband Harry hired me after a twenty-minute interview during which we mostly discussed Francesca's use of injectables—particularly the current state of her bottom lip—in keeled-over laughter. An HR person informed me that my title was account coordinator and that my annual salary would be $32,000. Lydia told me that was almost less than minimum wage, but I accepted the job anyway, because who knew if I'd ever get another job offer, and the sooner I got a job the sooner I could move to the city.

That weekend, Bree and I found a reasonably priced apartment on Third Street in the East Village. We signed a lease to move in the middle of June. That night, while Alice was at a work event and I was alone in my bed in Cold Spring Harbor, Stephen and I had a naked FaceTime session to celebrate.

40

STEPHEN

MAY 2014

Alice handed me a plate of steaming scrambled eggs, buttered toast, and two strips of limp, rubbery bacon. She climbed into bed next to me holding her own plate, which, as usual, contained an identical meal to mine. She rubbed her legs against my own, picked up the remote, and flicked on the television. *The Big Lebowski* flashed on the screen, one of my favorites. But Alice quickly changed the channel, surfing through until she landed on one of her beloved reality shows, this time a rerun of *The Real Housewives of New Jersey*. A woman with brown hair yapped at a woman with blond hair, and then the blonde yapped back at the brunette.

The eggs were watery and bland; they were a struggle to swallow. Alice was not a good cook, and her attempts to be domestic were sad. I placed my unfinished plate on the floor, picked up my copy of my contracts hornbook, debated shooting myself, and then began chapter fourteen.

"Oh, you're going to read?" Alice looked over at me and chewed a piece of bacon between her teeth, which I noticed she hadn't bothered to brush.

"Maybe I just don't want to eat breakfast in bed this morning. Okay?" I felt like being a dick. I wasn't sure why.

"Do whatever you want." She glanced back toward the TV.

I felt the stirrings of yet another fight.

"Look, Al, I have an exam on Friday. Maybe I'll just go to the library now and get a jump start on studying."

She shrugged and kept her eyes glued to the blabbing girls on the screen. "Suit yourself."

"The eggs were good."

"You didn't even eat them."

I wondered how she knew that without having peeled her eyes from the television.

I stood and brought my plate over to our pea-size kitchen, which was two feet from the bedroom, and dumped the uneaten food into the trash bin. I would get a roast beef sandwich at my favorite deli on the way to NYU.

"What are you going to do today?" I asked Alice in an effort to be friendly.

She shrugged, still not looking at me. She wore my old Baird College T-shirt, which was soft and frayed at the edges from so many washes. Her hair was tied up in a messy bun and loose blond wisps sprinkled her neck. For a second I wondered if I should go over and try to fuck her before I left, but decided it wasn't worth it.

"Maybe clean the apartment," she said eventually. "And I'll buy groceries for the week. What do you want for dinner tonight?"

I wished Alice would go out and spend a Sunday with her friends, go to brunch or have some Bloody Marys at the Frying Pan. But all she ever did these days was wait for me, like a faithful dog.

"What time will you be home?" she asked, not waiting for me to answer her about what I wanted for dinner.

"I don't know. It might be late." I didn't have any plans, but I could always make some. If I didn't stay late at the library I would probably grab a beer with some classmates—anything to delay the return to the apartment.

"Okay, so what time do you think?"

"Don't worry about dinner for me tonight, okay, Al?"

"Fine," she snapped, and I knew she was pissed again. She was always pissed about one thing or another, just like Diana, actually. She shoveled a bite of egg into her mouth.

"By the way, when's our lease up again, Al?" I asked warily. "July first, right?"

"What lease?"

"For our apartment."

"This is my grandfather's apartment. We didn't sign a lease. Why?" She shot me a threatening look.

"I thought I signed something. Wasn't it six months?"

"That wasn't a lease. It was an agreement to pay him a specific amount on a monthly basis."

"Oh."

"Why?" Alice's dark eyes narrowed.

"I just didn't know if we were supposed to re-sign," I lied.

"No," she said, turning back toward the television. "There's no time frame. He owns this place."

This dump, I wanted to say.

I knew she was annoyed at me but I didn't have it in me to try and patch things up right then, so I said goodbye. The usual relief of leaving my apartment filled me as I walked down our shitty Kips Bay block toward the subway, but it was only temporary respite. The words *no time frame* made my throat feel very tight and dry. I couldn't place precisely when I had gone from adoring Alice to feeling trapped and irritated by nearly every wavelength of her existence.

But I was usually horny and that was at least one thing Alice was still good for; despite my waning interest in her we continued to have sex. I think she took it as a sign that our relationship was still in good standing, but the truth was I needed sex more than ever that first year of law school. It was the one precious pocket of the day when I could forget my heavy textbooks and looming deadlines and cumbersome relationship and lose myself.

I rode the 6 train downtown, toward NYU. The grimy subway car was sparse for a Sunday morning, and I wondered how many times I'd ridden this train back and forth, back and forth. I wouldn't be riding this route much longer. What a fucking miracle we hadn't signed a lease. Once law review applications were done in July, I was getting the hell out of there.

41
LUCY
JUNE 2014

The Monday after I moved into my new apartment on Third Street and Avenue B, Stephen asked me to meet him for a postwork drink. I'd moved in over the weekend; Bree wasn't moving in until Wednesday.

> STEPHEN: Morning pretty girl. Meet for a drink at 7 tonight?
> 135 Avenue A is the address of the bar. I have news.

Stephen's messages to me—the simple sight of his name on my phone or email address in my in-box—never ceased to send a judder of excitement through my insides, even when our communication was regular.

It was spitting rain as I strode toward 135 Avenue A under my umbrella, confidence dusting my heels. I had made it all happen, and faster than planned. Job, apartment, and now Stephen. I'd seen him a few times since I'd been back east, for coffee or drinks, but we couldn't fool around, not with my commuting back to Cold Spring Harbor and his living with *Alice*. I hated the sound of her name.

Stephen and I had only hooked up once since Bear Mountain, in the side stairwell of Lydia's apartment building on a night when I'd been staying there, because there was nowhere else to do it and we were practically already screwing on the street after dinner at Tacombi. That kind of chemistry—God, nothing compared.

But now I had my own apartment, and Stephen was on the brink of leaving Alice, and everything was different and fresh and even the smallest daily tasks, like buying water at the bodega or swiping my MetroCard, were tinged with a sense of purpose and possibility.

I had to smile when I came to a halt in front of 135 Avenue A; the outside of the bar was black and in magenta cursive above the entrance a sign read: *Lucy's*.

I opened the door and as I walked through the bar the air seemed to move around me, filling the spaces where my body had been as I made my way forward. He sat at one of the tables in the back, hands folded neatly on the polished wood surface, his expression complacent. In one untraceable flicker his eyes were fastened to mine, and a sudden memory filled me up: I saw that same pair of eyes watching me from the houseboat on Lake Mead my freshman fall.

It's funny how people don't change. I mean physically, how they don't change. For example, I could look at a picture of Georgia at age two and she'd have the same distinct pointed elf ears that are still part of her twenty-three-year-old body.

Stephen's eyes were the same crazy green as they had always been. I could see the afternoon sunlight drenching the deck of that houseboat, three and a half years ago. In my memory I felt the allure of those first weeks at Baird, how in utter awe I'd been of everything happening around me. Whoever I was then seemed like a long-lost version of myself, someone I didn't know anymore, and I couldn't figure out how I'd gotten to where I was. I'd been experiencing the same recurring thoughts since I'd moved back to New York: What was I doing? Why was I still chasing him? Did I even *like* him as a person? How could I ever bank on a future with someone I couldn't trust? There was that one stubborn, annoyingly veracious part of me that knew wanting Stephen had to be wrong. If you ignored the gray and got really honest, if everything in the world was separated into black and white, into good and bad, Stephen would fall into bad. For a fleeting moment, something foreign but persuasive filled me, and I debated turning around, leaving the bar, and never looking back. I could run six blocks to my new apartment and lock myself inside; he didn't know the address yet.

But my legs were moving forward, quickly, and the closer I got to the table, the more ecstatic energy rose behind my sternum. And that was my answer, forever. Maybe I didn't always like him, but there is a difference between liking someone and loving them, and the power in that difference is enough to shape your life.

I smelled his Old Spice. His bottom lip was wet with Scotch. I studied his familiar hand, how it gripped the glass, the half-moons on his fingernails.

"Lucy's, huh?" I glanced around.

"Fitting, right?" One side of his mouth curled. "Have a seat. Stay awhile. I ordered you a glass of pinot noir. A drink for Lucy at Lucy's."

"Clever." I smiled and sat. Was I supposed to be angry with him? I couldn't remember. I tasted the wine. It was just what I needed.

"You look good, Luce," he said. I studied his eyes, and wondered for a moment if it had always been about the way I looked. It wasn't a new thought.

"So do you," I said, meaning it. Cleaned up in a suit and freshly shaven, Stephen looked handsome. I fingered the silky fabric of his red tie. "How are you?"

"Oh, I'm fine. My internship is a nice change of pace from school. The only drawback is having to wear a damn suit again."

"I like the suit."

"And how is your job?" he probed. "I googled *The Suitest*. It looks cool."

"It's fine. It's a lot of grunt work."

"Well, you're an assistant. I know how that goes."

"*Coordinator*, actually."

"That's corporate America's gracious term for *assistant*, Luce. Hate to break it to you."

"Believe me, I know." I rolled my eyes. "My boss is the best, though. Harry. He's late forties and gay and hilarious."

"Having a good boss is important."

"Yeah. I can't complain. It's a job."

"That it is. You have a job. *And* an apartment. You're finally a real New Yorker, Luce. You're finally here."

The thought that I had the apartment to myself that night made me way more excited than I should've been, considering that Stephen still, technically, lived with Alice thirty blocks north. I studied his face. He really did look handsome.

"Thanks for meeting me," he said, interlacing his wide fingers in mine across the table. "I know you don't love this situation."

"What situation?"

"You know, me living with Alice . . ."

"While we fuck?" I whispered. I knew it turned him on when I said *fuck*.

"You know it's not like that. Cut me some slack, Luce."

"I am cutting you slack. I'm just tired of sneaking around. I just want to be with you."

"And I want to be with you," he said evenly, his eyes unblinking.

"Only a couple of more weeks." I drummed my fingertips against the wood surface.

"I actually need to tell you something."

"What is it?" Instant sweat coated my palms.

He exhaled an audible sigh. "I need to stay in the apartment just a little longer. Law review applications are due at the end of July, and I just need to put in a little more time at school before—"

"What are you saying?" My stomach was dropping like quicksand.

"I probably need to stay there through the end of July, early August at the latest."

"August. *August?*" The momentary mirage shattered, my words erupting unconsciously. "You told me you were moving out in June. First you said the beginning of June, then it was the end of June, and now it's *August*? How can you stay there for another six weeks? You talk so much shit about her. You're so full of shit it's a joke. *We* are a joke. You ask me for naked pictures every fucking day because you 'can't fall asleep without seeing them.' I'm a low-rate porn star, is all. Some girl in a photograph who gets you going before you go and fuck your girlfriend." I lurched back in my chair, livid.

"Lucy—"

"I don't believe anything you say anymore. All you do is lie. This entire thing—whatever the *fuck* this is—has been one giant lie."

I forced myself to stand. I knew people were staring but I kept my eyes locked to the dirty floor as I moved toward the exit. I thought of Dr. Wattenbarger, of how disappointed he would be in me for landing myself back here. I hadn't had an appointment with him in months.

Outside, the air had turned to fog, a dense mass of whiteness. In the hazy weather I couldn't see a foot ahead. A damp film covered my bare arms, and I realized I'd left my jacket inside. I shivered in the misty rain, my stomach a wrenching pool of sickness.

Stephen bounded out of the bar, and I watched him squint to find me in the fog. I wanted to hop in a cab to Penn Station and take the train home and crawl into CJ's arms and ask my mother what the hell I was supposed to do. I wanted this more than I could stomach, so much so that the reminder of CJ's betrayal eviscerated me in its full capacity all over again, and I knew I couldn't go home because that safe, unconditional space of love in my mother's arms had long since ceased to exist for me. All I could do was stand still and watch as Stephen's bright eyes found me through the mist, and he walked toward me, my jacket tucked under his arm. I knew he would say something that would make me feel better—whether or not it was true didn't matter anymore. He placed the jacket around my shoulders and smudged a tear from my cheek with his thumb.

"Lucy." His voice filled me. "Look, I know you want me to say that I'll move out tomorrow. And I would if I could; you have my word on that. But I have law review applications and I can't be homeless for a month—"

"Homeless?" I felt defeated; I was shocked at the anger and defense so ready to spew out of me. "You would move back to Long Island and commute if you were really that miserable."

"You're right, then," he said. "I'm not *miserable*. I'm definitely not happy, but okay, it's not *so* bad that I can't suck it up until I'm totally done with school and law review in July. I can't afford to get my own place right now—I'd have to pay first month's rent, last month's rent, a security deposit and probably a broker's fee, all with no income. And if I moved back to Long Island, I'd spend three hours of the day commuting and my academic life would take a detrimental toll. I understand that you think I'm being selfish, but law school needs to be my priority right now. I've invested a ton of money and time into this, and I can't afford to make a decision that risks losing what I stand to gain."

He looked like a lawyer who'd just given the jury his best argument. I willed my head to wrap itself around his logic. On paper it made sense. And Stephen was the kind of person who saw the world for what it could give him, for what he could take from it. Betrayal, shame, love—they were secondary hindrances, not even sacrifices.

"I get it." I stared passed his shoulder, not for a second forgetting that it was *his* shoulder.

"Lucy, I don't want her the way I want you. You have to know that."
Stephen looked concerned as he bent his head down toward mine.
Shadows from passing cars danced across his face.

"I've heard you say that before."

"Because it's true. With Alice . . . I feel like I'm driving a Honda. And
I want a BMW."

"Huh?"

"It's a metaphor. And you, Lucy in the Sky with Diamonds, are a
BMW."

"That's crazy."

"You and I both know I'm crazy."

I looked up into his eyes. A million thoughts passed through my
head, each of them like tiny invisible passengers clinging to a mass of
tiny invisible chains. I knew only that I was happier here than anywhere
else—the nonsensical, arbitrary, indiscriminate three centimeters from
his face—and I knew that meant it was love, and even though I had always known I was in love with him I let myself relearn it, partially so
that the psychosis of it could take responsibility for everything that I
had done wrong.

As Stephen enveloped me, I suddenly understood the other piece of
the truth—Stephen and I were the same. I was emotionally intelligent
enough to know that Stephen was not good, not objectively, but if I stood
face-to-face with myself in the truest light, I wasn't, either. For what I'd
done to CJ and to Marilyn's memory, for the way I'd treated Georgia and
my father and Lydia and Parker and all the people who'd loved me without
reason, I fell into the bad category. I'd internally justified all that behavior based on the rubric of CJ's behavior and the Unforgivable Thing, but
what I could finally feel now, surrendering in Stephen's arms, was that no
matter how justifiable that excuse was, it didn't make me a good person.
Maybe CJ wasn't good, but neither was I, and neither was Stephen, and
my love for Stephen finally made complete, wonderful, real sense, and if it
were possible, I loved him even more.

"So I'm a BMW, yeah?" I smiled up at him.

I didn't have to dislike myself anymore for indulging in the parts of
him that I found offensive, even cruel. I imagined Alice on the couch in
their apartment, flipping through TV channels and maybe having a glass

of wine. She expected him home later, after his dinner with work colleagues, which would turn into postdinner drinks and important lawyer
talk that he couldn't afford to miss. In reality the work colleagues were
me, and tonight she was a Honda, and her relationship was a lie.

"You're my BMW." Stephen pressed his mouth to mine, and I didn't
doubt anything.

We walked the six blocks back to my building on Third Street. Our
apartment on the fourth floor of the walk-up was newly renovated; it
was dark and empty and smelled of fresh paint. Patches of light spilled in
from the building across the street.

"This place is awesome," Stephen said, walking around. His voice
echoed since there wasn't any furniture yet. "A *dishwasher*?" He stopped
in the kitchen. "How much are they paying you at this hotel website,
moneybags?"

"According to Lydia, minimum wage." I shook off my jacket, which
was wet with mist. "But rent is reasonable in Alphabet City."

I led him through the small living area and Bree's room, then my
room. I walked over to the window next to my bed, which overlooked
Third Street below.

"It's not the worst view," Stephen said, standing behind me as I pressed
my forehead against the glass. "The window in my first New York apartment faced a brick wall."

"I remember."

He placed his hands on my hips. He planted small kisses on the
side of my neck until I turned around. I ran my hands over his smooth
cheeks. It was the first time Stephen and I had been alone together in
a real bedroom, with a real bed, in longer than I could remember. He
leaned toward me. His kiss weakened my knee joints.

"Stephen."

"Yeah?"

"We should wait. We shouldn't do this. I know we did it in the stairwell that time, but—"

"I promise this will be better than the stairwell." He slid his hands
up my shirt.

"Stephen."

"Luce. If you want me to go, I'll go. Just say the word."

"I just—Alice. Don't you feel guilty?" Maybe I was testing him. I definitely didn't want him to go.

"I don't feel guilt. Not about this."

The words hung in the air, like smoke. I wasn't sure what to do with them, but then Stephen peeled my shirt up over my head, and there was nothing left to interpret. We toppled onto the bare mattress, the only piece of furniture in the room. It still smelled new, like the thick plastic the men from Sleepy's had delivered it in that morning.

After we had sex he held me close and we watched the rain drip down the windows, cast with a vermilion glow from the streetlamps. He kissed the top of my back and let his mouth linger there, the heat of his breath soft against the base of my neck.

I got up and walked to the kitchen and took two Amstel Light longnecks out of the fridge. It was all that was in there; Bree had bought them for us the other day when we picked up the keys.

Stephen and I sat up in bed, sipping the beers.

"See, this is what I'm talking about," he said.

"What is?"

"This." He motioned his hand between us. "Us. In bed. Having beers. Naked. It's awesome. It just feels . . . right."

"It does." I smiled.

"I know I always tell you, Lucy in the Sky with Diamonds, but you are so beautiful. I think you're more beautiful every time I see you."

Affection drenched my insides. My body ached for him even though he was inches from me. The desire was insatiable. "You looked stupid hot in that suit."

"You must have been hammered."

"I had one drink."

I rested my head against his chest. An hour flew by.

Stephen rubbed my knee. "It's past two. I have to go."

I gripped his ankle. I thought I'd die if he left. I wanted him to stay the night, but knew I couldn't ask. I knew what the answer would be, and couldn't stand to hear it out loud.

I lay horizontal on the bed and watched him dress, savoring the time. He kissed me on the forehead.

"What about this?" I held up the red tie, which lay on the mattress.

"Can't forget that."

"Here, let me."

CJ taught Georgia and me how to tie a tie when we were younger. She said it was something that would come in handy later.

As I secured the knot Stephen touched the backs of my bare thighs and I felt that rousing tug from deep inside.

"What are you doing this weekend, birthday girl?"

"I'll be out in the Hamptons at Lydia's. She's saying something about throwing me a birthday party." Lydia's grandparents had a house in Sagaponack but were spending the summer traveling around Europe. Lydia and her cousins were allowed to use the house whenever.

"You don't say? I'll be at the family place in Westhampton. I'd love to come by and see you, if that would be okay." Stephen ran his hands over my bare back, and I nodded into his shoulder.

"Yes," I whispered.

He kissed me one more time before turning to leave. In the doorway he looked back, hooded in silver shadows. "Lucy?"

"Yes?"

"I love you."

I love you. I LOVE YOU. HE LOVED ME. I'd always known he did. It was all I had ever wanted to hear him say.

"I love you, too, Stephen." Finally, I could say it.

After he left I curled up on my new mattress in my new apartment. Happiness flooded me. I had the feeling that nothing would ever be the same.

42

STEPHEN

She sat on a wooden bench in Washington Square Park, her head tilted toward the pages of a book. The sky was still robin's-egg blue even though it was a quarter to seven and most people had left work for the day. A clashing combination of yuppies, students, hipsters, and homeless people populated the scene. Washington Square Park is overcrowded as far as New York City parks go, but it was right by NYU and close to the spa in SoHo where Alice had just gotten a postwork facial.

Alice's hair was pulled back in a tight ponytail that made her brown roots extra visible, her skin appeared slightly blotchy from her facial, and she wore a tank top that made her arms look chubbier than they might have in another shirt. I wondered if she would've put more effort into her appearance—and perhaps rescheduled the facial—had she known the reason behind this meeting.

I hadn't wanted to do it in the apartment; outside was cleaner, more final, there was less room for misinterpretation. I studied her from afar and reaffirmed my decision. I couldn't take it anymore; waiting until the end of July was not an option.

When Alice looked up and saw me, she waved and shifted to make room on the bench. She kissed me hello and, out of habit, I kissed her back easily, the way we always did. It occurred to me that we would probably never kiss again.

"It's so nice out." She closed her book and smiled, glancing ahead at the fountain and a group of kids splashing in the shallow water around it. "Summer just changes everything in this city."

I attempted to smile back but ended up gritting my teeth, something I'd been doing a lot lately. I just wanted to get this over with.

"My facial was fan*tas*tic," she trilled, even though I hadn't asked. "Just what I needed."

"Good. Good." I said it twice, accidentally.

"I missed you today, baby." Alice placed her hand on my leg.

Rip the Band-Aid.

I removed her hand and placed it on her side of the bench. She frowned.

Next to us a cluster of homeless guys were stretching out their dirty blankets over a patch of grass. A foul stench filled my nostrils.

Alice swatted her hand back and forth in front of her nose. "Maybe we should go get a drink somewhere, babe. B Bar and sit on the patio?"

I studied the details of her face. Her dark, almond-shaped eyes, her rounded chin.

"Alice," I said carefully. "We need to talk."

"Talk? Why? What's going on?" The color—red splotches and all—drained from her face.

"I haven't been happy lately, in this relationship. I feel that I need to move on."

The words stuck between us. Alice's expression told me that they might have come out a bit too harshly. A wet gloss sealed her eyes; they already looked red around the rims, as though she hadn't been sleeping well. Her voice was squeaky when she spoke.

"What?"

"I'm sorry. This isn't what I want. I am sorry."

I watched her collapse, heaving forward like she'd been hit in the gut. When she picked her head up so many tears covered her face that it might've scared me if I hadn't seen girls cry that way too many times before.

I suddenly felt so incredibly exhausted; I couldn't wait to have some Scotch on the train to Long Island and pass out. I'd already packed some clothes and my laptop and a fifth of Dewar's in my backpack, and my father was expecting me. I'd crash there and move the rest of my stuff out over the weekend. Commuting would suck, but I could always crash at Luke's or Carl's or probably Lucy's if I needed to.

"Why are you doing this?" Alice's voice was desperate, rattled. "Do you even realize what you're saying?"

"Yeah, Al, this is something I've been thinking about for a while. I mean, things haven't been great."

"We're having problems, sure, but you can't just give up like this. We *live* together. We love each other. You don't know what you're saying. Did you sleep with someone else? Is that what this is about?" She was practically yelling.

"*No.* Jesus. Keep your voice down."

"Keep my *voice* down? Is that why you brought me here? So I wouldn't make a scene in a public place? You're a piece of shit."

Another wave of tears dispensed; the endless, endless flood. I rubbed her back. It seemed like a decent gesture.

"Please don't do this," she said, choking on her words. "Please. We can work on things. Whatever I'm doing, I can fix it. We can fix this."

I sank my head down and stared at the overgrown blades of grass between my flip-flops. The problem with girls is that they always think there is something they can do to "fix it," and there never is. The end is just the end; it doesn't *mean* anything and it isn't necessarily the *result* of something. It isn't a decision so much as a natural alteration. Change is instinctual.

"You fucked that girl, didn't you? Lucy Whatsherface. The one who's always texting you."

"*No.* I've never cheated on you. I told you, she's a girl from school who I exchange notes with."

"I don't believe you. You're not friends with anyone named Lucy on Facebook."

"Maybe she isn't on Facebook!" I shouted, even though Lucy was on it, she'd just unfriended me at some point over the contentious years. "Jesus, Alice. You're acting crazy."

"*I'm* acting crazy? You're so messed up, and the sad part is you can't even see it."

Frustration seized me. I had known Alice would try and make me feel like a heartless bastard, just like Jenna and Diana had. Just like Lucy did, when she felt like it. I racked my brain for the right response.

"Alice, it's not fair for you to be with someone who isn't fully there for you. You deserve more than that, much more. I'm so sorry for the pain I'm causing you, but I know that soon you'll see this is the right thing." This made her cry harder. She sobbed into my shoulder.

We sat on the bench for another hour or maybe it was two, until the sun had dipped below the west side and the crowds in Washington Square Park began to disperse.

Alice and I had a slightly different version of the same conversation about ten times. I wished for once in my goddamn life I could've cried to help prove her heartless-bastard theory wrong, but as usual, the ducts remained dry.

I pulled a handwritten letter out of my pocket. It was Diana who taught me the efficacy of handwritten letters, and I thank her for that because they work like magical charms.

"It's hard for me to say everything I'm feeling in words." I handed her the folded note.

Tears slipped off Alice's cheeks in thick streams. I didn't think it was possible for her eyes to produce more liquid. Passersby in the park were sort of staring at us: the hysterically sobbing girl and the dry-eyed prick next to her.

"I think you should read it after I leave," I said.

"I bet you already have your stuff packed, don't you?" She looked up at me, her face pink and swollen.

"I packed a backpack. I'm going to stay in Bayville for a while."

"I can't believe any of this," she moaned. "I don't understand how you're not more upset."

"I am upset."

"*Not* like I am. Your fucking heart isn't breaking." Her bottom lip quivered. I decided I had to get out of there. It had been over two hours of this and I was starting to feel unbearably tense.

"Just read the letter," I said. "I'll be back in a few days to get the rest of my stuff and we can talk some more then, if you want. I do have to go now. I need to make the train."

Alice wouldn't look at me, and she didn't budge when I tried to hug her goodbye, so I ended up putting an arm around her awkwardly while she stared into her lap.

I walked through the giant arch at the north end of the park and headed west, my shoes slamming the dirty cement sidewalk. I was angry. It was naive of Alice to act like she hadn't seen any of this coming, to assume that I'd be there for her indefinitely like some loyal pet. She'd looked at me the way the girls before her had looked at me: broken and defeated at my departure, as though their lives would be forever changed. What they all failed to understand and what aggravated me the most was that none of it had been my fault. That kind of pain was the risk for choosing to rely on another person, and reliance is always a choice.

A bearded man handing out Christianity flyers practically mounted me on the street and I shooed him away. Fucking Jesus chasers. I suddenly didn't feel at all like catching the subway to Penn and going out to Bayville to spend the night at my dad's. He would just pester me with questions about the breakup, and the last thing I wanted to do was spend another second *talking* about any of this.

I turned around at the corner of Waverly and Sixth Avenue, now positive where I was headed. I pulled out my cell and texted my father.

> STEPHEN: Too much work tonight. Need to crash at a friend's. Be home tomorrow.

I stopped at a grocery store and got what I needed. I quickened my pace, continuing east and then south until I reached the corner of Third Street and Avenue B. I rang the doorbell to apartment 4C. She buzzed me up and appeared to be alone when she opened the door.

Her hair was longer than I remembered it being two weeks ago. It fell loose past her bare shoulders, the ends silky and uneven. Her skin was sun-kissed from several weekends at the beach, and her blue-gray eyes popped arrestingly from her face. In a white tank top and cut-off Levi's she was more perfect than I'd remembered, even though it had been only a couple of weeks ago that I'd seen her out in Sagaponack at her birthday party. I'd tried hard to fuck her again, and succeeded for about three thrusts before she made me stop and said *No. No more. Not until you're out of that apartment.*

Well, I'm out of that apartment, honey.

"What are you doing here, Stephen?" Her eyes searched my face.

"Can I come in?"

Lucy hesitated before opening the door all the way. It clicked shut behind me.

"Where's Bree?"

"In San Francisco for work."

"Oh. Then you're here all alone?"

"Stephen, what do you want?" I recognized her quintessential annoyed-but-intrigued tone of voice. She backed into the kitchen and leaned her elbow against the black marble counter. There was a candle burning on the coffee table that made the apartment smell delicious, like vanilla and patchouli.

I set down the bag of groceries I'd just purchased and shrugged. "I bought shrimp and bok choy and white wine. I want to make you dinner, if you'll let me."

Her eyes grew large; I could almost see through them into the patterns running wildly inside her brain.

"We talked about this," she said. "I know we hooked up the other week but I told you in Sagaponack, I want to wait until you move out. I mean it. It's too complicated for me otherwise, can't you—"

"It's over, Lucy."

"What?"

"I told Alice. I couldn't handle it for another second. Remember when I told you I loved you? Well, I meant it. I'm going to move back to Bayville and commute until I can find a new place. And I thought maybe I could stay here every now and then . . . if that would be all right with you."

I watched the news and the second *I love you* melt into her spongy heart and she nodded, a smile creeping into the corners of her perfect mouth. I was growing hard inside my khakis and had the feeling we wouldn't get around to cooking the shrimp and bok choy until later.

I pulled her in close, interlacing my hands around the small of her back.

"That's why I'm here," I said softly. "It's just you and me now, Luce. And I want it to work, for real this time."

43

LUCY

Stephen pressed his foot to the gas and the Ford Explorer accelerated down Montauk Highway. It was the second to last weekend of August and the Hamptons were in their prime. Crowded but still magical, especially during the golden hour around seven. The green cornfields stretched into the distance as the fading light danced on the tips of the stalks, signaling the end of another flawless summer day.

From the driver's seat, Stephen reached his hand over and squeezed my thigh. After two and a half months of having him fully back in my life, I was still in awe of reality, still astounded by the simplest moments with him. It was as good as it had ever been.

The wind whipped my hair. I wore a white sundress of Georgia's that I'd snagged from her closet the previous weekend, when I'd been home for the first time since June. I remembered the day Georgia got the dress, because CJ had bought me the same one in navy. It was the summer before I went to Baird, and CJ had taken us to the sidewalk sales in Cold Spring Harbor. I tried not to think about CJ; it only reminded me of the crushing guilt lodged in my gut.

She and my dad had called the night before while I was packing for the weekend, with the news that Hickory was dying. Fifteen was old for a Labrador, and her hind legs had been shot since early spring. For months CJ or my dad would prop her legs up with a sheet—a makeshift harness—and help her stumble outside to use the bathroom. But lately Hickory hadn't been getting through the night without making a mess on her bed. She'd stopped eating. She could barely drink water.

"Her front legs are gone now, too," my dad had explained on the phone. "She can't move. This isn't a way of life for her. She's suffering."

They'd decided to put her to sleep, he said, and the only appointment the vet had was on Saturday afternoon. My parents were going to Bermuda the following week; it couldn't be put off any longer. Hickory's death had become something that had to fit into my parents' schedule.

"Come home this weekend, Sass," my dad had said. "We'll all be here together with Hick. She needs us. Georgia Peach is taking the train down from Boston."

I heard my father's voice through the phone but didn't believe what he was saying. I examined the outfit I'd spread out on my bed for Friday night: a cherry-red Reformation dress with side cutouts and an open back. With the beige wedges or gold flats? If I wore the wedges I'd only be two inches shorter than Stephen.

"Lucy?" My dad sounded tired. I pictured CJ next to him on the floor of the kitchen curled into Hickory, her eyes bloodshot from crying, her face pressed into Hick's warm sand-colored coat as she begged our dog's forgiveness and understanding.

I remembered the autumn day we got Hickory with crystal clarity. I was seven, Georgia was eight, and CJ had driven us all the way to a farm in Amagansett where a litter of yellow Labs had been born. My father was at work. He'd grown up with yellow Labs and CJ wanted to surprise him.

The puppies were eight weeks old and there were nine of them. They were huddled together in a wooden whelping box in a big barn that smelled like fresh hay. CJ said we could choose whichever puppy we wanted. Georgia and I wanted a girl, of course, and we picked the smallest one, the tiniest ball of pale yellow fur. On the way home Georgia and I sat in the back seat and held her between us on our laps. I remembered the way she nuzzled our faces with her wet nose, and the way she smelled, warm and milky. My seven-year-old self had decided that her name should be Hickory, after the hickory tree that Georgia and I loved to climb in our backyard. Georgia, always the affable big sister, didn't object.

A colossal hole filled me. Hickory was going to die. The vet was going to come to our house and inject her with poison that would stop her heart. I had to be there. Not seeing Hickory one last time was not a choice.

But *this* weekend—why did it have to be *this* weekend? The weekend I was supposed to go to dinner at Stephen's grandfather's house in Westhampton, where I would meet his extended family for the first time. He'd invited me almost a month ago. I couldn't not go.

The decision was already made up in my mind; it decided itself. I pressed the phone to my ear and tried to avoid thinking of Hickory, constant and loyal on the front stoop; I tried not to feel the depth of a near lifetime with her.

"I can't, Dad," I said into the phone. "It'll just be too sad. I think it'll be better if I'm not there." The sound of my own lie disgusted me.

"Don't you want a break from the Hamptons? You've had a nonstop summer."

"Not really. It's been fun."

"Lucy." There was a tremor of frustration in my father's voice. He almost never got mad. "This is Hickory. Think about it. There's a lot of healing in being able to say goodbye."

I agreed to think about it, even though I knew I would call after work the next day and say that I hadn't changed my mind, that I thought it would be better to remember a buoyant, lively Hickory instead of watching her die, old and suffering.

A few days later, Stephen and I were driving toward Westhampton from Lydia's grandparents' house in Sagaponack, where we'd spent Friday night.

Lydia didn't have a problem with Stephen. Neither did Bree—not the way Jackie did.

"Weigh the consequences," Bree had said when I first told her I was seeing Stephen again.

"I have. He makes me happy."

"Then do what makes you happy. I don't have an issue with him. I mean, he's kind of a dick, but he's funny."

Unlike me, Bree was generally pragmatic when it came to emotions. Her advice was helpful, a dose of realism from the other side. She didn't mind when Stephen hung around our apartment. Unlike Jackie, she actually made an effort to be his friend.

The car slowed with the snarl of Hamptons weekend traffic. Stephen glanced over at me.

"Don't be nervous. Are you nervous?" He turned down a Cranberries song that was playing on the radio.

I wondered if Hickory had died yet. The thought haunted me.

I shook my head. "I like this song." I turned the volume back up.

What's in your head? In your heaaad. Zombie, zombie, zombie.

"Ugh, I can't stand it." He changed the station. "Luce?"

"What?"

"What's bugging you?"

"Nothing," I lied. "I'm not nervous. I've met some of your family before."

"I know, but this is the whole rowdy group. Well, minus my mom, but she doesn't count. Anyway, I know it's a lot." He squeezed my hand.

Since the day Stephen showed up at my door with the bok choy and wine, I'd reached a new level of happiness. It was the feeling I had known that only he could give me—the feeling I'd chased for years.

I wasn't upset about the really bad stuff. When I thought of Diana Bunn and Nicole Hart and the Unforgivable Thing and Dr. Wattenbarger and the Prozac and Billy Boyd and Marilyn's jewelry and fighting with Jackie, I understood that all of it was the means to this. I wouldn't have done anything differently.

We finally reached Westhampton, which according to Helen and Lydia was "by *far* the tackiest Hampton." And while my high school self might've once agreed with them, I was far removed from that seventeen-year-old girl, and I thought Westhampton was nice, and that Stephen's grandfather's gray-shingled beach house was charming and close to perfect.

"Remember this place, Luce? We came here that summer. We had sex on the beach off Dune Road. And in the outdoor shower." Stephen's eyes widened. "Think of all the places we've had sex." His cheeks and nose were sun-kissed, and his dark hair splayed unevenly over his forehead, salty and dry from the ocean. I'd never been so attracted to anyone.

"There are some strange ones." I nodded. For some reason I couldn't bring myself to tell Stephen about Hickory. I pictured her old, slouched face and knew I was going to be sick.

"That's because I can't be around you and not fuck you." He leaned over the middle console and gave me a kiss. Through the trees, dusk gathered in the sky, a wash of pale pink. "Come on. Let's go inside."

I remembered the house. The kitchen was simple, with sanded wood floors and awning windows overlooking the small backyard. Mr. De-Marco and a man I'd never met were emptying the dishwasher.

"Dad, you know Lucy." Stephen touched his father's shoulder. "And this is my uncle Daniel. Daniel, this is my girlfriend, Lucy."

"A new girlfriend?" Daniel wiped his hands on a dish towel and seemed to realize he'd said the wrong thing. My stomach clenched.

"It's hard to keep track, I know." Sadie, Stephen's younger sister, appeared in the doorway.

"Cut it out." Stephen pinned Sadie a look.

"Kidding." Sadie rolled her eyes before walking over and giving me a half hug. "Hey, Lucy."

Stephen introduced me to his grandfather, his aunt Amy, and his cousins, Vivian and Christina. Vivian, who I took to be a few years older, held an adorable baby boy wrapped in a beach towel.

"Cody!" Stephen gushed, grabbing the baby out of Vivian's arms and turning toward me. "Cody just turned six months."

I rubbed Cody's tiny cheek and he reached for a wad of my hair.

"Okay, bud." Vivian laughed and snatched Cody back from Stephen. "Time for your bath. Sorry, he loves hair right now," she said to me.

"It's totally fine. He's adorable."

"I'll take him, Viv," said a tall man with cider-brown hair who appeared behind Vivian. Stephen introduced me to Vivian's husband, Rod.

"There's liquor and beer out back," said Daniel. "Help yourselves."

"Sorry about Sadie," Stephen whispered in my ear when we'd gone outside. "It's not you."

"Seems like it's sort of me." I watched him fill two glasses with ice.

"No." Stephen sighed. "She just thinks I'm a jerk for dumping Alice. And she knows I cheated on her. With you."

"*What?* Sadie knows about that night in Bear Mountain? At Jared's house? In that bedroom?"

"*No*—God no. Sadie was comatose in that bedroom. She doesn't know the full . . . extent. She saw us kissing earlier in the night, at the concert.

But that's it." He handed me a cold drink, full to the brim. "Vodka tonic on the rocks with a twist, miss."

"Great. So your sister thinks I'm an adulterous whore."

"*No.* She thinks *I* was an asshole. But it doesn't matter what Sadie thinks, anyway. She doesn't understand how I felt about Alice, or how I feel about you." His green gaze pinned me. "She's only seventeen. She doesn't get it."

I shrugged. "I feel weird. Did you bring Alice out here this summer? Before you broke up? Is that why your uncle said that?"

"Not this summer." Stephen paused. "The last time I brought her out here was in May, I guess. It was before you even graduated."

"Oh." I sipped the top of my drink.

"Please don't feel weird, Luce. Daniel knows all about you. He's not judging you. Nobody is."

"Okay."

"Come on." He took my hand. "Let's help Amy set the table."

Dinner was served on a long table in the backyard—pasta with fresh clams, arugula salad, and garlic bread. Stephen kept his hand on my thigh underneath the table.

"I can tell my family loves you," Stephen whispered at some point. "And so do I."

"I love you so much."

"After everyone goes to bed I'm gonna fuck you in the outdoor shower." His voice was hushed in my ear. "Round two."

He poured me more wine. His eyes were heavy and mollified. Even in my tipsy stupor I could sense the alcohol cloaking the creeping anxiety surrounding the fact that it was not possible for things to get any better—the vaguely unsettling helplessness of needing nothing.

I knew Hickory was dead by now, but it was okay because she was no longer suffering. She was in heaven. She would have been sixteen on the sixteenth of September, her golden birthday, I realized as Stephen slid a plate of blueberry pie in front of me, vanilla ice cream melting into the warm wedge. And then I realized with a start that the date was August 16, that Hickory had lived to be exactly fifteen years and eleven months.

August 16 was the date of Macy's death, too. The night I saw her and the night she died. I'll never forget it.

44

STEPHEN

I got the call at three on a Tuesday morning. I was having the same vivid dream again. In the dream, which is partly a dream within a dream, her long red hair is wrapped around my throat, choking me, the sickening bubble gum smell saturates my nostrils and *Zombie zombie zombie* won't stop playing and I can't get free, and then I wake up and the doorbell's ringing and the police are there, always two of them, red-and-blue lights blinding my eyes. One of them asks: *Where were you the night of August 16, 2008?*

I woke up in a full sweat to my phone's Für Elise ringtone. I keep the ringer on through the night—always have, always will. You never know.

When I answered it was my father's voice on the other end of the line.

"It's your mother," he said, his voice panicked. "She's been injured."

"Injured how?" I pretended to care, but my mother's well-being had long ceased to interest me.

"She just got out of surgery. Can you come meet us at Mount Sinai? Everyone's coming. I just got off the phone with Luke. And Amy and Daniel are driving in."

"Right now? What happened to Mom?"

"She was . . . she got into some trouble. She was attacked in Port Jefferson. She was *stabbed.*" My father's voice was nearly shaking.

"Stabbed? Jeez. By who?"

"They don't *know,* Stephen." My father sounded rattled beyond reason. "Her friend Pauline—you remember Pauline—found her all beat up and bleeding near the waterfront, right behind her house. She called the cops, then called me. They don't know what happened, but Pauline thinks your mother owed some people some money."

I'm sure she did, Pops. Just like she owes you money. Just like she owes Uncle Daniel money. Unfortunately most people don't tolerate evasion, and assault is cheaper than litigation. And no, I do not remember Pauline.

"Yikes," I said. "Sounds like some sketchy business."

"This is *serious*, Stephen. Your mother is *unconscious*."

"What do you mean? Like in a coma?"

"Not exactly. She's stable, thank God. They performed emergency surgery and the doctors said she got extremely lucky that the knife didn't slice any major arteries. But she's got broken ribs and a fair amount of internal bleeding. They don't know when she'll wake up—it's too soon to tell. It could be a couple of days. Christ, Stephen. Whoever did this to your mother . . . the shape she's in, I barely recognize her. I feel like I'm in a living nightmare. Please get to the hospital immediately."

"Dad, listen, I can be there at eleven thirty tomorrow morning but I have an exam at nine. It'll take me two hours and then I'll head up there. It's really important. Can't miss."

"Are you kidding, Stephen? Your mother is in the *hospital*. She needs us."

"Dad, she's not even conscious. You just said she's not going to be conscious for a couple of days."

"*Maybe* a couple of days, the doctors said." My father was practically yelling now. "They don't know for sure. She could wake up at any time. And when she does she's going to be terrified and in pain."

I closed my eyes and momentarily debated powering off my phone and slipping back into a deep slumber. It was no use trying to reason with my father. Why he wanted to be there for his psychotic, freeloading maniac of an ex-wife who hadn't given him the time of day since 1988 was truly beyond me. But it didn't matter. Going to the hospital was my only choice; if I didn't, I'd be deemed the heartless brother and son.

"All right, Dad," I said. "I'll be there in half an hour."

I hung up the phone and switched on the bedside lamp, light piercing my tired eyes. I scanned the floor for some clothes to put on.

I was still shaken from my dream as I gathered my stuff and left my apartment in the dark. The place was a dump in Chinatown that I shared with a random classmate from NYU, but it was cheap and a quick subway ride to school. I didn't spend a lot of time there anyway, between my classes and workload and staying at Lucy's.

I rode the subway uptown, even though it was late and a cab would've been faster. I felt like going underground, for some reason. And I can't afford cabs.

Forty-five minutes later I arrived at Mount Sinai. A fat nurse directed me to the fifteenth floor. Why are nurses always fat? It couldn't be more ironic.

Room 1521 was at the end of the hallway. My mother, Nora DeMarco, lay unconscious in the hospital bed. She looked very small and shriveled under all the bandages wrapping her torso and arms. A dark purple bruise covered one of her eyes and there were smaller bruises and lacerations around her face. An IV was plugged into her left inner arm below some bandaging. My father and Luke and Kathleen sat in plastic chairs around the bed. Sadie wasn't there because she was a plane ride away at school—lucky bitch—and Amy and Daniel were still en route from Long Island. Kathleen wore an extremely low-cut top that was certainly not spontaneous-middle-of-the-night-trip-to-the-hospital appropriate, but knowing Kathleen she was probably trying to seduce all of the attractive male doctors.

The room possessed the stuffy hospital smell of cleaning chemicals and sick sweat. In the corner, several flower arrangements sat on a wooden table, which baffled me. You'd have thought my mother had been holed up in this shithole for months instead of less than twelve hours.

Was this some twisted joke? I would've laughed out loud if I weren't so exhausted. There weren't any free chairs, so I slumped onto the windowsill. I glanced out the window down to the street and got that pinched, tingling ache in my toes signaling acrophobia. Fifteen stories below the cars were tiny blurred lights moving leisurely down Fifth Avenue. The city, truly, never slept.

My father's eyes were red around the rims, fixed on my unmoving mother. I glanced at my watch, which read 4:11 a.m. My exam would start in fewer than five hours.

"She's going to be okay, right?" Luke was staring at my mother, his face pallid.

"That's what the doctors say." My father gave a pained smile. "They're running more tests. They'll be back with an update soon."

I studied the battered woman lying on the bed and almost couldn't believe it was my mother. We shared the same green eyes, but hers were firmly closed. Her straight dark hair was shorter than I remembered, and streaked with strands of silver. She'd always been a small woman, but she looked even smaller now; her body had begun to collapse in on itself, like old paper that starts to curl.

Muffled into Luke's shoulder, Kathleen began to cry. She said all of this reminded her of her grandmother's battle with breast cancer when she was sixteen. How breast cancer and getting stabbed in the chest were related I did not know, but my family dutifully consoled her.

Amy and Daniel arrived at five, out of breath.

"We're parked illegally but we had to see her," Amy panted, rushing over to the bed where her ex-sister-in-law lay unmoving. "Oh, *Nora*. Who would do this to her?"

Nora was still in a deep sleep three tedious hours later when a young, good-looking doctor came to deliver an update. He introduced himself as Dr. Everett, and Kathleen stuck out her chest and batted her eyelashes. Dr. Everett sounded as bored as I felt as he explained the ins and outs of the surgery they'd performed, a procedure called a thoracotomy. He said the surgery had been successful, but that my mother had lost a lot of blood and would require several more transfusions.

"So she's going to be fine?" Luke asked.

"It's going to be a long recovery, but yes, she will be fine."

Everyone exhaled relief.

"And you're in touch with the police, Mr. DeMarco?"

"Yes," my father said. "But I want to wait for Nora to wake up before dealing with any of that."

Dr. Everett nodded. "I want to emphasize how lucky Nora is to be able to make a full recovery from this accident. Of course she's the victim here, but I do see in her chart that she's bipolar one, prescribed lithium. However, there's no trace of lithium in her blood, which leads me to believe she hasn't been taking her medication. I don't know if this circumstance has any bearing on what happened to her tonight, but regardless, I strongly advise that Nora take her medication regularly."

My father explained that my mother had been averse to her prescribed treatment for a number of years.

"I suggest you speak with a counselor here at the hospital, then," Dr. Everett replied flatly. "They can best advise you on ways to approach the subject with your wife."

"Ex-wife." My father's face had turned as white as the bandages glued to my mother's torso.

"Right, yes." Dr. Everett shifted uncomfortably before excusing himself and promising to return soon.

The clock on the wall read 7:50. I told my family that I had to go back downtown for my exam.

"You'll come back after, though?" my father asked, though it wasn't a question.

Luke jogged down the corridor while I waited for the elevator.

"Stephen," he called. "Wait."

"Hey, Luke."

He stopped in front of me, his expression weary but self-assured. Luke the firstborn. Luke the caretaker. *Pure of heart*, Aunt Amy liked to say of him.

"Mom is still family," Luke said. "That's why we're all here. I can tell you think all of this is stupid, but we can't just give up on her." He blinked.

Luke's self-righteousness had always been grating, but was even worse now that he wore a wedding ring. Luke the superhusband. Luke the family man. The epitome of convention.

A *ding* sounded the elevator's arrival. I shrugged at Luke and walked inside, the metallic doors clipping closed behind me. I didn't feel like giving my brother the satisfaction of agreeing with him, especially when I didn't agree with him at all.

It was a relief to leave the airless hospital. Outside, the sidewalk sparkled, early-morning sunlight catching bits of silver mica buried in the concrete. Papery red-and-golden leaves hung loosely from the branches of the trees lining Fifth Avenue.

I crossed three blocks over to Lexington. There was a problem with the downtown 6 train, so I walked down to Eighty-Sixth Street to catch the 4/5. There wasn't time to go home and sleep before the exam; I'd have to go straight to NYU.

On Lex, shopkeepers were beginning to open up for the day, the iron-chained gates lifting from the storefronts. The smell of smoke from a hot dog vendor on the corner filled my nostrils. I bought one with relish and mustard and ate it as I walked.

I got on the express train at Eighty-Sixth. The subway was so crowded you couldn't move, and the kid next to me was chewing gum and blowing big pink bubbles right in my face. It was undoubtedly Bubblicious, the smell was just too strong, and I'd know that scent from a mile away. I could taste it. It took me right back to the night of August 16, 2008, and there I was, in the car, in the driver's seat, plastered, broken glass everywhere but not a scratch on my body. Not a scratch. How was it possible?

I couldn't stand the sweet, juicy aroma a second longer. I got off at Fifty-Ninth Street and pushed past people on the escalator until I made it up, out of the underground, back into the light.

August 16, 2008, was the last night I ever spent with Macy Petersen. Beautiful Macy, with her deep, shiny red hair, a striking contrast against her porcelain skin.

It had been the night of Carl's everyone's-going-away-to-college party. Jenna got too drunk and took a cab home early, and Macy picked me up. She was sober, on her way home from some babysitting job. She was chewing bubblegum. Bubblicious—I saw the opened pack in the center console. I told her I wanted to drive so she could give me road head, and she pointed that she was driving her brother's manual car, and asked if I could drive stick and I said that I could—Carl had taught me—and so she let me. And I'd had too much to drink, and though I was doing a fair job of masking it, I shouldn't have been behind the wheel.

I'll never forget how Macy removed the pink wad of gum from her mouth and placed it in mine before unzipping my shorts. I hate the memory, but it still gets me hard. Her lips were moving up and down at an exquisite pace and my mind slipped into oblivion, and then all too suddenly her brother's Jeep was off the road, Carl's stick shift tutorial a distant black hole, my foot uselessly pounding on the brake, the car sliding hard and rolling once, twice, then coming to a juddering halt at the bottom of a small hill. The Jeep was undoubtedly totaled; I still don't know why the radio didn't shut off. *Zombie zombie zombie*—I can't fucking stand that song.

I knew she was dead right away because her neck was snapped

against the gearshift, her pale eyes open, unblinking, my dick still hard against her white cheek. The end of Macy's short life. There was no point in calling the cops. It wouldn't have saved her.

What I did next was never a choice or an internal debate. There was college, law school, my whole future. The fact that it was her car was my greatest stroke of luck. Some people don't get a way out of these situations, but life had handed me one. When the cops found Macy the next morning she was sitting in the driver's seat, her neck wrapped around the steering wheel, her head cut open. I was warm in my bed, tired from the three-mile walk home in the middle of the night.

What's in your head, in your head
Zombie, zombie, zombie

Pieces of that night still surface and when they do they're as vivid as they were then, even though I was drunk. Macy's smooth face. The taste of Bubblicious bubblegum. My erection rubbing the back of her wet throat. My hands too loose on the steering wheel. The petrifying realization that the wheels were spinning out of control. Macy's terrified scream-gag. Swerving hard to avoid the tree. An impossible amount of glass. Her fixed eyes, like marbles. Creeping home in the misty dark, the dewy grass wet around my ankles. The feeling of knowing I'd escaped. Jenna's tears soaking my shoulder the next day when the town learned that Portledge's rising junior Macy Petersen had died in a car crash the night before. She was the driver and sole passenger. Her parents didn't want a full autopsy—they didn't want anyone cutting into their beautiful daughter—but authorities did measure her blood-alcohol level. It was zero; Macy had been sober.

Zombie zombie zombie zombie zombie zombie zombie zombie zombie.

Making my way down Lex I suddenly felt so sick I could barely walk, and the sun was so bright I could barely see, and when I hunched over and squeezed my eyes shut I felt something warm and unfamiliar between them, and when I touched my fingers to my eyes they were wet.

I sat down on some stoop and buried my head between my knees. I let the tears run until my eyes dried up again. I don't know how long I sat there.

I couldn't stomach another attempt on the subway, so I hailed a cab. I wanted to go home and sleep forever, but the sane part of me knew I couldn't miss my torts exam.

I made it to my classroom just before nine.

The exam was hard but not impossible, and after it was over I decided to walk back to Chinatown. The midday sun splintered down through a thin wedge of clouds; it had turned into a nice autumn day. I listened to my father's voice mail, which said that my mother was still out and I didn't need to come back uptown until she woke up. Thank fucking God.

I felt my appetite again and stopped at my favorite deli on Mott Street for a roast beef sandwich. Luckily my roommate wasn't at the apartment, so I sat down at the table in the tiny living room to eat my lunch. I got a cold beer out of the fridge, set my laptop in front of me and turned on an episode of *House of Cards*. My sandwich tasted delicious; the roast beef was cold and fresh, and there was just the right amount of mayonnaise between slices of meat. I felt myself relax for the first time in days. Pent-up tension from the exam rolled off my back, and the beer helped diffuse any lingering agitation from earlier.

Just then my phone rang. *Lucy*, the screen read.

"Hey, Luce."

"Hey." Something in her voice was off, I could tell immediately. I didn't think I had the energy to deal with another problem.

I paused *House of Cards*. I waited for Lucy to say something, but she didn't. Of course she was going to make me press her and *then* she would reveal the nature of the issue. My Budweiser was already gone; I walked over to the fridge to grab another.

"What's up?" I asked. "Aren't you at work?"

"I'm on my lunch break. I'm sitting in Bryant Park."

"Nice day for it." I cracked open the new beer.

I heard her sigh through the phone. I imagined her sitting on one of the benches in the sun, wearing her jean jacket and a pair of brown

leather boots over fitted pants, her hair pulled back. Maybe she was nib-
bling on a salad or an apple with peanut butter—something healthy like
that.

"What's up, Luce?"

"Look, I need to ask you something and I don't know how to approach this, so I'm just going to come out and say it."

She sounded shaky but proud, as though she'd been rehearsing her
words.

"All right, what is it?"

"Well, Lydia's friend Charlotte—the one you met in Montauk this
summer, remember? That night at Ruschmeyer's? Charlotte said she
saw you out to dinner at Crif Dogs with some girl last week. She said it
seemed like you were on a date—that you were basically holding hands
across the table."

The trill in her voice told me she was scared in her defiance. I
drummed my fingertips on the surface of the table. The other half of my
sandwich sat there in all its mouthwatering glory. I considered hanging
up the phone and eating it.

I'd become so bored and weighed-down by Lucy's concerns about
me, about the so-called shady things I had done and the shadier things
she anticipated I would do. I often wondered, especially lately, why she
wanted to be with me at all. Lucy had proof that I cheated, proof that
I lied, and though I could persuasively promise not to do those things
to *her*, she still knew, at the end of the day, that I had those abilities
within me.

Last week I'd gotten dinner with a girl. A very *casual* dinner, but I
suppose it could be called a date because I paid for our hot dogs and
beers at Crif Dogs. The situation had unfolded naturally and I hadn't
thought much of it at the time. What happened was, a couple of weeks
ago my buddy Dave from school had a birthday party at a bar in Red
Hook. I didn't invite Lucy. I just needed a night off. I hadn't felt like dealing with her and having to introduce her to everyone while she flaunted
her legs in some short dress.

So I went to the party alone and met a girl named Jillian. Talking to
her was refreshing. It was *nice* chatting with a girl who wasn't scouring
my eyes for signs of trouble; there was absolutely zero at stake. I found

myself telling her about my mother and her mania, my father's depression problems, and Luke and Kathleen's obnoxiousness. She listened without judgment. I bought a round of gin and tonics; she bought the next. At the end of the night I asked for her number. I suggested we grab dinner sometime.

A few days later I found the piece of paper with a scribbled phone number in my pocket. Without a thought I dialed. We chatted. She lived on St. Mark's but had never been to Crif Dogs, which seemed like a crime. We made a plan to go the following week.

When I walked into the restaurant I realized I didn't fully remember what Jillian looked like. But I recognized her once I saw her sitting on one of the red stools: she was broad-shouldered, like a swimmer, with chin-length strawberry-blond hair that brought out the freckles dusting her narrow face. We ordered our food and sat. Jillian's smile revealed straight teeth, and I counted four studded earrings on each of her ears. She was pretty but not stunning, attractive but not beautiful.

From the moment I sat down the *feeling* was back—the liberating notion that I could say anything and be anyone and she would accept me. When it came time to pay at the end of the meal I laid down my credit card. A part of me hoped to fuck her, I suppose. But we just walked and kissed a little on the sidewalk in front of her apartment building.

It had been innocent, an isolated incident, except for the fact that *Charlotte* had seen us. I barely remembered Charlotte. I swear, New York is the fucking biggest and smallest city in the world.

Still, it caught me off guard that Lucy knew about the so-called date, because in the moment it had felt so private, so detached from reality. I lingered in the limbo of my options. I could've lied; I could've easily said it was a girl from school who I was eating *hot dogs* with—Crif Dogs doesn't exactly evoke romance. I could've convinced her that Charlotte had been mistaken about the holding hands. But I was suddenly so *tired* of defending myself—it was all I'd been doing for years. From Jenna to Diana to Lucy to Diana to Alice to Lucy—it was a long, tangled web, the problems with one relationship somehow always infiltrating the next, a never-ending knot of toxicity, and I was too exhausted to keep trying to fix it. Lucy's appeal had always been that she wasn't truly my girlfriend; in the back of my head I'd suspected a relationship with her wasn't sustainable. We'd been running in circles for too long. What was the fucking point anymore?

"I went to dinner with someone, yes," I said. "But I wouldn't say it was a date."

Lucy exhaled. "You *wouldn't say* it was a date? Then why were you *holding hands* with her? Like what the fuck?"

Like what the fuck? My temples ached, and I felt flooded with pent-up exhaustion from the previous night and morning. All I wanted was a shower and a long, long nap.

"It was nothing, Lucy. Believe me; don't believe me. Your call." I felt like being a dick suddenly.

"But you went to dinner with some girl? *Who* did you go to dinner with? I don't get it." Her voice wobbled.

"She's this girl I met. It wasn't really anything."

"What the hell, Stephen?"

"It wasn't a *date*, Lucy. We went to *Crif Dogs*. They barely even have tables there!"

"You've never taken *me* to Crif Dogs!"

"That's because you don't eat hot dogs!"

"That's because hot dogs are disgusting! They're processed sacs of pig intestines and God knows what else."

"Jesus *Christ*, Lucy. What is the point of this conversation?"

"You're just being so weird. I have to go back to work."

"Okay."

"Can you come over tonight? I want to talk in person. I feel weird right now."

"I don't know. I have to work on my brief." I didn't feel like telling her about my mom. She would just offer to come to the hospital with me.

"Cool." Her sarcasm wasn't effective, and I almost felt sorry for her then.

"Look, I just finished my exam and was up all night at the hospital because my mother got hurt, okay? I'm going to take a shower and finish up some work. I'll call you later."

"Shit," she said. "I didn't know. Is she okay? What happened?"

"She's fine, it's just a few stiches," I lied. "Not worth getting into the specifics."

"I'm sorry."

"It's honestly not a big deal. I have to go. I'll call you later."

"Okay. Let me know if there's anything I can do."

"Thanks."

"By the way, we're still on for Gramercy Tavern with my parents on Thursday, right? I know you have a lot going on, but this dinner has been rescheduled so many times already."

"Thursday. Right. I'll make it work."

I hung up with her and ran a shower, hotter than usual. As the water trickled down my back, I dreaded the dinner at Gramercy Tavern— having dinner with Lucy's parents was the *last* thing I wanted to do at this point.

I scrubbed myself with soap and thought about how *wrong* Lucy was for me—she had always been wrong for me. Whatever Lucy expected from me in her naive perception of our relationship was laughable. I would never give her what she wanted. Didn't she know that? And why should I? It wasn't as if Lucy had ever made me feel like my best self; she'd never made me truly happy. And she never would. She was pretty, but sometimes, lately, when I really looked at her, she wasn't *that* pretty. I'd let the sex get in the way. Again.

By the time I got out of the shower and wrapped myself in a towel, I knew what I had to do. In the meantime, maybe I would ask Jillian on a second date. I craved a fresh start, and she seemed cool enough.

45

LUCY

My phone buzzed on my desk like a mosquito.

>   LYDIA: Call me.

Something in those two words was urgent. I peered into Harry's office; he was still tied up in meetings. Melissa—the girl who worked under Harry, who pretended to be my boss whenever Harry was busy—was parked at her desk, barricading me from the exit with her hawk-eyed glare. When Melissa finally surrendered her post, I grabbed my phone and lunch and fled the office.

"What is it, Lydia?" I said when she picked up.

"Don't panic," Lydia said, which made me panic more.

"Just tell me."

"Okay. So I saw Charlotte last night, and she told me that last week she was with Max at Crif Dogs—you know that hot dog place everyone is obsessed with in the East Village? Anyway, she saw Stephen. She said he was having dinner with some girl and that it seemed like they were on a date. Maybe it was nothing, but I had to tell you."

My stomach seesawed. I'd wandered into Bryant Park for my lunch break. I sat down on one of the wooden benches.

"That doesn't make any sense. How does Charlotte know they were on a date? She barely knows Stephen." Charlotte was Lydia's friend from Amherst who I'd met in the Hamptons a couple of times over the summer.

"She doesn't know for *sure*. She just said it looked like they were—"

"*How* did it look like they were on a date? I don't understand."

"I dunno. She said they were, like, holding hands over the table or something."

"That doesn't make any sense," I repeated, my insides wrenching. "Maybe it wasn't Stephen."

"She seemed pretty sure it was Stephen, Luce. But who knows. Just ask him about it. It was probably nothing."

"Do you remember what day Charlotte saw him?"

"Lucy, don't spiral."

"I'm not spiraling. But do you remember?"

"*Lucy.*"

"What, Lydia? I've dealt with your shit enough times. You'd be freaking out about this, too."

"I don't remember. I'll ask Charlotte, okay? But I think you should just talk to Stephen. Don't freak out yet."

"Fine."

"I'm getting nervous for the race. Are you guys ready?"

"I guess." Lydia, Bree, and I were running a half marathon in East Hampton that Saturday. We'd been training all summer. "I just want to get it over with. Stephen was supposed to come out and watch."

"That's right. Is he not anymore?"

"Not now that he's apparently dating other people."

"Lucy, stop," Lydia sighed. "I told you, don't jump to any conclusions yet."

"Ugh. Fine."

"I should go back to work. *Don't* worry. I'll call you later."

I hung up with Lydia. I couldn't blame her for thinking it was nothing. She didn't know Stephen the way my friends from Baird did, the way I did. She didn't know what he was capable of; she didn't know the extent to which I'd lowered myself for him in the past. Lydia was my oldest friend and though we'd grown up telling each other everything, there were things I'd started to omit.

I decided I had to call Stephen—I couldn't wait until after work. It had to be a misunderstanding; at the least he would deny it or explain it. Or maybe he hadn't even *been* at Crif Dogs. Charlotte was probably wrong. Charlotte was kind of dumb. She'd only gotten into Amherst because her dad was some oil heir.

As the phone rang, the qualms and anxieties continued to creep in, and I felt sick to my stomach. I'd sat by for years and watched Stephen go behind Diana's back, then Alice's back. Why had I thought anything would be different for me?

I heard Dr. Wattenbarger's voice. *People like Stephen, they don't change.*

But isn't the whole point to believe that people *can* change? To believe that we can all become better versions of ourselves? Otherwise, what hope is there for anybody? Maybe Dr. Wattenbarger didn't know everything.

Stephen picked up, his voice interrupting my reeling thoughts.

"Hey, Luce."

I knew I should keep my mouth shut. I finally had what I wanted and accusing Stephen of going behind my back would only cause tension.

But I couldn't, and before I could change my mind I was repeating what Lydia had told me about Charlotte and Crif Dogs and the so-called date.

Worry encased me when he didn't deny having gone to dinner with a girl, and even though he said it hadn't been a date, there was a nonchalance to his tone that pooled my gut with dread. Something in Stephen's voice sounded unfamiliar and very far away. I asked him to come over that night so we could talk in person, but he seemed preoccupied with a paper and casually mentioned that his mother was in the hospital. He said he'd call later.

I felt a little better after we hung up, but only a little. Clearly Stephen was distracted because of his mom—they'd never had a good relationship and seeing her in the hospital was probably complicated. Still, I'd lost my appetite, and I tossed my salad in the trash on my way back to the office.

After work I went for a run along the East River path. The sky turned a dusky gray and I cut the run short when I felt raindrops prickling my arms.

Bree was making fish tacos when I got back to the apartment. I checked my cell but Stephen hadn't called or texted.

I took a hot shower and let the day wash off me. Afterward I combed my hair in front of the full-length mirror and looked at myself. My body was still lean but packed with more muscle from running. My breasts were bigger. I didn't hate it. I wasn't going to let myself go or anything—I'd still never look at a carbohydrate in the same thoughtless way as before—but I couldn't run fast if I didn't eat.

I put on sweatpants and Marilyn's sweater. Bree had made me a plate of tacos, and I joined her on the couch. I was still anxious but starving after my run, and I devoured the tacos.

"Bree."

"Yeah?" She didn't peel her eyes away from *Mad Men*.

I wanted to tell her about Stephen and the whole dinner/date ordeal; I needed a dose of Bree's pragmatism. But I decided against it when I remembered she might tell Jackie, who still wasn't happy about my dating Stephen.

"Never mind."

After Bree went to bed I rinsed the dishes in the kitchen. The apartment was silent except for the hum of the dishwasher.

I climbed into bed and stared at my phone, willing him to call. When it finally rang it was CJ calling, and I was so disappointed I whined out loud to no one and let it go to voice mail.

I had to hear from Stephen. I wouldn't be able to sleep otherwise.

I tried to read *Cutting for Stone* where I'd left off, but I couldn't concentrate. I read the same sentence ten times. When I couldn't stand it any longer, I sent a text.

LUCY: What's up?

When he answered several minutes later, relief filled me to the bone.

STEPHEN: Still in the library, I'm swamped. Let's talk tomorrow.

I tossed and turned through the night, waking every hour. I couldn't shake the feeling that something was off with him. The next day at work I couldn't focus; dread loomed over me like a dark cloud. Melissa eyed me suspiciously and I put my phone away.

When I left the office at dusk I was so anxious I was practically shaking. Out on the street I finally checked my phone, and my stomach sank in another round of disappointment. Still nothing from Stephen. I decided to call him. It was already Wednesday and my parents were coming in for dinner the next night. Stephen still hadn't met my dad, so the four of us were going to Gramercy Tavern. CJ was already annoying me with questions about what she should wear and whether I thought she should drive or take the train to the city.

"Hi." He picked up, but sounded bothered.

"Hey." I wanted to jump through the phone and punch him in the face.

"What's going on?"

"Just saying hello. I've barely talked to you in the past couple of days."

"I haven't talked to anyone in the past couple of days," he replied defensively. "I've been cooped up in the library writing this fucking brief."

"You could at least text me. You were supposed to call me last night."

"I'm really fucking busy, Lucy."

"I know that, Stephen. But what the hell? If we're really trying to make this work like we say we are, then you can't just leave me in the dark and act like an asshole because you feel like it. And I'm really fucking busy, too, by the way. You're not the only one."

"I'm sorry," he sighed. "I'm just stressed."

"Whatever. We can talk about it later. I'm checking in about dinner tomorrow. It's Gramercy Tavern at seven thirty, okay?"

"You're going to kill me."

"You're not coming." My stomach dropped.

"I can't. I'm not even a quarter way through this brief and it's due early next week. There's no way I'll be able to take a break for dinner tomorrow. I'm sorry."

"I don't understand. Is everything okay with your mom?"

"My mom?"

"Is she still in the hospital?"

"*No.* I told you that was nothing. This is not about my mom. This is about *work*."

"Okay, well, I thought you wanted to meet my dad and ask him about law review. But whatever, we'll reschedule *again*."

"Are you trying to blame me for this? You're the one who's been so fucking weird about me meeting your family. You don't want me to meet them. Admit it. You know they won't like me."

"Are you joking? You already met my mom. It was fine."

"It wasn't fine. She clearly thinks I'm not good enough for her pre-cious perfect privately educated daughter. It was written all over her face, Luce. Wake up."

"What the *hell*, Stephen? Why are you being such a dick? Don't turn this on *me*. This is your fault." I felt close to tears, practically shouting on the street.

"I'm sorry," he muttered finally. "Can we talk about this later?"

"Good idea."

"Tell your parents I'm sorry. It was bad planning on my part. Okay?"

"Fine."

"I really am sorry, Lucy."

"You're still coming to Sagaponack this weekend, though? For the half marathon." My voice was small.

Stephen sighed again in a way that made me cringe at myself. I could palpably feel his annoyance at my neediness through the phone.

"Possibly," he said. "I'd like to, but I have to see how much work I get done. This brief is a huge part of my legal writing grade and it's due next week."

"You can work in the Hamptons. You can go to the library or work at Lydia's. We won't bother you." I hated myself for sounding so desperate.

"I'll see. I'll call you tomorrow and let you know. Okay?"

"Okay."

"Bye." He hung up abruptly.

I felt more alone and dejected than I could stomach. It was before seven and the light was already slate gray. I shivered in my thin jacket and could feel winter coming, the cold, lingering stretch of it. I called CJ and explained that Stephen had to reschedule because his mother was in the hospital. She asked a million frantic questions and I made up answers to all of them.

Bree was at the apartment when I got home, already packing for the weekend. She talked my ear off about hydrating properly and what we should eat for dinner to carbo-load the night before the race. I managed one-word answers and she appeared in my doorway with a serious ex-pression on her face.

"If you're nervous about the race, don't be," she said. "You've been running more than I have."

"It's not that."

"What is it, then?"

"Nothing. Work stuff."

"Melissa again?"

"Yeah. Same old."

"She's such a bitch. She's not even your boss."

"I know."

"Is Stephen taking the Jitney out with us tomorrow?"

"Maybe. I don't know if he can come anymore, actually. He has a brief due Monday."

"Oh. That's too bad."

"We'll see. He might come Saturday." I forced a smile.

I didn't sleep all night. I couldn't understand why Stephen wasn't texting me. He always called or texted to say good night if we weren't spending it together. The hole of angst in my gut was growing larger by the second. I wished I could rewind time to just a week ago when Stephen had surprised me with last-minute Sigur Rós tickets and a bouquet of pale pink roses. What could have gone wrong in a week?

Maybe it was his mother and he just wasn't telling me. His mother was bipolar—bipolar I, the most severe type—and maybe there was something he wasn't admitting about the real reason she'd been in the hospital. My mind spun through the night with various scenarios. Every time I did drift off I dreamed about Stephen. In one of them we were having dinner at a fancy restaurant; in another we were sleeping entwined on the beach in Sagaponack, under the stars. I hated all of them because I woke up and he wasn't there and it was just me, hot underneath my sheets, my eyes stinging from light spurts of sleep.

The next day I struggled through work again. I kept my phone on my desk in plain sight, practically hooked to my bloodstream. With each passing minute that he didn't call, it seemed less and less likely that he would, and by the time I was hauling my weekend bag toward the Forty-Fourth Street Jitney stop on Friday evening, I knew I wasn't going to hear from him.

The Jitney rolled out of Manhattan and headed east, leaving the city in its dust. Lydia and Bree passed out almost instantly, leaving me alone with my spiraling thoughts. I pulled out my phone. In between my misery were surges of anger. This wasn't fair. I typed another text.

> LUCY: Is everything ok? What did you decide about the
> weekend? Call me.

I made an effort not to sound as angry as I felt, because maybe there was a real problem with his mother. Still, it was Friday night and the half marathon was starting in twelve hours. A week ago he'd said he was making a sign for me—LUCY RUNNING IN THE SKY WITH DIAMONDS.

I pulled out *Cutting for Stone* and didn't bother opening it before shoving the fat paperback back into my purse.

I checked my phone every thirty seconds like someone with Tourette's syndrome. At nine thirty the bus pulled into the Watermill stop near Sagaponack.

I hadn't been out east since Labor Day weekend. Now that it was October the air was much cooler, the streets strangely empty.

The inside of Lydia's grandmother's house was stuffy from several weeks of sitting unoccupied with closed windows. I took in the familiar, woody scent of the kitchen and felt gutted, like I might crack open with sadness. Stephen and I had spent many summer nights at this house, in this kitchen—we'd covered the big wooden table in newspaper for crab dinners with Helen and Bree and other friends and relatives of Lydia's who visited. I'd sat on his lap during games of Cards Against Humanity and Bananagrams around that table. One afternoon while everyone was still at the beach, we'd had sex on it.

I ran my hands over the smooth walnut tabletop where we'd been just weeks before. My fingers traced the indentations and knots of the wood, and my heart hurt so much I could barely stand it. Where was he? Why wasn't he answering? Why wasn't he here with me?

It took me hours to fall asleep but when I finally did I dreamed of a brand-new BMW station wagon, its silver hood gleaming. Sets of ambiguous hands held thick, soapy sponges that wiped down the sides and its windows and surfaces. A black cloth polished the blue-and-white logo on the hood until it squeaked. The car started but instead of headlights there were Stephen's eyes, scorching green, and then they became Dr. Wattenbarger's, gray like the sea when it rains.

And you, Lucy in the Sky with Diamonds, are a BMW.

I woke up in a full sweat to the sound of my 5:00 a.m. alarm and a light rain falling on the tin roof above my head.

Lydia and Bree were already in the kitchen making coffee and toasting bagels while cheerfully discussing their running playlists. Bree handed me half a cinnamon raisin bagel and I spread a layer of cream cheese over its crispy surface.

We left the house just after six and drove down Montauk Highway toward East Hampton. The rain had stopped and the sun was a yellow line burning the horizon, illuminating the wide green cornfields in a buttery wash. I rolled my window down and the earthy scent of dew and manure filled the car.

Lydia seemed collected, but I could tell Bree was nervous the way she kept tucking loose strands of white-blond hair behind her ears with her toothpick arms. None of us had run 13.1 miles before, and I had been nervous, too. But now any nervousness I'd felt had morphed into the mind-numbing dread that seized every cell in my body.

As Lydia sped along the empty highway, she and Bree chatted effortlessly up front, like best old friends, even though I'd just introduced them over the summer.

"You've barely said a word since we left Manhattan," Lydia said, glancing at me in the rearview mirror. She turned down the radio, the same way CJ did whenever she wanted to talk in the car, as if it were impossible to have a conversation over the slightest amount of volume.

"Yeah," Bree stated in agreement. "Are you sure everything's okay?"

"I'm just nervous about the race," I lied.

"Me, too," Bree said. "But think about how much we've been training. We'll be fine. Hey, what'd Stephen end up doing? Is he coming out today?"

"No, he had to stay in the city and work. He has that big brief due at school."

"That's a bummer. Sorry, Luce." She looked back at me with a small frown. Unlike Jackie, Bree never questioned what I told her. She expected honesty the way you expect water to flood from a faucet, and around her I sometimes felt shady and deceptive.

The half marathon was a blur. My legs felt heavy and dull as I pounded along the rain-slicked roads of East Hampton. For the last five miles of the run my calves and feet ached so much that I forgot about Stephen for forty-five whole minutes. I crossed the finish line in one hour and fifty-eight minutes and was greeted by Lydia and Bree, who had finished the race side by side in an hour fifty.

"Luce!" Bree shrieked. "We did it! Let's get a picture!"

Lydia's boyfriend and some of her friends met us at the finish line. They were mostly city kids I knew from the summer, but I couldn't have been less in the mood to socialize. The sun was shining and only a few clouds hung low in the sky. I wished it were still raining. Everyone wanted to get breakfast sandwiches and beer and head to the beach. We got our stuff from the baggage tent and when I pulled out my phone my stomach was such a mess of knots I was hunched over like someone with a hernia. I scanned through my messages, my eyes running over the congratulatory texts and missed calls from friends and home and Georgia and CJ. Nothing, nothing, *nothing* from Stephen. Still nothing. Maybe he'd lost his phone. That was a legitimate possibility. Maybe I should get in touch with Carl and make sure everything was okay.

We stopped at the deli before heading to the beach. It had unfortunately turned into a perfect day—every lingering cloud had disappeared from the spotless blue sky by the time we laid our towels out over the sand, and the temperature was uncharacteristically warm for October. I forced two bites of a bacon egg and cheese, but it tasted like rubber. I finished a beer and felt dizzy with depression. I knew if I had another I'd try calling Stephen again. I watched everybody go swimming in the ocean.

Jackie called.

"I can't believe you guys ran thirteen miles. You're insane." The sound of her voice made me feel a little better.

"It wasn't that bad. You could do it if you really wanted."

"Not a chance." Jackie laughed. "But I'm proud of you guys. Is Bree there?"

"She's swimming."

"In October?"

"It's really warm here. It's weird."

"Well, tell her congratulations for me."

"I will. I miss you, Jack."

"I miss you, too, Luce. You need to come visit like, now."

"I wish. I'm so poor at the moment. Maybe I can convince CJ to buy me a ticket and come for New Year's."

"You need to. You have to see our spot in Santa Monica."

"I know. I miss California. Also, Jack, I've been meaning to tell you . . ."

"Yeah?"

"Well, I've been meaning to say that I'm sorry. About Stephen. I know it's messed things up between us. I know you think I did the wrong thing and I know you don't want to talk to me about it and the thing is, maybe you're—"

"Lucy, that's crazy. It hasn't messed things up between us. You're my best friend."

"I know." I felt my voice crack. I dug my toes into the sand.

"Seriously, Luce. Stephen might not be my favorite person but I'm not going to love you any less because you're with him. And besides, Bree says you've been really happy lately. She says Stephen is really nice to you. Which I guess is weird for me to imagine but I dunno, maybe you were right. I don't really know him. The times we hung out I was probably coked out and being a bitch. We did too much coke at that school, don't you think? It got bad at points . . . and Pippa wasn't the greatest influence. I told her she had to cut it out once we got to LA and she hasn't done it since graduation, did you know that? We all just needed to grow up. Anyway, I'm getting off track. What I meant to say is that maybe you were right when you said you and Stephen had bad timing before. Maybe people can change . . ." She was rambling. She sounded a little tipsy.

"But, Jackie—"

"Luce, I just want you to be happy. Nothing else matters. I have to go. Sorry, Pip and I are drinking mimosas and we have to go to this brunch thing . . . but I love you. So does Pip."

I hung up with Jackie as Bree scrambled out of the water, her tiny body shivering.

"Holy shit, the ocean is *freezing*." She grabbed a towel. "Who was that?"

"Jackie. She says to tell you congratulations."

"You look pale," Bree said, drying off. "And you're not talking to anyone. What's going on?"

"I don't feel well. I should go back to Lydia's and . . . rest."

The world tipped. I saw Bree saying something to Lydia. I heard Lydia's voice from a very long way away. "Lucy, take the car keys. Go back to the house and lie down."

Back at the Sagaponack house I took a shower, then buried myself under the covers in the guest room bed. It was too sunny, even with the shades closed. I felt guilty and lame and weak for being indoors on such a beautiful day, but being at the beach had been unbearable. All I could do was lie in the fetal position, a metal weight inside me, obliterating me to the core.

I checked my phone for the billionth time. I tried to be practical. I assessed the facts. The last interaction I'd had with Stephen had been the phone call on Thursday evening, nearly forty-eight hours earlier. Since then I'd called him four times, left two voice mails and sent seven texts, all of them unanswered. He'd probably lost his phone. There was actually no other explanation. But then why hadn't he emailed me, or called me from a friend's phone?

CJ had called again and left another voice mail. I knew she wanted to ask me all about the race, but I couldn't bring myself to call her back. I couldn't force another minute of simulated enthusiasm, but I listened to her message.

Hi, Luce, it's Seej again. Just calling to say congratulations . . . thirteen-point-one miles, I just can't believe it and I am so impressed! I want to hear everything but you're probably out celebrating with your friends, so no need to call back if you're busy, just call later when you can, okay? I love you so much, G and Daddy say congratulations, too. We are all so proud of you, baby girl! Talk later. Bye, Sass.

CJ's voice, all maternal and bursting with genuine pride, sent me over the edge. I lay back down on the bed and sobbed silently.

When Lydia and Bree arrived home hours later I had fallen asleep, and I woke to them laughing about something. In the past twenty-four hours the two of them had become some kind of synced-up unit.

"Are you feeling better?" One of them cracked the door open.

"Not really. I feel a little feverish." I propped up on an elbow.

"You don't look so good." Lydia frowned. "No offense."

"Do you want some Advil? Or tea? Or soup!" Bree's voice had risen several octaves, which told me she was several beers deep.

"I'm okay, but thanks."

They went off to shower, and when they reappeared next to my bed they were dressed and ready to go out. They were going to the Surf Lodge in Montauk and asked if I was up for it, but I said I didn't feel well enough.

After Lydia and Bree left I caved and called Stephen one more time, but it just rang and rang and went to voice mail. I turned on the TV in the living room and gazed at it inanely. An old Julia Roberts movie was playing but I couldn't absorb a minute of it. I was pathetic, I knew, more than pathetic. In the bathroom I looked in the mirror and barely recognized myself; puffy bags hung under my eyes, my skin was blotchy and my hair a tangled, sweaty mess. I looked horrible. I was suddenly ravenous and devoured a bag of Tate's chocolate chip cookies, too distracted to make an actual meal. I felt like a creature, a rabid thing.

All I wanted to do was get the hell out of Lydia's house and the hell out of Sagaponack. I closed my eyes and willed myself to pass out so that it would be morning, but I couldn't sleep. A chill floated through the window and I listened to the wind rustle the trees against the glass. I heard Bree and Lyd come in late, heard them rummage through the kitchen for a snack and remembered I'd eaten all of Bree's Tate's cookies—those were her favorite. I listened to them giggle and chat for a while until they finally went upstairs.

The next day I was grateful when Bree said she wanted to get back to the city on the earlier side because she was going on a second date with Evan Donovan, Stephen's old roommate from Baird who had recently moved to New York. Bree had had a crush on Evan forever, so Stephen had set them up and the four of us had gone on a double date the week before.

We took a late-morning Jitney back the way we came, worming through the clogged Hamptons traffic onto the LIE and back through the Midtown Tunnel, into the heart of Manhattan.

I was so relieved to be back in the city and out of the stuffy, memory-filled Sagaponack house that I nearly kissed the sidewalk.

After Bree left for her date, delirious with butterflies, I sat in my bed like a dejected, anxious freak. My legs ached from the run. It was Sunday night, seventy-two hours since I'd last spoken to Stephen. I decided that something could be seriously, seriously wrong. If I didn't hear from him that night, I was going to call one of his friends. I would have to. I picked up my cell and sent him One. Last. Text.

LUCY: Are you alive?

My phone vibrated thirty seconds later.

STEPHEN: Yeah. Been at my dad's in Bayville all weekend. Needed to get out of the city to study. Sorry, I know you're probably upset. I have a ton of work this week, but can you meet me on Friday? We'll talk.

———

Five excruciatingly long days passed. On Friday evening I ducked out of work at 5:45 to make it to the Lower East Side by six. It was earlier than I should've left—we had a big pitch on Monday—but Harry had pulled me into his office and asked why I looked like I hadn't slept in a week. After I broke down and told him everything, he gave me the green light to leave early, not without a discerning Harry pep talk and a spritz of Acqua di Parma.

It had been two full weeks since I'd laid eyes on Stephen. I was so nervous I could barely walk because I was shaking, my gut a hollow pit of doom. I reread his text.

STEPHEN: Meet at Dudley's on Orchard at 6.

I didn't bother trying to negotiate a later meeting time. I had been cooped up with my thoughts for too long, forming one elaborate scenario after the next, making myself insane. I just needed to talk to him. Things had gotten all fucked up again, but we would fix them. We always did.

He will always come back for more, Lucy. He won't give it up until he has to. Dr. Wattenbarger's words resounded in my head—he had meant them as a warning; I savored them as hope.

I took a cab downtown so I'd have time to reapply makeup. I was wearing my jean jacket and fitted white pants that Stephen always said made my legs look good. I needed to make him remember how crazy he was about me, to make him feel regretful and sorry for acting like a self-involved jerk for the past two weeks. But it was hard to apply eyeliner and mascara with the cab swerving down Broadway, and I didn't feel pretty by the time the taxi pulled to a stop on Orchard. My eyes looked small and overdone from the sloppy eyeliner job and lack of sleep, but it was too late to do anything about it.

When I walked into Dudley's Stephen was already there, sitting at the bar sipping a Scotch and soda. It was a relief just to see him. The scene was too familiar. How many times had I walked into a bar to meet Stephen and slid onto the seat beside him, my heart thrashing inside my chest?

Except this time his eyes didn't light up when he saw me, he didn't say *Lucy in the Sky with Diamonds* in the enchanting way that only he can.

Instead, he barely glanced up; he subtly raised his eyebrows to acknowledge my arrival and my relief was replaced by pure panic. Stephen spun his almost empty glass around in his hands, the watery ice clinking.

"Hey." One side of his mouth slid into a forced smile. I removed my jacket and folded it over my legs.

"Hi." I wanted my voice to sound confident, but I knew he'd be able to trace the nerves.

"How was your weekend?" he asked finally. He didn't look at me but stared vaguely past my shoulder, shifting uncomfortably on the barstool.

"It was fine."

"How was the half marathon?"

"It went well, thanks for asking about it a week later." I hated how sarcasm made me feel—like a spiteful, small person—but I couldn't help it. Underneath my trepidation I was manically livid. I had been alone with my thoughts for so long that saying them out loud was shocking, almost comical.

Stephen sighed. The bartender appeared and asked what I wanted. I didn't know or care. A bottle of Xanax. A loaded gun. I ordered a vodka tonic. Stephen drained the rest of his glass and ordered another Scotch. At least he was ordering another drink, which meant he was staying. That was a good sign.

"Stephen," I began calmly. I vowed to stay calm. If I lost my cool, I wouldn't get anywhere with him. "I can't just sit here and pretend to have a normal conversation with you about the half marathon. You were supposed to be there. You've ignored me for the past two weeks and I have no idea why."

I studied his face for signs of remorse or guilt. His face was like magic to me, it always had been. The emeralds he had for eyes, the good, even nose, his ample cheeks and soft, rounded chin. But nothing about his expression was regretful or even defensive. Instead he appeared completely impassive, almost bored. *I don't feel guilt.* I remembered him saying those words the night we first slept together at my apartment. While he was still living with Alice.

"I'm sorry, Lucy," he said. "I've been busy as hell. Law school is a real bitch."

"I know, I've heard," I said, my cool swaying off-kilter at his stark indifference. "But guess what? You're not the only busy person in New York. I have a full-time job. A full-time job is also a real bitch."

"Lucy." He looked me straight in the eye for the first time since I walked into the bar, his expression hard. "This just isn't . . . I can't. I can't do this anymore."

It was in moments like this that time seemed to stop—moments so vividly painful, almost surreal in the pain that they promised. My insides lurched. My breath slipped out of my throat and I thought I was going to choke. Every part of my body went numb, and I had the sensation that I was deep in a lucid dream. I blinked several times but still found myself in the dimly lit bar, bad rock music playing in the background, the back of my head woozy from the sip of vodka on an empty stomach.

"What?" When I spoke it wasn't my voice but a foreign growl, the sound of a wild animal.

Stephen stared at his hands resting neatly on the bar.

"Are you serious?" My voice shook so much it was barely audible.

"Yes, Lucy."

I sensed the well of tears pressing behind my eyes, but I was too shocked to cry. None of this made a speck of sense. It was the most irrational thing I'd ever heard. I willed myself to speak. Calmly, reasonably.

"Stephen," I exhaled. "I understand that you are in law school and are swamped, but we can fix whatever isn't working."

"No we can't, Lucy."

"That's ridiculous."

"I can't do it, Lucy."

"Why?" The shock was slowly lifting and I began to feel out of control, on the edge of sanity. "Is this about your mom?"

"What? No. Why would it be about my mom?"

"I just—I mean I don't understand—I don't get it." My words crashed into each other.

"I don't know, Lucy. Something isn't right."

"Stop saying my name at the end of every fucking sentence. I don't understand. Is this a joke?"

"No."

I couldn't look at him. I stared ahead and watched the bartender shake up a cocktail and pour it into a martini glass through the strainer.

"I don't understand," I repeated. I felt so queasy I was almost seeing double.

"What don't you understand?"

"Stephen," I said, my voice hoarse. "We are finally in a place where we can make this work. We've been through too much of this crap. You can't just give up like this."

"There's something off," he sighed. "I want something more."

"Something *more*? What the hell do you want? You owe me more than this."

"No I don't, Lucy." He stared at me apathetically, his mouth a neat line.

I glared at him. I hated him. I wanted to punch him in his smug, average Joe face.

"Two weeks ago you were acting like a different person."

"Things change."

"Not overnight. I—this is crazy. I don't understand. Is this about the girl you went to dinner with?"

"*No.* I told you that was nothing." He frowned. "I'm sorry if I'm hurting you in some big way."

Hurting you in some big way.

You are killing me. You are destroying the fibers of me.

The bustling bar fell silent, the way it does in movies. I felt the hope I'd stowed up and stored burst within me, draining out of me as rapidly as blood from a deep wound. I would die, I knew. I would not go on. I would suffocate on my own breath. My own life would kill me.

I lifted my eyes to his bottle-green orbs, flecks of chartreuse glowing in the irises. I would have to finish this. I would have to have something to tell everyone. There was a part of me on autopilot who knew this, and I heard her speak.

"I hope you know that if you do this now, this is it," I said. "This is really it, this time."

"I know."

"You're acting like you don't even care. After all this time. You act like I haven't known you for four years."

"Do you really know me?" he snapped defensively, his eyes narrowing. "Do we *really* know each other?"

"I guess you're right," I sputtered. "I really don't know who the fuck you are. Two weeks ago you were telling me you loved me."

"Things change," he repeated.

"And you have no explanation for why?"

"No." His tone was clipped and curt. There was a trace of satisfaction in his voice, like he was glad to be inflicting this pain on me. Like I was a stupid, useless pawn. "Something about us together isn't right. There's something missing, and I can't put my finger on it." He motioned to the air between us with his hands. "We didn't actually love each other, Lucy."

My mind spun like a torrential cyclone, a spiraling stream of thoughts I knew I wouldn't be able to absorb until later. I bit the insides of my cheeks as hard as I could to keep from crying in front of him.

"You're so messed up." I couldn't look at him. "You're twisted."

"You want to make me out to be evil, go ahead."

I glanced in front of me at my full vodka tonic, a limp orange slice hanging weakly off the glass rim. I hadn't even asked for an orange. I hated him. I hated him in a way I hadn't before. He wanted to hurt me. He lied and lied and he didn't feel guilt. He was sadistic at his core. I had always known it. I was so, so stupid for thinking that our shared defiance of goodness was strong enough to equal love. There was always good in love. There had to be. But then maybe there wasn't, and maybe that was the whole problem with the world.

"I can't stay here," I said.

"I understand."

But my body felt glued to the stool. I couldn't leave. I loved him. I loved him more than anything. This had all gone terribly wrong. Stephen and I were supposed to order several rounds of drinks and sit at the bar for a few hours and work everything out. After a drink or two we'd shift closer to each other and interlace our fingers, and eventually we would start kissing, and the bartender would be jealous, and then we'd go back to Avenue B and have makeup sex all night.

I could still fix it. There was time. He was here and I was here. If we both stayed at the bar, it wasn't too late.

But I looked into Stephen's eyes again and they were like ice. There was nothing in them that wanted me to stay. There was no flirtation or lust or acknowledgment of a secret that only the two of us shared. I knew it was over forever this time.

I forced myself to stand and move. I kept my eyes on the floor and walked out of the bar and only looked up when I was out on the street, lost in the crowded shuffle. Rowdy groups drifted in and out of bars on Orchard. Choppy salsa music played loudly from a restaurant. I didn't know which direction I was walking, only that I had to keep moving. When I finally stopped I collapsed in on myself, the tears breaking loose, dry racking sobs heaving through my body. I was so sad I wanted to laugh. I thought of my freshman year English class with Mr. Levy, Intro to Shakespeare: all tragedies are comedies; all comedies are tragedies. All truth is a paradox.

I took out my phone and called Bree. I hadn't told her a thing about Stephen's behavior over the past two weeks. I hadn't told anybody. Her phone went to voice mail. I remembered that she had another date with

Evan. People were out doing things, Friday-night things. I staggered down the street and passed faces that looked like clowns. Giant mouths opened wide as Frisbees and cackled in drunken laughter, staggering around me, their faces red, their hair like strands of yarn. It felt like a Tim Burton movie.

I don't remember hailing a cab but I must've, because that's how I got home. Bree wasn't at the apartment. I was still crying ferociously, salty tears dripping down my face and into my mouth. I felt like a hysterical child. I curled into a ball on my bed and sobbed into my pillow. What I had been most afraid of had happened. I had spent the past two weeks in a state of debilitating worry for a reason.

I cried so hard my nose started bleeding out of both nostrils. I could taste the blood before it hit the pillow and I covered my nose and ran to my dresser for tissues. I lay on my back on the wood floor and stuffed Kleenex up my nostrils. I swallowed snotty streams of blood and salt.

The tears wouldn't stop. I closed my eyes and let them run over my face. In the blackness behind my eyelids I saw Stephen's eyes that first day on the Lake Mead houseboat freshman year, the way they'd promised me something uncharted. I felt his mouth on my neck in his bed at Slug. I saw his face light up when I opened the "Lucy in the Sky with Diamonds" poster on Carl's boat. I heard him whisper in the dark, *I love you, Lucy.* I saw him in the doorway of my apartment holding groceries and wine. I tasted him in the outdoor shower in Westhampton. I felt his thick body curled around mine in the mornings.

My heart hurt so much it scared me; it seared with pain behind my sternum. I don't know how long I lay there on the floor but I must've fallen asleep, because the next thing I remember was Bree shaking me awake.

"What the hell happened?" she was shouting. There were bloody tissues all around me and there was blood on my shirt, and my eyes were so swollen from crying I could barely open them.

"Evan's not here, is he?" I whispered, already imagining Evan's text to Stephen.

"What? No. Why? What *happened*, Lucy?"

My nose had stopped bleeding, and I propped myself up to stand, back in a living nightmare.

Bree yanked me up when I tried to sit down on the bed. "You need to go to the bathroom, Lucy. You need to wash your face."

When I saw my reflection in the mirror I screamed out loud. I looked like I had been attacked. Bree held my hair back as I rinsed the dried blood and tears from my face, and I was suddenly filled with the memory of Macy Petersen holding my hair back that drunken night in high school, the last night of her life. I closed my eyes and let the water wash over my forehead, and suddenly I saw her, leaning against the wall of that bathroom, so many years ago but the memory still mysteriously clear. *I'm just giving him a ride home, because I was babysitting nearby and he lives around here. . . . He's no one you know. He's this older guy, from Bayville.*

I pulled my face out of the sink and turned off the faucet. No.

My eyes still closed, I saw Macy twirling a lock of long red hair around her finger. *He sort of has a girlfriend. He says they're breaking up and that he's not into her, but we're keeping it really quiet for now. It's shitty, I know. I wish I didn't like him so much.*

No. It was impossible. I kept my eyes sealed shut and clenched my jaw and dug into the depth of my brain for other memories of that night. I'd been with Antonia and her brother, but whose party had it been? In Bayville? Who were we with? Kids from what school?

And then I saw Macy glancing back from the doorway, gesturing to the beer I was offering her from my hand. *Can't. I'm driving, remember?*

And then she was gone.

I grit my teeth and burrowed deeper. Tried harder. But there was nothing else from that night. Nothing. Only too many vodka pulls, and Macy, and blankness. Maybe I hadn't seen Macy at all. Maybe I'd made the whole thing up in my psycho crazy head. And then Bree was shouting something in front of me, and when I opened my eyes she was staring at me like I had three heads.

"Lucy? It's Stephen, isn't it? What happened tonight?"

Stephen. The bar. Tonight.

Bree gave me water and helped me into boxers and Marilyn's sweater while I told her everything. I was suddenly so tired and slurring the words, but she nodded, her hazel eyes kind and understanding.

"I wish you had told me before," she said. "That explains why you were sick last weekend."

"Well, I wasn't actually sick."

"I know."

"I'm sorry, Bree . . ."

When I woke hours later, orange light filtered through the blinds. I heard the sound of my dresser drawers opening and closing, and when I looked up I saw CJ in my room, throwing clothes into a canvas tote.

"CJ?"

"Morning, Luce," she said casually, as if it were perfectly normal for her to be standing in my bedroom in the East Village at the crack of dawn.

"What are you doing?"

She walked over to the bed and leaned down to kiss my forehead.

"Bree said you had a tough night."

"Bree called you?"

"Yes. She was worried."

My head felt muddled as I tried to absorb everything. My thoughts shot to my phone. Maybe Stephen had texted me telling me he'd made a huge mistake. He probably had.

"Where's my phone?" I scanned the side table and the floor next to the bed.

"This it?" CJ took the phone from my dresser and handed it to me. There were no texts or calls from Stephen, and my stomach plunged in a new wave of misery.

"What are you doing?" I asked again.

"Packing you a weekend bag," she said. "We'll go up to the Cape. You can clear your head. Maybe the water will still be warm enough for a swim. Salt water fixes everything, you know."

"What? Why are you doing this, CJ?"

She looked at me from across the room, her eyes a strident aquamarine blue. She looked irritatingly perfect in a black cashmere sweater and some expensive Parisian scarf.

"Because right now you need to get out of this apartment. We'll get away and be by the ocean and talk. We'll figure this whole thing out. Now get up and get dressed. I don't want to hit traffic. Are you wearing Marilyn's sweater? I love that you still wear that. She would've adored you."

I ducked my head into Bree's room but she was still sleeping when we left the apartment at quarter past seven. CJ cruised up the FDR, which was empty so early on a Saturday morning. The low-hanging sun shimmered over the East River, casting glittery flecks on the water's surface. It was a chilly morning and CJ cranked the heat. She turned on an old mixed CD. Fleetwood Mac's "Never Going Back Again" filled the car.

The music was too much; it reminded me of being a little girl riding in the back seat while CJ sang along to the lyrics, the same way she was now.

"'Been down one time, been down two times, I'm never going back again.'" She smiled. "I forgot how much I love this song."

Tears streamed down my face, so many that I couldn't see.

CJ reached over and squeezed my hand. "He broke your heart, didn't he?"

I couldn't speak.

"You loved him. I had the feeling you did, but I wasn't sure until now. I'm so sorry, my girl."

We zoomed along the Triborough Bridge across the river. I wanted her to let go of my hand. I hated her. What right did she have to be my so-called rescuer? What right did Bree have calling her?

I leaned my head against the window. The sun was too bright; it stabbed my eyes. I squinted and watched the city disappear until the Empire State Building was as small as a thumbtack. I was glad to be out of Manhattan.

"You'll feel better tomorrow, I promise." CJ turned down the music.

I stayed silent.

"You can talk to me, you know."

"Where's Dad?"

"He's at home. Georgia's home, too."

"She is?"

"She has Monday off for Columbus Day."

"Why aren't they coming to Chatham?"

"Georgia wants to catch up with friends in the city. And I figured it would be nice for you and me to have some alone time. We haven't really had that lately, you know?"

I said nothing.

We sped by tiny houses that sat right on the highway, houses smaller than our garage. I'd always felt sorry for people who had to live in houses like that.

"Sass, you learn almost everything from your relationships," CJ said. "They're how you figure out who you are."

I couldn't think of a response that wouldn't keep the conversation going.

She went on. "I know you wanted it to work out with Stephen, and I know you thought it would."

"Yeah. I did."

"But the thing is," CJ continued. "Love—real love—isn't something you construct or hope or imagine or plan for the future. Love is something you live and feel in real time, in every single moment, big or small. It's reciprocal and often unglamorous. But we bank on it because it's what gives life meaning."

"That sounds a little underwhelming for love."

"I wouldn't call it underwhelming." She laughed. "But I see what you mean. Maybe it's not always the most exciting thing in the world. But I guess that's what happens when you trust someone completely."

"Excuse me?" I picked my head up from the window and sat up straight as a pole, as a buried switch flipped within me.

"What?" CJ glanced at me. Her eyes were covered in huge dark sunglasses that slid down the bridge of her enviable nose.

"Trust? Really?" I suddenly felt more alert than I had in days.

"Yes, trust. You can't have a relationship without trust. It's impossible."

"So *you're* going to talk to me about trust?"

"What the hell, Lucy?" CJ removed her sunglasses and looked at me with a bemused expression. Her eyes were the color of the Caribbean Sea.

Anger seized me. I was brimming with a fury so intense I was shaking. I didn't care anymore. The words erupted out of my mouth. The wrath of eight years.

"You *slept* with someone!" I yelled. "I *saw* you!"

My eyes had flooded again—they seemed to be involuntary at this point—and liquid ran down my cheeks in torrents.

CJ pulled the Lexus over to the shoulder of the highway. Something flashed across her face, and she looked broken. It was just past eight, and more cars were populating the interstate, rushing by us like rockets.

"What?" Her voice sounded hollow, unfamiliar.

"My freshman year of high school. I saw you." I was crying so hard I could barely speak, my sentences choppy blocks of words. "Soccer practice was canceled and Mrs. Montgomery dropped me off and I went upstairs and I saw you with—with—you were with Gabe Petersen."

CJ's face turned white as a sheet. I sank my head between my knees and wailed silently, hot tears glazing my face. Nothing would ever be the same. I'd said it. She knew. It was over.

An eternity passed.

"Oh God, Lucy," CJ said finally, her voice cracking, an unfamiliar pitch. "Oh God. Oh God. I had no idea."

I looked up; her face was covered in tears.

"Why didn't you tell me?" she gasped. "That was so many years ago. Why didn't you tell me?"

"I couldn't."

"Jesus Christ . . . my God . . . Georgia . . . does Georgia know?"

I shook my head.

"I can't . . . I can't imagine what that must've been like for you. God, how did I not know? I'm so sorry. I'm so, so sorry." CJ choked out her words, and I knew I was breaking things inside her, the same way things had broken inside me. "Oh, Lucy. It's all my fault." The rims of her eyes were pink and wet, and up close, she looked older than I remembered.

"What made it even worse," I continued. "Was that I had this huge crush on Gabe. I know you didn't know that, but I kind of thought I loved him, that summer he gave me tennis lessons. He kissed me once. We started to fool around—it was just one time. I mean I was only fourteen and it was totally stupid, in retrospect, how much I liked him. But that made it even more horrible, when I saw you. Because of Dad but also because it was Gabe."

"Oh, Lucy . . . oh *no*. Of course I didn't know any of that." Tears spilled down her face as she explained how her affair with Gabe had lasted one month, how he'd shown up to her Pilates class one day after the summer he gave me lessons, how they'd connected, how it was the worst, dumbest thing she'd ever done.

"I told your father about it—he didn't find out on his own or anything. That's when he went to stay with Uncle Pete in Cambridge. Remember those two months he spent in Boston, your freshman year?"

I racked my brain for memories of ninth grade. The Unforgivable Thing clouded most of that year, but I did recall my father being gone for work a lot at some point. There'd been a big trial in Boston.

"That trial in Boston? That wasn't real?"

CJ shook her head solemnly. "He worked remotely for a couple months. He was devastated—we both were. He just needed time and space from me—from everything—to work on forgiving me. He came home most weekends to see you guys. We should've told you. Oh God, I was such a wreck, too. I was so humiliated and confused." CJ wiped her cheeks. "I was going through my own stuff, stuff from Marilyn and my parents that I'd never worked through. It doesn't excuse what I did, not for a second, but I made a terrible mistake. Your dad and I went to therapy. A lot of it. And he found it in his heart to forgive me. We've moved past it—we *so* have—but oh, I hate thinking about it."

"I didn't know that Dad knew." My memory wound, my perspective splintering. "I assumed he didn't know. I thought it was a secret you were keeping from all of us."

"That's why you never brought it up with me?"

"I guess, mainly. I didn't know what to do. I didn't want you guys to get divorced or something because of me."

"Oh, Sass . . . oh, love. I'm so sorry. We should've told you everything. It's just . . . you and Georgia were in the thick of it in high school."

"So you lied."

"I know it was wrong, but yes. I don't know . . . somehow it seemed like the right solution at the time. We knew we could fix our marriage and we didn't want to confuse you."

"So what about the Petersens? Do Mr. and Mrs. Petersen know? Did you stop being friends with them? Does Dad hate Gabe?" I had too many questions; they toppled out.

"Yes, the Petersens know. It hasn't been easy between us, running in similar circles at Cove Club and whatnot. And then Macy died. It's all so horrible. I want you to know, Lucy, that I love your father very much. I never stopped loving him."

I watched CJ's face, the tears clinging to her thick eyelashes. The way her bottom lip trembled. I didn't hate her, I thought. No matter what happened I didn't hate her. People messed up. People were allowed to mess up. CJ wasn't a bad person.

I closed my eyes. Behind the lids I saw dozens of beloved objects sinking into a dark, deep river, and the guilt that had been absent for over a year was suddenly a force against my lungs, a weight so crushing I knew I had to speak.

"I did something horrible, too." I let the confession and the tears tumble out of me at once, and I let CJ catch me in her arms across the center console as I told her what I'd done with Marilyn's jewelry. I felt her small, strong body sobbing lightly against mine. I inhaled the familiar scent of her face cream.

"It's okay, Lucy," she whispered. "Jesus. Fuck. It's okay."

"I wasn't thinking," I said, pressing my cheek against the softness of her cashmere. "I'm so sorry."

"It's okay." She whispered it over and over again. She held my head in her hands, shrouding me with invincible love, the love that had never stopped for either of us. "I forgive you."

"I want to forgive you." I picked my head up. "I know I can."

"I know you can, too. I'll help you. It's beyond complicated, I know, but Dad and I will explain everything to you and Georgia."

I nodded.

"Does anyone know about . . . me?" CJ asked. "About the affair? Any of your friends?"

"No one." I couldn't bring myself to say his name. I swore to myself it was the last lie I would ever tell her.

I brushed my hair away from my face. Dried tears stuck to my cheeks, but I wasn't crying anymore. My gut churned; I was suddenly hungrier than I'd felt in days.

"CJ, can we get some coffee? And some breakfast? I'm starving."

"I'm hungry, too." She wiped her eyes and smiled. She pulled the Lexus back onto I-278.

"Hey, CJ?"

"Yeah?"

"Can we go home and pick up Georgia and Dad? Can they come up to Chatham with us? I think it would be nice if we all went. We could spread the rest of Hickory's ashes. She loved the Cape."

"Okay. Yeah. I like that idea." CJ sniffled and pulled her sunglasses back over her eyes.

We turned around at the next exit and headed south, toward home. It was still early in the morning and I couldn't wait for a hot cup of coffee with milk and sugar. I couldn't wait to be up on the Cape and play gin rummy with Georgia and smell the ocean from the deck. Maybe I would wake up the next day and feel better, like CJ said I would.

Sunlight flooded the car as we headed home. My mother held on to my hand and I hoped she would never let go. I watched the gold-and-red trees fly by and I saw a little girl lugging a bright pumpkin up her front stoop. Fall had descended while I wasn't looking. CJ lowered the windows and the air smelled like wood smoke. My heart felt empty and full at the same time.

EPILOGUE

LUCY

AUGUST 2017

"What the fuck? Jackie. What the *fuck*?"

Jackie pulls me into the black town car waiting to take us back to the Donovans' for the reception.

"You look pale," she says, which doesn't surprise me because I've felt the blood draining from my face for the past thirty minutes, all through-out the ceremony.

"You ladies want to leave now, or wait for the rest of the wedding pahty?" The driver speaks in a thick New Jersey accent.

"Now," Jackie says. "We need to leave now."

"Jack, aren't we supposed to wait for the rest of the bridesmaids?"

But the driver is already pulling out of the church. Jackie digs around in her clutch, pulls out bronzer and starts applying it to my face. The car hits a speed bump and the bronzer brush jerks up my cheek.

"Jackie!"

"Sorry!"

"*Ugh.* He's married. This is great. This is just great."

"He's *engaged.*"

"You ladies okay?" The driver glances back at us in the rearview.

"She'll be fine," Jackie says. "She just needs about six shots of vodka injected into her bloodstream."

"Weddings, I tell yah."

"Do you think Bree knew?"

"Not a chance. She would have told you." Jackie is wiping the excess bronzer off my face with a Kleenex. "There. You look way less pale."

"Here we ah!" The driver pulls to a stop in front of the Donovans' mansion.

"We're here already?"

"Want me to drive around the block a coupla times, miss?"

"That won't be necessary, but thank you," Jackie says. "Lucy, get out of the car."

Everything is happening too quickly. Jackie leads me through the Donovans' massive foyer to the terrace and the massive white reception tent. It's all so perfect I want to mess something up. There's a raw bar, a bubbly bar, two regular bars, a cheese station, a caviar station, a giant cake pop tree, an elaborate swan ice sculpture, and a chocolate fountain that looks like something out of Willy Wonka's factory. The centerpieces are elaborate lilac sculptures and the two dozen round tables frame a huge dance floor facing a twelve-piece band. Little signs are displayed throughout the tent that read:

Help us capture images throughout the night & share them using our hashtag: #BreecomingaDonovan.

The place cards/table assignments are personalized engraved crystal champagne flutes:

Lucy Albright

Bree & Evan

8.26.17

Table 8

The band has begun to play light, toe-tapping jazz, and the dusky sun fills the tent with a golden wash.

"This is insane," Jackie says as we beeline for the bar. "The last wedding I went to was my cousin's and it was, like, hamburgers and hot dogs in a community-center rec room." She shoves a whole cake pop into her mouth. "What? I'm starving."

"Where the hell did you guys go?" Pippa appears behind us, and I'm suddenly conscious of the rest of the guests beginning to fill the tent. "The bridesmaids were supposed to ride back *together*. You left me alone with Bree's Ohio people who think I'm a professional prostitute."

"I'm sorry. There was an emergency," Jackie says. "Three vodka sodas with limes, please," she tells the barback.

"Stephen's here, and he's engaged." I feel surprisingly neutral saying the words out loud.

"He's *engaged*? To who? To that girl he's with? That's his girlfriend?"

"Yes. Well, fiancée. *Jillian*."

"Oh fuck. You saw the ring and everything?"

"Yes."

"Fuck. And you didn't know? Bree didn't know?"

"Bree couldn't have known," Jackie says. "She would've told us."

"But wouldn't Evan have told her?"

"Maybe he just forgot." I sigh. "They've had a lot going on."

"Fuck," Pippa repeats. "I can't believe Stephen fucking DeMarco is engaged."

"That poor, poor girl," Jackie says.

"You guys, it's fine." I take another sip of my drink, my nerves jangled at the sight of Stephen and his fiancée near the entrance of the tent. Her dress is marigold and boxy and what CJ would call "a disaster." I watch him study the ice sculpture while he clutches his drink in one hand. He holds the tumbler firmly with the same fingers he'd used to hold the back of my neck when he kissed me.

"I can't really see her," Pippa says, glancing over. "But that dress is nightmarish."

"Pippa." I sigh.

"Luce . . ." Jackie links her elbow in mine.

"I'm fine. Really. Let's go get some appetizers. I need to eat something."

I keep my eyes peeled for Stephen and Jillian, but it becomes harder to spot them as the tent fills with guests.

Back at the bar, a tall guy with a blond buzz cut taps my shoulder, and I smile when I look up to see Mike Wrigley's face.

"Lucy Albright," he says. "You look great."

"*You* look great, Wrigley." We hug.

"Cranberry juice," he says to the bartender, pointing to his empty glass. "Eighteen months sober," he says to me.

"I think I heard that somewhere. Good for you."

Wrigley and I catch up for a bit before he says he's going to say hi to Pippa.

"So good to see you," I say honestly. I'd always liked Wrigley. He and Pippa hadn't had the best relationship, but I'd learned not to cast people into designated boxes. As it turns out, the world is not black-and-white. There's a whole lot of gray.

"You, too, Luce. DeMarco's around here somewhere. Just a heads-up."

"I saw him from afar," I said, nodding. "Is he really engaged?"

"Yeah. Pretty recently."

"Wow," I say. "Good for him."

"For what it's worth, Luce, he never deserved you."

"Thanks, Wrig. I wasn't being spiteful, though. It's been awhile now. I'm over it."

"I know you are. I just wanted to tell you that. DeMarco's a good friend of mine, sure, but he's a dick. You're a unicorn." Wrigley touches the tip of my nose.

"Thank you, Wrig. You're a good man." I clink my glass against his before he turns to find Pippa.

Evan and Bree's first dance is to "Loving You Easy" by Zac Brown Band. I've never heard Bree listen to Zac Brown Band, but the song is somehow perfect, because *easy* is just the word I would use to describe Evan and Bree's relationship. It was easy from the start—from that very first night he kissed her on the street outside Schiller's after Stephen and I had gone home. And that easy love had carried them through to this moment, here and now, dancing their first dance at their beautiful wedding, to their perfect song.

Bree looks more stunning than I ever could have imagined, and it isn't just her dress and makeup and Grecian-goddess hairstyle. I can see in her face just how much she loves Evan, in the way her smile is bursting from every part of her. And Evan, too, handsome in his tux—God, the way he's looking at her as he spins her around and around in his arms, mouthing the words to the song.

Every morning when you come downstairs
Hair's a mess but I don't care

And whatever it is that I'm seeing in front of me—the thing I made a point of not looking at too closely as it unfolded over the past three years—is again bringing tears to my eyes. So I'm caught off guard when, as the song ends and people are clapping and wiping their faces, I hear the voice behind me.

"It's funny, I never cry at weddings."

I know who it is before I turn around—that voice could probably wake me from the dead—and a jolt of electricity runs up my spine. But I'm shocked at how calm I am by the time I complete the turn and clip my gaze into his—that impossible green.

"Apparently I do," I say.

"Leave it to Lucy Albright to look hotter than the bride." He raises his eyebrows. The comment, which would have, not a couple years earlier, drenched everything inside me with crack-like lust, now seems typical in a way that makes me sad.

"Hey, Stephen."

"Hey, yourself."

I study him. He looks mostly the same, except older, maybe. Tired in his face. Maybe five or six more pounds packed around his middle.

"It's been awhile, huh?"

"It has."

"A couple of years, I think."

I nod. At the Christmas party, he'd wedged away from Jillian long enough to say hi to me, and I'd felt so sick I'd nearly dropped my drink. There were too many things I'd wanted to say but of course he'd done the talking, touching on law school and his overwhelming workload, a two-minute surface-level conversation that demolished me with its lack of intimacy.

Now, I realize, I have nothing to say to him.

"Have you been here all weekend, Luce?"

"I got here yesterday morning. I had the bridal lunch and the rehearsal dinner."

"Ah. How was the rehearsal dinner? I heard Evan's speech was very touching."

Even though the sarcasm isn't obvious in his tone, I know it's there. Stephen has always scoffed at Evan's earnestness.

"It was really nice."

"So, Luce. You gonna make me jealous, strutting around with your date in that dress all night." He looks me up and down, not inadvertently. He sounds a little drunk.

"Stephen."

"Sorry. Old habits, ya know?" He sips his Scotch and soda and gives me a coquettish grin.

"Well, don't worry. No dates even for bridesmaids unless we have something here." I clutch my left ring finger. "But I see you dodged that problem."

"But if that wasn't the rule you'd no doubt have some stud on your arm," he says, avoiding my insinuation of his fiancée. "And he'd be glaring at me for having this conversation with you."

I shrug, imagining Dane and how absurd it would be if he were here. I sip my drink. I can see in Stephen's face that he's working to conjure his next comment, his next *move*, because that's what life is to him—one big chessboard. It's suddenly so uninteresting to me—our "conversation"—which isn't a real conversation at all, and I'm racking my brain for an excuse to leave it and find my friends. And it isn't because I'm nostalgic or upset or even uncomfortable; the shock I felt in the church has lifted, and what's left isn't pain, but apathy. Stephen is just another guy who needs to shave and lose the beer belly, another corporate lawyer who gets his kicks on payday. Maybe he was magic to me once, but he isn't anymore. The pedestal has finally vanished, yet somehow, the relief in knowing I'm over him doesn't make me want to sing from the hilltops. It just makes me want to go and do something else.

"Congratulations," I say. "I'm happy for you." I'm not actually happy for him, but maybe I will be, one day.

"So that's it?" He cocks his head, and the old girlfriend part of me wants to smack him in the face, not for myself but for her. *Acknowledge your engagement! Acknowledge your fucking engagement!*

"That's it."

"You don't want to catch up more? Take a walk or something?"

I look into his narrow green eyes, his gaze as steady and uncompromising as ever, and instead of an internal collapse something quiet but true clicks within, and there is my answer. I can see now what I am to him, what I've always been to him, and the part of me that would be desperately thrilled to take a walk with Stephen and find out what would happen is no longer even subliminal—it's just gone. In his amused, absorbed expression I can see the risk and the rush that talking to me provides him. It's something that is not remotely about me.

And then there's a familiar voice echoing in my head. A teenage girl's voice.

He's no one you know. He's this older guy, from Bayville.

And all of a sudden I know, because when you figure out the truth you can *feel* it, hot and deep in your bones, and it feels different and familiar at once, like déjà vu, like opening your suitcase in a foreign place and smelling home.

"Can't take a walk," I say. "I have to tend to the bride." I give him a small smile and turn on one heel. But then I twist the heel further and complete the circle. I can't not say it.

"I always meant to ask you . . ." I lock his gaze. "Did you know a girl named Macy Petersen in high school?"

"Macy Petersen." He says her name slowly, lingering on each syllable. He puts a finger to his chin and scorches me with his eyes, which are smiling. "Hmm. Doesn't ring a bell."

I know he's lying the way you know it's going to storm, the electrical charge in the air that precedes lightning. I know what he did to Macy— it's an instinct in my gut so overpowering that it has to be Macy knowing, too; silently passing this knowledge to me from her side. There are no specific details I can grasp in my mind; there is no proof or evidence, only inexplicable yet incontestable certainty.

"Why do you ask, Luce?" He doesn't blink.

I shrug, and that's it. I feel him staring at me as I turn and walk away for good this time. Knowing he's watching me doesn't do anything for me anymore.

Maybe it's seeing Bree and Evan in love the way I always imagined was possible for myself, or maybe it's seeing Stephen so blatantly unchanged and capable of worse than I ever imagined, or maybe it's just a part of growing up and realizing things when you're ready to realize them, but I feel flooded with profound conviction as I grab my clutch from Table 8 and exit the tent.

The late-summer light is fading but the air is still warm, and I take out my cell phone and wander out past the swimming pool onto the Donovans' luscious acreage.

CJ picks up on the first ring. "I've been waiting for your call! Tell me everything."

I do tell her everything, not skipping a detail, because by this point, CJ and I both know that skipping the details is too risky. I tell her all about the bridal luncheon and the rehearsal dinner and the ceremony and seeing Stephen and Stephen's *fiancée* and his fiancée's tacky dress and Bree and Evan's first dance and how spectacular the wedding has been— and sharing it all with my mother is everything. Part of me wants to tell her what I know about Macy's death—about Stephen being there that night—but it's the one thing I leave out. Somehow, it felt like a message that was only meant for me.

"His fiancée *would* be tacky," CJ says.

"I said her dress was tacky."

"Which means *she's* tacky because she chose it!"

"This isn't about insulting his fiancée, Seej."

"Well, you're being very mature. I would've thrown a drink in his face."

"If I did that I'd look like a psychopath. Besides, I don't care enough. I thought I'd care—I was practically sick leading up to this weekend, and when I saw the ring, I thought I'd be sick right on the altar. But then it all just went away. I was watching Bree and Evan dance their first dance, and all the Stephen stuff just stopped mattering. I don't know, it was like, nothing changed except that suddenly I was seeing things differently, and then I just felt stronger and better."

"Well, time and space give you clarity, and sometimes you don't realize things until . . . you do."

"Yeah. I just don't know what I was thinking, all those years. I do and I don't, I guess."

"Everyone has that guy, Luce. That *one* guy you think you'll never be able to shake—the one who gets under your skin and epically fucks you up for a little while. I know I did."

"You did?"

"*Oh* yeah. Cole Hammond. I've told you about him, haven't I? I barely think about it now, but when it was happening, it was big-time. But guys like that, in the end, when all the smoke has cleared, just make you realize what you don't want."

"Yeah," I say, leaning against the trunk of thick maple, its leaves casting early moonlit shadows at my feet. "I get that now. Talking to Stephen tonight, I understood that, to him, I was always just this source of entertainment—this *thing*—and that he sees relationships as just these useful things, and I would never want to be that to anybody, not in a million years. I don't even hate him, not anymore. It was just sad or something."

"Well, it is sad." CJ sighed through the phone. "I'm proud of you, Luce. You sound very Buddhist."

"I dunno, Seej. It's been really good to be here—seeing Jackie and Pip is amazing, I *miss* them—but I'm just exhausted. I don't want to go back to the city tomorrow."

"So don't. Take the train out here. I'll pick you up. We can do yoga or nails or something."

"I don't really want to go back to the city on Monday, either."

"So take the day off. Can you?"

"No way. There's this big pitch."

"Hmm."

"The thing is, Seej . . ."

"Spit it out, Sass."

"I think I want to leave New York." Saying it out loud, I know it's true. "And it's not because any one thing is going particularly *wrong*. I mean I don't like my job, so that's part of it. But I used to have all these dreams about traveling and writing and journalism school and I feel like at some point I just abandoned all of that, and I can't exactly pinpoint when or why. I know I'm freelance writing a little bit, but I can't pursue it seriously while I'm working in sales, and let's face it—I'm not getting anywhere with editorial at *The Suitest*. I don't know, CJ. I think I need to go and be somewhere else for a while. Figure out what I want."

"Well, I think you have to listen to those feelings. I always thought you'd make a fantastic writer, and I *know* you can do it, if that's what you want. The last thing you should feel is stuck. It's never too late to make a change."

"So you don't think it's a bad idea? Leaving New York?"

"I think the opposite. I love having you close, but, Luce, this is your life. It's a giant world out there. You gotta dream really, really big."

"You're right. I just . . . I don't even know where to start anymore."

"We can brainstorm when you're home tomorrow. Let's just take it one day at a time."

"Okay." I smile into the phone. "I should probably go, CJ. I can't miss the toasts. I'll call you from the train tomorrow. I love you."

"I love you more."

I hang up and gaze back toward the reception, the pearl-colored tent glowing in the dusk, alive with dancing and the twelve-piece band. I smooth the front of my dress and walk back toward the music.

ACKNOWLEDGMENTS

Sarah Cantin and Allison Hunter, interchangeably, I will never be able to thank you enough. The two of you have made this book so much better than I ever dreamed it could be. Sarah, thank you for being my brilliant editor, sharing my vision, and seeing what was special about this book from an early stage—and bringing that to the forefront. Allison, you are fearless and savvy and extraordinary, and I am beyond lucky to have you as my agent; I couldn't have done any of this without your solid advice, constant enthusiasm, and unwavering support.

Amelia Russo, thank you for reading more early drafts of this novel than anyone should've had to, and for our insightful conversation on top of Aspen Mountain that prompted me to write the first pages of *Tell Me Lies* five years ago—I'll never forget that moment. Enormous thanks to Joycie Hunter, Ryan Payne, Hannah Thompson, Ginger Nelson, Sangeeta Mehta, Stefanie Lieberman, Emily Finnegan, Elsie Swank, Claire Abbadi, and my parents and siblings for reading various drafts of the manuscript along the way, and providing invaluable feedback and enthusiasm that kept me coming back to my laptop. Joycie, thank you for believing in this book during times when I couldn't. Ryan, thank you for believing in me when I couldn't believe in myself—it will always mean everything.

To my friends—you know who you are—thank you for being just that. I am eternally grateful for the many long and immensely helpful conversations I've had with you about this book. Joanie Choremi, Dru Davis, Maggie Seay, Julia Livick, and Charlotte Hardie—you are my sisters, and you helped bring the characters of Pippa, Bree, and Jackie to life. Kacey Klonsky, thank you for our photography sessions and for being such a solid source of support and friendship in my life. Thank you to Eliza Crater. Thank you to Chloe LaBranche for your willingness to help. Thank you to Laura Van Ingen, and Lily Haydock for your knowledge and input on all things Long Island.

Thank you to Danielle Lanzet, Rachel Crawford, and Duvall Osteen—your early advice and agent wisdom was more helpful than you know. Thank you to Susan Breen and my unforgettable group at the New York Pitch Conference for your early support. Thank you to Eric Rayman, Haley Weaver, Clare Mao, Sherry Wasserman, Felice Javit, Judith Curr, Albert Tang, Bianca Salvant, and everyone else at Simon & Schuster, Atria, and Janklow & Nesbit who contributed to this project—I am grateful, including Stephanie Mendoza and Ann Pryor.

Stevie Nicks, thank you for creating music that has been such an inspiration for this book, and myself. Thank you to my loves at CorePower Yoga, near and far—our community will always feel like home. Thank you to my professors at Taft and Colorado College for teaching me how to write—especially Jennifer Zaccara, Steven Le, and Lisa Hughes.

Philip and Alexandra Walsh—you were both beautiful writers, and I will never stop being inspired by your talent, courage, and grace. To my uncle Philip, an extraordinary writer, thank you for your soulful wisdom and encouragement. To VSL and JSL, thank you for your unconditional love—I carry it in my heart. To Rob—for being my sounding board and my love, thank you. I'm the luckiest to have you by my side. Last: Mom, Dad, Charlie, Ellie, B, and R—thank you, thank you, thank you. I love you to infinity. I could never find the words to explain what you mean to me, and I won't even try.